PRAISE FOR MEGAN O'KEEFE

"Megan O'Keefe's prose is so full of fascinating twists and delights, you won't want to put it down. Go ahead, open it up: I dare you!"
   David Farland, author of the bestselling Runelords series

"Blend two lovable rogues, a magical doppelganger, and a nasty empire, and you have O'Keefe's Steal the Sky. It's like an epic steampunk *Firefly*."
   Beth Cato, author of The Clockwork Dagger

"Come for the heist, stay for the inventive world building."
   Kirkus Reviews

"A fun, page turning debut."
   SF Signal

"The tension rises throughout, leading up to an action packed third act, with some characters living up to their full potential. Mysteries keep unfolding, and you never truly learn the whole story, which means that there is now yet another series that I'm eagerly anticipating the follow up to."
   Fantasy Faction

"It's a buddy tale, a heist caper, a socioeconomic thriller and a steampunk-seasoned fantasia all at once. And it fires beautifully on all cylinders."
   NPR

"Megan O'Keefe's stories are always vivid and compelling."
   Tim Powers, author of Declare *and* Three Days to Never

-world adventure with
g twists, and wonderful
throughout the story."

MEGAN O'KEEFE

Inherit the Flame

A SCORCHED CONTINENT NOVEL

ANGRY
ROBOT

ANGRY ROBOT
An imprint of Watkins Media Ltd

20 Fletcher Gate,
Nottingham,
NG1 2FZ
UK

angryrobotbooks.com
twitter.com/angryrobotbooks
Seize the city!

An Angry Robot paperback original 2017

Cover by Kim Sokol
Set in Meridien by Epub Services

Distributed in the United States by Penguin Random House, Inc., New York.

ISBN 978 0 85766 496 9
Ebook ISBN 978 0 85766 497 6

9 8 7 6 5 4 3 2 1

For Sam "Secret Agent Man" Morgan

CHAPTER 1

The really annoying thing about being tortured was that Detan had volunteered for the experience. He hung from the ceiling of a nasty little room in the yellowhouse, ropes digging into the tender flesh of his wrists. Slowly, he spun, toes brushing the grit of the floor, body twisting as he struggled to grip the rope and haul himself up to relieve the pain. No use. He'd been there too long, and each time he managed to lift himself the muscles of his arms and shoulders trembled until he fell again. The ropes bit all the deeper for the extra weight jerked upon them.

Aella laughed. He tried to glare at her, but with the sack pulled over his head he probably just scowled at a blank wall.

"Sadist," he said.

"Need I remind you this was your idea? Though I'm beginning to think it was a poor one. We're to test your control, Honding. If you keep lipping off, remaining calm, then greater measures will need to be taken."

The butt of Misol's spear scraped pointedly against the

hard stone. He swallowed.

"I can't help it if you can't get a rise out of me, Aella. I suppose your flavor of fear just isn't my type."

His body screamed at him to shut his mouth, to button up to stop the pain from coming. But he'd asked for this. Needed it, if he were being honest with himself. Needed to know where the fine limits of his control rested, and just how hard they could be nudged.

Aella tsked. Her bare feet pattered against the floor as she paced. She'd taken her slippers off to keep the blood from staining. "A full shift of the moon, and we haven't been able to push the limits of your temper. A pity, for you, that Pelkaia taught you her calming techniques. If you'd come to me ignorant, then we could have kept our measures mild. I wonder," she hmmed to herself, "if I shouldn't have kept Tibal after all."

He went rigid.

"Oh, he was useless to me, really," she continued. Her tunic shifted, the slight rustle of fabric telling him she was circling. Like a shark that'd scented blood. He tried to keep his head down, his body loose, while she paced. "No sense in his thin little body. No sense in his head, either, to have followed you around as long as he did. I wonder how much it hurt him, to hear you tell him off? I wonder: just where did it cut? Is he still bleeding inside? Or is he done with you already? Found another capering idiot to keep alive with his spare time?

"Perhaps I should have kept him, just to put him out of his misery. There is still time, I suppose. Misol, how long do you think it would take to reach Hond Steading?"

"Monsoons are in," Misol replied. "On the *Larkspur*, maybe two weeks."

"Oh, but I doubt he took the *Larkspur*." Her fingers brushed Detan's jawline through the bag. He flinched away. "No, he took the flier, didn't he? I'm sure he had that contraption stashed somewhere, he's such a sentimental sack of bones. A month, easily, to get to Hond Steading in the monsoons on that thing. I bet he's not even there yet. I could send a message along, quick as an arrow. Have him scooped up, brought back to make you sing for his pain. Would you like that, Honding? To see your little friend again? To see him bleed?"

"Don't you fucking dare." Anger sang through him, thrummed just beneath his skin, choked him with the urge to lash out, to grab at the thin sheet of selium hovering just above the yellowhouse.

She clapped. "Ah, there it is! Aren't you a soft soul? Your own pain won't do it, but those of others whips you right up. Pity we don't have anyone you value close to hand."

"I think you're just precious, Aella. Why don't you string yourself up here? I'm sure my heart will burst from sadness."

"You see? It's that attitude that keeps us from testing you as you are. Misol, prepare a message for Thratia's network. Send word that Tibal's presence is requested here at the Remnant, with all haste."

Detan's stomach sank, cold sweat dripped between his wrenched shoulder blades. He had to get angry. Had to work up a righteous fury. It shouldn't be hard. He knew Aella was serious, knew she'd do just exactly what she said she'd do to break him. Images of Tibs hanging in his place, dripping sweat and blood and bile onto the hard floor, filled him. He shivered, nausea threatening to rise, unable to shake his shame when what he desperately wanted was a good outburst.

Misol said, "Pardon, Miss Ward, but I've an idea that's a bit closer to hand."

"Oh? Don't tell me he's developed a soft spot for you."

"Hardly. But there are two women here at the Remnant I've been keeping an eye on. Friends of Ripka's. Without their help, she would have been torn apart in the riot on that last day. I bet Honding would feel just terrible if they were to suffer for his insufficiencies."

"I'm willing to try it. Go collect these women."

Misol slipped from the room, letting the door bang shut behind her.

"Those women." Detan licked his cracked lips. "They have nothing to do with this. My control has grown much in the last few weeks, I hardly think it's necessary to bring them into things."

"No, they don't." Aella sighed. "And while your control is admirable, it has not been tested under true duress." She gave his ropes a jangle, and he winced from the hundred tiny lances of pain that raked through his arms. "We must be certain, or would you rather risk blowing the head off some poor innocent because you believe yourself under control?"

"It's unnecessarily cruel." His voice drifted into a soft growl.

"That is the *point*." She stroked his cheek with the back of her hand. "And isn't it just heaps of fun?"

CHAPTER 2

Hond Steading lay like a pearl without the shelter of its shell upon the horizon. The great city, the first city, the heart of all the Scorched continent, was a cracked open thing. Broken and spread across the wide valley between its renowned firemounts, it sprawled and breathed and pumped, citizens filling out its flush lanes, the figures indistinct from a distance but merging together to make a whole as alive and vibrant from above as it must be from up close.

It should have been beautiful. But all Ripka saw, as she squinted over the forerail of the *Larkspur*, was an indefensible mess. A loose-knit cluster of urban living threaded between the most valuable resource of the Scorched – its firemounts – ripe and ready for Thratia to pluck.

"Looks bad," Nouli said.

He stood beside her, rubbing his hands together as the city sprawl came into view.

She gave him a sidelong glance. "You think?"

He puffed out his cheeks and chuckled. "Forgive me, but I have to start somewhere. This city you've brought

11

me to defend, did you know it was so..." He waved a hand over the disparate pieces below.

"This is the first time I've seen it. Detan assured me you'd be able to figure something out."

"I appreciate the man's faith, but some things–"

"Prepare to dock!" Coss bellowed from the nav podium.

Activity burst across the deck. Pelkaia's crew scrambled to their tasks, the ship turning on a knife's edge to slew toward its destination. Desert air gusted against Ripka's cheeks, sweeping her hair from her face and neck. She breathed deep of the rock-and-dust scent, caught a hint of the weedy greens that flourished below. After so long on the Remnant, setting down in a proper Scorched city again felt like coming home.

"That's better," Nouli said.

Ripka had to agree. As the *Larkspur* swung about, the ship pointed them at the city's core, the dense urban center that swarmed around the Honding family palace. It backed up against the largest of the city's firemounts. The palace itself stepped up the side of the mountain, but the city stayed resolutely in the belly of the valley. A wall swaddled the dense-packed heart of the city.

Compared to the wall that had encircled Aransa, it was a meager thing. It must have been some vestige of the city's earlier life, when it was little more than a frontier outpost. Now the gates stood wide open, disgorging citizens in both directions. While Ripka doubted those gates had been shut in decades, the mere sight of them eased her worries. At least they had some sort of defensive measure to work with.

From one of the palace's many high towers a straight blade of a dock awaited them. The *Larkspur* sidled against it, timbers shivering at the contact. Heavy thumps drummed the air as the crew tossed anchors and tie lines over the sides.

Three men in the sharp, black livery of the Honding family approached the ship. Their uniforms gave Ripka pause. She'd known Detan was a lord of an old family, but around him that was easy to forget. He was a flippant man, caring but unpredictable. Half the time he was in desperate need of a bath.

But these guards – their weapons might have been hidden, but Ripka knew a fighting force when she saw one – who arrayed themselves on the dock wore the insignia of his family with pride. The same sword and pickaxe crossed over a ship's sail that was burned into the back of Detan's neck. On them it was dignified. Red and gold embroidery stitched into black coats trimmed with crimson. On Detan, the scar had been a dirty, greasy mess.

"Ho, *Larkspur*," a man with a head of iron-grey hair called out. "You've been expected."

Whether that was a good thing or not, Ripka wasn't sure, but she'd come all this way to keep Thratia from taking another city. Whatever was waiting for her in the Honding family palace, she would prevail.

By previous arrangement, Pelkaia, Tibal, and Ripka were the only ones to leave the ship. Though Hond Steading was supposed to be friendly territory, they had no idea what they faced within those walls – what the rumors of Detan's misadventures would do to their welcome. The more of them left to man the ship in case of a quick escape, the better.

Ripka gave Nouli a pat on the shoulder and followed Tibal down the gangplank. Pelkaia drifted after them. While her back was rigid, and her chin held with regal bearing, Ripka found something odd about her posture, as if she were trying to hide some sort of pain. Just a few weeks ago, Pelkaia had swung down from the ropes of the *Larkspur* without care. Now she looked shy of so much as a stubbed toe.

The iron-haired man bowed to the three and fixed his gaze on Pelkaia.

"You are Pelkaia Teria captain of the *Larkspur*, am I correct?"

Pelkaia inclined her head. After the disaster on the Remnant, she'd stopped bothering to hide the ship's distinctive lines. "I am that. This is Ripka Leshe, and Tibal."

"Well met," he said, bowing his head to each. "I am Gatai, keymaster of the Honding household and personal attendant to Dame Honding. The Dame awaits you in her meeting room. Do you require ablutions before we proceed? I can also send for fresh water to be brought to your ship."

Ripka raised her brows despite her desire to remain aloof. This kind of hospitality was common on the Scorched: fresh water and a cloth to clean your face were the simplest of pleasures in the desert, but rarely were they offered to those who were unwelcome. She hoped this offering was a good sign for their future, and not just a Honding family matter of pride.

There was a scuffle of feet behind them, and the group turned as one. Honey made her way down the gangplank, Enard's hand half-extended as if he'd tried to grab her shoulder and missed. The woman's curly mop of hair caught the sunlight with unsettling brilliance, as if someone had set her alight. She hummed to herself as she strolled along, unmindful of all the startled gazes upon her, and came to stand beside Ripka.

Pelkaia gave Ripka a look that said, quite clearly: can't

you control your pet? While Tibal refused to look at her at all.

Gatai cleared his throat gently. "A pleasure to meet you as well...?"

Honey just stared at him, humming a little lullaby so soft Ripka wondered if she were the only one who could hear it.

"This is Honey," Ripka offered to cut the tension. "She..." Ripka faltered. What in the pits was she supposed to say here? She's a woman with a lust for blood who follows me around like a suckling kitten and we're all worried that if I send her back she'll make roasts of the crew in my absence? "She's a friend."

Honey beamed. Gatai didn't seem convinced – he had a pucker between his brows that even careful training couldn't smooth away – but he gathered himself and bowed his head to Honey.

"You are all," and here he raised his voice to be heard by the crew crowding the rail, "welcome to Hond Steading."

Unsteady murmurs from the crew. They'd spent all their time aboard the *Larkspur* avoiding cities like Hond Steading, hiding out in places where imperial reach was imperfect, where their deviant abilities were less likely to get them run out of town or killed. Ripka, having no selium sensitivity herself, wondered what they felt now, to be both known and welcomed in the largest city on the Scorched. She'd be wary, in their place. But there must be some relief. Some fragile hope that at last they may have found a place to belong.

"My ship will take water. We, however, are anxious to greet the Dame."

One of Gatai's men broke away, crisp-stepping into the palace to place the order for water without so much as

a glance from Gatai. Ripka watched him go with hungry
eyes. Here was a well-oiled machine, a force trained to
respond without direct interference from their leader.
She was desperate to pick Gatai's brain on his training
techniques. But then, it's not like she had a group to
train any more.

"After me, please," Gatai said, and led them with
practiced formality into the palace. Ripka's heart
thumped away in her throat, excitement thrumming
through her despite the cool disposition she cultivated.

This place was legend. And though most legends
failed to live up to their grandeur once seen up close, she
found the Palace Honding did not disappoint.

Its walls were carved of native rock, set so close and
fine she could not tell if they were mortared at all. Oil-
fed candelabras grew from the ceiling, wrought iron
twisted to look like lavish vines, their light bright and
warm and pure in the wide hall. A simple stretch of fine
wool made up the rug cushioning her feet. It would be
unremarkable, except that the whole length of it had
been dyed a brilliant, emerald green. Such color she
had never seen before outside of nature. She imagined
Detan as a child, running wild through the palace, and
wondered if he ever really understood what privilege
he'd been gifted until the day it had been stripped from
him.

Dame Honding's meeting room was no less elegant,
but the Dame herself held Ripka's eye. Ripka had
expected a battleship of a woman. What she found
instead was a spear.

Dame Honding stood at the head of the room, one
hand resting on the back of a chair it seemed obvious the
advisors fidgeting by her side would much rather she sit
in than stand beside. Her hair – gone wholly to silver –

had been piled atop her head in an elegant bun, framed by the crossed pickaxe and sword carved into the wall behind her. She was the tallest woman Ripka had ever seen. Despite age lending a slight stoop to her shoulders, she towered over all gathered. And though her arms were wrapped in navy silk, the slight curve of muscle along her bicep betrayed an active lifestyle.

She had Detan's eyes.

"Welcome to my home." Her voice was clear, strong. She must be in her seventies, Ripka marvelled, and yet looked ready to race a rockcat.

"Your hospitality is most welcome," Pelkaia said, pausing two strides before the Dame. "If surprising."

The Dame smiled. Ripka could not help but study every line of her face, seeking out other traces of Detan hidden away in the aged countenance. "All the little birds of the Scorched whisper in my ear. Your arrival was expected, and anticipated."

"You understand the nature of my crew, my ship?" Pelkaia tensed, fingers curled as if ready to form fists, or grab for a weapon. The Dame's advisors shifted restlessly. Gatai flicked a piece of lint from his collar. The Dame inclined her head.

"I know what you and your crew are, and that your ship is stolen property. It matters not to me. You are free in my city, and Thratia's ability to keep what's hers is her own business."

"If we stay here, she will come for it."

Dame Honding graced them with a grim smile. "She will come regardless."

"We have come to help you, if we may," Ripka said.

The Dame's gaze snapped to her, and in that proud stance and steady stare Ripka saw a shadow of what Detan might become one day. Could become, if only he'd figure out how to keep a handle on himself and accept the responsibility he'd been born into. Watching those eyes, Ripka was not sure that that would be a good thing.

"You must be Captain Leshe. I heard a rumor that my wayward nephew took your life in the firemount of Aransa. I'm pleased to see you recovered."

Ripka cracked a small grin. "It seems your little birds have incomplete information, Dame. I will be happy to fill in the details when you wish."

"There is only one detail that matters to me." She turned her hard gaze upon Tibal. "Where is my nephew?"

Tibal lingered toward the back of the hall, the drooping edge of his hat tugged down to shadow his eyes. "Exactly where he always is: wherever he wants to be, and to pits with the consequences."

Stiff backs all around, a slight flush of anger rouged the Dame's cheeks. Ripka started to say something, saw Gatai shake his head behind the Dame, and sealed her lips shut. Whatever was going on here was older than Ripka's relationship with Detan.

"Have you failed me after all these years, then, little bastard Honding?"

CHAPTER 3

Aella had cut him down from the ceiling, but left his wrists bound behind his back and the sack slouching over his face. She'd plopped him down in the center of the room, told him merrily there were shards of glass strewn across the floor, and traipsed off to join Misol in concocting whatever foul plan they had in store for him next.

He wasn't about to let a threat of glass and the fact he'd consented to this madness keep him corralled.

Rolling his shoulders to loosen his stiffened neck, Detan unfolded his legs and slowly, carefully, felt forward. Grit so thick it might as well have been glass dragged at his toes, at the soles of his feet. Aella must have had some poor grunt haul sand up from one of the island's beachheads.

Painstakingly, he edged out the boundaries of his new space. Aella had left him maybe a stride in all directions clear of the sand and glass. A little halo of safety that was, at best, a paltry illusion. Really, she needn't bother. No matter how much rope she gave him, he wasn't about to hang himself by running off. He'd made this trade willingly, bent knee to her not only to free his companions but to find out all there was to know about himself. Such fences as the glass, as the ropes and the chains, were laughable. If he wanted to leave, he could. And though he desired to leave with every fiber of his being, greater forces held him at bay. Locked him in place.

He was corralled tighter by fear than he'd ever be by iron or glass.

Worldbreaker.

Misol tapped her spear butt against the ground, alerting him to their return. Knowing she was there, he could just pick out the whisper-soft patter of Aella's bare feet against the stone.

"Welcome back. May I fetch you some tea, or some cakes?" he drawled, amused by the sharp halt of Aella's tread. He could kiss Misol for her subtle announcement. Any chance to startle Aella was one worth taking. "I wouldn't want you to find my hospitality lacking."

"I've found you some friends to entertain. Misol, bring them."

Aella stepped beside him, her small body a heavy presence in the air to his left. She yanked the bag off his head. He blinked in the light, twisted until he could see the door.

Two women in Remnant-issued beige jumpsuits shuffled into the room, everything about their posture taut and wary. One had straight black hair cut short, the other hair like wet mud clinging to her cheeks. Both appeared to have taken up the strange hobby of repeatedly getting their noses broken. He'd never seen them before, and for their sake wished he wasn't seeing them now.

Detan forced a smile and inclined his head to them.

"Welcome to my sitting room."

The brown-haired woman took one pointed look at the circular pit that had been Detan's training ground for the last few weeks and snorted. "You need a better decorator."

He grinned. Leave it to Ripka to find friends with cheek, even in this monstrous place.

"This here's Clink," Misol said, nodding to the brown-haired woman, "and this is Forge. Ladies, say hello to Detan Honding."

"Ain't that a fancy name?" Clink asked.

Forge snorted. "I faked a manifest for a Honding ship once. Big load of dehydrated cactus, tasted like candied diarrhea. More money 'n sense in that family."

"Ah. Auntie Honding has always had a questionable palate. Wait. Did you say faked?"

Forge gave him a look like she'd give a slow child. "What you think I'm doing on the Remnant, sightseeing?"

"Speaking of." Clink narrowed her eyes at him. "What are you doing here?"

"Would you believe sightseeing?"

Both women smirked. Detan decided to like them. He had to like someone around here, and it might as well be these women who had supposedly helped Ripka out during her stay.

"Detan is here to learn the nature of himself," Aella said.

"Sounds like a waste of time," Clink said.

Misol hid a smile by turning her head away, but Detan didn't bother. He laughed out loud. "Feels that way, most of the time. But I'm afraid it's best for everyone's safety if I get myself figured out."

"Everyone's?" Forge asked, incredulous.

"Everyone's," he agreed. Their smirks vanished.

Whether they believed him or not, they certainly believed he meant what he said.

"And you're going to help him."

"We ain't the altruistic type," Clink said, eyes narrowing, but Aella had already shifted her thoughts to the experiment to come, and was deaf to her protests. For all the brainpower that girl was packing, she could be remarkably single-minded at times. Focus like that was a rarity in the adults Detan had stumbled across in his day, but common enough in any hunting viper's path he'd had the misfortune of crossing.

Aella stepped through the minefield of sand and glass on the tips of her toes, light as a stone skipping across still water. Taking her cue, Misol dug around in a pouch slung about her hips and produced two leather sacks, stitched up tight and bulging all around at the seams. Detan licked his lips. He didn't need to use his sel-sense to know there was selium in those bladders.

"One for you," Misol said, and gave the first to Forge. "And for you." She passed the other to Clink. The women turned them over in their hands, brows furrowed.

"This is sel, isn't it?" Clink asked.

"Yes it is," Aella confirmed. Her eyes shone as she leaned toward the two women, practically radiating curiosity.

"What you want us to do with it?" Clink demanded. "We're not sensitive. Wouldn't be here if we were, would we?"

"You'd be surprised," Detan muttered.

"Hush," Aella ordered him. "All you have to do is to stand on opposite sides of the room, and hold those tight. Can you do that?"

The women exchanged a look. It was Clink who asked the pertinent question, "Why?"

"We're going to put Detan here through his paces. See how much he's learned."

"And if we refuse?"

Aella's excitement dimmed like a snuffed candle. "There are quite a few people in this prison who would like dearly to have some time alone with you two, after your assistance in Ripka Leshe's escape. I can arrange that meeting, if you'd like."

They swallowed in unison. "That won't be necessary."

"Excellent." Aella was all warm smiles and friendly chatter as she ushered the women to their places. "Now, Detan, this is for you. Get to know it well, you have only a few moments."

She thrust a third bladder of selium into his hands. He turned it over with care, tracing his thumb along the seams, extending his sel-sense just enough to know the exact shape of the selium hidden within. How it pushed against the leather, how it'd found a little weakness in one of the seams and was bunching up against it. Selium was good at that. At finding the weak points and pushing, pushing. Maybe he was kindred spirits with the gas after all.

Aella snatched it from him, and before he could complain the sack was back over his head.

"Now." Soft footsteps, fading to silence. "You must work your little deviation upon just this sphere, understood? It alone is not being held by the women. It alone will not harm anyone, if you manage to control yourself and set fire to it and only it."

"Set fire?" Clink blurted.

"Erupt may be a better word," Aella corrected with slow care.

"*Erupt*?"

"Hmm? Yes, erupt. Like the firemounts. Now hush,"

Aella ordered. "I'm shuffling the women's positions now, so that you cannot rely on their placement from before the bag was pulled over your head. If they speak, or make the slightest noise, they will be moved."

Detan closed his eyes and strained, struggling to listen for the patter of their footsteps. Aella was the lighter of the three, and her step was soft against the stone, but she paced and paced, until he couldn't tell where she'd begun and where she'd ended up.

"There," she said. "The sphere is placed. Find it. Destroy it."

Sweat beaded across his forehead, sticking to the bag. "And if I can't?"

"Neither of these women will eat again until you do."

Right. He really hadn't known what he'd expected, but it wasn't that. Pain for himself he could handle, but watching the two women who saved Ripka starve to death just wasn't something he was willing to do. But neither was he willing to blow their hands off. Which, of course, Aella knew.

Get it over with, he scolded himself, and let his body relax, slumping, as he gradually grew in awareness. He started with his toes, feeling and flexing every muscle, working his way up until he was aware of every last crease of his forehead. That was the easy part.

He waited until his breath came smooth and easy, then reached out. His sel-sense flared within him, drawing from an old well of anger and hurt. It boiled through him like fire, seared his soul like something far worse. He wanted to flinch away from the power, from the potential that lurked within him. Had spent the past few years of his life doing just that. But he couldn't. Not any more. That was why he was here, after all. To examine that fire, that great gaping maw of rage, and bend it to his will.

Detan probed his anger. His arms tensed. He forced himself to ease them, struggling to find a balance. If he relaxed too much, he lost his edge, couldn't force the selium to slam itself together and burst apart. But neither could he grow too tense. He knew all too well the devastation he was capable of when he let his rage take the reins of his talents.

He was cold. Absolutely shivering. Sweat streaked down the muscles of his bare back, coalesced in a river along the valley of his spine. How long had he sat there, sweating and fretting? He couldn't think of that. Couldn't let the passing time worry him. Someone shifted aching feet, impatient. He zeroed in on the sound and couldn't pinpoint who it was. Not that that was the point. If he cheated this test, he cheated himself.

He gave up on hesitance, reached his sense with deliberate care to examine the sources of sel in the room. Three, as promised. All of them hauntingly familiar. Which one had been his? Which one had Aella let him hold in his hands?

Cruel as she was, she wouldn't have cheated him in this. Wouldn't have given him an impossible task to solve. Though her reasons eluded him, she desired to know the secret of his abilities – and its limits – just as sorely as he did. Perhaps more, he sometimes thought. There was little that woman wouldn't do to achieve her goals, and Detan had his boundaries.

He let the three globes fill his mind. Held them like shining stars in the dark, fireflies disrupting the wave of his sense reaching out from the center of his being. Five strides away, six, and five again. Three points of a triangle of which he was the heart, the center, the core of destruction. He held them all, turned them over.

Compared them not to his memory but to each other. Equal in size, Aella would have made sure of that. But one... One felt denser, somehow, crammed tight, bulging against the seams with eager gluttony. He discarded it.

The second and third hung in his mind now, and he imagined a bright line of light bridging them as he weighed them against each other, sought new methods of comparison. Aella would not have made the trick so obvious as to pack two of the globes tight-full. Or would she? Devious creature that she was... He jettisoned the thought. Nothing to be gained down that path, nothing at all. Aella's psychology wasn't what he was trying to figure out. This wasn't game theory, this wasn't a gambling hand. He either had the flavor of the globe, or he didn't. And if he didn't, some poor woman would die.

Some woman who had helped Ripka. Saved her life, most probably, when the Remnant was boiling with riot over the rumor of a blue coat in their midst. Her face filled his mind, the harsh regard of her stare when he said something irritating a warm balm. He pushed her away. This wasn't about her. Wasn't about Tibs or his Auntie or New Chum or any other soul that had the misfortune of having earned his affections.

Focus. Weigh the two. Feel them out. Identical in density, or as near as could be achieved by human hands and talents. He suspected that if he dug deeper, if he reached into that miniscule level of the world that bare eyes couldn't see – that he only glimpsed when the injections were fresh in his veins – that he might find a difference otherwise undetectable. Nothing intentional though, unless Aella had much more refined sensitives hanging around here who he had yet to meet.

She didn't have that. But she knew he could push himself that way. Had been trying to make it second nature to him. An idea struck. Stoking the coals of his rage, banking them to keep them hot, he focused in on one sphere and reached for those fine particles. Nothing. He turned his attention to the other. Imagined what he was looking for like dust in the air, drifting, invisible until the glint of sun hits just right. Imagined his anger as that light, his rage the source of that sun.

Found what he was looking for, in miniscule amounts, woven into the fabric of the bladder's interior in tiny pockets, like quilting. Like what Pelkaia'd done to Ripka's jacket so she'd always know where she was.

Detan didn't hesitate. He flared his anger, directed it into those tiny pockets. Heard a whoosh and a cry and a gasp. Aella – for who else could it be? – clapped for joy.

"Well *done*," she cooed as she yanked the bag off his head. He looked around, blinking, came up out of his meditative stupor to discover his legs cramped, his head pounding, his feet two clumps of tingling, limp meat. A great maw of hunger crooned in his belly, and his mouth was thick with dryness.

Forge and Clink eyed him like a rockviper that'd suddenly reared up and started hissing. They held their intact globes gingerly, away from their bodies as if that'd do any good at all. In one corner of the room, a smear of soot marred the wall, charred fragments of leather curling on the ground.

"How long?" he asked, and had to stop to cough and lick some moisture into his lips.

"Only seven marks." Aella beamed, proud. "Impressive for a first try."

Seven marks. When Aella'd first dragged him into this room for his daily testing his belly had been warm with breakfast and his eyes dry against the rising sun. That sun was gone, now. Hidden behind the curve of the world for a mark or two at least. Gingerly, he unfolded his legs and winced as the blood flowed back to his feet. Felt like he'd stomped all over a cactus, but at least he could still feel something.

"Did he do that?" Clink demanded, thrusting a finger at the fiery smear.

Detan forced himself to crawl to wobbly feet. Misol was beside him in an instant, propping him up. He almost laughed. Couldn't let the merchandise get any more damaged than required.

"I did that," he confirmed, watching her eyes widen and her nostrils flare.

."Sweet skies," Forge murmured.

Detan drew himself up and turned to Aella. "Feed them. Shelter them here, in the yellowhouse. They've earned that much."

"Yes, yes," she said, waving a dismissive hand. "Skies know we have the room. And I'll need them close at hand for further testing. I wonder if we could shave a mark off your time on the next attempt."

He winced at the thought. Seven marks. Seven long marks sitting on that floor in nothing but his pants and his sweat, huddled up under that sack on his head and thinking, thinking. It had felt like only moments to him. He'd have been surprised to hear it'd been a single mark, let alone seven. How could he ever become effectual, and safe, if it took him so long to master himself, to gain control? A man who takes seven marks to fire an arrow at his enemy is a dead man.

"Problem with that," Misol said. "A letter came for you around mark four, Miss Ward. I looked to see how urgent it was, and figured it could wait until this was finished, but you'd better see for yourself."

Misol passed Aella an envelope with a broken wax

seal Detan recognized as Thratia's. His stomach dropped. Nothing Thratia had to say to Aella could be any good. The girl's eyes flicked over the missive, a faint tension thinned her lips. With a sigh she snapped the paper shut, propped her hands on her hips, and set a heavy glare on Detan. He met her gaze, calm and easy. After seven marks rooting around in his own head, that girl didn't much disturb him any more. He'd seen darker things.

"Thratia requests the Lord Honding's presence in Aransa. In all haste."

"For what purpose?" he asked.

She rolled her bony shoulders. "No idea. But I jump when called, don't I? Misol, pack up, we leave in the morning."

Misol eyed Forge and Clink. "And these two?"

"Oh. Bring them along. Why not? I suppose we can get some work done along the way. And pick out whoever you need to help you handle the lot."

"Yes, Miss Ward."

Detan swallowed. He'd seen darker things than Aella's glare, that was true, but a whole lot of them had to do with Thratia Ganal.

CHAPTER 4

Ripka gawped. Couldn't help herself. All these years she'd come to know Tibal, and his last name had never been mentioned – not once. She'd assumed the lack a simple refusal on Tibal's part to acknowledge his patronage, and hadn't dug much deeper. She knew his past had been fraught with violence and hunger, known that even though he'd been press-ganged into joining the Fleet, he'd welcomed the steady meal schedule. And then he'd left, he'd retired from Fleet work and returned to his hometown where he'd worked on airships and any other old thing he could fix up until Detan had strolled along.

Not once. Not once in all their back-and-forth had either Detan or Tibal let slip that Tibal was a Honding himself. Pits below, but Tibal had often ribbed Detan for being of noble blood. Did Detan know?

Pelkaia went quiet, staring at Tibal like she'd plucked a flower and found an angry spider inside. It wasn't that Pelkaia feared Tibal, Ripka wasn't fool enough to think that. No, she knew real well what had to be running through Pelkaia's mind, and it wasn't pretty. She would be wondering, as Ripka was, just how close those familial ties were. Tibal had once told Ripka he and Detan had tempers like two pieces of a puzzle, similar in strength but different in expression – complements to each other, and it was too hard to tell which was more dangerous. She'd never seen him reach for selium, never seen him manipulate it, but that was no guarantee he didn't know how.

"Name's Tibal," he said slowly. "And I did what you asked of me. Not my fault your nephew's a man who can't ever tell what's good for him. Ran off to join Thratia, he did. Bent knee right down before Thratia's pits-cursed whitecoat and damned near kissed her slippers. You want to know where your nephew is? You send a letter along to Thratia, I'm sure she'd be delighted to let you know how well they're all getting along now. But I don't want to hear it, understand? Detan's his own man. He's made that clear enough."

"You lost him." Tibal was too wound up to see it, but there was such profound sadness in Dame Honding's voice, lurking just there at the edges, simmering below the surface, that Ripka's heart actually ached for the spear of a woman.

"He lost his own self. You need me for anything that matters, Dame, you know where I'll be."

"Your mother–"

Tibal raised a hand to cut her off. "You're a woman of your word, Dame. I know you won't let an old woman starve because her bastard son lost someone else's."

"That is not what I meant," she snapped. Whatever stoop age had lent to her back disappeared as she straightened up, and Ripka had the distinct impression that she was shouldering the weight of the crest carved into the wall behind her. "Your mother vouched for your heritage, and your father has not disowned you, absent though he may have been. If you have lost my heir, then you are next in line."

"You want to stick that brand on me, Dame, you're gonna have to find a whole battalion willing to hold me down."

Tibal stomped off like he owned the place, took a turn he obviously knew well and disappeared down another hallway. Ripka choked on questions, sorted them, and realized she'd have to wait to deal with Tibal. Nouli was on board the *Larkspur*, awaiting permission to set up shop here, and Ripka was his advocate.

Into the silence that stretched behind Tibal's leaving, she said, "Dame, forgive me, but I believe Detan sacrificed his freedom to Thratia."

Her shoulders twitched, her gaze snapping from the direction Tibal had taken, back to Ripka. "Dear girl, do not attempt to soothe me on his behalf. I will discover my nephew's intentions in due time."

"I have evidence of his loyalty to you with me, now, on the *Larkspur*. He arranged for the rescue of Nouli Bern, the engineer who built the Century Gates of Valathea, from the Remnant prison – and has entreated him to serve for Hond Steading's defense."

A curl tipped up the corner of her lips. The same crooked smile Detan put on before he was about to tell a particularly large lie. "My nephew did all of that?"

"He arranged for it."

She shook her head, smile locked in place. "I see. Well, it is something, at least. Bring this Master Bern to me and I will arrange rooms for him. I suppose he needs a workshop and materials?" Ripka nodded. "Very well. Though I cannot see how much help he will be on the balance."

"He has intimate knowledge of many machines of war, and Commodore Ganal's tactics." "I'm sure he does, my dear, but Valathea comes to Hond Steading's aid. His efforts will be appreciated, in concert with theirs."

Ripka's throat went dry. "What do you mean?"

"A delegation from Valathea arrives tonight to discuss the city's defense."

"Those people tortured your nephew." The words tumbled out before she could stop them, hot with anger. Pelkaia cleared her throat, and Ripka realized she'd taken a step forward without meaning to.

Dame Honding's head jerked back, her eyes narrowed. "I respect your work, Captain Leshe, but Hond Steading is not your city to protect. It is mine. This is an era of alliances. One cannot stand alone on the Scorched. Not with Thratia Ganal running wild across it."

CHAPTER 5

Monsoon season made its presence known with a toothy growl. Sticky winds rocked the transport ship Aella had commandeered for their travel, pitching the deck to and fro. Detan hunkered by the cabins, his ass on the deck and his back shoved against the wall, head in his hands. He wasn't sure what was more nauseating, the buck of the ship or the incompetence of the pilot.

"It's not that bad," Misol said. She leaned her back against the deck-rail with her elbows propped up on it, head tipped back to feel the full extent of the winds. Droplets of moisture collected on her bald head, making it gleam. Not a hint of green marred her cheeks, the bitch.

"Trust me, it's worse when you know everything the pilot is doing wrong."

"Didn't think you had a perfectionist nature."

"My dear woman, there are some disciplines in which I will not put up with sloppiness: the piloting of airships, the brewing of ale, and making love to women."

"What about making love to men?"

"Haven't yet had the pleasure."

"Pity for you." She picked at her teeth with one thick thumbnail. "Too bad you skipped dinner. Aella may not be much for domestics, but the girl can cook."

"Of course she can. How else would she know what meals pair best with which poisons?"

"Aww, she's not that bad, either."

"You weren't the one tied to a ceiling with a bag over your head."

"Not my fault my deviation doesn't require that sort of training, and it ain't Aella's fault either. You don't like what you gotta do, blame yourself."

"I hardly see how it's my fault."

"Don't you?" Misol whistled low and slow, then shook her head. "I know you're not stupid, but sometimes I wonder if you might be blind. You think Aella had to wrap me up in chains to get me to figure out how to make my face look like a man's?"

"I'm not exactly free here, Misol."

She snorted. "Sure you are. Got that crap in your veins leashing you, but both Aella and I figure you could probably whip up your own brew if you really put your mind to it. It's not to keep you close, anyway, it's more to help you with your training. Skies above, you think I'm watching you because we're afraid you'll run? I'm just along to be an extra set of hands – and keep an eye on Forge and Clink, now. Aella's got no worry you'll bolt."

"If I left–"

"She'd do what? Hunt down that little friend of yours? Girl's got no time for that bullshit. She'd come after you, sure, but she'd come with an offer in hand and it wouldn't be chains. She wants you compliant. Makes it easier when she's got to rile you up, you know she's just working to figure out what you can do – not being mean for the sake of it."

"That girl's cold as a glacier. You expect me to believe she's not taking at least a little pleasure in this?"

"Pleasure? Maybe, I don't know. But if she's getting any joy out of this it's not because she's putting the heat to your toes, it's because she's getting answers for once. It was harder for her, trying to pin down her theory when it was just us regular deviants. Not a lot to suss out in people like me and that blue guy. But you? You're malleable, and quick to change. It's that quickness that she's counting on."

"Took me seven marks to figure out her last puzzle. Ain't quick by any stretch."

Misol sighed as if she were trying to explain herself to a particularly slow child. "Stay with me now. You got a temper in you, don't you? Keep it locked down with jokes and other bullshit but you've got a streak in you hotter than a firemount flow. That right?"

He shifted, the scars of his back hot against the wall. "I got a handle on it."

"More or less. Don't matter how hard you squeeze it down, it's still in there. And when you touch sel, if you're not careful, you make things burn right up with the heat of that anger.

"Now, take me. I'm a doppel, I can change my face around anyway I'd like using sel. All my life I had a hard time trying to decide what I wanted to be. Spent some time farming, some time bartending, and a half dozen other things before I picked up the spear and Aella stumbled across me. Things starting to look clear?"

"Doesn't hold up. You call yourself a doppel, but that's Valathea's word. I knew a woman like you – called herself an illusionist – was Catari through and through. Could do a whole pits-lot more than just change her face, and didn't have to mess about shaving her head, either. She made the hair she had work."

Misol whistled again. "Musta' been real good, and I wonder what her personality was like, but she's not here to test, so that ain't the point. Look at Callia. I didn't know her before her accident, but she's got a deviation almost as rare as yours. She can do this twisting thing – make anyone manipulating sel feel like it's perverted, disgusting. She makes it feel like raw corruption, like chugging a flask of rotten water. Now, woman like that musta been a real piece of work when she had her wits about her, but look what it did for her. She survived that poisoning, maybe even thrived from it. There's not another body alive I know of that could take the dose Aella said Callia consumed and come out the other side alive. It's like her body welcomed it, sucked it up like a sponge. She's rotten all through, and thrives on it."

"I'll give you that Callia's rotten, but what about Aella? That girl's cold as a night is long, but she can't make sel feel cold. Can only shut it down."

"You got your metaphor confused with reality there, Honding. She ain't cold – she's *empty*. Cultivates indifference like it's a sport and she's its top athlete. Doesn't feel a damned thing, half the time. You watch her react to something. She always takes an extra beat, this little hesitation while she figures out what reaction she wants to have that'll get her the result she wants."

"What in the pits does that have to do with me?"

"You really don't get it, do you?" She rubbed her fuzzed scalp with one hand. "If she can teach you to be calm, to douse your temper, and still control the flame you wield? Then maybe she could try to feel again, without fear of losing the talent that defines her very existence."

Aella marched toward them, a forced smile on her

face, slippered feet scuffing the deck in the unsteady gait of those who weren't used to airships – as if their feet being in contact with the wood at all times would keep them from flying off.

"We will reach Aransa before nightfall," Aella said. "I haven't a clue why Thratia wants you, but if she's going to make use of you then I won't have you embarrass me with ineptitude."

"Wouldn't that be a disaster," he drawled.

She fixed him with a narrowed gaze and clasped her hands to her hips. "Get up, now, and come along. We've some time yet to put you through your paces before we reach the city."

Detan groaned. "I still say my practicing on a live, selium-bloated ship is a terrible idea. A better test of my refinement, I'm sure, would be to relieve the poor pilot of his post for just a while."

She slashed a hand through the air. "You're not flying this ship, Honding, though I suppose there's something to be said for your enthusiasm."

"Only thing I'm enthused about is not throwing up on my shoes. Where'd you find this pilot, anyway? Couldn't be a Fleetie."

Aella fixed him with a scowl. "Stop attempting to distract me. You're overdue for a dose, and I want to test your fine control while you're waning."

Detan looked at her. Really, really looked, since the first time he'd seen her sitting barefoot on a barrel aboard Callia's ship. She was just as neat as ever, her clothes finely made and the seams perfectly pressed, the colors all working together to harmonize with her natural hues. The white coat smoothing out her silhouette was jarring, sure, but she wore it with confidence, like it was armor, the pockets heavy with the tools of her trade. She coiled her hair up tight against her head, and plucked every stray strand from her youth-dewy face.

She gave the impression of total control, everything in its right place, nothing out of line or harmony. She was, Detan realized with a start, a walking doll. And she'd done it to herself. Even the annoyed creases between her brows were false. There was an aloofness in her eyes he'd always ascribed to the same flippancy he felt most of the time, but, no. Her detachment was something deeper, everything about her exterior a carefully planned and executed show. He felt a little sorry for her, then realized it didn't matter. She wouldn't be able to relate to his sympathy anyway.

"Come on," she said, tapping her foot with calculated impatience.

Misol was watching him. He met her eye, and nodded understanding even as he grunted and levered himself to his feet. "Bank your coals, girl, I'm coming. Things are stiffer than they used to be."

The scar tissue on his back pulled, the length of his forearm itched with raw puncture wounds. There was an ache in his joints that'd never been there before, a radial warmth that both worried and distracted him. He'd lost both his parents to bonewither. He knew too well it was a sorry way to die.

"Say, Aella," he said, as he stretched out and followed her back toward the cabin she'd commandeered for research purposes. "You think all this messing with sel, and the injections, could speed up the onset of bonewither?"

Aella flicked the needle of her syringe with one finger, watching the little bubbles within burst and sputter. She glanced up at him over the point of steel, brows pinched, and shrugged. "Oh. Definitely. Now sit down on that bench. I want to see if you can identify all the sources of sel on the ship before we renew your injection."

Wonderful, he thought, and closed his eyes, reaching for his sense slowly, carefully. Ignoring that bright, magma-hot vein of anger that threaded through everything he'd ever been. Forced himself to forget the face of his mother, sunken as her cheekbones dissolved, even as he touched all the sources of sel on the ship with his mind.

Drone-like, he began to count them off, and wondered if Aella suspected he knew her secret fear.

CHAPTER 6

Ripka had no job to do. She paced the streets of Hond Steading, peeking in dark alleys, warning citizens of unsecured money pouches that would make for easy picking. The streets of the city twisted all around her, the natural sprawl of a city that grew up around itself; unplanned, unshepherded. Hond Steading's rapid growth in its early days had left it a scattered division of neighborhoods, dead ends, and narrow roads that were once little more than goat paths.

The meander of the streets made her jumpy, expecting bad neighborhoods around every corner. For all Aransa's flaws, the stepped nature of her home lent it to easy division – a blessing and a curse. With class barriers entrenched, the lines where trouble brewed grew clearer. Made her job easier, in theory. But it'd made her watchers lazier, too. At the end of the day, when a crime had been committed, she knew full well her watchers were more likely to go poking around for evidence in the nearest adjoining poor quarter. In her long experience, the vast majority of offenses were committed by those who knew the victim. The division, the poor quarters, just made for easy scapegoats.

As much as Hond Steading unnerved her, a semblance of order emerged as she stalked its winding streets. The city was not a sloppy mishmash, as she had originally thought. Its subtle melding and gradation of culture and class fascinated Ripka. So many here. So many pushed up against each other, but not drawing hard lines in rock and sand. However the Hondings had managed to foster this sense of togetherness, she admired them.

The more she walked the dusty streets, scents of honey and cactus and crisp-skinned goat heavy on the air, the more she began to see the city's twisting paths as a benefit to their defense. Thratia would be just as thrown as Ripka had been upon arrival in the city. The hodgepodge nature of Hond Steading was unique on the Scorched, where most cities were laid out to best facilitate the mining of their firemounts. Hond Steading had been the first – organic in its growth, massive in its current scale. For any soldiers Thratia managed to bend to her banner, they would be Scorched-born, used to well-ordered streets and clear hard lines. Dealing with Hond Steading would not be an easy shift for them.

Ripka turned hard on her heel, angling back up the dusty road she'd wandered down toward the Honding palace. Nouli, for all he was clever, was Valathean born and raised. His tactics would focus on the clear, hard lines of the Scorched cities he knew well. And because he was too unwell to wander the streets himself, Ripka had to be his eyes and ears. Had to let him know what she'd observed.

It was a purpose she could serve well, and it added a little spring to her step.

As she looped up a curving side street toward a stone-laid thoroughfare, a blue-coated woman stepped into her path. Ripka stopped short, startled. A watcher. The woman had the weather-beaten appearance of one who roamed an outdoor beat, her age made difficult to discern by the sun-bitten wrinkles at the corners of her eyes.

Ripka'd never been stopped by a watcher before. She felt naked without her own blue coat, and tugged self-consciously at the long caramel sleeves of the tunic Pelkaia had loaned her. She'd have to buy new clothes, soon. Clothes meant not to fit underneath a layer of blue.

"Good morning, watcher," she said.

The watcher's smile grew a little wider. "Good morning, Captain Leshe."

Ripka stood straighter. "Miss Leshe is appropriate, please."

"If you insist. Have you been enjoying our fair city?"

Ripka bit her tongue to keep from divulging all her revelations. The watcher was after small talk, not a detailed evaluation of the city's civic planning. "It is blessedly cooler than Aransa, without being as cold as–" She cut herself off just short of saying the Remnant. "Some southern cities I've visited."

"We do partake of the Darkling Sea's breezes during monsoon season, but I'm sure you've realized a discussion of the weather isn't why I stopped to chat with you."

Indignation and fascination warred within Ripka. So this was what it was like to be on the other end of being suspected of mischief in a watcher-controlled city. Fascinating. "Have I done something wrong?"

"Not as such. My captain has sent me to fetch you, to discuss your continued presence in Hond Steading."

"Dame Honding has given me her blessing."

"We understand. Would you come with me, please?" She spoke in the well-practiced tone that gave the polite illusion of question without being an outright command.

For just a moment Ripka was tempted to tell her off, return to the palace and complain to the Dame that her watchers had for some reason not gotten the message that Ripka was welcome in their city.

But Ripka'd never been one to hide under another's authority. And besides, her curiosity was well and truly piqued. The watch could very well be a deciding force in the city's defense. If she could bend this captain's ear, make him see reason and urge his working with Nouli... So many possibilities unspooled within her mind that she caught herself grinning, wiped it away, and gave the watcher what she hoped was a respectful nod.

"Please, lead the way."

The watcher wasted no time. They cut through the city at a crisp near-jog, Ripka struggling to memorize all the twists and turns.

The watcher delivered Ripka, breath coming a little quickly due to the pace, to the front doors of the station house and bade her enter and ask for the captain – she was expected – then disappeared back into the city to see to her other tasks.

Ripka forced a deep breath, and steeled herself. Too long on the Remnant had made her jumpy, wary of imprisonment of any kind. She was fine. Even if things went wrong here, Enard knew she'd gone out walking. With Dame Honding's power behind him, it wouldn't take him long to discover where she was being held.

Curiosity overrode caution, and she shoved the station house door open. A large room splayed out before her, high of ceiling and brightly lit with dozens of gleaming oil-fed candelabras. The grandeur of Valathea's aesthetics infused the room's size and scale, but the austerity she'd seen on display at the Honding palace was present as well. Every stick of furniture was needed, every piece well-made, if a little worn from use.

Ripka caught herself doing an inspection – cleanliness of the floors, easy access to a restraints cage – and stopped. This wasn't her station house. This wasn't why she was here.

Watchers buzzed through the room, files tucked under arms or prisoners ushered before them. A few harried citizens sat at tables, distressed and talking with their assigned watcher. Everything, so far as she could tell, seemed in order here. Running smoothly.

With a pleased smile, she stepped up to the room's primary desk and addressed the sharp young man standing at ease there.

"I'm here to see your watch-captain."

Surprise registered, but was gone in a flash. "I see. Do you have an appointment?"

"I might. One of your watchers collected me and told me he wished to see me." As she spoke, she realized how ridiculous the story sounded. She didn't even know the watch-captain's name, let alone the name of the watcher who'd corralled her here. Ripka's stomach soured as the young man's face grew tight with confusion. That watcher could have very easily been playing a prank on her, making the disgraced watch-captain feel important, then ripping the rug out. She might be making a fool of herself. She cleared her throat and started again. "My name is Ripka Leshe."

"Oh," the man said. "My apologies. I didn't think they'd find you so soon. Please, follow me."

The watcher opened a door and stepped aside so that she could pass. Laughter rolled out, young and bright. Ripka stepped into the well-lit room and blinked. A man sat behind a desk, shirtsleeves rolled to his elbows and a spatter of grey in his short-cropped hair. She marked him in his forties, and the young girl sitting on his shoulders at five, maybe six. The girl grinned at Ripka, revealing a wide gap where a front tooth should be, and the older man looked a touch embarrassed.

The air smelled of clean oil and fresh ink, the floor beneath her feet was swept clean and all the furniture polished to a high shine. If ever there existed an office meant to be the complete opposite of the Remnant Warden, Radu Baset's, this was it.

"I'm Kalliah," the little girl said.

"Am I interrupting…? Ripka asked.

"No, no, not at all." The man swung Kalliah from his shoulders with ease and the girl whooped. "Watcher Yethon, please take Kalliah to her mother. She's probably worried sick."

"Any idea where she's at?" the watcher asked, taking Kalliah's hand and leading her toward the door.

"Swimming at the hole, more than like."

Kalliah brightened. "Can I go swimming too?"

"Only if your mother says you can."

"Yay!" Kalliah dragged her watcher escort behind her like a kite. The man sat back down behind his desk with a rueful laugh.

"I apologize, miss. She gets away from her mother sometimes, but always to come to see me. Could be worse acts of escape, I suppose. Now, what can I do for you? Did we have an appointment?"

"I'm not sure," she confessed. "One of your watchers asked me to come see you. I am Ripka Leshe, formerly of the Aransa watch."

"Captain Leshe!" The man was on his feet in an instant. He rounded the desk and held her hand in his before she could blink. He shook it like it had something foul on it he was trying to kick clean, a huge smile splitting his face. "I should have known, shouldn't I? Sit, sit, please, can I get you a drink?"

He was gone as soon as he'd come, disappearing back behind his desk to rummage through a drawer that produced the telltale clink of bottles. Feeling like she'd just been swept up in a monsoon wind, she took the chair opposite his desk and sat. It didn't even creak.

"No thank you, Captain…?"

"Lakon. Falston Lakon. I'd say you could call me Falston, but Lakon's less of a mouthful on the balance. Are you sure you won't drink? I've fizzed Erst Pear juice, new stuff, no booze in it if that's what you're worried about."

"I'll try the juice, thank you, Lakon."

He produced two glazed clay cups half-full with something sweet and fizzy. As the bubbles popped against her tongue, she recognized the bitter-tannic taste of selium bubbles. Before he could throw another flurry of conversation at her, she gathered herself.

"Captain, I apologize if I've done anything to disturb your watchers. I understand the presence of another captain – even though I've lost my post – can be worrisome to some watchers. I mean no harm to you or your organization."

He chuckled. "They hide it well, but my people are all in a tizzy that you're here. The Dame sent me a letter last night to say you'd arrived and would be staying at the palace indefinitely. Of course she didn't seal the pits-cursed note, so half the station knew about it by morning and the other half by midday. There's no worse gossipmonger than a watcher.

"When we started getting reports of a plain-clothes woman roaming the city, acting suspicious by checking out dark alleys and warning citizens against easily stealable items, well, I confess there was a bit of a betting pool on who would find you first – I guess Halka won. She'll be insufferable about it.

"You really riled up the populace, you know. It's one thing to be told to mind your goods by a watcher, but when a perfectly sane and healthy-looking woman comes up to you and tells you the same it really puts the wind up these desert flowers. The High Ridge Ladies' Club is all afuss – they think it's some grand conspiracy, though skies know what the conspiracy they've dreamed up is for. You've caused quite the stir in the city, Captain Leshe."

"Please, call me Ripka. I apologize for frightening your citizens; that really wasn't my intention."

He held up a hand to forestall her. "You misunderstand me. I'm *glad* you did. This city has been too cursed safe, and all the older generation are set in their ways, not thinking at all that anyone could dare do anything to harm them, or steal from them. But Hond Steading's getting big, and with the refugee problem spilling over from Aransa and some of the smaller cities Thratia's people have been snatching up in her name, well, desperate people are here. They're hungry and they're scared and our regular populace just doesn't know how to deal with it. I'm glad you scared 'em a bit. Maybe they'll watch themselves now."

"You've a refugee problem?" she asked, embarrassment buried beneath professional interest. He grinned like a man who'd just snagged a fish on a hook.

"'Fraid so. I know you did the best you could for Aransa – please don't think I'm disparaging you for what happened there – but the fact is Thratia's takeover wasn't as complete as she thought. People got scared, they ran, and there aren't a lot of places to run to on the

Scorched, you know? Lots of them came here, looking for new lives – or at the very least safety. And the Dame is a kind soul, beneath all that iron she carries around her, so she let them in with open arms, started training programs for them to get jobs in spots we're lacking here in the city. But there's just so many, and every day the numbers grow. We could shut 'em out, it's been discussed, but the Dame doesn't want them to die in the desert on their own. And anyway, they've got nowhere else to go. They'd likely camp on our doorstep, and just get absorbed into Thratia's army when it arrives. None of us want to see them turned into cannon fodder, even if they are kicking up a spot of trouble here and there.

"We suspect some of Thratia's supporters are getting through too, of course, but there's no real way to tell. Nothing to tie them together, if you know what I mean. But we've found a bunch of her trash kicking around the city. Posters, leaflets, things like that. I'll hand it to the old girl, she knows how to write a piece of propaganda."

Ripka remembered stacks of crates, loaded with liqueur and weapons. She'd discovered them too late – the weapons had already been distributed throughout the city. Though she doubted Thratia would risk using the liqueur as her cover again, she thought it a safe bet that the method would be more or less the same. And here, in Hond Steading, she had time. They were in the early days of Thratia's aggression here; she hadn't come knocking yet. If Ripka was lucky, she could poison the roots of Thratia's uprising before they ever took hold.

"I don't mean to be presumptuous," she said carefully, watching Lakon's expression with every word. "But I have some experience with Thratia's techniques. If you'd allow me to consult you on these matters, I think we could puzzle out what keeps her people connected here in your city."

Lakon grinned and drained his glass. "I was hoping you'd say that. Consider yourself hired, Captain, though the issue of rank might be a tricky one."

She waved him off. "No. I won't wear the blues again. But I will help you as best as I can."

"As some sort of private watcher?"

She shrugged. "Think of it as undercover work. People may know my reputation, but they don't know my face, and looks are an easy enough thing to alter anyway."

"Hmm. I like it. Where would you start, though? You've hardly been a day in the city. I suppose I'll have to give you a tour."

Ripka leaned forward and set her empty cup down, eyes bright and a new intensity burning in her chest. "Tell me, have there been any new food or drink crazes in your city lately?"

CHAPTER 7

Pelkaia lay dying. Every bone in her body ached. Every pore of her skin bled hot sweat into the fine linen of her sheets. The steady thrum of her heart was a stutter-stop drumbeat in her chest, marching her to her grave.

She twisted, feeling her back peel away from the sweat-puddle it had left throughout the night, the fresh air a blessed, cool kiss over her heat-tired skin. Movement sapped her strength, made her limbs shaky with exhaustion. Fingers jittery, she reached to the trunk bolted alongside her bed, slumping, fumbling with the catch.

So early. Sunlight slanted like blades across her cabin floor, pressed at her eyes and made her vision milky – no, that wasn't the light. Old eyes. Old, stupid, failing eyes.

Been alive too long. Been moving and breathing and fucking and fighting longer than she'd had any right to. Even of the long-lived Catari, Pelkaia was an anomaly. Must be. Couldn't even imagine the whole of her people stumbling through old age like this, wretched as she was.

How many years? Her fingertips brushed familiar bottles, body going through the motions even while her mind wandered down old, dusty hallways of memory.

Really – how many years? How many children raised and, halfbreeds that they were, left to the dust? Except Kel. Sweet Kel. He'd died before his youth was through, died to hide Thratia's plans.

She pulled stoppers with her teeth, drank bitter concoctions she hardly remembered the names of. Every morning, she forgot them. By night they'd be back again, filling up the empty spaces that now echoed in her brain. Full formulas, names, methods of growing the plants to make them. Each one was bitter, acerbic. A healthy throat would have rebelled at their abuse, but hers was long past healthy.

Ritual complete, she dropped the last of the bottles into place and flopped back into bed, arms splayed, feeling the potions that would be poison to any other body course through her. Eyes half-closed, she imagined them filling her veins, replacing her blood, re-inflating her vitality. Stolen time. That was all she had left, now.

But a little bit of stolen time might just be enough to do some good.

Or punish some wrongs.

The cabin door banged open, and she was amused to realize she remembered the sound. Coming back up, now, she thought. Raising herself from the dead. Her skin was growing cooler, almost clammy, the sweat that sheathed her turning into chilly condensation. She cracked an eye, saw her vision clear, then risked cracking the other. Took a breath, and noted her lungs inflated fully.

Functional, then. At least for another day.

"Pell?"

Oh. Right. Coss. She'd been so busy raising herself from near-death she'd forgotten he came in to wake her every morning. Well, ostensibly to wake her. She suspected he insisted on barging in as soon as the sun was up to make sure she was still alive.

"I'm here," she said, which was a rather stupid thing to say because, really, where else would she be?

"I see that." His voice was soft, amused. Not long ago that voice had made her knees weak. It still made her head swim, her heart thump, if she were being honest with herself.

But that was before she started dying. She'd had to kick him out of her room, then. Couldn't let your lover see you rot from the inside out. Poor dear thought he'd done something wrong. Probably thought Pelkaia was drinking herself to death, or something, with all the bottles she kept locked up in her room. She almost giggled at the thought, then remembered she had company.

"Give me a hand?" she asked, after she moved to swing her legs over the bed's edge and realized they weren't quite ready to obey her yet.

Coss was at her side in an instant, his big hand enfolding hers while he slipped the other behind her back, between her shoulder blades where the sweat was still thick, and helped her upright. Either he didn't notice, or he pretended not to, when her legs thumped weakly over the edge of the bed, heels dragging on the floor.

Gods below the dunes, but the worry in his eyes almost broke her faster than the age taking its dues on her organs.

"Are you well?" he asked, which seemed a stupid question, because obviously she wasn't.

"Stomach upset," she lied easily, giving him a lopsided smile as she pushed a sweat-damp chunk of hair off her forehead. No one ever asked detailed questions about stomach troubles.

Except Coss, apparently. "What did you eat last night?"

She sighed and rolled her eyes, wiggling her fingers to get the feeling back in them. "Same thing as everyone else, just didn't take well to me."

The look he gave her was clear enough. He thought she was full of donkeyshit. Which she was, but that wasn't any of his business.

As clarity seeped back into her overheated mind, she began to realize just what was wrong with this scene. Why Coss was seeing her so weak and shaking when she'd taken great pains to push him away from this, away from the truth of what was eating her up inside. Coss came to her every morning, sure, but after she'd raised herself from the dead. After she'd had her bath and her elixirs and had a moment to sit just breathing, gathering herself against the plain exertion of living.

Essi. Little pouf-headed Essi was supposed to bring her a bucket to wash with in the morning, supposed to knock on the door to raise her from her sleep long before the sun got high enough to glare through her window like it was doing now. Pelkaia blinked, taking in the room through clearing eyes. There was the bucket, full up to the brim by the shut door. But no Essi. And here was Coss. Frowning at her like he'd said something and she hadn't answered. Probably the truth, that. She forced herself to focus. She was the captain of this ship, and a protocol she'd initiated had been broken. Find out the reason. Find out why Coss was looking at her like he'd seen a ghost, when he wasn't meant to realize she was teetering on the edge of the pits until she'd fallen into the dark of them.

"Where's Essi? Why did she not wake me?" And, unspoken, *why are you here now*? But she didn't need to explain that. He knew her well enough to scrape the meaning from the surface of her words.

"Essi hollered at your door for a half-mark before Jeffin came and got me. Thought you were dead."

She was, of course; the timing just hadn't quite caught

up with her yet. But that wasn't any of his business. "So you decided to let yourself in. Without permission."

His expression locked down. Well, as locked down as he could make it. Even stoic, practical Coss couldn't hide his feelings from her. She'd spent too long making a study of faces, the way they ticked away every emotional beat coursing through a person. It was what she was. Doppel. No, that wasn't right. Illusionist. Yes. Better.

"I thought you were ill and needed assistance." He gave her a slow look, making a point of taking in her still-trembling limbs and the human-shaped imprint of sweat on her sheets. Just as she didn't need to say everything she was thinking to get her meaning across, neither did he. What a sweet pair they'd made. She missed that. Missed him filling in the blanks of what she didn't say, missed him supporting her in all the hundreds of subtle ways only a person who has become your other half in truth ever really can. Missed doing the same for him.

Like now. A few months ago, if she'd seen that look on his face, she'd reach out. Brush his cheek. Give his hand a squeeze. Or even just smile in that way she knew made his belly loose. A little upward quirk of the lips, a sideways peek through her lashes.

She caught herself halfway between smiling and reaching for him. Shook her head to clear it.

"I was ill," she said, realizing she needed to back up her lie about her stomach. "Thank you for checking on me. I'm strong enough to wash now, if you don't mind…?"

It wasn't a question, they both knew that. He pursed his lips at her, shifted his weight uncomfortably in his crouch. He didn't want to leave, probably feared her drowning in her wash water, but she was captain. And though she hadn't exactly given him an order… well. She had, really.

"Call for me if you require help." So formal. So stiff.

Not bothering to hide a grimace he pushed to his feet, knees popping, and made a show of rubbing the small of his back. She almost laughed. How old was he? Thirty, forty? She'd never been good at guessing ages, but whatever his small aches, they were nothing compared to the bonewither eating her alive. She envied him his sore knees, his knotted back. Envied him the time he had left.

Envied, too, whoever would get to spend that time with him once she was gone.

He left her there, shutting the door gently behind him, and it took her longer than she'd ever admit to find her feet, to shuffle over to the bucket of sun-warmed water and wash the sticky sweat from her body. The trembling of her limbs sprayed droplets across the floor, sprinkled wet darkness on her walls, her shelf. She grit her teeth, breathed deep and even, and by the time she was washed and dressed in clothes loose enough to hide the bone braces she wore all the time now, she was stable. Calm. Something like her old self.

Whatever that meant. Standing before her mirror as she forced her hair into a tight queue – Ripka's style, part of her recalled as she worked – she wondered if the madness that had driven her mother to raving fits was finally taking root in her own mind. She'd caught glimpses of it during those days in Aransa, when Kel was left cooling beneath the sand and she had only her vengeance to nurse. Felt the intoxicating lilt of mania speed her heart and sharpen her mind every time she picked up a blade to draw blood. If it wasn't for the responsibility of the *Larkspur* and its crew – she had given up hiding it after the Remnant, given up on being the *Mirror* – then she would have devolved into her mother's madness in the days after Aransa.

Or dedicated her life to destroying Thratia Ganal.

Maybe that was what she was doing, after all. She had gathered a cadre of skilled deviants, stolen them away from Thratia's reach, trained them up to be stronger and more refined than they had any right to be as non-Catari.

In those moments she had felt calm. Centered. As if in rescuing her little collection of deviants she was doing a good thing. And she had been. Still was. Rumors swirled about deviants hiding in Hond Steading, after all. That was the only reason they were still lingering here. Fishing, fishing.

But maybe those were just the reasons she gave them all. Lies she'd told to herself. Maybe... maybe the madness had never really left her. Could it ever? She recalled islands of sanity in her life, oases of peace raising her children bracketed by hard rage and desperation.

She had done good, in the literal sense. Had saved lives. But she was doppel – *illusionist* – and duplicity was bred into her bones. Bones that were leaking their true nature throughout her now.

She had been saving people, yes. But she had also been gathering them. Gathering weapons.

Weapons Thratia Ganal was coming to meet.

Pelkaia smiled at herself in the mirror, and did not bother covering her Catari features with a false face today. When she opened her cabin door to gaze upon her crew, to issue the orders for the day, she looked upon them all – each in turn – and saw them for the truth beneath the veneer.

Sharpened spears, under her command. Weapons the likes of which hadn't been released upon the Scorched since the time of Catari dominance.

And as they smiled at her, waved good morning and asked after her recovery from her so-called stomach troubles, she realized the true extent of her command, here and now. They trusted her. Implicitly.

Pelkaia looked upon her unknowing soldiers, and was filled with joy.

CHAPTER 8

Ripka was being followed. At first she suspected the watchers, tailing her to report back to their captain, but not a hint of blue flashed in the corner of her eye. No, someone else was shadowing Ripka's heels, and it wasn't likely to be anyone friendly.

She didn't dare pick up her pace or start weaving through streets, lest she alert her tail that they'd been spotted. She kept her gait a slow, easy stroll. Just a woman new to the city out for a little exploring. Anticipation tingled in her fingertips. She wished she had her weapons – a cutlass, a baton, anything really. But she was no longer a watcher, and normal citizens didn't roam the streets armed to the teeth.

Despite her unease, a little thrill went through her. It'd been a long time since she'd played any flavor of cat-and-mouse game. She meant to win.

The street opened up into a stall market, hot spices and pungent dyes heavy on the air. She cut close to the right-hand stalls, weathering the clamor of excited vendors with polite, but firm indifference. She had no interest in their goods, she just wanted to see what her follower would do in a denser crowd.

The crowd congealed behind her as she passed, as it always did in busy marketplaces, but this had a different feel to it, a touch of tension. Someone was moving quickly back there, trying to keep Ripka in their sight. She grinned a little, pretended to finger a light-woven scarf, then stepped into the narrow space between two stalls, flicking her gaze back the way she'd come. A hint of an arm as a person – by build she suspected a woman – slithered back into the crowd. Nothing recognizable. Nothing even inherently threatening. But that arm had been clothed in russet, not watcher blue.

While her follower was busy avoiding Ripka's backward stare, she slipped behind a pile of rugs and darted into a side-alley, drawing raised eyebrows from the rug seller, but nothing more. Back pressed against the stone of the alley wall, she waited. A smear of a shadow approached, movements halting and furtive. The shadow stopped to finger the same rug Ripka had.

The shadow drew close. Ripka tensed. An arm swung into the alley and Ripka was upon it in a second, yanked hard on the forearm and pivoted, swinging the woman like a club into the alley wall.

She smacked the stone with a grunt and a yelp of surprise, bush of pale blonde hair catching some of the dust that showered down upon her. Ripka's eyes widened.

"Honey!"

She released her and stepped back, wary. Honey was her ally – or had been, in the Remnant – but the woman's lust for violence wasn't something to be ignored. Ripka wouldn't have been surprised at all if Honey'd decided to hunt Ripka through the streets, just for fun.

"What are you doing following me like that?"

Honey peeled herself off the wall with a little grunt and adjusted her clothes, wiping away grit and bits of slime as best she could.

"I was bored," she said in her whisper-soft rasp. "Dame Honding says I'm not to play with the knives, they're for the kitchen staff."

Ripka swallowed a laugh. "Well, she's not wrong. Did I hurt you?"

Honey's eyes widened as she prodded at the forearm Ripka had yanked on. "Just a little bruise."

"I'm sorry about that, I didn't know it was you."

"I don't mind." She lapsed into her usual silence, watching Ripka with those wide, reverent eyes. Honey, bored. In a city of hundreds of thousands. Ripka swallowed. In bringing Honey here she had, inadvertently, released a viper into a nest of pinkie rats.

Before they had arrived at the city, Ripka had made sure Honey had a new set of clothes outside of the worn old jumpsuit the prison had given her. They were a little big; the new clothes hung down around her body making her look like an underfed urchin.

"Hey, you two!" The proprietor of the rug stall stuck his head down the alley, pinched eyes narrowed with suspicion. "I don't like no one sneaking around my goods, understand? Get lost a'fore I call the watch."

Honey began to hum softly to herself.

"Took a wrong turn. Don't mean any trouble!" Ripka grabbed Honey by the wrist and yanked her along the alley to the other side. This street was quieter, a residential neighborhood with a sparse scattering of foot traffic. Ripka huffed the warm desert air and breathed out with a heavy sigh.

"Honey," she began haltingly. "This city is in danger, and I have a lot of work to do to try and keep it safe.

You–" she bit her lip, cutting off what she was going to say: *you can't keep dogging my heels.* What else was Honey going to do? This wasn't a woman who made easy friends, and for some reason she'd taken a liking to Ripka. "You want to help me?"

Honey visibly brightened. "What do I do?"

Ripka knew of Honey's more violent skills, but the fact remained that she hadn't a clue how the woman had come to be the way she was. What Honey's life had been before the Remnant was a mystery to Ripka, but she might yet be harboring some skills that could be of use.

"What did you used to do, before we met?"

She frowned. "Hung with Clink and the girls."

"Yes, but, before that – before the Remnant?"

Honey buttoned up her lips and just stared. Ripka knew better than to think that it was because she didn't understand.

"All right then, you don't have to tell me. I have to go and stake a place out. It's watcher-work, but I think you could help. All you have to do is be quiet, and remember everything you see and hear. Can you do that?"

Honey, always a riveting conversationalist, nodded.

They found the bright berry cafe at the end of the market, tucked under a faded garnet overhang in the shadow of Hond Steading's forum, a place the Dame had built to allow the intellectuals of her city to debate the problems of the time.

Ripka hadn't known what to expect, really. The taverns of Aransa that had sold Renold Grandon's honey liqueur, hiding weapons of Thratia's loyalists in the bellies of the crates, had been middling places. Places where the working class of Aransa gathered to drink, gamble, and talk out their worries. Bright Eyes, as the cafe's slapdash painted sign declared itself, was packed with men and women whose nails Ripka found suspiciously clean.

Small round tables spilled out into the street, barely large enough to support two of the small sienna-glazed mugs of tea the cafe sold. Patrons leaned over their steaming mugs, either engaged in animated conversation with their partners or bent over sheaths of ragged-edged papers. The tannic-sweet aroma of the tea was so heavy on the air that Ripka felt more alert just by taking a deep breath.

A harried waitress emerged from the cafe's doors, spotted Ripka and Honey standing there, and bustled right up to them. She'd piled her hair atop her head and speared both sides with two charcoal pencils. She bared her teeth at them in a forced smile.

"Got a table around back that just opened up. You want it?"

"Sure," Ripka said.

The waitress turned on her heel so sharp she'd make a watcher look sloppy, and stormed the doors of her cafe. They were deposited at a tiny round table with precariously high stools on the cafe's back patio. The waitress vanished, returned with a couple of matched cups and saucers, and hit them with a hard stare.

"You want it hot?"

"Uh, sure," Ripka said.

The waitress snorted, disappeared, and returned with a piping hot pitcher full of bright eye berry tea. She doled out both mugs, then dashed them off with something from an amber glass bottle. Something that, as soon as it hit the hot liquid, sent up a steaming curl of biting alcohol. Ripka wrinkled her nose.

"What's that?"

The waitress scowled. "That's your heat. First tea refills are free, rest cost you a small copper grain. Want any more heat, and it's double that. Cause any trouble, you're banned for life."

"Lot of people cause trouble here?"

The waitress puffed a curl of hair from her eyes and pursed her lips like she'd kissed a cactus. "Lady, there's nothing worse for trouble than a couple of bright-upped brainiacs."

With that pronouncement, she swept from the patio and left Ripka and Honey alone with their drinks. Ripka gave hers a tentative sniff. Bright eye berry was a common enough staple at all watcher station houses. She'd never been a regular drinker herself, she preferred her teas heavy with spice, but the bright eye taste never quite managed to offend her. She took a sip. Couldn't much taste the sweetness of the tea over the acrid bite of the dash of whisky.

Honey stared at her cup like it was a viper rearing to strike.

"Everything all right?" Ripka asked.

"Smells sweet," she said.

"Not a fan of the sweet stuff? Unfortunate name choice, then. Go on and give it a taste. It's not too bad – the whisky cuts the sweetness."

Honey gave it a taste, and a flicker of pleasure crinkled her face. "Oh. That's nice."

"See? Drink it slow, now, I want to get a good look at this place."

Honey sipped quietly while Ripka leaned back, cup in hand, and took in the view. The interior of Bright Eyes Cafe hadn't been much to look at. It'd been a cramped space, just a handful of tables and narrow chairs, the air heavy with smoke. But the patio was wider than she'd expected, and whoever owned the place had put some effort into the details. The stone walls hemming them in were crawling all over with spiny-leaved vines, sporting the tiny buds that could be harvested and roasted to make the eponymous tea. Huge umbrellas dotted the patio, dropping and faded, but well patched and providing much-needed shade. Whether by chance or choice, the patio was angled to take advantage of the evening breeze.

Ripka sighed, leaning into her seat, truly relaxed. Here, she couldn't see the Honding family palace. Here, she could pretend the city would carry on like this forever.

"I say, it's not right. The old Dame has got to see sense."

Ripka searched those gathered for the voice and found the source. A man no more than twenty leaned across a table toward two companions, gesturing with every word. A rat's tail of a beard clung to his chin, and he wore a drooping hat that the poor soul probably thought gave him a rakish air, but really just gave off the rather unappealing message that he was, as it were, limp.

His companions did not seem half so moved by the man's words as he'd hoped they would be. To his right, a woman in a cheap beige shift with hints of ink and paint about her fingers leaned back to put distance between them and snorted. To his left, a man just slightly the speaker's senior toyed with the rim of his cup, fingers drumming against his knee under the table. The nervous man wore a suit coat despite the steamy monsoon warmth, the elbows and hemline patched with ruddy brown to contrast the overall hue of mustard. The colors would have made most complexions on the Scorched look as if they were suffering from sand scabies, but this man was dark enough to carry them off.

"Let it go, Dranik," the woman said. "The Dame knows what she's about."

"Does she?" the young man pounced. "She's what, seventy-five? She could be going raw in the head and no one would dare point it out. We need a new system in place. A representative law code."

"My own grandma's near ninety," the patched man offered, "and sharp as Valathean steel."

"Bully for her, but I don't see how that's relevant."

"I don't see how *any* of this is relevant." The woman shook her cup for a refill and clucked her tongue. "The Dame will do as she wills. It's not for us to decide."

"But it *could* be, that's the whole point!"

Ripka caught Honey's eye and mouthed, "What do you think?"

"Thunder, no lightning," Honey murmured.

Ripka nodded agreement, but kept an ear on the conversation anyway. The young man's tone was unusually earnest. She'd come across a lot of people with that kind of earnestness in their voice in Aransa. Nine times out of ten, they were just dying to tell her all about whatever strange conspiracy they'd stumbled across that week, and their evidence was always in the dying off of a tree, or the presence of game tracks where they were convinced nothing could have made them. Nonsense, on the balance.

But something about this man told her that he wasn't prone to that particular flavor of conspiracy. For one, he was quite a deal cleaner than the usual type, and for two, there really was something afoot in Hond Steading. She thought about approaching him outright, expressing interest in the ideals she'd overheard, but that'd raise suspicion. He must meet with more like-minded individuals sometime. If she managed to cross the lad's path at just the right moment, then maybe…

"Republicanism is dead," a wiry-bearded man at a table near Ripka's suspicious trio declared. The young man, Dranik, bristled all over.

"There's no proof of that," Dranik said.

"Fiery pits there isn't. Look at what happened in Aransa!"

"That was a success! Commodore Ganal was voted to her post, in case you've forgotten."

"Voted," the older man slurred, making air quotes around the word with both hands as he swayed toward Dranik's table. He thumped a hand down and made all three cups jump. "That previous warden of theirs – *he* was voted in, right and proper, then Thratia comes along and gets him killed and scoops the city right into her pocket. Tell me, who was running against her in this fair and enlightened election?"

"That mine-master–"

"Also dead! Murdered, his sel-hub burned down around him. You think that's coincidence, I got something shiny to sell ya."

"Knock it off, old man," the woman said. "It's all just an intellectual exercise anyway. People like us don't make these calls."

"People like us can!" Dranik jumped to his feet and wagged a finger at the older man. "Ganal was still elected! I'd rather a contested election than a line of succession, wouldn't you?"

"Pahh. Nothing wrong with a bloodline at the head. Got a lot of sense to pass down through the generations. Can't elect experience like that."

"Oh, and that's working out well. Dame Honding's a grand woman, I'll grant you, but that nephew of hers is a discredit to the name. Where's he been? He doesn't care about this city. Hardly stepped foot in it."

"Heard he's hustling gambling tables in the south," the woman drawled.

"I heard he's *murdered* someone," Dranik threw in. "What kind of leader would that be? We need a new system in place, before it's too late and we end up with the likes of that buffoon."

"You want to run elections like the other un-founded cities?" The old man snorted. "Know what they call the leaders of those places? *Wardens*. Like they run a prison! Hond Steading ain't no prison. It's a jewel. The Scorched's jewel."

"That's only because the wardens operate under the yoke of the empire. If we were to shake off Valathea's rule, then–"

"Whoa, whoa, whoa," the old man sneered at Dranik. "You some kind of secessionist?"

"I'm only saying–"

The older man grabbed Dranik by the front collar of his shirt and gave him a hearty shake. "Saying what? Saying that bloodthirsty Ganal would be better for us than the Dame and her lineage?"

"I didn't mean *that*," he squeaked.

Ripka was on her feet without realizing. Between the sedative effects of the alcohol and the energizing nature of the tea, she felt a weird disconnect in her body – as if she were at once sleepy and alert, sharp but slow. Dimly she was aware of Honey rising alongside her, of the woman and the man at Dranik's table shouting protests.

She closed the distance. The old man was weakened by drink and age, so he put up no resistance as she peeled him off a flush-faced Dranik. No physical resistance, anyway. He spun around and loomed over Ripka, yelling into her face so that spittle flecked her cheeks. She grimaced.

"This is no business of yours, girl!"

Honey sidled up alongside the old man and pressed something shiny down low against his hipbone. Not too hard. Just enough to be clear of her intentions. Her voice was soft as always, but from the way the old man's eyes widened he didn't have trouble hearing.

"Don't yell at the captain."

Dranik brushed off his clothes and scowled, oblivious to the real reason the old man had gone pale. "This brutish behavior is the inevitable result of just the old-fashioned kind of thinking I was talking about."

"Out!" The waitress reappeared, her serving tray wielded like a battering ram. "I said no trouble, understand? I'm sick of your brains and your squabbles. Take it to the street, now, you're barred for the week."

"But–" Dranik protested. The woman with painted fingers whooped a laugh and jumped to her feet. The man in the mustard coat had managed to fade away to another table during the scuffle. Ripka caught his eye, and he winked, then hid his face with his mug and turned away.

"Knew this would be a good time," the woman said.

While they scurried to gather their things, the old man stood stock still, a little bit of sweat on his pale brow.

"Honey," Ripka murmured, "that's enough."

She pouted, but slipped whatever implement she'd found into a pocket and slunk away from the old man to take up her usual position in Ripka's shadow. Tray held before her, the waitress ushered all of them out onto the road and slammed the gate behind. The old man stomped off without another word. The woman gave a whoop and clapped Ripka on the back.

"Haven't seen you 'round before, lady, but that was a fine showing, twisting up old Hammod like that."

Ripka flushed. "I didn't want anyone to get hurt."

"Sweet of you, but Hammod's all bluster. I suppose now you know. I wouldn't be surprised if he's running home to change his pants."

"That's unkind, Latia," Dranik said.

"True, though, innit?" She flashed him a grin, and he rolled his eyes.

"So sorry to get you involved," Dranik said, turning to shake Ripka's hand, "but thank you nonetheless. Hammod may be toothless, but he's got to learn that that kind of behavior is no way to argue a point."

"You really believe all that stuff you were saying?" she asked, keeping her voice carefully neutral.

Latia snorted. "He believes it well enough, it's what he's willing to do about it where it all falls down."

"Now, that's unkind," Dranik admonished. Latia rolled her eyes, but lapsed into silence. "I am a believer, it's true. Say, you didn't get to finish your teas. May I buy you another?"

"And bend our ears?" Ripka asked. Dranik shoved his hands in his pockets and made a close survey of the ground.

"Hah," Latia said, "don't let him pick the place, he's got terrible taste. Let's all go back to my studio. I've got the tea, and Dranik hasn't got the grains to treat you both anyway. Could barely afford his own cup today."

"I afforded my cup just fine!"

"Then why were you nursing it so long?"

Dranik scuffed a kick against the dirt floor. "Fine. But I'll replace the tea we drink."

"Sure you will. Care to join us?" Latia turned to Ripka and Honey, eyebrows raised expectantly.

"What about your other friend?" Ripka asked.

"Oh. *Him*." Latia threw her hands in the air dramatically. "He'd only drink the tea to be *seen* drinking it, if you catch my meaning. So, what about it? Coming along?"

"We'd love to. I'm Ripka, and this is Honey," she said. Latia gave Honey the once-over and harrumphed.

"Don't hear a name like that every day."

"It's for my voice," Honey said. Ripka held her breath, but they seemed to take this at face value. Despite Honey's muted rasp, she had an undeniable sweetness to every syllable.

As they followed the two through the city, listening to them rehash old arguments, Ripka leaned close to Honey and whispered.

"Did you get a knife?"

"Found it." She flashed Ripka a quick glimpse of a worn fruitknife and then slipped it back into her pocket.

"Where?"

"The waitress's apron."

Ripka coughed on a laugh and grinned despite herself. "Honey, you little thief."

"She wasn't using it," Honey protested, a faint pout on her lips.

"Keep it close," Ripka said, eyeing Dranik's back. "And hidden."

CHAPTER 9

Aransa. City of fire. City of blood. City of Thratia Ganal. It slid into view upon the horizon just like any other city, the sharp crags of its skyline a black blot under the bowed head of the setting sun.

Such a city should not appear so docile, so sleepy under the lowing of the day's light. Detan wanted to hate the sight of it. This was the city that had almost trapped him, almost enslaved him. This was the city where he dug deepest, reached out and rendered the sky in flame.

This was the city that broke him, though it took a while for the cracks to show.

And yet he could not hate it. Could not even summon up a mild disgust. Aransa was beautiful, with its dormant mountain cut through with streets and city life facing the relatively blank face of its commerce-supplying firemount. Those black shards of obsidian that stretched between the city and the firemount gleamed even in the setting light, their heat twisting vision into smoky waves. Somewhere beneath those shards a vast chamber of magma dwelt, merging with the desert heat to create a killing field.

He'd walked that field, once. Walked it with Ripka, for Ripka, and had come out the other side a different man.

No, he couldn't hate it. Aransa was the city that'd forged him. He was only gaining temper, now. Honing his edge for what was to come.

Closer, and the differences began to show. Thratia's compound had expanded, bled out across the level below. The first time he'd seen it, the size had struck him as ostentatious. Now, with her walls consuming half of a whole level, he realized how wrong he'd been that first time. She'd just been waiting. Waiting to consume the city whole.

And, in a way, he'd let her. He'd scooped up Ripka, Tibs, Pelkaia, and New Chum and sailed out across the sands, leaving Thratia to do whatever she willed. He hadn't stayed. Hadn't even considered the possibility of staying to fight back. He'd been consumed by the need to escape the whitecoat's scalpel looming over his head. A fate he'd bent knee to, willingly, when the opportunity had suited him. Shame burned in his throat.

He was coming back, now. Coming back to set things to rights, if he could at all manage the task. That's why he'd bent knee to Aella, after all. Not just to save his friends, not just to discover the secrets of his own abilities. But to begin to balance the scales he'd left so terribly out of whack.

Standing beside him on the airship's forerail, Forge whistled low. "Looks like she's ready to march." Her hair obscured her face, but Detan could hear a hint of disdain in her tone.

If Thratia'd bled her presence all over the upper levels of the city, she'd gone and thrown up on the mid-levels. An entire level once given over to rental docks and mercer berths was swarmed with ships of war. Where

Thratia'd found the wood to construct them all on such short notice, he hadn't the slightest clue, but they existed despite their impossibility. Probably she'd had the source for that wood lined up years in advance. Even before her exile from Valathea, Thratia had been admired amongst her peers in their Fleet for her tendency to obsessively plan all her maneuvers.

The ships weren't things of beauty, not like the *Larkspur* had been. But then, they hadn't been built to impress – they were built for one purpose; troop transportation, and to rain fire from above. Each hull was long and lean, the cabins sparse and the rails speckled by heavy harpoon stands. Detan tried to count them, but the curve of the city hid the bulk from his view.

"Not a fan of old Commodore Throatslitter, are you?" he asked Forge.

Her long fingers, the nails trimmed down to stubs and the cuticles splitting, curled tight around the rail. "I got a certain amount of respect for a woman like that, you understand. No one can say she does anything by half measures, and that's the skies' truth, but you can't trust her. Got no honor for anything save her own goals, and those she keeps tight to the chest. A woman like that, she'd do anything if it meant achieving her goal. Anything at all."

"Says the convict," Detan mused.

She snorted. "Your hands can't be clean either, little lord. And anyway, I only did what I had to to make a living. Wasn't ever quick to kill or anything like that."

"And how did you make your living?"

She turned to regard him, and when he met her eyes, her look said he was the biggest idiot she'd ever met.

"Oh. Forge. It's in the name, isn't it?"

She laughed. "Now he gets it. Wrote up some false

contracts, identity papers, things like that. Nothing too
cutting, at least not that I knew of, and I confess I rarely
looked into the outcome of my works. I was good. Real
good." She picked at her curling, dry cuticles and flicked
a bit of skin over the side of the ship.

"How'd you get caught?"

She shrugged. "How's anybody get caught?
Overreached, is what I did. Wrote up a fake manifest for
some ship, real bit of bloated nonsense, and the mercer
who bought it couldn't pull it off. He got hauled in, and
I didn't find out about it until he'd already squealed and
the watch was knocking on my door. Usually it's just a
jail stint for that kinda work, but Valathea thought they
might want my talents someday and kicked me to the R
to keep an eye on me. Lucky girl I was, meeting Clink
and Honey straight off."

"Clink I know, but who's Honey?"

Forge shook her head, slow and ponderous. She stuck
her gaze on the approaching city and kept on picking
at her nails. "Don't know her real name, or her whole
story. Never bothered to ask – got the feeling that she
didn't want to talk about it, you know? Of the group –
me, Clink, Honey, and Kisser – Honey was the first of
us. She'd been at the Remnant a long while before she
hitched herself up to Clink.

"I asked Clink about it once, how they met and
decided to roll along together. She said Honey just came
up to her one day, sat down beside her, and that was
that. It was Clink's second day in, and she wasn't a fool –
she could tell everyone in the place was wary of Honey.
So she figured it wasn't such a bad idea to stick with the
girl. Then I came along, then Kisser, then the captain –
that's Ripka. Honey liked the captain right off, saw her
fight, you know. Honey likes that kinda thing. Escaped

with the captain, I think she did, anyway. Never saw her again in the Remnant and we know she wasn't killed that day. Only Kisser was."

"Is Honey a short, sturdy woman with a mess of blonde curls?"

"That's the one."

Detan nodded. "I saw her that day. As far as I know, she walked out with Ripka."

"You know... Part of me's happy she's free, the Remnant's no place to live. But the smart part of me... Well, I wonder if the world wasn't better off with her tucked away there, you know?"

"If Ripka's got her, it'll be all right."

Forge clucked her tongue against her teeth and leaned back to stretch. "Wish I shared your faith, little lord."

"You two." Misol snapped her fingers at them as she approached. "Get away from the rail now, we're preparing to dock."

"Straight to the compound, then?" Detan asked.

Misol shrugged. "There's not exactly room on the eleventh, now is there?"

They retreated from the fore rail, but Detan lingered nearby, watching the massive structure that was Thratia's home and stronghold grow closer and closer. The pilot was fidgety with the controls, yawing the ship at random angles as he approached. Detan grit his teeth to keep from yelling at the man for being a moron.

They angled toward the old u-dock, the very berth where he'd first sighted the *Larkspur*. The dock upon which Bel Grandon had died, just to make Detan's life a little harder.

He swallowed a lump in his throat. It didn't go anywhere.

The crew called out to one another, hauling ropes

and throwing anchor, as the ship slid into port. Those huge, hugging arms of deck reached out to give the ship shelter, though this ship was considerably smaller than the *Larkspur* had been. Where once crates of supplies – smuggled weapons and uniforms – had littered the ground, there was only empty space, now.

Empty, aside from Thratia Ganal and her entourage.

Ignoring Misol's warning about being near the fore rail, Detan stepped forward. He didn't have a lot of pride left, nowadays, but he'd be damned to the pits if he cowered in a cabin while they docked. He wanted to be the first thing she saw, as this ship of hers came running to her call. Wanted her to know he'd come back, and though he'd bent knee to Aella, he wasn't cowed. Wanted her, above all else, to see him grinning like he owned the world she'd threaded her fingers through – she just didn't know it yet.

Thratia stood at the spearpoint of her group of guards and attendants, posture as straight and sure as ever, chin lifted to meet the incoming ship. She wore granite-grey leggings, a bloodstone-hued tunic cut close to her lithe body. No weapons. Not even a wisp of armor. He wasn't the only one faking confidence, then.

Her hair was braided, pulled back from her shoulders to reveal the burn-scar that marred her cheek. The flesh rippled from the left side of her chin all the way up to her ear, the skin a warped pattern of shiny waves and eddies. Detan wondered if it hurt – if she pulled her hair from it to keep the ache at bay – but no. That wasn't Thratia's way. Even if it did ache, she'd still pull her hair back to display the injury.

The injury he'd given her.

They stared at one another as the ship tied in and the gangplanks were thrown down. She'd tried to kill him, or capture him, more than once. And here he was, strolling into her home under the power of one of her lackeys. Knee already bent, head bowed to her whims. She had called for him, reached south across the Scorched to a knobby little island in the middle of the Endless Sea and said: come.

And he had. He'd come when she called. Because he desired nothing more than to make her regret it.

He was on the dock, couldn't even recall walking down the gangplank, standing in front of Thratia. Trying real hard not to look down, not to spare the boards beneath his feet a glance. He didn't want to see the stain of Bel's blood there. Didn't want to see that it'd been scrubbed clean even worse.

"Thratia. You're looking better every day."

She cut her gaze to Aella. "You told me he'd changed."

"He's *started* to," the girl corrected.

A sane woman would have sighed. Would have glared at him and told him to shove it, or otherwise admonished him for mocking the very wound he'd dealt her. Thratia's lips didn't even twitch. She cocked her head to the side, looked him over real slow, and nodded to herself. "You'll do."

"Excuse me?" he asked, but she had already turned her back on him.

"See Aella's people settled," she said to her entourage. "Get secure facilities for the two prisoners, and show the guards where the training grounds are. Upper floor rooms for Aella and the Lord Honding. Honding has free run of the city, do not detain him. Aella–" She turned back to the girl and jerked her head to the side. "With me. My people will make sure Callia's settled."

And just like that, Thratia was gone, Aella floating along at her side like a ghost. Her people swarmed Aella's guards, the ship, bundled off Clink and Forge and set to carrying Callia away to be looked after. Detan found Misol directing the unloading of the ship and looked at her, open-mouthed.

"That's it?" he asked.

Misol shrugged. "I don't make the rules. Explore the city, if you'd like." She grinned a little. "I won't stop you."

"Lord Honding?" an attendant sidled up to him. "Would you like to be shown your rooms?"

"I..." he stammered, annoyed that Thratia, of all people, had managed to put him at a loss for words. "No. No. I'm going to go for a walk. Get my land-legs back."

"As you wish. When you return, any of the house staff will be able to show you to your rooms, you have but to ask." The attendant dipped her head and raised her palms above her head. "Skies bless," she said, and bustled off to see to her other duties.

"Skies bless," Detan responded by rote, numb with shock. Whatever he'd been expecting in Thratia's home, it hadn't been a household holding to the old functions of politeness. He certainly hadn't expected to be turned loose to do as he pleased just like any other guest.

Time to test the leash, he thought, and turned his back on the ill-omened dock to greet the streets of Aransa.

CHAPTER 10

Latia's studio nestled in the cool shadow of one of Hond Steading's many firemounts. Though Hond Steading's firemounts lacked the impressive, steep angles of Aransa's Smokestack, hints of the wealth they generated for the city clung to the sides of each and every one of them. Even from Latia's studio Ripka could see the fittings of pipework that snaked down the firemount from its mouth, moving selium and gathering it into central confinement chambers as sel-miners urged it along.

"The view's a bit rubbish," Latia said, as she swung open the door to her studio. "But I own the place outright."

"Built it with her own two hands," Dranik threw in. Latia scoffed.

"Mine and a half dozen others. Used to be I let other artists flop at my place when they were hard up, so when it came time to build my own studio they were all keen to help out. Some of 'em still drop by, but it's rare. They think I'm a snob now that I own property. Figures."

She ushered them into a wide, round sitting room with arched walkways hung with gauzy curtains leading out onto a patio. The walls were mud-plastered, but every inch had been enriched with vibrant frescoes in reds and yellows and blacks. Rare birds, lush flowers, and fish that Ripka suspected were purely imaginary, danced on every available surface.

"Is this your work?" Ripka asked.

Latia flicked the back of her hand through the air, as if brushing away their existence. "Old stuff, but yes. I like to keep the shadows of my past failures close."

"Failures? But they're beautiful. I've never seen anything like them."

"Latia is too modest." Dranik drew back one of the curtains to let in the breeze. "She believes everything she does is her best work while she's making it, and her worst as soon as it's done."

"Piddle. You don't make anything, my dear, and so you cannot possibly understand."

"I make no objects, that's true, but I *am* trying to make a new future for this tired world of ours."

Latia rolled her eyes to the sweet skies. "If I could have but half your confidence, I'd have taken over the world by now."

"What future?" Ripka asked, all curious innocence, as she traced a fish's tail through the mud-plaster with the tip of her finger.

"*Don't* get him started," Latia admonished.

"Not everyone has their head in their paints, Latia dear."

"At least let me get them their tea, first."

After much fuss, Latia situated Ripka and Honey in creaky chairs of woven scrubgrass and deposited heavy cups of bright berry in their hands. The packed dirt patio was soft under Ripka's feet, the breeze coming down off the firemount crisp with an edge of creosote. Latia might not have been fond of the view, but Ripka enjoyed it. It focused her, reminded her why Hond Steading mattered. Why she was making friends with these people, to discover if they knew any of Thratia's loyalists.

"I don't know why Dranik insists on meeting at cafes all the time," Latia said, swilling her cup in her hand. "I make a much better brew here at home."

"For the atmosphere, darling."

"Do you enjoy it when Hammod chokes you then?"

"Is that a regular occurrence?" Ripka asked.

Latia grinned fiercely while Dranik squirmed in his seat. "We disagree often, Hammod and I, but usually he has the sense to take it to the forum for a proper debate. I haven't a clue why he's so wound up as of late. He's never raised hands before," Dranik admitted.

Latia said, "Could have something to do with the army marching to our doorstep."

"Bah." Dranik waved her off. "Thratia won't crush us. She'd hardly want to take over a city that's been kicked to pieces."

"Oh, and does she write you personal letters to tell you as much? With little smooch drawings on the bottom, I bet. 'Don't worry, I won't grind you beneath my heel. Hugs and Kisses, General Throatslitter.'"

"Don't be so flip, Latia, this is important stuff. Dame Honding has had her run, but let's face it, the dynasty's dead. We need someone who will let us hold proper elections, debate city policies openly–"

"You mean like the forum the Dame opened, that you're so fond of?"

"Yes! But imagine if we could debate the merits of our officials as well as small civic matters."

"You forget, my dear, that people like Hammod would have just as much right to make arguments as you do."

They fell into a pattern of bickering that felt old and

comfortable. Ripka leaned back in her creaking chair, watching them battle out their differences with good-natured affection. Something like what they spoke of – that forum – might have done some good in Aransa. She wished she'd heard of it before Warden Faud's death. Then maybe all those angry souls who'd secretly worn her uniform would have been able to talk about their grievances with the empire, and find solutions, before a tyrant took the reins.

But it was too late for Aransa. She scrubbed the past failures of that city from her mind for the time being. Though they were what kept her up in the dark of the night, they helped her not at all now. She was here to find out how far Thratia's fingers reached. She let her mind wander, stoking the coals of information she'd gathered.

In Aransa, Thratia had smuggled weapons in the bottom of liqueur crates. Here, where Detan had written to his aunt about Grandon's honey liqueur, she would have had to find a different method. According to Watch-captain Lakon, these bright eye berry tea shops were the place to be seen amongst the young and vibrant of Hond Steading. The pattern might not be exact – it'd been the poor and working class Thratia had reached for in Aransa – but it needn't be. Thratia was a flexible woman, and Hond Steading was a very different city.

"Listen to you prattle on, Dranik, we're ignoring our guests." Latia turned her languid gaze upon Ripka and Honey. Her eyes were set just a touch further apart than Ripka felt was strictly normal, her lashes thick and a dark, dusky brown. In the half-shade of her patio, lounging against the scrubbrush furniture with a mug in her hand, Latia reminded Ripka of old etchings from fairytales. A queen of the fae, perhaps. Or a poisoner. Ripka's mother hadn't exactly been coy with the stories she'd sung Ripka to bed with as a child.

"Don't change your habits for our sake," Ripka protested. "We're new to the city, and happy for the company."

"New?" Dranik sat forward, fingers tight around his mug. "Where did you come from?"

Ripka doled out the bait with care. "Honey's from Petrastad, and I'm from Aransa."

"Aransa!"

"Petrastad!" Latia was suddenly alert. "What's it like?" She directed her question to Honey, who'd been running a thumb around the edge of her mug, but not drinking.

Ripka held her breath as Honey looked up, frowned a little in thought, then said, "Cold."

"Oh!" Latia said, "It must be more than that, surely?"

Honey stared at Ripka, begging for help with her gaze. Ripka just shrugged.

"Damp, too," Honey amended.

Latia arched one eyebrow at Ripka, who offered a helpless smile and another shrug. "Honey's a woman of few words."

"Never found much use for them," Honey said, her rasp growing in depth the more words she strung together.

"Oh, you have a throat injury! My poor dear girl. I had a friend like that. She wanted to sing on stage, but blew out her voice – something about not hitting the high notes right. Ah! I'm such a terrible host. That bright berry's no good for your throat *at all*. Here." Latia swept to her feet, swooped down upon Honey and snatched her untouched mug from her hands. "Let me brew you something a little more soothing."

Honey caught Ripka's eye and murmured, "I don't like the stage."

Ripka had absolutely no idea what she meant. She gave Honey's hand a pat, as if they were old friends discussing past heartaches, and the woman's pouting lips swung up in a smile. Ripka caught herself smiling back. As much as Honey unnerved her, Ripka was convinced there was a streak of good in the woman. A streak she'd like to get to know.

"Never mind the stage," Dranik said all in a rush. "When did you come from Aransa? Were you there for the takeover?"

"I was there when Warden Faud was murdered. I left shortly after that."

"So you've seen it in action! The well-oiled machine of the populace, rising together to elect a leader more fit to listen to their needs than the old aristocracy."

Ripka bit her tongue until she tasted iron. This young fool was her best bet for discovering Thratia's network in Hond Steading, or at least the only lead she'd stumbled across so far, and she didn't want to alienate him. Even if she thought he was a proper moron. And yet, she just couldn't bring herself to sing Thratia's praises. Ripka smiled a little, thinking of Detan. That willingness to deceive was where their paths diverged. She hoped he was having better luck than she was.

"...Thratia certainly disrupted the old ways. But I can't say how well it went, I was gone long before she took complete control."

"A pity you didn't get to see it." His shoulders slumped.

Latia glided back to the patio, dropped a fresh mug in Honey's hands and actually squeezed the woman's shoulder affectionately. "There you go, my dear. Drink up, drink up. I can't undo old damage, but I've got a few tricks up my sleeve to make living with it easier." She pinned Dranik with a look. "Living with old pain's the best anyone can hope for."

Dranik shifted, took a drink, coughed into his elbow

and adjusted the collar of his coat. "I was just asking Ripka here about her time in Aransa. Seems she left before things really got cooking."

"Oh?" Latia sank back into her seat and laid her arms out on the wide arms of the chair. "And why did you leave? Though I can think of a half dozen good reasons."

"I had a job to do," Ripka said.

"Really?" Latia grinned. "Come now, what kind of job? You've been traveling with your muted friend too long, I think. You can't just leave it like that – *a job*. By the sweet skies, woman, you do leave one's imagination to *spin* with that kind of talk. Fess up, now, what's your work?"

Watcher. Prisoner. Con-woman. Ripka blinked, slowly. None of these would suit her purposes here. Detan had told her, before she'd gone to the Remnant, to stick to half-truths when faced with the need to tell a lie, something she was likely to remember, to be able to supply details for. And she'd had work before she was a watcher. She'd just tried hard to forget it.

"I fought for prizes, for a while. I guard convoys now, if I can find the work."

Honey's eyes widened, just a touch.

"A prizefighter!" Latia leaned forward and clapped. "That explains your killer instincts with Hammod. Are you any good?"

"The best," Honey said, firmly.

"My, my, she speaks. How's that throat?"

Honey cleared her voice carefully. "Better," she said, and though her tone was still soft, it was clearer.

"Marvelous. And what about you? Surely we don't have two prizefighters before us tonight?"

"I used to sing," Honey said, and hummed a little under her breath. Ripka really, really wished she'd taken the time to work out a proper backstory agreement for them both before she'd gone storming off to the cafe. She'd spent too long with Detan, had grown too used to winging her maneuvers. That would have to stop. She had watcher training to fall back on, and to ignore it now would do more than herself a disservice.

"Of course you did, dear." There was a patronizing sadness in Latia's tone that said clearly that she'd seen this sort of thing all too often: women who thought they'd be great singers, great performers, cut down by faulty voices. Ripka wondered how much pity would fill Latia's heart if she knew Honey only sang when she was shedding another's blood.

"We met in Petrastad," Ripka said before Honey could explain herself further. "Both out of work, and decided to head to Hond Steading for a fresh start."

"Pity," Dranik said, "that you chose this place. There's nothing fresh in these streets."

"Piddle," Latia said.

"You don't know how beautiful it is," Honey murmured.

"I know," Latia insisted. "It's this tosh-head who can't see the beauty through his own self-importance. Say, where are you two staying?"

Honey's lips parted. Ripka said, "The palace district."

Dranik coughed over his cup. "Prizefighting must pay well."

"I was very good." At least that much was true.

"Well! I was going to invite you to stay awhile, the studio has been so quiet lately."

"You never ask me to stay," Dranik protested.

"Quiet of *worthwhile* conversation. But! You are new arrivals, yes?"

"Just last night," Ripka said.

"Marvelous. Let me be your ambassador to this sweet

city. Tonight, the Ashfall Lounge, around the seventh mark a friend of mine will sing. Please do join me."

"I don't know..." Ripka demurred, tried to catch Honey's eye but the woman was staring down at her cup.

"We'll come," Honey said.

"Wonderful!" Latia leapt to her feet and swept the empty cups from their hands, stacking them one atop the other. "Now I must usher you out, I feel all bursting with desire to paint – shoo, shoo, all of you. *Yes*, you too, Dranik. I shall see you tonight!"

Before Ripka could so much as thank the woman for her tea and invitation they were, all three of them, back out on the street, staring at the door that'd been closed in their faces.

"Well," Ripka said.

"You get used to it." Dranik ran a hand through his hair. "She gets... creative fits. Runs off in the middle of dinner sometimes."

"You've known each other long?"

He stared at her, wide-eyed, and barked a laugh. "She's my little sister."

"*Little?*"

"I know. She takes after our father." He paused. "You don't want to meet him. See you tonight?"

"Yes," Honey agreed.

Dranik gave them both a quick bow and took off at a brisk stroll. From within the studio, the sound of banging pots echoed. Ripka frowned at the door, then looked to Honey.

"You really want to go tonight?"

"Yes." Her expression grew wistful. "I miss singing."

"No cutting anyone who doesn't try to cut you first."

Honey sighed the sigh of a long-suffering child, kicked at the dirt, and gave a sullen nod.

CHAPTER 11

Aransa settled into darkness. Detan paced its winding streets, following the dusty, twisting paths cut into the side of the dormant mountain as if finding the right path would reveal to him just what in the pits he was supposed to do now.

He'll do. Thratia's words filled every silent moment of his mind. Whatever that viper was up to, he didn't want anything to do with it, but he could hardly run off now that he'd taken things so far. He had Thratia's trust, insomuch as she allowed him to wander her city a free man, and that was a prize he wasn't quite ready to squander. With her trust, he could do a lot of damage to her plans from the inside – if only he knew what they were, what angle he should take.

Aransa was quieter than it'd been since he last walked its streets. A strange hush encapsulated the city, swathed it in muted cotton wool. Last time he'd been here, night was the time to be on the streets, to be seen. There'd been raucous parties and overflowing bars. Except for one night, the night Thratia took control. And it seemed the fear of that night had yet to die out.

A red door appeared to his right. Detan stopped cold, drawing a curse from a man who had been walking behind him. Dust hung heavy on the air, clung to his boots and his hair. He shoved his hands in his pockets, stared at that red door a little longer.

The Red Door Inn. Not the most imaginative name, but in a city full of working-man taverns and rough-and-tumble gambling halls, it stood out for the simple fact it wasn't an allusion to a curse word or a carnal act. He'd been through that door once. Invited by a sharp-eyed woman who'd wanted to ask him how he'd lost his sel-sense, so she could save her daughter from working the mines.

He hadn't lost his sense, of course, and though he didn't tell her that, he'd tried to make her understand that chasing that path was a dangerous one. What she'd decided to do to keep her daughter out of that hard, hot life, Detan didn't know. Whatever her plan had been, she'd died before she'd had the chance to see it through. Cut down, bleeding her last on Thratia's dock, all because Thratia wanted to pin the murder on Detan.

The parlor of the Red Door Inn was cool, kept insulated from the desert heat by its thick mud-stuccoed walls and lack of windows. He didn't recall opening the door, but the brass knob was in his hand, and he stepped into the chandelier light of the entry hall.

"May I help you, sir?" A man in the red-vested livery of the inn hovered at his shoulder, his smile pure solicitation. Of course the welcoming was warmer than last time. Despite the dust on his boots, Detan was a whole lot cleaner than he'd been the last time he'd stepped through that door. Aella hadn't let him take any of his old clothes with him to Aransa, and so he'd been trussed up in upperclass wear – slim, dark trousers, a contrasting cream vest, and matching dark jacket. Sometime along the way, he'd started dressing like the man his auntie had always wanted him to be. Too bad the inside didn't match the exterior.

"A table, please," he said. The thought of cloistering himself away in one of the Inn's private booths drew him like a moth to a flame. Something strong to drink, and a curtain to pull against the world. In one of those little booths, he could almost pretend for a moment that the world outside was friendly.

The attendant led Detan down the steps of the inn, deep into the bottom levels where only the richest patrons lingered. Detan wondered, fleetingly, if Thratia had put the word out amongst high-brow places that he was residing in her compound now, but cast the thought aside. No, this wasn't Thratia's doing. Between his clothes and the brand on the back of his neck, Detan had enough cachet on his own to warrant this flavor of treatment. Didn't much like being reminded of the fact, though.

A familiar voice shook him out of his moping, brash and male, behind the cloak of a curtained booth. The man called for an attendant, slurring slightly, not reaching for the bell meant to do the job for him. Detan froze.

"Sir?" the attendant asked, all professional concern.

"I..." he cleared his throat. "I'm going to say hello to an old friend."

The attendant followed his glance to the booth with the slurring man and frowned, weighing the guest's probable desire for privacy against both rebuking Detan's wish and having to deal with the drunken man. He eventually shrugged, and gestured toward the booth.

Detan moved before he could think better of it and pulled the curtain. He sat.

Renold Grandon peered at him across the thin, lacquered table. Smoke curled around the man's eyes, and a glass dangled from his swollen fingers – twin to a litter of empty glasses filling the narrow table. Red blotches bloomed like storm cells across his cheeks, and cactus-prickle stubble clung to his sagging chin.

Detan did not believe in ghosts. But sitting in that booth, that same booth where Bel Grandon had summoned him to to ask a question all that time ago, he thought he could feel her. She was in the smoke swirling between him and Renold now, in the heady-sweet scent of alcohol in the stale air. The very memory of her stern gaze forced Detan to sit straighter with some foolish hope that, if only he presented himself well, he could do honor to her memory.

He bore Renold's drunken stare, and thought of the first time he'd seen the man. Bloated on his own importance, swaggering with his mistress as he gallivanted through the Salt Baths. Renold had done nothing to offend Detan, save being a likely target when Detan was in need.

Detan had looked at Renold Grandon, and thought, *he'll do*.

And an innocent woman had died.

And countless futures were snuffed to dust with her passing.

"You," Renold said, but there was very little malice in it. Just a wan sort of tiredness that bit deeper than anger ever could have.

"Me," Detan agreed.

Renold looked at him. Really looked. His swollen face puckered up as he squinted, digging with his gaze into all the details that made up Detan now. His clean hair, his expensive clothes. The leanness of his frame, and perhaps even the slight hunch he harbored due to pain in his shoulder from Aella's careful administrations. He swept all this up, counted it, and with a snort dismissed Detan as irrelevant. Little more than a fly drawn to the stench of his sorrow.

"I didn't–" Detan began, but Renold cut him off with a sharp gesture, spilling dribbles of liquor down the side of his hand.

"You didn't hold the knife that split her throat," he sneered. "You don't have the steel in you. But she does, our fearless commodore, and you riled her up as sure as a man pulls back a knife hand to strike."

Detan swallowed, laced his fingers together under the table to stop their tremble. "Thratia killed Bel to make you hate me. To make you hunt me."

Renold studied the depths of his glass, as if he could see his dead wife's face lurking within. "Told you that, did she? And you believed her? Dumber than I thought. No. She knew I'd never believe a floundering fop like you could have ever spilt real blood. Not Bel's, anyway. That was a warning for me, not you."

A little flare of anger sparked in Detan's blood, fleeting but sharp. Sel's presence loomed in the liqueur, in the lanterns, in the… He shut his sense down. Forced himself to focus. "And this is how you answer her?"

Renold's bloodshot eyes roamed the empty glasses on the table that his wife had used so often to host her private meetings. He breathed deep, let out a slow breath, and pierced Detan with a stare. "Virra, our daughter, captains a ship in Thratia's fleet as a sensitive pilot. It was Bel's greatest ambition to see that Virra never had to work the mines. Yes. This is how I answer her." He bared his teeth. "And aren't we all just one big happy family?"

Ill with revulsion, Detan pushed to his feet and

staggered through the curtain that separated that booth from the rest of the world. The cool opulence of the Red Door Inn pressed all around him, mirroring a deeper cold, one which ensconced his bones and chest and made him gasp despite the delicately perfumed air.

Ignoring the concerned queries of the valet, he dragged himself up the stairs to the final floor, legs growing heavier with every step, and only when he was out on the blistering hot streets of Aransa, dust on his shoes and dry air whipping the moisture from his eyes, his lips, did he feel he could breathe again.

He had been so very tempted, walking down these beaten streets to this pristine door, to flee. To take to the open skies once more. To find another flier, another path to freedom from duty and consequence. Now the very thought churned his stomach, broke sweat across his chest and brow.

What good was his freedom, when he had done as Thratia? What good was he, when he had looked at a man and thought: *he'll do*, without ever considering the breadth and depth of the consequences?

Whatever freedom existed for him out there in the empty sky, he had not earned it.

Detan straightened his lapels, stood tall and brushed the dust from his coat sleeves. Aransa stretched out around him in all directions: the shanty towns downward, the tenuous government-worker class upward, and topping it at its very peak, lower only than the city's highest garden, Thratia waited.

She'd looked at him, and said, *he'll do*. He knew not what for, yet, but with the memory-scent of Bel's cigarillos warm in his nostrils, he was going to find out. And whatever the consequences were, wherever the pain fell, Detan would see it through, or break himself trying.

CHAPTER 12

Enard caught Ripka by the arm in the hall on her way to Dame Honding's sitting room, causing her to nearly jump clear out of her skin.

"Enard!" she gasped, then stifled a laugh when she saw the embarrassed shock in his eyes.

"I apologize, Captain, I thought you had seen me."

"Ah, no, that's my fault." She ran a hand through her hair and offered him a small smile. "Between the bright berry tea, and my adventures with Honey this morning, I'm wound up tighter than a harpoon spring."

He frowned. "Tell me."

She did. It was so very easy to spill her thoughts to Enard. He listened attentively, asking pertinent questions, and as she expressed her suspicion regarding Thratia's influence in the city via the cafes, his growing alarm reassured her she had not been mistaken, there was a real threat lurking within Hond Steading's walls.

"That is troubling news. Are you going to report to the Dame?"

"I had thought as much, I have a few marks yet before that performance Latia wants us to join her for."

"May I go with you? An extra set of eyes and ears couldn't hurt."

She grinned, just a touch. "Are you worried about me?"

"I – ah – well. You're perfectly capable, of course, and Honey–"

She squeezed his shoulder. "It's all right, Enard. It's even a little sweet."

He clamped his mouth closed so hard she watched his lips disappear.

"Come on, let's see what the Dame thinks."

They found the Dame surrounded by her attendants, head bowed as she listened to a portly young woman explain something that, by the way she was gesticulating, was of grave importance. Ripka pinched Enard's sleeve and they found an out of the way spot toward the back of the room to wait, just within sight but not intruding. When the five people who had come to beg the Dame's ear had said their piece and been sent away, the Dame fixed her gaze – Detan's gaze – upon Ripka and curled her fingers to gesture her forward.

"Ripka Leshe, Enard Harwit. How are you two finding my city?"

"It is in danger, Dame."

She pursed her lips in a tight smile. "I am aware of such matters."

"Not from Thratia's advance, though that is an obvious threat. No, you have an insurgency brewing from within."

She stiffened, fingers coiling tight around the ends of her chair's armrests. "It is only due to my great respect for you as Aransa's watch-captain that I ask, so tread carefully: explain, quickly."

Ripka began with her time in Aransa, and her too-late discovery of the honey liqueur crates in which Thratia had hidden her weapons, then moved onto her brief interview with Captain Lakon, and her trip to the bright eye berry cafe. She left out the names of Dranik and Latia, but the implications were strong enough. A taste for revolution was brewing in Hond Steading, and Thratia had lit that spark.

The Dame leaned back in her chair, regarding Ripka and Enard in a silence so stretched Ripka had to resist an urge to fidget. At last, the Dame said, "Do you know how I spent my morning?"

"I do not, Dame."

She gestured vaguely toward a door to the right of her meeting room. "Negotiating. Treating. Hammering out plans with my empress. Or a representative of her, at any rate." She sighed. "Her highness is unfortunately unable to travel, and her surrogate leaves much to be desired, in my opinion. Do you know her? Ranalae Lasson?"

Ripka shook her head.

"Ah. Then you don't quite understand." Her expression twisted, but she was quick to school it into indifference. "Ranalae. I knew her father, a kind man, but she is no child of his. She has joined the Bone Tower, and spearheads the whitecoats. Yes, I see your horror. I would not treat with them, were there any other option. Rumor has reached me from Valathea in regard to their methods, and I know Detan was in their vicious care, tricked away from me. I should have never let him go, but... They said they could cure him. I should have known better."

She pulled herself up, rolled her shoulders as if shaking off a great weight. "Regardless, Ranalae is who my empress sent, and while she inquired about Detan's health she otherwise left the subject alone, she knows it is thin ground on which to tread. She comes offering me troops, fortifications. And if Thratia's insurgency has taken root in my city, as you claim, then I need Valathea's aid more than ever."

Ripka swallowed around a dry throat. "At what cost?"

"Ah." The Dame smiled. "I knew you were no fool. They ask I rescind Hond Steading's independent status. That we become a vassal of Valathea in whole, turned over to their rule and their law." She waved a hand. "No more forums. No more watchers hired by my choosing. It'd mean Fleetmen taking over the streets, while the power transitioned. And, upon my death, they'd appoint a warden of their choosing. Certainly they would allow the illusion of a vote, but the matter would be settled long ahead of time. The Hondings would no longer own this land, we would lease it. And Detan would never be able to return to his home without fear of capture by those–" She cleared her throat. "By his enemies."

Ripka's stomach soured. "You would do this?"

"Valathea's hand on Hond Steading's tiller, or Thratia's. I am honestly not convinced that either is the better option. Now I lean toward Valathea, as they at least I know well. The Honding family was once ruled by that governance, and I trust my empress, if not her envoys. We would only go back to how things were in the early days of the city's settlement. I do not think the upheaval would be so great."

"How long until the Valathean troops arrive?"

"Two weeks, perhaps. The monsoons may hold them back, but they were already prepared to fly."

"And when must you give your answer?"

"My dear, I have already given it."

Ripka clasped her hands behind her back so that the Dame could not see her tighten her fists. "They would have to pass the message. Even with signal flags and the finest runners it would be a while before the troops received orders to move. Thratia is already on her way, or so I surmise. She may be here before them."

"And if she is, Valathea will be the hammer that smashes them against the anvil of our city. But I have faith that Thratia is not completely mad. She will see reason, I hope, and realize her defeat has already been made."

"And in the meantime, do I have your permission to root out Thratia's network here in the city?"

She flicked her fingers, as if brushing the idea away. "If it entertains you, yes. I know you are a woman of action. And the information will be very useful to Valathea, once they arrive."

Ripka tucked her head in acknowledgement. "Thank you, Dame."

The Dame dismissed them by turning to a nearby attendant. Back in the hall, heart pounding in her throat, Ripka made a sharp right and angled for the stairs that led up to the smaller airship docks. Enard jogged at her heels, and though her breath came hot and her legs burned from the speed at which she took the stairs, she did not slow down. Not even for a moment.

"Where are we going?" Enard asked, a little breathless.

"To find Tibal. I find myself in sudden need of an airship."

"What for?"

"I'm going to stop that messenger."

CHAPTER 13

With every step she took up the long tower stairs, Ripka cursed Tibal for picking a room so high above all the others. Enard's steady panting at her heels cheered her, for at least she wasn't the only one struggling with the climb.

"Why he chose the top of this hideous tower..." she muttered.

"I believe he did not wish to be bothered."

She snorted. "Should have known better. Now I'm just going to be annoyed when I finally get to him."

"I would not wish to be on the other side of your ire."

The simple admiration in his tone both warmed her and sent a thread of nervousness throughout her. She had no time to think of such things – to explore the fine edges of her affections. The task she had set herself, saving this doomed city from both Thratia and Valathea, securing its independence as a beacon in the Scorched, was too great. The fall of Aransa, her failure to protect those people, shadowed every crevice of her thoughts. To succeed here, to save Hond Steading, would do more than fulfill a duty. It would return to her a piece of herself.

She reached the top of the tower, damp with sweat, and took a moment to lean over her knees and catch her breath.

The door to Tibal's suite of rooms was shut, a foreboding silence leaking out all around it. The harsh rasp of her breath and the steady thump of her heart were the only sounds, so high up in the squared-off tower of the Honding family palace. Dame Honding had called this tower the crow's nest, for its height and the airship moorings along its top. Ripka wondered just how crow-like Tibal had become in his self-imposed isolation.

When her breath was settled, she straightened her back and knocked. Nothing.

"Tibal," she called, "it's Ripka and Enard. Open up."

A soft scraping – boot leather against stone? – and a rustling of cloth. She held her breath, swallowing impatience. Every moment that ticked away she imagined that messenger flying away from Hond Steading, coming closer to completing his task and delivering the future of this once independent city-state into the hands of Valathea for good.

The door jerked open. Tibal was silhouetted in bright sunlight, his dusty hair gone ragged and twisted out in all directions. Pale dust limned the cracks in his dark hands, his cheeks, and the wrench hanging from his fingers seemed as if it had grown there, forever a part of him. A wildness whispered in the corners of his eyes, a glint of something feral – something that had rejected human company.

The light shifted under the stroke of a wooly cloud, and the harsh lines of him were smoothed away, that animalistic gleam faded to dust. He was just Tibal again. Tired, and grieving, but Tibal all the same.

"Captain," he said real slow, dragging his gaze over

the two winded friends that stood in his doorway.

"I hate to bother you, but I need use of the flier. Quickly."

A sour twitch took up residence at the corner of his lips. He glanced down at the wrench in his hand, turned it over so the harsh sunlight falling into the room from behind painted sunsets in the tool's oil.

"She's not ready."

In that moment, she knew he was talking about himself. Dancing around the gnawing pain in his chest, using the little flier as a shield between him and the world he'd shunned. She took a breath, knowing that what she had to do was unkind, but that she had to do it all the same.

"She's right there, Tibal. I can see her, docked over your shoulder. She's buoyant, and you wouldn't stake her out there if she didn't have navigation abilities, would you? I know you. You'd bring her in, deflate the sacks and lay out all her pieces to be put back together again."

He glanced over his shoulder to the airdock that was the balcony of his room, and the little flier beyond, drifting lazily in the stale breeze. His bushy eyebrows raised, as if seeing it for the first time, and he nodded to himself.

"That's the next step. Taking her apart to see what needs mending before I build her up again."

"Tibal," she said, "*please*."

He blinked at her, as if seeing her for the first time. There was more between them than she could ever address in this moment – her questions about his heritage, her want to soothe his pain. But Tibal'd always been a practical man. She willed him to feel her desperation, to put aside the storm between them and help her now, when time was so crucial. He weighed the wrench in his hand, and nodded to himself.

"What do you need her for?"

She explained the Dame's plans in brief – the fleet of Valatheans waiting on the northern coast, the messenger flying to them now with the terrible invitation to come, to set up their stakes in this city that had been so long independent of greater powers. Tibal pursed his lips and shook his head.

"Don't see the point. And anyway, the *Larkspur* would get you there faster. Go talk to Pelkaia."

"You know damned well Pelkaia's moored to the north. She's faster, but by the time I got to her the damage would already be done." Ripka gave up on swallowing her anger and stepped closer, pushing Tibal back, letting her voice show her scorn. "Valathea comes in here, it won't mean protection for the city. Reinforcements, sure, but Valatheans in the streets will just churn the waters for Thratia. I don't know what happened to her to make her scorn them so, but she hates the empire – and seeing them set up in the city she desires won't keep it safe. It'll just encourage her to dig in deeper, to roll us all back into the sand."

"Thratia's rule, Valathea's. Who says the Dame has a healthier grip on this city than either of those two forces? They all look the same from where I'm standing, don't see much point in throwing in a chit with either faction."

"You can't mean that. You saw the terror Thratia infused in the streets. You heard Detan's horror stories of his time in Valathea. Anyone – any institution – that would treat another human being like that, like tools, like puzzles meant to be broken out and pieced back together again, they're not worthy of rule. The Hondings aren't perfect but they're willing to listen to their people – that's the right path."

"If they're so keen on caring for their citizens, then why's Detan running around willingly under Thratia's power?"

"You know damned well he made that trade just to get us off the Remnant."

"You weren't there." He flung the wrench to the side and it clanged against the hard stone floor. "You don't know how his mind had changed leading up to that moment. If you'd seen him, if you'd heard him–" Tibal cut himself off, shook his head and scowled. "He left this city to rot, so why should we care what happens to it?"

"You mean he left you."

They stared at one another hard, letting tension build between them until it was twisted up tight enough to snap. Enard cleared his throat delicately.

"The messenger?"

"Right. You got a choice, Tibal. You fly me after that messenger, now, or I take the flier on my own. No other option."

His lip curled, and without another word he turned and stomped toward the dock. Ripka swallowed her guilt down. This was desperate, important, and she didn't have time to argue about Detan's motives.

Not so much as a rug softened Tibal's room. Tools speckled the floor, and every available flat surface. His bed was smooth, the sheets pulled with military precision. She wondered if he'd made the bed, or if he simply hadn't bothered sleeping in it.

The flier had been stripped down, every ding, every stain, every hint of the personality it had garnered over the years sanded away into so much dust. The sight of its wood, bare and gleaming as if new, in the harsh desert sun grew a knot in Ripka's chest. Piece by piece, layer by layer. Tibal was excavating Detan from his life.

"Where is this damned messenger headed, exactly?"
Tibal hauled ropes and manipulated the dozens of little
wheels and levers attached to the nav podium Ripka still
had only the fuzziest of ideas on how to use.

"Left the palace fleet docks and headed straight north,
I'd guess. The Valathean delegates are anchored just off
the coast."

"Figures they'd stick to where the air's cooler," Tibal
muttered to himself. "Yank the anchor rope, and let's get
this over with this. You got a plan?"

"Not yet," she confessed.

Tibal snorted. "Bad habit."

She ignored the jibe as she yanked the anchor rope
free. The flier slid out into the hot sky, thready cloud
cover doing little at all to shield them from the sun's
glare. Ripka wrapped her hair in a scarf, tugging the
front of it out and down just enough to shade her eyes.
Tibal had his hat, singed and grey, and Enard found a
beaten old straw thing that looked ridiculous atop his
perfectly coiffed black hair.

As the flier gained speed, wind cooled the sun's bite.
Knowing she risked a burn, Ripka tipped her head back
to the sun, let the warmth of it seep through her skin
straight to her bones. She liked to imagine the Scorched's
sun could erase the chill that'd taken root in her marrow
during her time on the Remnant. Liked to imagine the
warmth that had been a part of her life since her birth
would welcome her home.

Months she'd been back on the mainland of the
Scorched, and still she felt a chill ache in her fingers, a
lingering stiffness in her knees.

"There's our bird," Enard said.

A sleek, thin-bellied flier painted brilliant russet
smeared the blue of the sky like an old scab. From its

buoyancy sacks flew brilliant banners boasting the seal
of Hond Steading, and by extension its ruling family. A
few other small craft dotted the sky, most dark and low
and obviously behaving as ferries for goods or people.
There was no other official ship in sight, and the narrow
flier was straining hard for the north.

"Can we catch her?" she asked Tibal.

He rolled those wiry shoulders and cranked hard on
the wheels, letting the fine gear ratios add urgency to the
propellers. The flier lurched forward eagerly. "Hope you
got a plan," he said, but there was a gleam in his eye like
hunger. Like he'd scented his prey and was warming to
the hunt.

Ripka turned away so he wouldn't see her smile.
She positioned herself toward the fore of the flier, the
semaphore flags for boarding gripped tight in her fists.
She felt a little silly up there, wearing little more than
snug-fitting breeches and a plain tunic in shades of ochre.
Her arms were bare to the sun and the breeze, only the
wrap around her hair giving her any real defense against
the Scorched's weather.

Without the borrowed authority of her watcher coat
ensconcing her, she wondered just how she'd bluff her way
through this. No weapons. No badge. No right to make any
orders at all. She didn't even have a fruitknife on her.

At the thought of kitchenware, her thoughts turned
to Honey and she winced. She should have brought that
woman along, instead of leaving her to her own devices in
the palace – or worse, the city. Loyal as Honey was, there
was no telling what she'd get up to if she grew too bored.

"Fast as she'll go," Tibal called out.

And not fast enough at all. Ripka caught herself
leaning forward as if the cant of her body could urge the
little flier onward. The Honding messenger had grown

closer as Tibal's flier gained speed, close enough for Ripka to make out the lone man on its deck – a sel-sensitive, no doubt, one of the city's elite pilots sent to deliver the message with all haste and care – but they could draw no closer. A gulf of empty sky hung between the two ships.

"No luck, Captain," Tibal said.

"What if we were to wave an emergency flag?" Enard asked.

Ripka *hmmed*. The messenger was the closest craft in the sky, and as an official delegate of the city would be honor-bound to come to their aid. There was risk in explaining away the deception once the messenger grew close enough to board, but Ripka thought she might be able to wave the messenger's suspicions away with explanations of urgency.

She found herself wishing for Detan's easy charm, and pushed the thought away. Whatever he was up to, he was no immediate help to her now. And anyway, she'd spent weeks stewing on the Remnant, hiding who she was, masking her real purpose. Though her watcher training still chafed at the deceptions she'd woven, she'd come to accept that a few little lies were nothing in the face of a worthwhile cause. Especially if they were the only way to achieve her goal.

"Wave the flag," she ordered.

Enard pushed to the fore rail and waved the emergency flag, a brilliant splash of crimson against the pristine sky. There was nothing subtle in this message, no effort at communicating detail. The empty stretch of red screamed one thing only: help. Ripka had only ever seen it waved once before in earnest, and even though she knew they were safe, the jarring stretch of it made her palms sweat with unease.

Squinting against the brightness, Ripka could just

make out the hesitant tilt of the messenger's head as he caught sight of their flag, then scanned the horizon to see if any ships were nearer. No luck for him. He came to their aid, or no one did. To add emphasis to their distress, she waved her arms above her head, feigning excitement that he had seen them.

The messenger visibly sighed, then began the process of swinging the ship around.

"Got him," she said, and caught herself grinning. She really was developing a taste for deception.

The messenger's ship closed the gap quickly, slipping up alongside Tibal's heavier flier. The messenger himself was a stocky young man in the tight-cut uniform of the Honding household, the only item about his person less than pristine were the well-worn boots on his feet denoting his position as messenger. No messenger worth their salt would be caught dead in stiff, unbroken-in shoes.

"What trouble?" he boomed in a deep, clear voice.

Enard and Tibal both looked to Ripka, and for just a moment she froze, having no idea what to say next.

"Dame Honding sent me," she blurted.

The messenger's brows shot up and he took a wary step backward. "I don't recognize you, and this is no official ship."

Ripka summoned all the easy arrogance of authority she'd ever possessed, cocked her hips, and sauntered toward the rail. "Do you not know me?" She swept the wrap from her hair dramatically, as if revealing the whole of her face should spark some memory. "I am Ripka Leshe, watch-captain of fallen Aransa, advisor to your dame. Please tell me you are not *that* oblivious to palace matters."

The messenger's cheeks flushed deep and he twisted his sleeve between his fingers. "I'm sorry, but I wasn't informed. Miss? Captain? I, uh–" He cleared his throat and glanced toward the navigation podium. "I have orders to attend. If your ship is in no danger, then–"

"I am delivering you new orders," she snapped. The poor young man flinched and visibly repressed an urge to snap her a salute. She held out her hand across the space between the ships, fingers unfurled. "Hand me your parcel."

He went white as his sails. "That is very much against protocol."

She snapped her fingers impatiently. "War is coming to Hond Steading, young man. Do you think your precious protocol will remain unchanged? Quickly, now, this ship is slower but we may still catch the delegation before the sun sets."

"You're to deliver the message?" he asked, torn between relief and incredulity.

"Of course I am! Do you think for a sand-cursed moment it's a good idea to send a green-chin like you to a delegation from the empress? Skies above, this city is such a mess – forgive my saying so – but this is *no* way to handle diplomacy."

"I, ah – I didn't think it was so important, you know, just following orders…"

"Less jawing, more handing me that parcel."

She snapped her fingers again, and he scrambled like a sand flea dunked in a booze bath. The message was removed from a locked chest tucked behind the podium, its creamy paper tied off with a thick, silken ribbon stamped over with Dame Honding's personal seal. The messenger passed it to her, hand trembling, and she hoped he was too nervous to notice she held her breath.

"Finally," she said, and tucked the message under her arm. "Back to your barracks, now, and tell your master the message was delivered with care."

"Yes ma'am!" He snapped her a sloppy salute and scrambled off, pointing his little craft toward the Honding palace docks.

Ripka let loose a breath so deep her shoulders slumped from the force of it leaving. Enard grinned at her, but her own smile was snuffed by Tibal's sour stare.

"Almost saw the ghost of Honding, there."

"Funny. I see a real flesh-and-blood Honding right here."

He went very, very still. She swallowed, hard, regretting the words as soon as she'd said them. She was too jittery. Too anxious over what she'd done to keep her damned mouth shut. The parcel under her arm dragged at her, heavy as the treason she'd just committed. It was one thing to con her way into a prison; that was to free a good man. It was another entirely to undermine the direct orders of a lawfully ruling woman – one whom she respected, at that. She felt sick. Tibal's hard stare made her feel sicker.

"Point us toward the north," she said crisply, covering her anxiety with a veneer of professional calm. Seemed all she had left was a collection of veneers, nowadays. She wondered if this was what it was like to be Pelkaia, never quite sure of which face she was going to wear for the moment, let alone the day. "We don't want the messenger thinking we're doubling back so soon. Then we'll bring the flier home, so you can tear her apart."

"Don't be coming to me for help with this nonsense again."

"Hadn't planned on it."

Ripka faced the sea-kissed northern winds, her back to Tibal so she wouldn't have to see the hurt in him, and wondered where things had all begun to fall apart.

CHAPTER 14

Given the opportunity to be elsewhere, not even Thratia's lackeys were populating her compound. Detan's boots echoed in the empty entryway, the angry brightness of the chandeliers not enough to penetrate the shadows that gathered in the high ceilings. A few staff dotted the place, seeing to the type of menial chores Detan had spent most of his life trying to pretend didn't exist. If Tibs hadn't made him dust the flier on occasion, he probably wouldn't know which end of a broom was up.

Despite the meager audience, he sauntered past the single, half-asleep guard at the door and slapped a pompous grin on his face. Body language wasn't just about fooling onlookers, after all. The demeanors he switched as often as he changed his longjohns – often enough, thank you kindly – were just as much about convincing him of his adopted role as they were about fooling others.

And he could really use some convincing now.

A glimpse of pale blue silk caught his eye, the silhouette under the long robe tickling his memory. The young woman's head was turned down as she flipped through a heavy ledger, her body canted away, but he recognized her all the same.

"Aella."

Her head lifted, and she scanned the room until she found him coming toward her. She placed a tight, practiced smile on her small face. "Did you enjoy your wander through the city?"

He wasn't about to let her drag him around with smalltalk the same way he did everyone else. "I didn't recognize you without your coat."

"Ah. That." She looked down at herself, as if seeing the pale dress for the first time. It fit her well, ending just above the ankle bone, the shoulder seams crisp at the top of her arms. He'd never seen her in anything like it before, though there was no way she could have had something made for herself so quickly since their arrival. Thratia's work, then. Seemed Detan wasn't the only one concerned with maintaining appearances. He just couldn't figure out what angle Thratia was working.

"Warden Ganal reminded me that I was no longer a whitecoat. And while she allows Callia to wear the garment – she *does* moan if you take it away – the Warden wants her people to bear as little resemblance to that particular institution as possible."

"But you *are* a whitecoat."

She shook her head, hand slipping across the ledger she held to obscure the words written there. "I gave them up when I entered Thratia's employ. They would not welcome my return now, and I am pleased with my current position. The Warden treats me well."

"Does she? Or does she just treat you less poorly than Callia did?"

"I see no point in the distinction."

A flare of anger, just a brief simmer, that she would

embrace the role she'd been crafted for so thoroughly while he fled from his own mold. "You are perpetuating what she did to you, what she crafted you to be. Callia's mind is gone, Aella. You don't have to please her, to follow in her shadow. There are places in this world Thratia and Valathea cannot reach, and you of all people have the strength to reach them if you so chose."

She lifted both brows at him, tucking the ledger beneath her arm. "I am no more a prisoner here than you are. Or will you tell me now you are being held against your will? That you desire to flee and cannot?"

"Why do you stay?" His breath rasped, his fists clung to the air at his sides, color rashed his collarbone and cheeks.

"I think…" She pursed her lips at him, tilted her head to the side. "I think you're asking yourself that question."

With a condescending pat on the arm and a faux-sympathetic smile, Aella turned and made her way up the steps to some upper room, some inner sanctum to which he was not privy. Detan watched her go, breathing slowly, trying to calm his twitching nerves. The functions of the compound moved on around him. Servants tended to household needs while Thratia's people worked on all the little plans that made her interests move forward.

Not a one of them paid him any mind. He was certain that if he stopped one, asked direction or assistance, they would provide it to him. Perfunctorily, as a matter of their duty to their mistress. Surely he had a room, somewhere. Surely he could take a meal if he so chose – demand fresh clothes, a bath, any of the little everyday facets of a life.

But he did not belong here. They had no need of him, no care for him. Not even Aella seemed interested in him any more, now that she had other tasks to attend to. He stood rudderless in a sea of someone else's making and felt himself come adrift.

Detan could bear a lot of indignity, but being ignored was simply galling.

He strode across the wide hall that'd once hosted a gala he'd crashed and angled toward the steps up to the airship dock. If he were going to be forgotten about, he'd use the time to prepare something for them to remember him by.

He swooped out onto the dock, pushing the doors wide, prepared to charm his way past guards and caretakers to make his way onto Aella's transport vessel. He hadn't expected to see Thratia herself, leaning against the soft curve of the u-dock's rail, the dock clear of every other soul.

If she'd heard him enter, she made no sign of it. She rested her forearms against the smooth rail, fingers interlaced, stooping to lean against the railing. He'd never seen her slouched before, had never seen her in any posture save ramrod straight.

Desert wind pushed her short hair against her scarred cheek, the ebony flesh tinged pink even in the warm glow of the oil lamps. Night crept in, reaching to meet her from across the horizon, bruised-purple and blue fingers of darkness lying in sheets against her skin. There was something intimate in the way she merged with the encroaching night.

"Did you enjoy your walk?" she asked.

He flinched, glad she wasn't looking at him, his bravado evaporating. Here was the woman he meant to undermine. To keep from his home as if she were a viper and he the charmer, tangled together in a dance that could leave either one of them killed. And in that moment, watching the colors of the sun bleed out across her pucker-scarred cheek, he knew he did not understand her. Knew nothing about her, truly.

She was strong and brave and fierce and cruel, and rumors about her spun themselves into sand-devils all across the Scorched. They called her General Throatslitter. She'd been too hungry for power for Valathea to keep her. Exiled, kicked from the isles that'd been her home, to this dusty stretch of endless sand and sel she'd come, and rebuilt herself. And he did not know why, save that she wanted it. But want alone wasn't enough to move most people.

Something had moved Thratia Ganal. Something besides the stories people told about her, something she kept close.

Something he could use.

"City's gotten quiet," he said. She didn't move, didn't so much as cock her head his way, so he sauntered over, adopting all the lazy affectations he'd refined over the years, to stand beside her.

Aransa really was beautiful from up here. Purple shadows draped the brown and yellow stones of the city's deep-cut layers, smearing into hints of red and black spotted through with the warm glow of hearth fires and the sharper punch of candles and lamps, scattered like stars. Last time he'd seen this view, he hadn't been properly positioned to appreciate it. It was hard to admire a landscape when you were pretty certain you'd just jumped to your death.

"They're frightened," she said.

"Because of you."

She snorted. A warm burst of air, shoulders jerking forward. Her breath smelled of bright berry tea, and he was brought back to that terrible moment when she'd leaned into him on this dock all that time ago and whispered, hot, against his ear: *I'm going to forge you an enemy.*

"I won't deny that. But this is better than the alternative."

"Living without fear?"

"Blissful ignorance. Blind vulnerability. They're safer now, whether they realize it or not."

"Because General Throatslitter has claimed them as her chattel? Better to be slaves, than enemies?"

She shook her head, slow and sad, like a parent disappointed in a particularly thick-headed child. When the sun had given itself up to the night she half-turned, leaning her hip against the rail, and regarded him with slow care. He bit back a wisecrack and turned to face her instead.

"It's funny. You almost look like a lord."

"Almost like I was born to it."

"Raised to it, maybe. You know better than most it doesn't matter what womb you pop out of, so long as you act the part."

"And what part have you been acting?"

Her smile slipped like a faultline. "Why don't I show you?"

He swallowed. "What do you mean?"

Thratia pushed away from the rail, stood straight once more and turned her knife-sharp gaze down upon him. "It's time you met the Saldivians."

CHAPTER 15

Ripka opened the door to her room to find Honey sitting at the foot of her bed. She clutched a linen-wrapped bundle to her lap like it was a life raft, fingers tangled in the twine holding it together.

"Honey?"

She jerked to attention and skittered to her feet, holding the bundle tight with one arm. It was just the right size to have wrapped up a head, or a couple of hands. Ripka pushed the thought away and forced herself to step into her room.

"I couldn't find you," Honey murmured. It wasn't an accusation, just a simple statement of fact – I couldn't find you, so I waited here. Ripka shrugged and adjusted the weight of the messenger's orders in her pocket, trying to keep a sudden surge of guilt off her face.

"Sorry, I was up on the flier with Tibal. Did you need me?"

"Here." Honey thrust the bundle toward her. She bit back an urge to recoil from the package and took it gingerly. It was lighter than she'd expected from the size, and squished pleasantly in her hands like an overstuffed pillow.

"What's this?"

"For you."

Ripka raised both her brows at Honey in question, but she just watched expectantly, her lips pursed as if she were humming an internal tune. The last gift Honey had given Ripka had been a shiv carved from a wooden spoon. At least this bundle didn't have any suspiciously hard edges.

She placed it on the bed and wiggled the knotted strings free, peeling back the shopkeeper's muslin. Fabric spilled out, in deep tones of crimson and sienna, and it took Ripka a moment to register what she was looking at. Clothes, civilian clothes, cut to modern style in long body-hugging tunics over complementary slim-legged trousers. There was one tunic in bloodstone red, leggings in mustard ochre, and another tunic in rich burnt sienna with crimson leggings. Not the most expensive of dyes, but the depth of their color spoke to their cost.

"These are for me?" she asked dumbly, running the rock-polished material between her fingers. They were thick, sturdy, and smooth.

"You dress like a watcher," was all Honey said.

Ripka looked down at her undyed trousers and loose tunic, both of which were common off-duty wear for watchers in all cities across the Scorched, and burst into a fit of laughter. Even without her blue coat, the messenger had been able to recognize her for what she was. It seemed Ripka was the only one who felt she'd lost her authority with her jacket.

"I... Thank you, Honey. Where in the pits did you find these?" She held up the red tunic and pressed it against her torso. No surprise, it fit perfectly.

Honey's lips twisted into a skewed smile. "I know how to find a market, Captain."

She flushed. "I didn't mean–"

"It's all right. I know you wonder about me. But I'm fine, Captain. Honest."

Whatever 'fine' meant to Honey, Ripka couldn't even begin to guess. The woman's motives were as opaque to Ripka as an afternoon sandstorm. With care, she took one of the crimson head scarves from the package and wrapped her hair. Honey watched with avid eyes, though her fingers never stopped drumming against her thigh.

Sunlight slanted through Ripka's half-pulled window, setting the room alight in golden rays that emphasized the amber tones of Honey's fluffy hair. She'd chopped it to chin length on the trip north to Hond Steading, so that the curls grew tighter without the weight of length and sprang and bobbed about her cheeks as if they had a mind of their own. In her civilian clothes, without the stigma of a Remnant jumpsuit, Ripka mused that they almost looked like sisters. Two daughters of the Scorched, with light-toned hair and darker skin, though Honey ran to a fuller figure than Ripka ever had. In the domestic intimacy of her room, the sweet scent of beeswax candles on the air, Ripka found a question she'd avoided bubbling to her lips.

"Honey, why did you help me, when the riot broke out? You must have known I had been a watcher, just like the warden said, but you told that man that I wasn't."

Honey stopped drumming and tipped her head to the side, round eyes glinting as she shifted her gaze to the window. Sere air gusted in, ruffling her hair. She pursed her lips and shrugged. "I liked you. I didn't like them."

Ripka bit back an urge to point out that *them* in this case meant the entire population of the Remnant. "Maybe you shouldn't have. It put you in a lot of danger. I'm still worried about Forge and Clink. We should never have left them behind." Her voice caught, and she swallowed a surge of pain.

"They'll be fine."

"How can you know?"

"Clink likes to start trouble. Has lots of practice."

Ripka grinned a little. "Is that why she brought me into her fold?"

"No. Because I asked her to."

Ripka bit her tongue. What she wanted to know, the question that gnawed deep inside her, she couldn't dive straight toward. She'd tried that once, on the trip up to Hond Steading. In a quiet moment, when no one was near enough to overhear, she'd asked how Honey had come to be in the Remnant, and why the other inmates had been so frightened of her. Honey'd just smiled and hummed to herself until Ripka changed the subject.

"How did you meet Clink?"

"I ate by myself. Then Clink came, and I sat next to her. She didn't mind."

"Did she say why?"

Honey shook her head.

"And Forge?"

"She came later. Clink picked her."

"Why'd you pick me?"

Honey's head swiveled until she was staring straight into Ripka's eyes, a little smile twitching up the corners of her lips. "You're interviewing me, Captain."

Ripka flushed. "I'm sorry, Honey. Old habits – it's just, there's so much about you I don't know."

"Likewise."

The point stuck. Here Ripka was, drilling Honey for her past, while staying tight-lipped about her own. It was her watcher training. She'd identified Honey as potentially dangerous – and reasonably so – and immediately shifted her into the category of suspect, skipping over the possibility of a friend. Honey *was* dangerous, she had no doubt of that, but if Ripka looked hard enough at herself, she had to acknowledge she wasn't much different. Maybe her flavor of violence was worse, too – she justified it, used the common good as an excuse to condone all her actions.

She shook herself. Her watcher coat was gone, there were no more legal justifications for her to ease her conscience with. Any heads she cracked would be done so illegally, any infiltration without government approval. She'd been cut loose, mind stuffed full of tools she no longer had the legal right to use, no matter Watch-captain Falston's implicit endorsement of her actions.

And yet she was using them. In the defense of Hond Steading, yes, but using them without allowance all the same. She was playing this game from Detan's level, now, outside the law and also free of its constraints.

She eyed Honey. Whatever that woman had done to end up in the Remnant, Ripka was desperate to know. But in the end it wasn't really any of her business. So long as Honey kept her knives to herself, or pointed at throats that meant her real harm, Ripka had no right to police Honey's past. She was here, now. Had thrown her lot in with Ripka and her cause. And Ripka was rapidly running out of allies.

Not to mention friends.

Ripka unrolled the bundle of clothes onto the bed. "Help pick an outfit for tonight. We'd better hurry or we're going to be late to meet Latia and Dranik."

Her eyes brightened. "We're going?"

"Said we would, didn't we? And anyway, I think Dranik is into something. I'd bet my blues – ah, I mean pride – that Thratia is using the cafes to smuggle weapons to her supporters, same as she did with the honey liqueur in Aransa. If we can catch her at it, feel out the extent of her network, we might be able to stop an uprising happening the moment Thratia arrives at the city's gates."

"Is she really that bad?"

Of course. Honey must have been imprisoned long before Thratia's rise to power. Ripka nodded, sorting through the clothes with Honey at her side. "She's an efficient ruler, I'll give her that, but she takes choices away from people, uses them like commodities, and that's something I just can't stomach."

Honey nodded, firmly. "We'll stop her."

In that moment, with the sun gleaming down upon a selection of new clothes gifted to her by a friend – quite possibly the first real friend Ripka'd had since the watch, since Detan and Tibal – she found herself smiling as a warm curl of hope unfolded within her. "Yeah. I think we might just pull it off."

CHAPTER 16

Detan was disappointed to discover that the Saldivians looked rather a lot like the rest of the peoples of Valathea and the Scorched. He'd been hoping for something a little more extreme: perhaps a squat people, or maybe a wild skin color like red or blue. But the people sitting before him now looked positively normal by Valathean body standards, if a little strange in the clothing department.

Thratia's guests enjoyed a suite of rooms on the top level of her compound, large arched doorways leading out to thin patios so that they could survey the city. The curtains on those doors were drawn now, fluttering in the night breeze. The pale linen looked as if clouds had blown into the room. The Saldivians sat cross-legged on cushions on the floor, a mat containing a bright berry tea set and plates of baked goods between them.

They were, he supposed, a little shorter than Valathean standard, but they still had the thin limbs and narrow features common to the region. Two men and a woman looked up at him, blinking with curiosity, teacups cradled with ease in the palms of their hands. The woman put her cup down and stuffed a pastry into her mouth, chewing noisily.

Their clothes were not in the slim-cut style Valathea and the Scorched favored – a style evolved for easy work, and safety around the many whirling gears and machinery of airships and their correspondent technologies. The Saldivians had gone wild with bolts of fabric, swathing themselves in great voluminous wraps. Detan rather thought they looked as if they'd tangled themselves in the curtains and just decided to live with it.

"Hullo," he chirruped at them, and gave them a wiggle of his fingers. He'd be damned if Thratia made him go through the dance of politic introductions. He only bowed his head over his hands for those he felt deserved the respect that gesture signified, no matter their station in life. Or those he wanted to believe he respected, at any rate.

"This," Thratia interjected smoothly, "is Lord Detan Honding."

There she went, calling him a lord again. She'd been trotting out that title at every opportunity, as if it really meant something any more, and the realization was beginning to make his skin crawl. What leverage did she think she could wrangle from having a disgraced lord press-ganged into her entourage?

"Seas bless our meeting," the youngest of the men said. His accent startled Detan, who was used to hearing only the rolling syllables of Valathea and the clipped speech of the Scorched. The Saldivian had a muddied way of speaking, as if each syllable was a heavy thing and left a coating in his mouth. He was maybe in his thirties, though Detan'd be hard pressed to bet on the fact, with the other man old enough to have some deep wrinkles and his hair all wave-crest white. The woman was about the young man's age, maybe younger, though it was hard for Detan to pin anything down on them for sure.

Thratia inclined her head to the older man. "This is Ossar, once a chieftain of the Saldive Isles and now functioning as a diplomat here in Aransa. Iessa," she nodded to the girl, "is his daughter, and Rensair her husband. Rensair's Valathean is the best of the bunch, though Iessa's is much improved since their arrival."

The young woman smiled, recognizing both her name and at the very least the tone of a compliment. Their names sounded strange to Detan – soft and hissy, like a wave breaking against a stone.

Before Thratia could make her presence more keenly felt, Detan plopped to the ground cross-legged at the empty edge of their tea mat and rested his hands on his knees, offering big smiles all around. Whatever reason Thratia had for dragging him here to meet these strange people, he was not about to let her take the reins. Purely on principle. He might be under Aella's thumb, but he had his pride to think about.

"What brings your lovely family to sunny Aransa?" he asked, high-toned, as if this were just a friendly chat between tourists passing one another in a tavern.

Rensair leaned toward him, foam-grey eyes brightening with interest. Detan chose to focus on the young man and ignore the scowl Ossar threw him. "We come on Thratia's invitation." Rensair spoke slowly, constructing his sentence with care.

"Matters in the Saldive Isles–" Thratia began, but Detan held up a hand to cut her off.

"You want me to hear what they have to say, then let them say it." He spoke quickly and without taking his gaze from Rensair, Detan's cheery smile plastered firmly in place. But there was no hiding the fine tension in the lines around his eyes, forced to crinkle to make a casual observer think his smile spread naturally to them. And no matter how quickly Detan spoke, Rensair's soft frown told him he'd picked up the gist of what Detan had said. Thratia gestured grandly, sarcastically handing control of the room over to him.

"And how did you get to be so chummy with ole Thratia?" he asked, but Rensair just frowned in response. "I mean – how did you make friends with Thratia?"

"Ah, friends, yes." He smiled, back on familiar footing. "She has worked very hard to keep the Valathean menace from the Saldives."

Detan coughed politely into his sleeve to cover a choked-off laugh. "I would have called her the Valathean menace, before she grew so boorish that Valathea couldn't even stomach her."

Ossar said something, fast and liquid, and though Detan couldn't understand the words the tone was clear enough – and the blush of embarrassment on his daughter's cheeks.

"What's the old man have to say, then?"

Rensair grimaced. "He says you are impotent."

Thratia roared with laughter while some colorful heat painted Detan's own cheeks.

"You mean… impudent?"

"Yes, yes, that. What did I say?"

Detan grimaced. "Never mind that. Your dear ole father-in-law isn't exactly wrong. On the impudent front, that is." He shot Thratia a glare and she wiped tears from her cheeks, snickering softly.

"And for that, I apologize." Detan shifted internal personas, moved from the glib con man that had shielded him for so long back into the skin of the lord, the child of privilege and politics. The man his aunt had always wanted him to be. He'd buried that old skin deeper than he'd thought, and it felt tight on him now. Constrictive in a way it never had before.

Just rusty, he told himself. Just need some time. He laced his fingers together and canted his head at an angle meant to signal solemnity, and watched the body language of the Saldivians shift around him to comfortable attention. All save Iessa, at any rate. She was looking at him hard, now. Like she'd seen his internal shift laid out bare at her feet, and didn't much like the implications.

He cleared his throat and continued, "Please, tell me what happened when Thratia came to your country."

"We are small," Rensair began. "Little islands, you understand? Not big like here, the Scorched, or like the bigger islands of Valathea. Just little islands. We have no selium." He pronounced it sa-lee-um, dragging the word out as if it were delightfully unique. "But we have great shoals of fish to feed us, and sugarcane and yams." He flashed a little smile. "Your food here, it is so bitter. But, I ramble. When Thratia came on her airships, we knew not what to think. She introduced herself as a commodore of a great empire, spreading across all of the known world, and promised they came seeking only trade. A little speck of a country, so far across the sea, was not worth the effort to conquer."

Detan had his doubts about Thratia's intentions in that regard, but he nodded understanding all the same and motioned for Rensair to continue.

"She stayed a long time, brought people to help with the teaching of Valathean." His smile grew with pride. "I was the first to gain mastery. To be con-ver-sant. Things were well, and we were trading our sweets for your liquor and your grains, but then these people – they wear white coats – came to visit us."

Detan's face went cold, bloodless, his stomach sinking to the bottom of his being.

"You are all right?" Rensair asked.

"Yes." He cleared thickness from his throat and wiped clammy palms against his knees. Though he could feel Thratia watching him, he didn't dare meet her eye. "Please, continue."

"They had learned that we had none of your selium. Our mountains have been dead a long, long time. So they came to find out if we still had sensitives. We had none, and they found this very curious so they..." He leaned back, pressing a hand to his chest while he took a deep breath. The man was near tears. Detan bit his tongue to keep from interrupting.

"They told us they had a way of inducing sensitivity, and wouldn't that be great? We could have pilots then, like your people. Take a greater role in worldwide trade. Maybe even find some selium deposits on our own land, if we were very lucky. Many people volunteered, and they took all of those who lived very close to the mountains.

"They had no such method." Rensair caught Detan's gaze and held it, testing to see if Detan realized the implications of what he meant. Detan nodded, slowly, not trusting his voice. Not even trusting himself to breathe without devolving into a stream of curses.

"But they had tests, experiments." Rensair's voice caught on the last word. He cleared his throat and soldiered on. "Many were hurt, many driven mad, and the people with the white coats were not happy. They couldn't get anyone to become a sensitive. So they took more volunteers, and more, and when the volunteers dried up they began just taking. They kept it very quiet, for a long time, but families began to talk amongst themselves. People spoke up.

"My father-in-law, he went to Thratia, demanded she find out what was going on. She was honest with us, even though she knew the horrors she'd uncovered would mean an uprising. Our king is, and was, a very old man used to peace. He did not know how to go about throwing out the whitecoats, or even if he could. Thratia promised him she would get rid of them, if he let her stay, and she did so. Her people, those working directly under her, were disgusted by what they found their fellows doing, and so they kicked them out.

"Eventually, Thratia had to leave. She said she feared those white-coated people were doing the same things elsewhere, and she needed a stronger base from which to stage her fight. She left her army with us and came here, to Aransa, to start again. We were not a very militaristic people. We could not have supplied her with the manpower she needed. You are very lucky, Lord Honding, that she comes to save your city next."

Detan stared at these friendly, well-meaning people. Their smiles, some cautious, some open, seemed very far away – phantom grins, all teeth and lips floating in the air, mocking him with their friendliness.

Sweat dripped across his brow, soaked through the knees of his trousers from the palms of his hands. He'd begun to shake, just slightly, a subtle all-over tremble that threatened to make his teeth clack. Every word of Rensair's story fell like lead, like iron, into his mind. Threatened to batter down old barriers he'd only recently begun to peek hesitantly behind.

Thratia had refused to relinquish control of the Saldive Isles.

Everyone in Valathea, in the Scorched, knew that story. A story of a commodore gone too thirsty for power, her greed and ruthlessness outmatched by anyone else her rank. The very thing, the very power-move, that had seen her exiled from the empire she'd been born and bred to serve.

Thratia had refused to relinquish control of the Saldive Isles *to the whitecoats.*

And there was nothing, nothing at all, in the tone or the faces of the Saldivians watching him now that led him to believe their story was anything else than the truth as they knew it.

"Excuse me," Detan rasped. "I need air."

Worried expressions dogged him. Expressions of concern from Rensair and Iessa blended with the slow, languorous words of Ossar as he pushed to his feet, swayed a moment, then set his gaze on the open doorway and locked it there. His ears buzzed. White encroached upon the corners of his vision.

He staggered to the hall, vaguely aware that he pushed past Thratia, and planted one hand hard against the stone, duck his head down, doubling over so that the blood would rush back into his head again.

However much time had passed, he had no idea, but when the storm of flies in his skull subsided and his vision cleared, Thratia was there, standing beside him, her face as carefully neutral as always.

He straightened, fancy new clothes sticking to him all over from sweat. She seemed smaller to him now, delicate yet fierce in a way he'd never noticed before. She was all persona, he realized with a sinking gut. Just as he put on his mask of bravado or seriousness, she was forever shrouded with how she wanted the world to see her: fearless, ruthless, a creature of power and strength.

And she was those things, was them so fully that he'd never been able to see where the rough edges lay. Where the mask ended and the real woman began.

Because she was all those things, and more. And that was the real terror of her.

"What do you want from me?" he demanded through the rasp in his throat. "Why am I here?"

"Come. It's time we talked."

She turned and walked up the hallway, not for a moment doubting he would follow. And skies help him, he did. Dogged her heels like a puppy in desperate search of a bone.

CHAPTER 17

The skeleton of the Ashfall Lounge was a burnt out warehouse on the outskirts of the city; the flesh was something else all together. Its performers had swathed the building in garishly painted linens, hiding the worst of the damage with sheets of fabric painted with the names of the performers, and the cost for entry. They'd crowded the soot-stained eaves with paper lanterns, covered with squiggles and dots to throw patterns against the cloth and wood.

Patrons milled about the exterior, talking to be heard over the soft threads of music seeping through the ramshackle building. Laughter and song and the vapor of alcohol mingled on the breeze, tinged with something else. Something Ripka couldn't quite place.

"They're so happy," Honey murmured.

The shock of that statement stopped her walking. That was it, that was all there was. These people were happy, out enjoying the night and the company of others despite everything. Despite knowing their city was doomed to fight for its freedom, despite knowing full well that the armies of Thratia were only days away – perhaps even here already, if rumors of a convoy spotted to the west could be believed.

Unlike Aransa, these people hadn't suffered weeks brewing in tension. Hadn't strained under the fear of a doppel in their streets, of their warden murdered and who knew how many officials lined up next on that shadowy boogeyman's chopping block. The people of Hond Steading were used to coming up on top. Ripka wasn't even sure that they knew what it was to fear for a nation, for a people.

It should have brought her joy, to see so many of them without care. Instead, her stomach clenched. A people easy with themselves, mollified and convinced of their invincibility, were difficult to mobilize. Thratia would arrive to find a city full of fat goats, ready for the slaughter.

"Come on." Ripka urged herself forward. "Let's go find Latia and get some seats."

Progress through the crowd was slow, halting. People did not endeavor to block her path so much as be completely indifferent to the fact that anyone of their number might have a sense of direction, of urgency. Ripka's training ticked away, marking certain groups as more likely to cause trouble than others, rankling at the sight of knots of people blocking exits. Worse yet, vendors clustered in triangles around every door, hawking beer and wine and portable foodstuffs. Didn't they see that this place had already burned down once? Fire was a real hazard on the Scorched, if they kept the doorways clogged, then–

"Here." Honey's short fingers gripped Ripka's shoulder, stopping her mid-prowl of the perimeter. She pressed a lopsided clay mug of something dark and grainy and frothing into Ripka's hand. "You need to relax."

Ripka took a long sniff. The sweet aroma of fermented grains startled her – this was no backwater swill – and the smooth warmth of it going down eased knots she hadn't realized she'd been bunching in her shoulders.

"Thanks." She took a longer pull as Honey bought a beer for herself.

Someone banged a spoon against a tin cup and the collective heads of those gathered lifted to the noise, everyone turning to mill into the husk of a lounge. Ripka followed, hesitant, and every time she wondered about the structural integrity of the building she took a deeper drink of her beer. By the time they were gathered in the lobby, her cup was half empty.

"There you are!"

Ripka turned just in time to see Latia swoop down upon them. She'd piled up her hair in a mass of a bun, shoved a paintbrush through it to keep it in place, and donned the biggest, sparkliest set of hammered-copper earrings Ripka'd ever seen. A brief impression of the woman was all Ripka could gather before she was having her cheeks kissed in a dizzying rush, then Latia grabbed her by the shoulders and held her at arm's length, nodding to herself.

"This shade of red *does* become you."

Honey grinned a bit over Latia's shoulder and Ripka shot her a sour look. "Honey decided I needed an update."

"A woman of few words, and excellent taste. I love it!"

Latia gathered Ripka's shoulders under one arm, Honey's under the other, and steered them firmly through the crowd toward a scattering of wood pallet tables that filled the floor before a burlap-curtained stage. She claimed a table toward the middle of the room and ushered both Ripka and Honey into chairs. One look at their drinks, and Latia clucked her tongue.

"For you, Ripka darling, that brew is just fine, but Honey! My dear, that just won't *do* for that poor throat of yours. You!" She flagged down a harried-looking serving boy and thrust a finger at Honey's cup. "Get this poor dear a dark tea with whisky and honey, warmed up, now, and be quick. The dear girl is *injured*, for skies' sake."

Latia dropped copper grains into the boy's outstretched hand and he raced off. "There!" She collapsed into her seat in a puff of stone-smoothed linens and dust.

"Where is Dranik?" Ripka asked when Latia paused to take a breath.

"Oh, *him*." Her face screwed up as if she'd tasted something sour. "Off on one of his little missions of truth and right-thinking, no doubt. Probably haranguing some poor passers-by in the market about the glory of a representative government." She sighed heavily. "He is such an earnest, yet tedious young soul."

"Is he not your elder brother?"

"Pah. Age is in here, my darling." She tapped her temple with one finger, a bit of mustard-yellow paint dried on its tip. "And as such he is *decidedly* my younger fool of a brother. Poor dear. Mama poured a bunch of nonsense into his head, he hardly stood a chance."

Ripka pressed her lips shut to keep from inquiring, fearing that if she seemed too eager to learn about Dranik's politics she might stir suspicion. Latia was Dranik's gatekeeper. If Ripka could ingratiate herself with the woman, then maybe she'd let her get a closer look at what was really going on.

She was forming a tree of questions in her mind to peel away the truth when the waiter arrived and plunked Honey's new drink down. Before Ripka could find a proper opening question, the candelabras lining the walls were snuffed and all conversation fell to a soft murmur. While each table had its own guttering candle, the stage glowed with oil lamps, a brighter light than any of the candles could give.

The stage glowed like a stoked ember. Sorrowful notes from a violin moaned from behind the curtain, their hollow tone carving out a matching emptiness in Ripka's belly. She leaned forward, and noticed Honey doing likewise. Honey's eyes were rapt, glowing in the unctuous light from the lamps, her golden curls all aflame on the top of her head. Her bee-sting full lips moved, slowly, mouthing the tones of the violin.

Honey had seemed focused but bored when she danced death among the rioting prisoners of the Remnant. Now she was enraptured. Ripka swallowed a long sip of her drink, trying to tell herself her fingers trembled because she was overtired.

A woman's silhouette stepped behind the thin curtain. She stood in profile, one arm extended to the sky, the other crooked at her back. She'd curled and teased her hair so much it obscured the shape of her face, of her shoulders. Just the slim curve of lips and nose were visible beyond the ringlets. Ripka leaned forward, trying to discern some telling feature, and the lips moved. The woman sang.

The sound was low, haunting. Shivers coursed up Ripka's spine, trailing goosebumps across her entire body. Beside her, Honey mouthed the words, the barest whisper slipping past her lips. Neither the language nor the tune was familiar to Ripka, but the glaze over Honey's eyes was enough to tell her the woman knew every word.

She nearly jumped out of her skin as a shadow fell over her shoulder, the presence of a man behind her, body warmed with exertion, shocking her out of her reverie.

"What are you doing?" Latia whispered, a low hiss.

Ripka forced herself to wrench her gaze away from the figure on the stage and turn in her seat. She was a little jealous to see Honey ignore the interruption, so intent was she on the performance. Ripka went cold.

Dranik hunched behind her, alongside his sister, his hair stiff with sweat and his forehead gleaming. Even in the near-dark of the candlelight the angry bruise marring his cheek and jaw stood out.

"You have to hide me," he whispered, voice strained with urgency.

"I'd like to drop you down a well," Latia snapped, earning a sharp hush from the table next to them. Dranik's gaze flitted around, uneasy. Ripka knew that pattern of looking – he was checking to see if he'd been followed.

"Let's talk outside," Ripka whispered. If Dranik was going to interrupt the performance for her, she'd be damned if she was going to be left out of any juicy information.

Dranik paled a little. "Not out front."

Ripka bit back sarcasm and nodded. Luckily for them all she'd made a habit of checking every room she entered for entrances and exits while in the watch. "There's a door on the back end of the bar, a service entrance that dumps to the side of the building. We can loop around to the back from there."

Nods all around. These two clearly weren't used to handling themselves in any flavor of real crises, they'd handed the tiller of the situation over to her without a second thought. Ripka stood, careful not to scrape her chair, and soft-footed her way toward the door, drawing a few murmurs of annoyance from the other patrons. She'd expected Honey to stay behind, but the woman followed them, head tipped toward the stage no matter which direction they turned.

The bartender threw her a sour look as she grabbed a nearly spent candle from the edge of the bar, but said nothing. The door was unlocked and didn't so much as creak as she swung it open into the night. Though the place was half-burnt, someone had obviously put some thought into oiling the hinges.

She shivered in the night air, missing her watcher coat, and checked down both ends of the alley before ushering their little group out. The moment the door shut, Latia jabbed her brother in the chest with one finger.

"Just what in the pits are you doing?"

He shifted his weight side to side, glancing down the lane toward the front of the building. Ripka decided to save him.

"Let's talk around back."

Latia rolled her eyes and flounced her skirts, but followed Ripka all the same. A packed-dirt patio reached from the back of the performance hall to a haphazard stone fence stacked high as Ripka's shoulders. The sight of it made her uneasy – such structures were known to collapse in Aransa – so she sidled a little closer to the building. A door stood in the middle of the back wall, a few chords of music seeping out, and piles of cloth and broken or half-finished stage props dotted the area. Dranik made a complete survey of their environs before he dared to speak.

"We have to get away from here, Latia. They'll find

me any moment – you must hide me!"

"Hush." Latia crossed her arms and stared down her long nose at him. "It's bad enough you disturbed the performance, don't yell so that the whole theater can hear you from out here, too."

"Latia," Ripka said, watching yellow bile tinge Dranik's cheeks. "He's serious, I think. What happened, Dranik?"

"*Later*," he hissed, though this time he kept his voice down. "They don't know my name. If we go to your studio–"

"I am in the middle of a piece!"

"Shhh," Honey murmured.

They all stopped cold, every last gaze swiveling to the golden-haired woman. Her head was no longer tilted toward the building. She'd turned slightly, angling her body the way they'd come, head cocked as if listening. Ripka heard thudding, thought it was the sound of her heart, but it was too disjointed. And growing louder.

"Company," Ripka whispered, and slid into a ready crouch.

Dranik moaned and slunk back, grabbing his sister's sleeve to yank her towards a deadfall in the fence. She swore and stumbled, painted sandals twisting in the dust.

Precision echoed in those footsteps, a practiced pattern that thundered through Ripka's memory. Long shadows appeared at the end of the alley, the hint of firm-lined coats evident about the pursuers' collars. She did not need to see them to know those coats were blue.

Shit. The shadows stretched, drawing closer, and her breath came harsh between her lips. Honey's fingers grazed her arm, and the simple touch returned her to herself. She wouldn't have to fight them. She just needed to get Dranik and Latia out of here. Preferably without being recognized.

"Go," she ordered, jerking her chin toward the break in the wall. Latia was first through, shoved by her brother, Honey tight on their heels. Ripka hesitated only a breath. She threw the candle.

Her aim was true. The sputtering stub of wax crashed into a pile of stage debris. She pivoted and sprinted toward the gap in the wall. Honey gripped her wrists, helping her over a low mound of rubble, as the first shouts filled the patio area.

Shouts, followed by a gut-churning *whoosh*. Ripka winced at the sound of the flames, the shouts of pursuit shifting to shouts of alarm. Watcher coats were made to smother fire, she told herself. They'd be all right. The patrons in the theater wouldn't even notice.

Latia and Dranik were halfway down the road, Latia limping but pumping her arms as if her life depended on it. They cut a straight path down the center of the road. Ripka bit her lips and shared a look with Honey, who shrugged. Some people were just shit at situational awareness.

Honey at her side, Ripka jogged up to the siblings. "We need to get off the main road."

Dranik's eyes bulged. "Right. I, uh–"

"This way," Latia said. She tore off toward a thin side street, the windows facing the road shuttered. Honey scampered forward and slipped her arm around Latia's shoulders, supporting her to ease her limping, and Dranik trotted after.

A sharp whistle pierced the night. Ripka winced. She knew that sound. Though most of the watchers must have stayed behind to deal with the fire, they'd been tagged by a scout. No scout worth their salt would let a group of fugitives out of their sight before backup arrived to help.

"Go on," Ripka ordered. "I'll lose the scout."

Honey threw a concerned glance over her shoulder, brows pinched together, and Ripka gave her a little nod. It was all right. She'd meet them at the studio, later. A brilliant smile flashed across Honey's face and then she was gone, ushering the siblings down the road.

Ripka slowed her jog, taking in her surroundings. The streets were dark. Those who ran the theater must have chosen this district for its lack of population. Hond Steading's roads sprawled in all directions, the twisting maze of a neighborhood had sprung into life spontaneously, without any pre-planning. She could use that.

She toed the ground, feeling the packed earth, the slick smoothness of the fine layer of dust that covered everything in the Scorched. She'd missed that dust while she'd been on the Remnant. It had always served to remind her how tenuous her footing truly was at any given time.

The whistle sounded again. She ducked down an alley, pressed her back against the still-warm mudbrick, evened out her breathing, and waited.

CHAPTER 18

Pelkaia entered the house of her enemy.

By some trick of fate and misfortune of trust she was welcome here, welcome in the austere halls of the Honding family palace. Tibal had vouched for her, or perhaps Ripka, speaking of her exploits of the past and her goals for the deviants of the future. Or – and this gave her a little frisson of amusement to consider – Detan himself had, perhaps, written to his aunt and given Pelkaia praise.

The reasons didn't matter. They were all lies, anyway. What mattered was that, despite how she had come by the freedom, Pelkaia mounted the steps to the Honding palace and entered its doors a free woman, without suspicion.

She hadn't even bothered putting on a Valathean-bred face. She wore her own countenance, relishing the feel of the sere air on sand-dune smooth cheeks she'd been pressed to keep hidden for the vast majority of her adult life. The Hondings, and the citizenry of their city, did not fear her heritage. Though, truth be told, she drew a few questioning glances.

No, the people of Hond Steading had forgotten their past, and hers. Forgotten it was their arrival, the lure in their blood toward the firemounts of this cursed city, that had brought Valathea's hungry might down upon the Scorched continent. That had rolled her people back into barren lands, and mingled their bloods until an entirely new people sprang up on the intersection of Valathea and Catari.

The people of the Scorched.

Despite her distaste for their origins, Pelkaia could not bring herself to loathe them as she should. She had better enemies to fan her hatred with.

She spotted a likely black-jacketed guard lingering near the doorway and approached, all easy smiles and open body language. It'd taken her a while to reclaim an easy, non-threatening posture after she'd given up masquerading with Ripka's stiff formality, but once she had it back it came easily to her, though she could not articulate why that was. Perhaps some echo from her childhood, or from her first time as a mother. From a time before her world had begun to be shredded, slowly, to bloodied pieces.

Whatever the reason, her easy stroll put the guard at ease, receptive to her request. Detan's manipulation tactics must be rubbing off. But no, that wasn't fair. She'd been a serpent in a ball gown long before Detan Honding had ever had the misfortune of stumbling into her life.

"Good morning," she said to the guard and bobbed her head politely. "Could you point me toward Nouli Bern's quarters? This place is so large, I've already forgotten the way."

The guard hesitated, the slightest flicker of indecision. Nouli's presence here was protected, as Pelkaia well knew. Not even the citizens of the city knew their leading family's palace harbored the man who'd help engineer Valathea's greatest weapons of war. But Pelkaia was a known entity to the guards: accepted, safe. And she knew the man's name – simply knowing that he was here at all was key enough to open that door.

The guard checked to be sure her post was covered by fellow eyes, then inclined her head in practiced solicitude. Pelkaia had to hand it to old Dame Honding, she had her people trained to within an inch of their lives.

"This way please, miss."

Pelkaia threw the remaining guard a friendly smile and trailed after her mark, making sure not to look too eager nor too disinterested. She marked the path, letting the guard see as she murmured assurances to herself that this was the right route after all. It didn't matter that she'd never seen these particular halls before; she needed the guard to believe this was little more than a refresher.

"Here you are, miss." The guard paused in front of a door toward the end of a lower level, set well away from the bulk of the residences, so far as Pelkaia could tell, in a wing that offered a low, sloped roof over what had to be Nouli's rooms. No doubt he'd been sequestered here, away from the bustle of the palace's everyday happenings, to both keep him out of sight, and his experiments from affecting anyone should they go awry.

Pelkaia half-stepped toward the door, only to be met with an upraised palm from the guard. "You must enter without knocking – the door is always unlocked – and shut it carefully behind you. Stand with your back to the door, beside the candelabra, and wait for Nouli to acknowledge you. Do not speak to him, or startle him in any way."

Pelkaia flashed a smile. "Thank you, dear, but I'm familiar with Master Bern's peculiarities."

The guard shrugged. "Rules are rules, miss. Dame's orders that everyone who approaches this door be reminded of them. Got her nethers in a twist over the man's experiments, if you ask me. Worried he'll knock the whole place down if he so much as sees a sandrat."

"The Dame has reason for her caution, I'm sure."

The guard twitched at her weapons belt, letting the heavy weight of her tools reassure her. "Everyone has an extra helping of caution, these days. Holler if you need anything, miss. But not too loud."

Pelkaia ran her fingers across her lips as if stitching them shut, and the guard tipped her helmet before hurrying off back to her post. She let the guard's steps fade into the distance before she peeled the door open. The hinges had been well-oiled, it glided wide with only the tiniest of efforts.

The sight made her breath catch. Master Bern, it seemed, had been given every possible item he could ever need, and then some. She slipped within the cavernous room and shut the door, lingering in the position indicated, while she let her eyes adjust to the oily light.

More than the accouterments of a chemist or engineer dotted the huge room. This was a space gone over to experimentation. Aside from the litter of instruments and notebooks across all the tables, Nouli had also been granted a small greenhouse for plant life. Though the plants were clustered in a glass-lined corner far from where Pelkaia waited, she recognized some of those glossy, leafy fronds, and took heart.

Nouli, in his genius, had not neglected the study of apothiks. Ripka had intimated as much when she brought him aboard Pelkaia's ship. He'd trembled in those first few days, claiming need of rest but clearly needing something more. Pelkaia had suspected drug abuse of some kind. She'd never dreamed he had knowledge of some of her old Catari remedies, too. Their conversation had yet to begin, and already she was brimming with confidence.

Paper on paper rustled somewhere in the back of the work room, the subtle clinking of glass. Pelkaia stood stock still alongside the candelabra, waiting patiently for the master to sense her presence. She'd heard Ripka's story of the conflagration he'd kicked off in his workshop back on the Remnant, and did not wish to see a live demonstration.

She hadn't long to wait. Nouli shuffled forward, favoring his left leg with a hardwood cane, his thick glasses sunk low on a nose long-dented by the nose grips. He squinted at Pelkaia, taking in her purebred Catari countenance, and nodded to himself.

"Pelkaia Teria, isn't it? The captain of my rescue ship. What can I do for you, Captain?"

"I am that." She darted a look around the room. Though it was huge, and doubtless branched into an opulent set of sleeping quarters, Pelkaia was no fool to the workings of such things. Nouli Bern did not leave the Honding palace. Ever. "Though I wonder how successful I was in my rescue."

He shuffled over to sit on a stool very near her and leaned his cane against his knee. "Not a subtle woman, are you?"

She shrugged. "The older I get, the thinner my patience for delicacy of speech."

"A dangerous mood, that one. Careful wording is an art to be mastered, not a relic to be discarded when one feels they've outgrown it." He eyed her, slowly and carefully, as she had expected. "Though that is something you will learn in time. You are not nearly old enough to be so cynical of politeness."

And just like that, he'd sidled so easily into her trap. It was almost a pity, really. She missed a good head to fence with – a manipulator as keen on the craft as she was – but this would do. She hadn't expected otherwise, truly. Nouli was a genius in a practical way. He expected people to be as straightforward as his equations were.

"You flatter me, Master Bern. But you do forget – I am Catari, and of a particular line. Or had you not heard the rumors?"

"Rumors?" He leaned forward, fingers curled tight over the knob of his cane to steady himself.

"That the mixed-bloods of the Scorched live just as long, if not longer, than the pure of Valathea, despite the harsher climate. And, it must be said, put off the more aesthetic ravages of age quite longer."

"Tosh." He slumped back and waved a dismissive hand. "I've heard the rumors, everyone likes a good fairytale, but I'm of mixed blood myself, my dear, and as you can see such mingling has not been so kind to me as the stories would suggest."

A bitter undercurrent caught her attention and swept it away. Anger that had nothing at all to do with the fading of his looks, nor his health, lay like a frond of spines beneath his words. It was no grand leap to puzzle out what would make a man like Nouli so deeply resentful.

"It's a subtle effect in the mixed, diluted as it is, and distributed amongst people who do not live nor eat the way the Catari have."

He snorted. "Clean living and thick blood, those are

your suggestions? I could have told any fool the same, it is the thing most prescribed by all backwater apothiks. Good knowledge, yes, but hardly revolutionary."

"Incomplete knowledge," Pelkaia said, and saw his eyes narrow with interest. "Due to... poor relations between Valatheas and Catari early on, my people failed to share certain insights with their new neighbors. Certain... recipes."

From within her tunic pocket she produced a small vial of elixir. It was not enough to perform miracles, for it was diluted and extracted from plants not grown in the traditional ways, but it was enough to keep Pelkaia's mind quick. Or, at the very least, to restore it from abject sluggishness.

Nouli was not a slow man, despite whatever age had done to him. He licked his lips, eyeing the little thumb-thick cylinder of stoppered glass. "And that is what, exactly? Some potion of youth? If you've come to peddle me fables, Captain, I'd ask you to save the interruption for dinner tonight, when I won't be postponing important work for entertainment's sake."

"Your skepticism is welcome. There is no magic in this vial, no one remedy to heal all the ills of time. It is, if anything, a stopgap, a momentary measure of restoration. But it does work, Master Bern, I can promise you that. It may be no miracle, but it can make your thoughts move easier, for a while. Something about removing old oil from the brain matter – the true function has been lost to time and war. But I recall the making of it, all the same."

He scowled. "You expect me to what, exactly? Take your word and drink down this concoction? It could be poison, for all I know. Or some bitter tea that will only grant me indigestion."

"I expect you to do nothing blindly, Master. I expect

you to draw off samples, set it beneath your magnification glasses and probe around in its making. Perhaps even feed it to a sandrat to judge the results. What you do to assure yourself doesn't matter to me. Only know that you must have half this amount remaining, when you finally decide to drink it, for it to have any effect at all."

She tossed it to him, end over end in a gleaming arc, and he fumbled forward, knocking his cane aside in his haste to save the thin glass from dashing against the hard floor. "You Catari have kept your secrets close, always. Why now? Why give this to me now, if it is indeed what you say it is?"

Such a clever man. Perhaps he was not so blind to her manipulations as she had expected. She caught herself smiling. A lively mark in Nouli was going to make this game much more entertaining. "If I told you I was dying, would you believe me?"

His lashes fluttered as he blinked in shock. "I would have no reason not to, but you seem in good health, why do you…?" He trailed off, eyeing the vial in his hand thoughtfully. She could tell from the furrow on his brow she did not need to explain to him why she appeared in good health when she was, in fact, dissolving from the inside out.

"I wish for something of my people to live on, once I am gone."

He picked his gaze off the vial and stared at her. "Your people continue, out in the desert. They will not die with you, my dear."

"No, but knowledge is a tenuous thing. Better to store it in as many safe places as possible, don't you think?"

He frowned. "But that is not all."

"No, no, of course not. Someday – someday soon – I may require a favor of you in return."

She watched the balance of scales shift in his mind, watched the wary guardedness seep back into his expression and posture. Here was not a man used to wagering his future against his present. Or, perhaps, a man who had done that very thing one too many times and found the payoff wanting.

"What favor?"

"I cannot be certain yet, but nothing that would risk your position."

His eyes narrowed, his fingers closed tight around the vial, his arm drifted backward, preparing to throw it. She held up her hands, palms out, put on that easy smile she'd been practicing and said, "Nothing untoward. I swear it. But take some time to consider – the vial is my gift to you, regardless of your choice. When you're satisfied with your research, send for me, and I will bring you something new to puzzle over."

"I will not–" he began, but she had already slipped out the door, shutting its well-oiled hinges behind her. She paused there, breathing softly, back pressed against the door as she strained the very edge of her hearing. Waiting, Waiting.

A shuffle of feet, the scrape of a stool, the click of the cane.

But no breaking of glass, no tinkle of precious elixir bleeding out onto the floor.

He'd taken her bait. She had now only to wait for the payoff.

Her smile was an easy, natural thing, as she strolled out of the Honding palace.

CHAPTER 19

Thratia led Detan to her bedroom, and his stomach was tied too tightly to make any smart remarks on the fact. Night had well and truly come to Aransa, and a small part of him was glad he could no longer see the city he'd abandoned. While the curtains were pulled back to let in the moon and starlight, their natural shine was not enough to dispel the shadows lurking in the corners of the room which was Thratia's sanctum. The whole place, the whole night, made his skin crawl.

He hadn't been sure what he'd expected, but he had an unsettling suspicion that even ascetic hermits holed up in caves in the badlands enjoyed more luxury than Thratia Ganal.

She moved to the window, put her back against its frame, and watched him while he took in her private space. A low bed, just wide and long enough to hold her, huddled against the far wall, its foot pointed toward the singular window she occupied now. Shelves filled the other wall, bursting with rolled maps, books, and hand-written folios. A desk, a chair, a wardrobe. Nothing else. Not even a rug on the hard, stone, floor.

"Are you a prisoner?" he asked, just to shake that low-lidded, intense look off her face.

"Only of myself."

"Shouldn't you have some sort of map on the wall, of all the lands you've left to conquer? Or, I don't know, a tapestry of babies being chucked into a bonfire. Is there a special agency that handles interior decorating for mad bastards?"

A ghost of a smile, seen only in the brief gleam of her teeth. "I have all I need, and it is private."

He swallowed, recalling the heavy lock she'd opened to let them in. He was quite certain no cleaning crew ever set foot in this room, and yet, even with the surroundings bled of color in the pale light, he could not find a speck of dust or filth. Her fastidiousness irritated him almost as much as her conquest. Almost.

"I mean, there's not even a set of shackles. Or the ears of your enemies."

"Honding. You're rambling."

"Haven't you noticed yet that's *what I do*?" The anger in his own voice surprised him. His hands had coiled to fists at his side, though he hardly knew how to use them. Some niggling in the back of his brain told him he was missing something, a sensation like deep hunger or thirst, ramping his irritation as surely as if he'd gone without food for a day. But he'd eaten, and... And skipped his daily meeting with Aella. Forgone the injection of selium and diviner blood that Callia had once been convinced would leash him to her, help him refine his power.

He shivered. The room was cold, but sweat sheeted between his shoulder blades.

He could push her. Standing with that smug little smirk on her face, back pressed up against the open window, she'd never see it coming. Her arms were crossed. It'd take her too long to mount a defense, to dodge his advance. The room was small. Four steps. Four steps and she could be plummeting to the dark.

And take her answers with her.

Detan breathed deep, smoothed his hair with both hands, and forced his shoulders to unbunch, letting his whole body slouch down into the languid posture he used to play the disaffected dilettante.

"Is this where you suck my blood, then?"

She snorted, a brief little laugh. "Don't be stupid. I have lost count of the opportunities I've had to kill you. I suspect you even know why I've brought you here, though you're too much the coward to face it."

"You want me here, under your thumb, for the same cursed reason everyone else does. Why the whitecoats, why my own aunt, hounds my heels. Because I have a skill you want, a talent unique enough it cannot be replicated, and you want to make use of it. Chain me to your ships and turn me into a machine of war.

"But that's not why I bent knee to Aella, and through her to you. Whatever you want me for, whatever blasted damage you think I can craft on your behalf – I won't. Do you understand me? I will not be turned against innocents. I brave Aella's *lessons* to gain control. To be less of a threat. I will not be your weapon."

He stepped forward, heart thudding in his ears, anger making his cheeks and chest hot. At the vaguest edge of his senses he realized there was no selium nearby, nothing at all for him to channel his anger into should the desire arise. Just Thratia's small, sharp face, half scarred by the damage he'd wrought, smiling up at him. Amused.

"Is that what you think?" she asked.

He'd moved close enough so that he stood over her,

her head tilted up to meet his gaze, her breath a warm gust against his throat. He stepped back, unclenched his fists. "You may have the Saldivians fooled, but I've seen inside you, Thratia Ganal. I stared into those eyes of yours while you slit Bel Grandon's throat just to make a point, and a poor one at that."

The smirk vanished, and while her hard stare made his skin crawl he took small satisfaction in wiping any pleasure off her face. "You are, quite possibly, the most obdurate person I have ever met."

"Thank you."

"Detan," she said, and the sound of his first name from her lips sent uneasy ripples through him. "Listen very carefully." She peeled herself from the window frame and stepped forward, tightening the distance between them so that he could feel the heat of her. She cocked her head, put her lips by his ear, never touching – not even allowing her breath to gust – as she whispered. "I don't need you in order to crush Hond Steading."

He resisted an urge to reel back from her nearness. She was a rock-viper of a woman. Sudden movements triggered sudden strikes.

"Yes. You do."

She threw her head back and laughed, hands folded over her stomach. The very sound of it drove pins and needles into Detan's skin.

"Oh, my Lord Honding. You are but one man. An exceptional man, in some ways, but not at all instrumental. Unless you choose to make it easier for all involved."

He felt himself drawn up on the edge of a precipice, wary and uncertain. Thratia was dangling what she wanted from him like bait on a string, teasing him forward into asking, demanding, just what exactly she wanted.

Whatever it was, he would pretend to give it to her. Pretend to bend his knee, as he had to Aella, just so that he could be closer to the inner workings of her machine. Whatever she wanted from him, he would pervert it.

First, he needed to master himself. To calm his revulsion from the Saldivians' story and see her as she was, as she always had been: a puppet master, hungry for power. Even if he believed her reasons for taking the Saldive Isles, for taking Aransa, he was convinced they were only set-dressing. A flimsy framework to prop up her own hunger.

She wanted him to ask what she wanted of him, what she'd planned for him. And while he knew full well he'd have to give it to her – if only briefly – he'd be spit-roasted before he made it easy on her. "If the whitecoats are such a scourge to the well-being of the empire, then why did you not go to your empress? Don't tell me you didn't have the access, nor the will to make her listen. Your family's as old as mine."

The quick breath she took told him all he needed to know – he'd pushed her off balance. "My empress is dead."

He would have laughed in her face, if her voice weren't so obviously shot through with the brittle edge of real grief. "I would have heard. Everyone would have heard."

"Spare me your false naivete. Shortly after the whitecoats arrived in the Saldives, personal correspondence from the empress to me ceased, and her son began to answer in her stead. Such a stupid, pliable boy. I knew his handwriting, though he signed her name, and I knew the strings pulling his hand. I returned to Valathea at once, while my garrison stayed behind in the Saldives. I was denied all access to her, and Ranalae..."

She sucked air through her teeth. "Ranalae had her claws in the young prince's shoulder. The empress is dead, and Ranalae Lasson pulls the prince's strings. If you believe me ruthless, Honding, you have only to meet Ranalae to then think me a lamb. She desires the puzzle of sel-sensitivity solved, in whole. She will not stop until she's acquired it, no matter the imperial legacy she tears apart in the process."

He'd gone cold, the only sound in his head the steady thwump-thwump of his heartbeat. Thratia cocked her head, sensing his unease, but he ignored her regard. He licked his lips, ignored long-buried images surfacing through the many vaults of his memory. Ranalae Lasson. There was a name he'd buried, a woman he'd erased from his own mind – had thought only of in terms of her long, white coat. Director of the Bone Tower. Founder of the whitecoats. The woman whose scalpel had danced across his skin long before he'd ever fallen into the clutches of Callia and Aella his last time in Aransa.

That name. That horrible, horrible, name.

"We've met," was all he could manage to say.

Her gaze flicked to his arms, to his chest. She knew what lurked there, though she'd never acknowledged it outright. Had to know, to know where to look. No doubt Aella sent her back a detailed description of all the torturous injuries he had once endured, perhaps she'd drawn a cartoonish little map of his scars for her mistress.

"And did she find what she was looking for in you?"

"I don't know," he grated. "I escaped the night I heard her say the word *vivisection*."

Thratia winced. He was sure of it. She was a master at controlling her expression, her body language, but he'd caught her there – struck her hard. The subtle ripple at the corners of her eyes, the pressing of her lips. That was real. That was horror. A crack in her iron-fast facade.

He shoved a wedge in that crack, and pushed. "But you knew that. Maybe not about me, not specifically, but you knew what she was capable of by the time you came to Aransa. You kicked her agents out of the Saldives, kept those islands all to yourself while you came here to set up a base of power. And what did you do, Thratia? What did you fucking do?"

He couldn't help it now. She knew. She'd always known. And that realization was acid in his chest. "You sold them to her. You thought to yourself: *Hmm, I need some weapons. Some nice shiny swords. You know how I can get them?* Trading deviants, trading human-fucking-beings, to Ranalae Lasson to carve up for jollies. To the very woman you claim you want to stop. Pitsfuckitall, Thratia, you were going to sell her Pelkaia, going to sell her *me*, just to get a few crates of weapons in your bloody hands. What good is that? What's the fucking point?"

She'd gone still, her slim frame so very solid he half expected her to radiate cold as if she'd been frozen through. After a long pause, wherein the only sound was the panting of his own breath, she licked her lips. "A few, to save many. That was my trade. My bloody bargain."

His wrist was in her hand, her grip coiled so tight his skin bulged between her fingers. He stared, open-mouthed, at his upraised hand, his flat palm. He'd been going to slap her. Hadn't even thought about it. Hadn't even realized it.

And then, the sudden realization: he could have reached for selium. Would have, months ago, but with the sharpening of his anger that sense had closed down, a safety valve switched shut. Tibs would be proud. He almost giggled.

"I lost only two," she said.

"What the fuck does that mean?"

"Two went to the Bone Tower. The rest were still on Callia's barge."

It was rather hard to think through the thundering of the rage in his ears, but he got there, eventually. Recalled what little Aella had told him about her return to Aransa, her whitecoat mistress Callia struck ill, Thratia their only port of refuge. Detan had long suspected Aella of poisoning Callia to take her place, to take control of her research under Thratia's direction. He hadn't considered that Thratia had orchestrated the whole thing from the start.

"You're insane."

She smiled, and the expression was so genuine and girlish she almost transformed into another woman right before his eyes. "I am determined."

"And what do you want me for, then?" he demanded, hating himself for letting her push him into that corner but needing, so desperately, to have something real to hold onto. Some kernel of truth from which he could begin to spin a plan to undo Thratia and Ranalae and any other cold-hearted bastard he stumbled across on his way to kicking her teeth in. "Am I trade goods for your enemy as well? A way to fake yourself close to her so that you may strike?"

"Haven't you figured it out yet? Your blood is the only thing of use to me."

His blood. His deviation. The horrible perversion of his sel-sensitivity, twisted into a weapon to throw at his home city. The city he'd promised his mother he'd protect. His stomach churned. To pretend to be a weapon against them, well, he'd expected as much, but – no.

That wasn't what she wanted. She'd said as much,

when she'd laughed him off.

What what what.

She reached for him. His skin crawled all over as her fingers curled around his neck, palm pressing against his jugular, the rising beat of his heart heavy and hot against her hand. If she choked him, he could twist away, throw her out that open window. He'd escaped from direr places, it wouldn't take more than a week to reach Hond Steading if he could steal a flier –

Her fingertips, nails trimmed away to nothing, pads firm with callouses, traced the outline of the family crest branded into the back of his neck. The crest that marked him the sole heir of the city she intended to take. He swallowed, pulse kicking, skin heating.

There were other reasons to want his blood. Older reasons.

That smile returned, though this time there was nothing of kindness in it. "I see you understand."

"You can't be serious."

Once, what seemed like lifetimes ago, he spotted Callia's barge flying into dock at Thratia's compound and, not knowing what it was, cracked a joke about her finally giving in to a political marriage. He did not feel like laughing now.

"I am. Your family's city is unique of the cities of the Scorched, in its de facto independence from Valathea and its insistence on a hereditary leadership. Quaint ideals, but useful to me. I want Hond Steading whole. With one little contract, you can give it to me. No siege. No war. No one has to die."

He'll do.

The distance between them shortened, but did not close, the heat of her body radiating through a tunic that seemed, to his eye, suddenly too thin, his own clothes too tight. He cleared his throat, swallowed hard, tried to get a handle on – on – anything, and came up floundering. Perhaps for the first time in his life, he was at a loss for words.

"You have until we arrive at Hond Steading to decide, and make no mistake, I am marching for that city prepared to break it regardless of your answer."

So perfunctory. So matter-of-fact. He caught himself staring at the ripple of a scar that marred the side of her face, the brutalization that was his doing. The evidence of which she wore proudly, black hair pinned back to reveal the whole scope of the damage.

He'd done that. Hadn't meant to, not really, but he hadn't felt sorry about it, either. And here she was, the distance between them gone now, the hard warmth of her pressed against him, head tilted in question, fingers stroking, stroking, and he could hardly catch his breath let alone decide if he wanted to scream or laugh or weep.

He brushed her ruined cheek with his fingertips, and she did not flinch away.

And then they were together, merging, forceful and firm and breathless.

He forgot himself. For a little while.

CHAPTER 20

Watcher whistles echoed down the lanes of Hond Steading, raising conflicting prickles all over Ripka's skin. Old instincts urged her to run to that call, to assist her fellows. She pushed those urges aside, focused on what she must do to gain the trust of Latia and Dranik.

The sight of Dranik's face, bruised and terrified, firmed her resolve. He was into something, something that frightened him. And that fear alone was enough to confirm her suspicions that he meant well for the citizens of Hond Steading. He'd just been misguided about the best methods to achieve that goal.

Distract and evade. What she had to work with wasn't much – a vague understanding of the city's streets, the quiet of night. No crowds bustled through this neighborhood, the only nightlife seemed to be centered on the theater. And that was the answer. She mentally saluted the watchers pursuing her, and hoped Lakon hadn't trained them as well as she'd been trained.

Cloistered in the alley's shadows, she listened to the clatter of watcher feet, judged the whistle-blower's distance, and sprinted into view.

He yelped with surprise, and she almost laughed at the sound. She'd cut it a little too close, but she threw power into her legs and widened the distance, diving into the shelter of another alley. He couldn't ignore that. No way. She paused, panting, wired with tension until she heard the blast of whistles that meant he'd sighted one of the fugitives and was in pursuit. Answering blasts broke the night.

She was prey, and they were hunting dogs.

Feigning uncoordinated panic, she bumped a stack of crates with her hip as she fled the alley, sprawling the wood to the ground with a heavy crash. A neat little trail for them to follow. She couldn't risk staying too close, lest he suspect her intentions, but by now he must have lost sight of the others. In his position, she'd consider the panicked woman fleeing down random streets a likely target for questioning. Panicky people were quick to talk.

The alley opened up into another narrow lane, and she glanced at the stars. The theater had been to the north, and the sky was clear. She might not know the streets by name or number, but any Scorched girl worth their stones could navigate by starlight. Becoming lost in the Scorched meant death. No exceptions.

She jogged, saving her breath for the moment the watchers would catch sight of her again. No sense in sprinting until she had to, there was a lot of ground yet to cover.

Watcher whistles sounded behind her and to her right, echoing off the crowded buildings. Ripka picked up the pace. A shadow fell across the road, looming from a side-lane. She ducked at the last moment, skittered sideways and just barely avoided the swipe of a baton. The watcher swore, but she was already adjusting course, peeling away, the fear of nearly being caught adding fire to her veins.

Footsteps thundered behind her, closer now, and she risked a more circuitous route, ducking and diving between homes, kicking over the occasional planter to string them forward, but not too much. Ache grew in her legs, her breath came hot in her throat. Her body was slowing down.

They lost sight of her. She heard it in their strained shouts, and though she couldn't quite hear their words she could intuit their meaning: *she went that way, no that way.*

Ripka swung closer to the theater. The rock wall they'd escaped through earlier loomed just across the lane, the watcher's calls tantalizingly close. She pushed to her toes, risked a peek in both directions, then darted across to the wall. The stones were rough beneath her hands, scraping her palms, but she heaved herself over all the same and landed stumbling.

"Who in the pits are you?" a woman demanded.

Ripka froze, jerked her head up to find the voice. The theater's backdoor stood half open. A woman in a snug robe with a long mass of curls squinted out at her, a smoldering cigarillo between her lips.

The singer. But there was something familiar about that sharp, dark face.

"*Laella?*"

The woman squinted through a plume of smoke. "Ripka?"

They stared, open-mouthed, for an embarrassing moment, then recovered in synch and pulled themselves up and shut their slack jaws.

"What are you doing here?" Laella asked, a little breathless.

"Quick," Ripka said as she dashed forward. "Give me your wig."

"What in the pits for?"

"Just do it."

Laella rolled her eyes and plucked the long wig from her head, revealing the tight braids that were her usual style. Ripka tugged the mass of curls over her own hair, tucked her natural strands behind her ear, and faced Laella.

"How's it look?"

"Ridiculous. What is this all about, Ripka? Did Pelkaia send you?"

"Haven't seen her since we arrived."

The whistles started up again. Ripka winced, and Laella's brows shot straight up as she caught the motion. Before Ripka could explain, a panting, red-faced watcher stuck his head over the break in the wall and scowled at them both.

"You seen anyone come through?" he demanded. "Woman, about her height." He jerked his chin to Ripka.

Laella put on her impervious, Valathean aristocracy act and scoffed as she tossed her head. "Haven't seen a soul, save those already in the theater."

"Call out if you see her. Could be dangerous."

"I'm quaking," Laella drawled as the watcher snorted in disgust and dove away to pick up Ripka's false trail.

Ripka breathed out, limp with relief, and almost laughed. "Thanks for the loan, and the cover."

"Don't mention it. Mind telling me what's going on?"

"Rather not," she admitted. Ripka plucked the wig from her head, made a cursory attempt at arranging it, then handed it back to Laella. She stuffed it under her arm without another glance.

"Didn't think so."

"Mind telling me what you're doing singing on stage? Can't be part of your, ah, training with Pelkaia."

Laella's eyes narrowed. "Rather not."

"Fair enough."

They gave each other a good, long side-eye, and Ripka had no reason to doubt that Laella was brimming with just as many questions as she was. It was probably more than fair that Laella had questions – she hadn't been the one seen running from the watch, after all. Ripka shuffled her feet awkwardly, edging toward the alley that led around to the front of the theater. And to escape.

Laella sent her along with a flick of the wrist. Ripka ducked her head to hide a smirk and turned down the alley, toward the throng of voices gathered just outside the theater. When she was halfway down the alley, on a whim, she glanced over her shoulder and caught Laella's eye. The girl flicked ash from her cigarillo, frowning.

"You've a lovely voice," Ripka called.

Laella scowled, snatched a pebble from the dusty ground, and hucked it at Ripka all in one smooth movement. Stifling a laugh, Ripka dodged to the side and sped her steps, preparing to lose herself in the crowd gathered out front.

Which was, apparently, a poor plan.

At the mouth of the alley two obvious bruisers gave her a good long once-over, not bothering to obscure their glance Laella's way. Ripka didn't dare follow their gazes, but whatever assurance Laella gave them must have been enough. They turned up their noses at her dusty clothes and wind-blown hair, but they eased aside to let her sidle past.

Into a clamor of chaos.

Ripka winced as half of those gathered near the alley spun the second she was through the brutes, eyes avid with interest. They closed on her, all speaking at once. Ripka took an instinctive step backward, brushed up against the solid wall of the bodyguards and sighed. Might as well try to move stone with her mind than to convince those two to let her back to the patio.

She forced a smile, knowing it was more of a grimace, and tried to convince herself this wasn't any different than leaving the station house after a particularly public, and nasty, crime. Except then, usually, her blue coat and belted weapons were enough to part the crowds like a ship's prow through a wisp of cloud. It seemed every time she took a step, the theater patrons tightened up.

"Who are you?" the indistinct voices demanded. "How did you get back there?" "Where did you come from?" "Did you break in?" "What's your name?" "Do you know the songstress?"

Ripka set her posture firm and shouldered her way past a woman with far too much alcohol on her breath.

Of course. Latia had claimed the singer – Laella – was a complete mystery to the local art scene. She'd shown up just a few days ago – no doubt shortly after Pelkaia's ship took harbor in the north – and allowed no one but her guards and musician to see her outside of the obscuring stretch of the theater curtain. She was a growing local legend, a puzzle to be unraveled. Whatever her motives, Ripka had no desire to out the girl. She'd seen how Laella was treated on Pelkaia's ship: a second-class citizen, barely tolerated and trusted, all because her family had branched from wealthy Valathean stock.

Couldn't be much harm in singing a few songs. Ripka schooled her expression to cold neutrality and weaved through the crowd with force. Once they realized she wasn't going to feed their gossip, the crowd broke up around her, going back to their drinks and snacks and petty rumors. Ripka let the conversations wash over her, trying to pick up any hint that might be useful.

Unless what colors were in vogue for the season, and which art shows were absolutely mandatory, were facts crucial in the fate of Hond Steading, she was without luck. Ripka sighed, kicking at the ground as she blended in with the other theater-goers heading back to their homes for the evening. There was something sweet in the naivete of these people. Something innocent, sincere, that Ripka dreaded to pierce. Though Thratia marched to their homes, though the agents of Valathea lurked in their northern waters, the greatest worry in these peoples' lives tonight were if they were fashionable enough, if they'd found the greatest art.

Such simple pleasures, simple concerns, made Ripka's chest ache.

The traffic thinned out as she approached the neighborhood that housed Latia's studio. The night, now that she wasn't running for her freedom through it, was nice and crisp. A cool breeze brushed away the sweat and grime she'd picked up during her flight. Pity she'd have to go and spoil the pleasant evening by drilling into Dranik's activities.

She turned onto the little lane that led to Latia's house and nearly jumped out of her boots as the door slammed open, spilling light onto the walkway. Light, and Latia. The woman barreled out of her home, skirts flying every which way, and grasped Ripka to her chest in a hug so firm it crushed the air clear out of her lungs.

"Oof, easy!" Ripka squeaked, as she sucked down a replacement breath.

"My dear, we were *so* very worried about you!"

"I wasn't." Honey appeared in the doorway, arms folded lightly over her stomach, her expression bored. From any other woman, Ripka would take offense at that, but she knew full well Honey meant it as a compliment –

she trusted Ripka's skill completely, therefore she wasn't worried. Simple as that.

"I'm fine," Ripka said as she peeled herself out of Latia's arms. "Let's get inside. We need to talk."

"Of course, of course." Latia locked her arm around Ripka's and herded her into the house. "You *must* put your feet up, you poor dear. Did they hurt you at all? I bet you sprouted some nasty blisters from all that running. Oh! A cool drink for you, yes? Something strong in it?"

Before Ripka could get a word out, Latia thrust her into a lounge chair on her back patio and stuffed a cup of something cool, with a sharp bite she decided not to think too strongly about. It was good, and she was tired, and that was all that mattered. Wasn't like she was on duty any more, and honor-bound not to get drunk in the process.

Dranik scuttled out after them, pacing a long loop around the patio as he wrung his hands together. Whatever gentle ministrations Latia offered to Ripka, it was clear from the dirt on Dranik's face and his nervous ticks that she hadn't bothered offering him the same. The man must have been brow-beaten the moment he stepped over Latia's threshold. Probably sooner. Ripka winced and set her cup aside. An anxious man was never a good one to interview.

"Dranik," she said. His head snapped up, swiveled to find her, eyes wide as if he'd noticed her for the first time. "Please sit, you're making me dizzy."

He perched on the seat's edge as if he were sitting on cactus prickles, and the slightest shift of weight would dig them in.

"Thank you, for what you did. If you hadn't shaken them off then, then, oh, I don't know…" He trailed off and took to wringing his hands together again. They'd be red-raw by the end of the night.

She had to calm him down. Get him relaxed enough to spill the details of what had sent him running to them.

"Peace, it's all right. I shook them good, they won't find where you've gone." She winked at him. "I bet they're still out there, chasing the shadows I set up to distract them."

Dranik's shoulders eased.

"You owe her *everything*, Dranik, *everything*!" Latia clutched her hands together in her lap. "If we hadn't had dear Ripka then you'd be in the clink now for sure, you daft boy. How you manage to even put your shoes on in the morning I haven't the foggiest idea. Sweet skies, but mother taught us better than this."

Dranik tensed right back up again.

Standing to the side of it all, Honey cocked her head and frowned. "I want to know what's in the frescoes."

"What?" Latia blinked, throwing her gaze around at all three of them as if seeing them for the first time. "You want a tour of my art? Now is not the time, dear. Now is an emergency!"

"The urgency has passed," Ripka said, smooth as a calm wind. Then she lowered her voice and tilted her head to stage whisper to Latia. "Honey is frightened by watchers. Couldn't you show her your art? I'm sure it would soothe her."

Latia sucked her teeth so loud she sounded like a mud hollow toad, but eventually she jerked her robe straight and nodded, then whispered back to Ripka. "I'll take care of the poor dear." Then, raising her voice, said, "Come along, Honey! Let me show you all the strange fishes of my imagination."

As Honey passed by, Ripka mouthed 'thank you' that only she could see, and Honey winked. Actually winked.

The move was so startling it took Ripka a moment to gather her wits once the two other women were safely inside.

"Dranik," she said, soft and slow. His name hooked him like a lure, and he turned to stare at her. "What happened?"

An anguished groan broke free. He leaned over his knees, gripped his face in both hands and rubbed vigorously. "I had no idea the others were doing anything – anything *illegal* – please, you must understand that."

"I understand," she said, possibly a little too fast, but he was too wrapped up in his own pain to notice. "It's easy to get in over your head."

"Yes, yes, that's exactly what happened. I got in over my head, couldn't figure out what to do once I was in it so deeply."

He latched onto the line she'd fed him like it was a life rope, and she clasped her hands together to keep from clenching her fists. Dranik was no real criminal. Lines like, 'in over your head' and 'things got out of control' only ever got the innocent to confess to the crimes they'd stumbled into. They were, however, great anchors to use in sussing out the scope and nature of the criminal activity. Innocent people were quick to talk, often to their own detriment.

"It happens," she agreed in the soothing voice she'd used on hundreds of witnesses sitting across from her in an interview room over the years. She considered the next line to feed him, then said, "There's little you could have done."

"That's just the thing." He was suddenly animated, throwing his hands into the air in exasperation. "If I had just heeded my gut, paid attention to all those little smoke wisps, those pre-quakes, I know I could have realized what was really going on sooner. I *know* it. But I was so – so – wrapped up in the ideal, I made myself blind to the rest. I thought, well, I guess I thought that if anything shady was going on, it was ultimately for a good cause. That's stupid of me, isn't it?"

"No," she said quickly enough so that he wouldn't have a chance to interpret her silence as insincerity. "Wanting to believe in something good is never stupid."

"But it *is* good, I still believe that. I don't like their methods, but their minds are in the right place." He groaned, ruffling his hair. "Pits below, those watchers poured right into the middle of us, we never saw them coming. Skies! What if they recognized me?"

"Then they would have already been here."

That calmed him. He flopped backward, arms dangling along either side of the chair, his head tipped back to stare at the stars. He was working up to something. Rallying his nerve so that he could tell her, confess to her, what had happened. What he'd seen. What he had, though he hadn't wanted to, been a part of.

"Liberation should never be achieved through bloodshed," he said to the night sky.

She swallowed. Clenched her hands tighter. She had to find his limits. Had to make him believe she was sympathetic to his so-called mistake. "What if that's the only way?"

Dranik slammed his fist to the arm of the chair and exploded to his feet, eyes bright with fervor. "It must not be! We are not so oppressed as that. No, I understand why the Desert Wind is decided on the matter, I understand the history better than many others. But we are better than that, we are beyond the petty politics of Valathea. Just because... Because those poor people, the Catari, were unable to establish their freedom from tyranny peacefully does not mean we cannot succeed where they failed. They were few, and unprepared. We are many, some of the greatest minds on the Scorched – if not all Valathea – and we have had warning. There is no reason – none! – that we should reduce ourselves to violence."

Desert Wind. The importance he lent those words made them glow like a brand in her mind, a key fact to dig into later. If she pushed now, though, when he had whipped himself up so far, he would clam up, embarrassed that he'd let the name slip. She'd seen it dozens of times before. Now, when he was at his most vulnerable – wrought with emotion – was the time to be gentle. To lure him where she wanted him to go.

She thought, a little ruefully, that Detan would be proud of her. Had he been a watcher and received their manipulation training, then that man would have been unstoppable.

"What do you want to happen here, Dranik? What do you want to see Hond Steading become?"

He paced, heels hitting the ground hard enough to leave half-moon divots in the dirt. Under the gleam of the stars, he twisted his hands through his hair, glared at the clear sky, the calm night, as if its peacefulness affronted him. She let him do all this, let him stomp out his anger and wring free his fear. The cup Latia had given her was warm in her palms now, the brew stinging as it slid down her throat. He paced, and paced, and when even the fine edge of her patience began to strain, he stopped.

"I want Hond Steading free."

"And what does free mean to you?"

He half-turned, glanced down the line of his body at her with fresh awareness in his expression. Maybe she'd revealed too much. Maybe he was beginning to suspect that she was more than she presented herself as. Whatever his thoughts on her, he nodded to himself, and his hands fell slack at his sides.

"A governance chosen by the people. Representative of them."

"And do you believe that Thratia is likely to allow you that? The woman exiled from Valathea for seizing control of the Saldive Isles – an independent island chain – just because she could?"

The sigh that left him seemed to take all his strength with it. He folded himself back into the chair, hands dangling between bent knees. "No. She won't. But the Hondings aren't any better."

Ripka shook her head, and made her play. "I think you know better than that, Dranik. Think it through, now. Dame Honding is hale, but aging, and her heir is–" Her voice caught, and she covered this by taking a sip from her cup. "– is unpredictable. If you strengthen your forum, make a strong case for your representative government to take control once Dame Honding passes to the endless night, she might just agree. I don't know much about your city, Dranik, not personally. But I've heard of it, all across the Scorched. The Hondings have ruled you all with a fair and even hand, and I don't believe the Dame would leave you to scramble for the throne, or at the will of the empire, upon her death. This city is precious to her–" She caught herself expressing too much familiarity with the family, saw Dranik's eyebrows rising, and corrected. "The history of her family is here. She *must* care deeply for it. She won't leave you to drift, if you show her a viable alternative.

"But Thratia… I'm from Aransa, you know. Once Thratia has her claws around something she desires, she never lets go. It's not the people of this city she cares about, anyway." Ripka dropped her gaze, turned to stare pointedly at the humped silhouettes of the firemounts that lined up back to back along the city's southern edge.

Dranik pressed his lips together until the blood fled them, staring at those shadows. She needn't say the truth of the matter out loud. Hond Steading was valuable for its selium. Full stop. The people who lived there were incidental, perhaps worthless, if their lives were not conducive to selium mining.

"Thratia will destroy us."

Ripka held her tongue, lest he hear the eagerness she felt to encourage this train of thought.

"… I thought. Truly, I thought that she might wake the Dame up. Make her understand that the city is only as valuable as its people, and their input on civic matters is a right. But the Dame has always listened, if not always complied. Thratia will roll over us. Take what she needs. She won't ever let us be free, and she's too much the egoist to appoint a plan for after her death. Hond Steading will fall into chaos."

He was talking himself into it, now. She need only extend a small risk. "When we met, you were all for Thratia's arrival. What changed your mind?"

He flinched and brushed his fingertips over his bruised cheek. "I was with the Desert Wind, when…" He sighed, shoulders rounding forward as the information he'd feared sharing all night left his lips. "When I realized they were smuggling more than information into and out of the city."

Fucking got you, Ripka thought. But she kept her expression mostly neutral, allowed a fine line of concern to mark her brow. "What are they smuggling?"

"Into the city? Weapons. Weapons like you wouldn't believe."

"And out?"

He jerked backward as if someone had yanked on his hair, stuck his gaze on the sky above so that he would not have to look Ripka in the eye, and said, "People."

Deviants. They must be. Ripka's world lurched sideways. She sucked a breath, not needing to fake her shock and disgust, and gripped the cup in her hands hard to hide the shaking in her fingers.

"Will you let me help you undo this, Dranik? Will you let me help you take them down?"

He lowered his head to look at her, tears like stars sparkling in his thick lashes. "Please, gods, yes. Help me."

CHAPTER 21

Detan woke howling. Fiery pain lanced outward from his shin, shook him out of his dreams and crested his vision with white stars. He curled in upon himself, grabbing his shin, sucking air between his teeth.

He caught the faint scent of musk in each breath and, as the pain faded, grew aware of the silk-smooth sheets tangled around him. Thratia's bed. Thratia's scent. The pain fled from him in an instant, and he stumbled, flailing, to his feet. He was alone in the bed. He would have found that a relief, if he couldn't clearly make out the place where Thratia had curled in the night, her back pressed against him, her sleep-breath slow and even. Should have killed her in her sleep.

But he hadn't had the heart for that. No, that wasn't it. He just hadn't been brave enough to try.

"Good morning, sunshine."

He spun. Misol stood at the foot of the bed, her spear propped against the crook of her arm, a small smirk flattening her lips. He scowled at her, but that just made her smile. His sleep-slow brain took a few moments to connect the ache on his shin with the shape of her spear shaft, and then his scowl deepened to something more than a mask meant to irritate her.

"Sweet skies, woman, was that necessary?"

"You didn't wake when I called your name, and I'm not about to touch you while you're naked."

"I am not–" But of course he was. Detan swore while Misol laughed, and scrabbled to drag a still sweat-damp sheet around his waist. "Are you here for a reason, or did you just decide there weren't enough opportunities to be a demon-whipped ass outside of this room?"

She rolled her eyes at him. "Don't flatter yourself. Thratia's given you over to Aella for the day. Something about not falling behind on your testing."

"Oh, that's just fucking lovely."

Her smirk was back, slow and coy. "Thought you'd be in a better mood this morning."

"I don't know what–" but he did. There was no sense playing dumb, or coy, or any other cursed thing. He'd spent the night in Thratia's room. In her bed. Woke naked as the day he was born and, well, the windows were open but the scent of them pervaded still. His stomach twisted with the memory of what he'd done. For a moment, all he could see was Bel Grandon's throat lying open at Thratia's feet.

Long con. Keep it together, Honding. He only had himself to rely on here, after all. Without Tibs to keep him stable, keep him sane, he felt like he was breaking at the seams. Maybe that really had been the wrong move. Maybe he should have spit at Thratia's feet and refused her advances.

Maybe he was just disgusted with how eagerly his body had reacted, despite his ulterior motives.

Strength fled his limbs. Trembling so that his knees knocked, he staggered, lurched. Heat and bitter bile filled his mouth bare moments before he was at the window, hunched over and retching stomach waters to dribble down the side of Thratia's precious compound.

"Get yourself together," Misol said, and there was an even gentleness to her tone that startled him. It was almost a cousin to sympathy.

"Why are you doing this?" he blurted, then bit his tongue until he tasted iron. Just because he was desperate for an ally didn't mean Misol would be one. Wiping vomit onto the back of his wrist he turned to face her. Had to see the truth in whatever her expression betrayed.

She eyed him. Not to observe his nakedness, he knew that. She was taking in something deeper, using her doppel's instinct to peel away the layers of masks he wrapped around himself like a shield. Like a cage. He'd never felt so truly naked in all his life.

She sighed then, low and slow, and shook her head. That simple negation wrenched at his gut, made him ache with a renewed sense of loneliness. "My reasons are my own. Now get dressed. I'll be waiting."

As the door slammed shut behind her he stood a moment, gripping the sheet to himself like it could hide what he'd done, heart pounding hard enough to echo in his ears. Bile threatened to rise again, tears threatened to smear his vision.

Fuck that. He came here with a goal. With something like a plan. He wasn't about to crumble just because he'd boned Thratia Ganal. Just because Misol, with her bald head and big stick, wouldn't be his friend.

Skies above, he was Detan-pitsdamned-Honding. *Lord*, at that. And this was his game. He'd stumbled across the board mid-play, certainly. Had wandered unwittingly into Thratia's web. But he was pulling the strings now.

Or something like that. Tibs would have a better analogy – probably involving rocks or gears or shit like that – but none of that mattered.

What mattered was this: he had the upper hand. They just didn't know it yet. And that was exactly what he wanted.

Detan flung the sheet to the bed and strode over to the water bucket some well-trained but underpaid servant had left him and scrubbed up, each brush with the sponge cleansing away his lingering sense of regret.

By the time he was dressed, in the crisp clothes of a lord that had been left for him folded neatly on a chair, he was almost feeling human again. Though he hadn't failed to notice that, although the clothes were well-cut and of high quality cotton, they were dyed a smudgey, ashy grey. Like the sky after he'd set it alight.

Probably just a coincidence. Probably Thratia had picked those colors knowing they'd hide dirt more easily.

The worried glance Misol gave him as he stepped into the hall stopped him hard in his tracks.

"What? I know I look sexy in a suit, Misol dear, but–"

She snorted and waved him to silence.

"Don't worry about it." She hefted her spear and took off down the hall.

"You know, of course, that the moment people start saying things like 'don't worry about it' the intended target of their otherwise benevolent advice can do nothing but worry about it."

"You talk too damned much."

"You're such a stunningly engaging conversationalist, I can't help myself."

She rewarded him with dead silence, which was probably fair. The halls of Thratia's compound – he'd never think of it as her home, it was another species entirely – wound on for ages. Detan fidgeted. Plucked at the fine seams inside his pockets, twitched at the lay of his shirt's stiff collar. A collar that had been cut just so to reveal the brand at the back of his neck to any who happened to glance his way. He grimaced and pulled his hand back. These clothes had definitely been chosen by Thratia. Only she would turn him into a show-dog like this.

"Where are Forge and Clink?" he asked, and flinched when his voice echoed back at him off the hard stone walls.

"Safe."

"Could mean a lot of things."

"Means they're fine, and the rest is none of your business."

Well then. If they didn't want him fraternizing with the other prisoners, then making them his business was exactly what he was going to do. He hadn't a clue why they'd want them separated, or why they'd draw a hard line about it, but he could spin a lot of guesses – and every last one of them pointed to an advantage he could use.

Except for one reason: that they were already dead. Aella might do that, if she saw no further use for them, and he doubted Thratia would step in to stop her. Doubted Thratia would ever even know. The commodore – and why did she still call herself a commodore, when she held the warden's seat? – ruled her domain with an iron fist, but he suspected not even Commodore Throatslitter had the wherewithal to micromanage all of her bastard helpers.

The things Thratia counted on to keep her people in line; fear, loyalty, informants. These things didn't apply to Aella, unless Misol was an informant, which didn't seem likely. He doubted Aella could ever be properly scared. Pissed off, sure, but the day Aella Ward grew frightened was the day the world came to an end.

Misol thumped once on a heavy, iron-banded door with the butt of her spear, and Detan realized he really should've been paying attention to the path they'd taken to walk here. Big, heavy doors like that were hardly ever in his favor.

The door opened to light brighter than the gleam off a bleached bone. He stumbled back a half-step, brought his arm up to shade his eyes while they adjusted. Some fool-headed engineer had wrangled a circular shaft straight through this wing of Thratia's compound, spearing up all three levels to the daylight above.

No balconies marred the place where those levels should be, not even a window nor a faint discoloration of the stone. It was like being in a well, and judging by the thickness of the door jamb, a well meant to hold a whole pits-lot more than a couple of gallons of fresh water. Someone had gone and brought the desert inside, dusting the ground with mottled beige-and-brown sands, raked into a curling labyrinth. Aella waited from him in the heart of it all, a table propped up to her side with all sorts of nasty equipment he'd come to expect from these sessions. And Callia, of course. Couldn't forget Aella's sadistic shadow. The withered woman hunched under the table, drawing in the sand with one finger.

Thratia'd clearly gone a little soft in the head when she'd ordered this place built. It was no sort of arena, no testing ground for her warriors. Anyone standing on the sandy floor was just as likely to get tangled up in events as those being tested. A few good balconies wouldn't have gone amiss. Maybe a nice little dais from which she could lounge and observe her loyal sycophants fight for her favor.

But no one, not even Thratia, put walls this thick around a practice arena. Nor bothered to band the room's singular door with hard iron. This room wasn't built for fighting, it was built for containing. For dying.

For him.

His throat went dry as the sand under his boots. He stopped mid-stride, caught the smug look on Aella's face as she watched his realization take hold, and decided not to give the little witch the satisfaction.

Decided, most assuredly, not to think about the fact that Thratia had to order this thing built the day he left Aransa – the day she discovered what he was capable of – in order to have it prepared for him now. Busy, busy bee.

"Aren't you just a ray of sunshine?!" He threw his arms out in welcome and strode forward, owning every step he took with a mud-eating grin. He certainly ignored the derisive snort from Misol as she shut and bolted the door behind him.

Aella was wearing a civilian-styled tunic over a long skirt this time, both in refreshing shades of rare gemstones. Callia still wore her white coat, grubby at the hem, but he ignored her. Focused on Aella's even stare. Callia had been neutralized – by Aella's own hand. Whatever fear that woman once inspired in him, whatever tortures she'd visited upon his scarred flesh, she was no risk to him now, broken as she was. He could only hope that one day his own fears would be as beaten down as her body was now.

"You have come unprepared for our session," Aella said, cool as ever, one blonde little brow perked in probably-faked annoyance.

"My spirit is always ready for the pleasure of your company." Feigning clumsiness, he stumbled a step

from the table and kicked a plume of fine sand at Callia.
The broken woman shrieked and tumbled backward,
clawing at her eyes with both hands. Aella swore and
dropped to her knees to aid her. Detan took the moment
to get a look at the instruments on the table while being
unobserved. Well, mostly unobserved. He felt Misol's
stare on his back, but the doppel said nothing to alert
Aella to his intentions.

Aella'd brought the usual tools of her trade. Scalpel,
flint stone, pliers, bags of selium and empty sacks as
well. Rope and leather and other gleaming things that
looked threatening but he couldn't name. In the name of
research, that girl carried a kit that'd make a professional
torturer wet themselves with glee. Skies above, she
probably had some potion in there designed to make a
man wet himself against his will.

There was no sight of the syringe that carried his usual
injection of diviner blood and selium. He tried to ignore
the fact, he really did, but after missing his dose the night,
before anxiety was creeping in. A presence he had come
to expect, invisible but always there, was slowly slipping
away. A certain heaviness to the air, a tactile sensation
every time he drew a breath. That injection had made
him aware of all the tiny particles of selium suspended in
the air, even if he couldn't reach them, and losing them
now was like having swaddling stripped away and being
left bare-assed in a cold wind.

He swallowed his anxiety, recalling one of the
meditative exercises Pelkaia had practiced with him in
the time immediately after he'd set Aransa's sky on fire:
think of a singular goal, and breathe evenly. The goal
was easy enough – get that injection. That first part was
making the second markedly harder.

"Try to watch yourself, you clumsy oaf," Aella said

after she'd settled Callia's whimpers and given the woman a metal mixing rod to draw in the dust with. Callia shot him little glares every so often, hard to see through the sunken skin shriveling up her face like an old plum, but each one of those little glares he took small pleasure in.

Should have been ashamed of that but, well. Callia had tortured him. And Detan had never been above small pettiness.

"A thousand apologies." He held his palms to the glaring sky and bowed over them expansively. Already the heat was beginning to draw prickles of sweat between his shoulder blades. He considered asking Aella if she'd swap clothes with him, then decided better of it. She didn't appear in the mood to tolerate his antics too long, and he knew from hard experience that pushing her now could lead to greater punishment down the road.

And anyway, his one goal wasn't about being comfortable. It was about getting that injection. And finding out what had happened to Clink and Forge. So, fine, two goals. But Pelkaia wasn't here to scold him about lack of focus, so to the pits with it.

"You should apologize to whoever made you that suit, it won't survive this. Skies above, Honding, You've been given the run of the city. The servants answer to your needs. Did you not think you could ask for something a little less formal?"

He winced, subtly embarrassed that he hadn't thought about the fact that their training sessions were quite intense, and he was likely to ruin all the fine stitch work that been put into what he wore now – not to mention stain that ash-grey fabric with sweat. But, more importantly, Aella'd let slip that the servants would treat him as the Lord Thratia was parading him around as.

Handy, that little piece of information. Servants would no doubt have less compunction about being forthright with him than his current companions, and anyway, they always had the best gossip. Considering the pits-cursed nightmares he'd dragged himself through over the last few months, he was in desperate need of a juicy story or two to wind down with. Something with an illicit affair being walked in on.

"I wanted nothing but the best for our little chats, Aella dear. You do know how I look forward to them so."

The corners of her lips twitched – something like a smile, something like a smirk. When he'd first met her, minding his leash on Callia's airship of nightmares, he'd thought that expression was a smile. Normal little girls smiled when someone cracked a joke, after all. But Aella was no normal girl. She was cold straight through, worse if what Misol had intimated was true – not cold at all. Just… hollowed out inside. Empty. That lip twitch could mean anything. Annoyance, amusement. Pleasure at having witnessed someone – anyone at all – score a verbal point. She did seem to like to spar with him, though her patience with such things had grown thinner lately.

If she even had patience. If Misol's theory was to be believed, then Aella was a walking blank slate. But that just couldn't be right. The girl had passion, drive. They were just pointed in what Detan felt were rather unfortunate directions. He wondered, just for a moment, if he could manage to reorient those passions. Harness her drive for something that didn't end in him sweating blood for data.

Callia shuffled in the dirt, and those thoughts evaporated like so much mist in the desert.

"Let us begin," she said, and reached for a bladder of selium.

Detan made a show of stripping off his coat, laying it with care on a blank space on the table, and then rolling up his sleeves. He paced, cutting lines in the sand with his new, too-shiny boots, working up a proper coating of dust. Never could trust a Scorched man with shiny shoes. But the dust just wouldn't stick. Thratia'd had them polished sleeker than a crow's back.

"What's the rush?" He was sweating now in full force, dampness seeping through his back in ribboned patterns. The scars on his back never sweated. Most of the time, he could ignore that. But now the memories of the fire he'd set to the sky came crashing back, his imagination so strong he could almost feel the lick of the flames eating his shirt away, kissing his skin all over. The same flames that'd mottled Thratia's cheek.

Awareness of the selium seeped into his being, his senses reaching out on instinct, finding the bladder Aella held, feeling out its shape and its volume. Some small part of him lamented that there wasn't nearly enough there for him to set the sky afire again. Maybe... Maybe he could thrust it up. Make a little fire. Just fill in the top of this thrice-cursed well with some real life. Show the sun's rays what real heat could do.

Pain splashed over him, danced those thoughts away. He winced, hopped back, grabbed at his shin and cursed himself and Misol and just about any other handy name that came to mind. The doppel just looked at him, gaze hooded and bored.

Aella sighed and clucked her tongue against the roof of her mouth. "As I feared. As soon as withdrawal sets in, he becomes almost as unpredictable as before his training."

"What–" he sucked air, made himself put his aching leg down and resist an urge to blow all four of them to itty bloody bits. "What in the pits did you do to me just then? I wasn't even thinking about…" he waved a hand, describing the rough shape of a blob of selium with the edge of his palm. "And then I was ready to blow us all to smoke."

"I did nothing *to* you, I merely introduced the presence of selium. Made you remember its existence, its nearness. You have grown so unstable over the night without your dose that that was all it took."

"Donkeyshit," he snapped. "I've never felt that way before – never without reason."

"And don't you have one?" She gave him a real smile now, a coy little thing that he'd bet his right testicle she practiced in the mirror to get just right. "You have quite a lot to be angry about, Honding. All the time. We all do, really. All the petty injustices of the world, they just pile up. Mount and mount until we break. Some people reach for a bottle, some mudleaf. Some practice meditations, or skies forbid, talk their worries out with another sympathetic being. We're all simmering, just a little. You're just quicker to boil than others, and the injections have made you more sensitive. And yet, without them, your irritation comes so swiftly it's like you've never had them at all. Fascinating."

"Fascinating? Really? Would you find it just plum-bloody-interesting if I stubbed my toe and took all our heads off in retaliation? Skies above, Aella, you swore you could teach me control. *Real* control. This is moving backwards."

She shrugged, as if it mattered not at all to her. "You really can be thick sometimes. This isn't a regression – not technically. It's a revelation. A hint as to what exactly is pumping through those veins of yours, or going on in that tiny brain. Did you know, before I left the Bone

Tower, that the whitecoats had yet to discern just where exactly in the body sel-sensitivity originated from? I can't even tell you the amount of cadavers they mucked around in trying to find a source, peeling the brain layer by layer looking for any anomaly. They found nothing in all that long research, and here you are upset because your control slipped a touch. Pah. You're cleverer than that, though you try very hard not to be. Think it through, now. The injections gave you finer control, and the removal of them has shaken the baseline of ability you already possessed. Why?"

"I am not your tailcoat-clinging whitecoated pupil, Aella. This isn't some twisted school quiz – and don't expect me to believe for a moment that your esteemed colleagues in the Bone Tower were rummaging around in the bodies of just the dead."

An eyebrow twitched, her head jerked back just slightly. He'd scored a point against her, reminded her of things that broke through even her veneer of indifference and unsettled her. His small victory lasted only a breath.

She reached into the pocket of her tunic, produced a syringe, showed it to him, swirled it, let the sel mingling with the blood gleam in the light.

"I mixed it just a moment ago, before you arrived. Thratia has a whole stable of diviners, did you know? She cultivates that deviation, sends them out into the harsh and hot world to find untapped resources of selium. They were all happy to donate a sample, after Thratia explained the situation to them. This one's from a woman. Healthy girl. Keen sel-sense. She was eager to help."

Aella tucked the syringe back into her pocket and pinned him with a look. "Such a shame blood goes to poison so quickly in this heat." She glanced at the hot sky. "We'd better work quickly. That woman has gone out scouting, and do you want to know a secret?"

He grit his teeth and asked, "What?"

"There just aren't that many people in the world who can donate blood for these types of things." She stroked her pocket, cradling the outline of the glass hidden within. "Took us – apothiks and whitecoats both, you know – ages to figure out the secret. Some bodies produce blood of a certain, special flavor. It can harmonize with all other types. But try to mix any other two together?" She drew her thumb across her throat and made a croaking sound. "It's not a pretty way to go."

"Aella." He hated the rasp that'd worked its way into his voice but, to pits with it, if she thought he was dangerous – thought he verged on going out of control – then maybe she'd give him the injection for all of their safety. He caught himself scratching at his inner elbow, in the place where previous needles had left tiny scars, and forced himself to make fists instead. "It wasn't my fault I missed last night's dose. Whatever you're punishing me for, bring it up with Thratia. I have to do as she says, same as you."

"We are not the same," she snapped, fingers clenching around the syringe so hard he winced, fearing she'd break it. "And unlike you, I can do as I please. Thratia may have taken you to her bed, but do not confuse her use of you as a political tool with protection. You came to me – *kneeling* – to discover the secrets of your power and I have found something here, Honding. Found something *interesting*, and short of killing you I have free rein to do as I please, do you understand? I will make you understand yourself, whether you're willing or not."

"This can't be useful, please–"

She waved him off. "That's withdrawal talking.

Unfortunate, but we can work through it. Now—"

Detan lunged. Hadn't even thought about it. One moment he was standing there, trying to find another angle to weasel that syringe into his arm without losing too much dignity, and the next he was lurching forward like someone had yanked on his puppet strings.

But he'd never been a fighting man, and that was probably best for them all.

Misol swept his legs with the butt of her spear and he went down hard, chest-first into the hot sand. His instincts reached out, flung in all directions, mapping all the amounts of selium in the room. Numbness fell over him like cold water – Aella clamping negating power over his.

He shivered, clinging to the scorching sand, and tried to pretend that in the moment he'd lunged, in the moment Aella'd leapt back to avoid him, he hadn't heard the crack of glass. Wasn't seeing, now, the dribble of sel-infused blood pooling on the ground.

Aella sighed, low and disappointed. Detan picked up his head, forced himself to look at what he'd done. A red smear spread out from Aella's pocket and she was, gingerly, peeling off the over-tunic.

"If your little fit is over," she said, and he wanted to weep as she chucked the ruined garment to the ground and stood over him, hands propped on her still-small, childish hips. "Let us begin."

CHAPTER 22

The sun was threatening to rise by the time Ripka and Honey had hammered out their plans with Dranik and dragged themselves, aching and exhausted, back to the palace. Even at night it was a piece of art. Carved into the side of a dormant firemount, the wide terraces of the stepped structure were strung with glimmering oil lamps, faceted glass splashing brightness in all directions. A flagrant display of Hond Steading's wealth, but one the citizens seemed to admire. They struck Ripka as ostentatious, but then, this wasn't her city. She wasn't sure she'd ever have a city to call her own again.

The front steps were more in line with Ripka's aesthetic. They were broad and shallow, spaced in such a way that would make them difficult for an invading force to take at any speed. The builders of this place had carved it into a gleaming jewel, and its edges could still cut when required.

The guards lining the walkway were reminder enough of that. Jacketed in sharp black, spears held easy at their sides, they dotted both sides of the broad stairs on every third step, their gazes locked on all approaching visitors.

They appeared ceremonial to the average citizen, but Ripka saw the tension in their jaws, the spring in their knees, and knew them the deadliest warriors the city had to offer. And the city would soon need them.

Massive double doors loomed at the top of the steps, thrown wide despite the late night. Dame Honding welcomed her citizens to seek refuge in her palace at all times. In the few days Ripka had been in the palace, she'd stumbled across troubled souls more than once, pacing or praying or weeping in silence in the solitude of the Dame's home.

There was kindness here, amongst the harsh living of the desert. A kindness born from the seed of the ruling family's philosophies. She wondered if Dranik ever considered that.

She stepped into that place of welcoming, and a guard grabbed her arm.

"Miss Leshe, Miss Honey?"

"Yes? Is there a problem?"

A red-eyed man reading on a bench nearby looked up, assessed the two women being apprehended, and shuffled away to a far seat. She couldn't blame him.

"The Dame wishes a word with you."

"It is very late…"

"She has been waiting."

Ripka nodded understanding. They were escorted through the welcoming room and down a side hall Ripka knew well – the path to the Dame's private sitting room. Her heart thundered, wondering just what had kept the Dame up through the night to speak with her. When the door opened, her stomach dropped.

The messenger she'd intercepted stood alongside Dame Honding's chair, his pale face streaked with what might have been dried tears. Tibal lingered to the side

of the room, Enard on the other, and both had a set of
guards twin to the two escorting Ripka and Honey.

Ripka put a placid face on, and bowed over her hands
like this were any other meeting. "Good evening, Dame."

The Dame snorted and flicked the hem of her long
sleeve. "My patience has burned away with the lamp oil,
Miss Leshe. You know why you are here, do not insult us
both by pretending otherwise. You accosted this young
man and intercepted a message from me meant for the
Valathean Fleet. Why?"

Ripka wished she was facing this with a well-rested
head. After a moment's consideration, she decided to
gamble with the truth. "I find Ranalae's promises to
you impossible, and I fear what will happen to Hond
Steading if you invite her and her forces within your
walls. Frankly, Dame, once she is inside your palace, you
will never get her out again."

"Now that's unfair." Ranalae stepped from behind a
pillar. The dignitary looked ragged from lack of sleep, but
otherwise composed. Maybe even a little amused. "I do
have my own home to return to."

I bet you do, Ripka thought, but bit her tongue.
Antagonizing the woman without a point wouldn't win
her any good will from the Dame, and that was what she
desperately needed now.

Interfering with a Honding messenger was treason.
And she knew full well how treason would be handled
in Aransa: walk the Black, or face the axe. She licked
her lips, composing an argument to keep Honey, Enard,
and Tibal free of the fallout she'd brought down upon
them all.

"I understand," the Dame said, "that you faced a
great deal of hardship in Aransa. The stories you have
told me, and that I have heard from others, are quite

chilling. But I fear your experiences have biased you to reality, my dear. The Scorched exists because of the goodwill of Valathea. Even Hond Steading, though unique in its system of government, relies on the empire for trade and, yes, even protection, when it comes to that. Relations between our city and the empress have always been strong. And now, in our time of need, they have come to our aid. I will not allow you to insult our imperial friends to soothe your paranoia. Is that clear?"

"And where was their friendship, when they took your nephew and tortured him?" The words were out before she could stop them, thrown hard as knives against a woman she could not otherwise wound.

The Dame took a sharp breath, but Ripka's gaze was on Ranalae, whose smile turned decidedly predatory. Whatever Ranalae's position in the empire, she knew. She must know what went on in the Bone Tower. There was no hiding something like that from the higher-ups. And, in knowing and doing nothing, Ranalae had been complicit in Detan's suffering. Could even be held accountable for the wall he brought down during his desperate escape.

"Those rumors are unsubstantiated," the Dame snapped, "and the fanciful imaginings of sick minds. They tried to cure my nephew's loss of sel-sense, he did not take well to the treatment. That is all."

"Is that what Ranalae told you?"

Ranalae smiled knives at Ripka, but she pushed on. She'd already stepped in the quicksand, might as well get a few shots off before she was buried. "He was never a normal sel-sensitive. He was always deviant, and they dug around in his flesh to figure out why."

"That. Is. Not. True." The Dame's cheeks had gone scarlet, her fingers curling into the arm of her chair.

"Why don't you ask him, instead of this sycophant?"

"He isn't here!"

Ripka jerked back a step, the anger seeping out of her sails. That was real pain in the Dame's voice, broken and ragged, and it shook Ripka to realize she'd done that to the woman – that she'd ripped a scab right off a festering wound. While Ripka fumbled for words, the Dame shot a glance at Tibal and said, "Despite my best efforts otherwise."

"He ain't a pet to put on a leash," Tibal drawled and rolled his shoulders. "But." He hesitated, flicked a gaze to Ripka. "She's right, you know. Weren't pleasant little talks they were having with Detan in that tower. Talks don't make a man scream in his sleep."

"My nephew," the Dame grated out the words, "is beside the point. The point is your treason, Miss Leshe, and your accomplices in the act."

"I pressed them all into it," she said immediately.

The Dame waved this off with a flick of her fingertips. "Noble of you, but I do not care. You are all quite lucky that the only damage you succeeded in causing was delaying matters by a few marks. If it had been otherwise, I would have you struck down where you stand. Now, out of deference to the friendship you have all shown my nephew, you may leave this place with your lives. But you *are* leaving this place."

She snapped her fingers, and the guards brought forward finely made rucksacks and set them at the feet of all four. Ripka picked hers up, flicked back the top, and was unsurprised to see her new clothes stuffed inside.

"But you are not leaving this place completely free. Meet your new friends." She inclined her head to the guards, none of whom so much as twitched an eyebrow in response. "They will escort you out of the palace and into an inn in the market district. That's the other side of the city, you'll note. There you will be given two rooms to split however you please, and I will cover the cost for the duration of your stay. Which will be indefinite, as I will not have the time to figure out what to do with you four until well after Thratia has been repelled from these walls. The rules of your new lives are simple: you may not leave the grounds of the inn without escort, and then only for excellent reason. And you, Tibal." She swivelled to pin him with her gaze. "You will be watched exceptionally closely, and your flier will remain here for safekeeping until I decide what to do with you."

He bared his teeth at the Dame, an expression of aggression that shocked Ripka straight to the core. "Wouldn't want to risk losing your spare heir, would you?"

She drew back as if struck, then pressed her lips together and gathered herself once more. "You are of my blood, though it chafes you so. Whether you believe me or not, I care what happens to you. I will see you safe, even if I must imprison you to ensure that fact."

"Why not just lock us up? You've got a big jail here." Tibal's arms came unfolded, his head cocked to the side like he'd scented blood in the air. "Why dress up what you're doing to us like it's something better than imprisonment?"

"Because it is most decidedly temporary, and my jail is for persons who have been convicted of crimes."

And the only crime they could be accused of was treason. Which always, always, came with a death penalty – no matter how enlightened a city claimed to be. Ripka shot Tibal a look, but he must have figured it out for himself, because he shut right up and took a step back, folding his arms over his chest to start a good and proper sulk.

Dame Honding surveyed them all, let her gaze linger on every last so-called traitor she'd harbored under her roof, and a spike of guilt stabbed at Ripka's chest. Though she had been acting for what she felt was the greater good, still she had betrayed this woman's trust. This firm, kind woman, who was struggling to keep her city safe while what little was left of her family dissolved all around her.

Though her expression was stern, the Dame appeared so very tired in that moment, and not just due to the late night. In fact, Ripka doubted she got to bed at a reasonable time at all any more. The unsteady lantern light highlighted the crow's feet stamped around her eyes, the hard lines about her lips where she'd spent her life schooling her expression to careful neutrality. Here was a strong woman, a proud woman, worn thin by time and circumstance, looking for a future – any future with a positive outcome – for the people she had spent her life serving. And now, toward the end of her life, she had nothing at all to support herself with. No family. No army. Just a lot of scared people, and a tenuous alliance with an empire that'd always been hungry to reclaim control of her family's legacy.

But she wasn't alone, though she didn't quite understand that fact.

"Time to go," Ripka's guard said. Mechanically, she swung her pack over her shoulder, unable to take her gaze from the Dame.

Halfway to the door, she called, "You know how to find him. Write to him. Please."

The Dame's brows lifted, and then Ripka was ushered out of the room, and the door clicked shut behind her.

CHAPTER 23

When Aella had finished wringing his will down to nothing, Detan stumbled free of the arena and stood, bent over and panting, in the hallway. While he was busy trying to figure out how to make his feet work again, a grey-haired man in the livery of Thratia's household staff passed down the hall, took one look at Detan, and halted.

"Is my lord all right?"

Detan squinted up at him. Though the man was a bit stooped with age, he held himself with a stiff grace, wiry grey hair slicked back into a perfect, cloud-like swoop. Detan's first instinct was to tell the man off – he wasn't much in the mood for company after Aella'd put him through his paces – but something in the man's manner reminded him of New Chum and put him instantly at ease.

"Can I ask a rather stupid question?"

The man's expression twitched, hiding whatever his knee-jerk reaction would have been – probably a joke at Detan's expense. Detan grinned. Yes, he could get along well with this man.

"I will do my best to answer, sir."

"Do you happen to have any idea where my room is?"

The man's brows lifted. "Do you have a head injury, sir? I can take you to the apothik straight away, or bring one to your side."

He forced himself to stand, leaning his back against the cold stone of the wall, and threw him a lopsided smile. "Whatever damage's been done to my head was done ages ago, my good man. No, I just arrived yesterday morning and I – ah – have yet to spend an evening in my own bed."

"That I can assist with. This way please, sir."

Detan regained some semblance of dignity by smushing his hair back down, and followed. The servant kept a crisp pace, but the moment he heard Detan's breath rasping in his chest he slowed without a word. Detan was so starved for kindness that simple act very nearly made him weep with joy.

"What's your name, grey-fox?"

The servant's steady steps faltered at this nickname, and he turned his head to hide his expression – but not quickly enough. A little hint of a smile peeked through. "I am Welkai."

"Been here long, Welkai?"

The man threw him a bemused glance. Seemed most servants weren't used to having to do any part of the talking that wasn't yes sir-ing and no sir-ing. "I have been with the commodore a year, but I've lived in Aransa all my life, sir. As did my parents."

Ah, a proper Scorched native. A son of a family who'd set down roots in one of the Scorched's rapidly growing cities, who identified not as Valathean but as Aransan first and foremost. He thought of red-cheeked Jeffin, the young lad's anger boiling over at the thought of allowing someone who was not Scorched to partake of the safety of Pelkaia's ship. Such pride could be a dangerous thing. Could draw lines in the sand that could be exploited.

And if he were a proud Aransan, he may not be too keen on Thratia's transformation of the city, and that was something Detan could use. But first he'd have to let the man know he was sympathetic to civic pride.

"Nice to have that sense of history. Not many in the Scorched get that pleasure nowadays, with people migrating here and there for work."

"Indeed, sir. My brothers and I were lucky our parents chose Aransa to settle down in, as there are a wide variety of opportunities in this city that cannot be found elsewhere. Begging your pardon, my lord, I am sure such opportunities also exist in Hond Steading, but Aransa is big enough for our needs."

He waved off Welkai's social stumble with a smile. "My old homestead can be a bit too big for its britches sometimes. Aransa's a good city, a nice size and full of possibility." He'd once thought it was big enough for him to roam through without notice, to play his cons and ramble the streets free as the man he wished he could be. But he'd soon learned that the world was slow to forget him, and not even Aransa's shadows cast far enough to hide the fire in his past. "Your brothers work at the compound too, then?"

A twitch of the shoulders, a subtle hunch forward quickly hidden by turning down a rug-lined hall. "My brothers work the selium mines, sir."

"Ah," was all Detan could manage. The night he'd escaped from Aransa, he and Pelkaia had burned the mine's Hub to the ground – and with it Aransa's economic stability.

Welkai stopped. He stood perpendicular to the wall,

his body stiff all over with repressed emotion – emotions Detan didn't even want to guess at. Welkai knew who he was. And even though Thratia had made it clear as a blue sky to all of Aransa that Detan Honding hadn't actually been responsible for the fire at the Hub after all, it'd been the doppel… well. That hadn't been the story she'd spread originally. Originally, she'd let the truth fly through the streets, had let the people of Aransa learn to hate him. Didn't matter what she said now. Rumors were rumors, and anger was a real hard thing to let go.

"Sir."

Detan flinched. He'd braced himself subconsciously, preparing for a strike – physical or verbal – that he knew, really knew, that he deserved.

"I – I'm sorry," he stammered. He knew he owed them all an apology. Knew words weren't really sufficient.

Welkai shifted his weight, lips pressed hard together as if he were holding something back. Probably he was. Probably his family couldn't afford to lose one more source of income due to Detan fucking Honding.

"Your room, sir." Welkai unlatched the door that stood between them, let it swing open. "If that is all you need…?"

He hesitated, hating to ask this man for any more than he'd already taken from him. But if he were going to see Hond Steading safe from Thratia, he needed to leverage everything he had. Even if that meant leaning on a man he'd already taken far too much from. With a false smile plastered over his face, as if they were old friends and not potential enemies, Detan leaned on the door frame and tried to look abashed.

"Thank you for the escort, my good man. Tell me, I docked here with two other companions – Forge and Clink are their names. What rooms did they end up in?"

Welkai's brow furrowed in legitimate confusion. "I'm sorry, sir. Only yourself, Aella, and her staff took rooms here. If there were others, they may have sought rooms in the city. Perhaps the Oasis hotel."

Detan forced his smile wide to keep from grimacing. "Thank you, I'll check for them there."

Welkai bowed, all rigid formality, which was somehow more hurtful to Detan than outright anger. Anger he knew well. Polite indifference was another weapon altogether.

He let himself into the room and shut the door, hands shaking from more than exhaustion. Welkai. Renold Grandon. The faces of the havoc he'd wrought the last time he'd blown through Aransa haunted him. One he'd targeted simply because he hadn't liked his manner, the other an innocent casualty of his desperation to escape.

But not just to escape. He'd been trying to do some good. Trying to save deviants, if he at all could, from the same horrors he'd experienced locked up with the whitecoats. Trying to get his friends clear of the terror, too. How many people had he harmed, trying to set things right? What right had he, to decide what was best for a city?

He'd failed Aransa. Failed this city in a variety of ways he was now certain he wasn't finished discovering. But he wouldn't fail Hond Steading, too. Wouldn't let the city his mother had loved and his dear auntie protected fall under Thratia Ganal's control.

No matter her so-called reasons – and he wasn't yet convinced he believed her – she was a woman who couldn't be trusted. A woman who traded lives into torturous ruin just to reach her greater cause. A woman who let Bel Grandon bleed out at her feet, just to make life more difficult for Detan.

No. Thratia may think she was doing the right thing, but she was no salvation. Not for Hond Steading. Not for the Scorched. Not for anyone. He'd stop her. He had to.

And he was going to have to convince her he was willing to marry her to do it.

When he'd stopped trembling, Detan stripped off his dusty, sweaty clothes and pitched them to the floor, scarcely taking in the room he'd been appointed for his stay here. Bed, rug, wardrobe, window, wash basin. Wasn't too much different from Thratia's room, save the lackluster view looking out on the dusty warehouse district, but it was plusher than a lot of hovels he'd spent his time in. And still, somehow, more oppressive than the stinkiest jail cell he'd ever been locked in.

Methodically, he washed and dressed again, trying not to think too hard about the fancy clothes that'd been stuffed in his wardrobe. Trying not to think too hard about how well they all fit him, and how they'd been tailored in shades of ash and stark carnelian. Flame and smoke. Thratia knew what he was, what he could still become. And though she claimed she did not need his deviant sense to gain control of Hond Steading, she was no fool. She'd let her enemies know, through whispers, that little Lord Honding was all grown up, and hadn't lost his sel-sense at all. No, he'd been forged into something else. Something dangerous. Dangerous enough that not even the empire – though skies knew they tried – could keep him on a leash. He'd never be able to hide from the fire in his veins again.

Which meant he must own it, must truly master his own temper, to survive what was coming next. For Valathea would be coming for him in force, now that the secret was open, and he had no doubt that the simple fact of his existence would create for him enemies he'd never dreamt of. And worse, never see coming.

As he dressed, he recalled old lessons his mother had drilled into him before her death. Thought long and hard about duties he'd promised to uphold long before he'd blown the selium pipeline he worked to cinders and found himself a guest of the Bone Tower.

Power is no gift, she'd told him as her breath rattled in her chest. Power is a burden that must be leashed, always, to the good of those who do not hold it.

He'd never questioned her. Never dared to press her for deeper meaning. Everything she told him he absorbed like a sponge, hoarded it greedily in the vaults of his memory. His mother had never been well, not in his living memory. The bonewither took her early, set her trembling and pale and fragile. He'd used to hug her by circling his arms around her waist, and marveling how he could touch his hands behind her without ever touching her at all.

And now, dressing in the formal clothes she might have picked for him had she lived to see him through to adulthood, he wondered: did she know? Was she as prone to fire as he, though she hid it a thousand times better?

Pelkaia had intimated as much. Had claimed that his bloodline was meant to be extinct, that the only possible reason for his existence was a Catari exile who must have ended up in Valathea, fleeing those hunting them for the strength of their sel-sense.

What secrets haunted his family? What had his mother been trying to tell him, in all her quiet lessons on power? He had thought she meant the rule of Hond Steading. And she had, at least on the surface. But... But his auntie had never given him such lessons, and certainly never in the tone of voice his mother had used.

And his auntie had not a hint of sel-sense in her body.

Detan stared up at the sky through his sliver of a window and asked the smeared clouds, "Did you know?"

He'd pushed himself away from her lessons after he'd escaped the Bone Tower, assuming he'd never take his old family throne. But now he faced it, faced that future, and wondered if he'd ever really known his family at all.

He shook himself. One thing was as certain as the pits were molten, his mother would have slapped him upside the head for ever allowing Thratia Ganal to get within a step of Hond Steading's reins.

He needed a better lay of the land, a clear look at all his possible options. He needed to find Clink and Forge, and he knew damned well they weren't lounging around in a posh hotel like the Oasis. They were dead, cast off by Aella for running out of usefulness, or else the more likely reason Welkai hadn't even heard of them: they'd never left the transport ship at all.

Detan drank from a cold cistern that some poor sod like Welkai had left in his room, wondered briefly if Welkai might ever consider poisoning him, then shrugged. If he kept on jumping at every little fear, he'd never get anything done at all. And skies knew, he had as much to do as there were grains of sand in the Black Wash. And very, very little time left to do it in.

CHAPTER 24

No one could ever accuse Dame Honding of treating her prisoners to cheap accommodations. The guards saw them settled in the upper floor of the Hotel Cinder, a quaint building of grey stone in the shadow of the city's second largest firemount. The smoothness of the carved walls spoke of quiet pride in the city's selium miners, who moved selium from the belly of the firemounts at just the right pace to keep quakes from rumbling their footing. The Cinder was a monument to those miners: crafted fully of stone, not a single wooden support beam to absorb an errant shake, and so very close to the firemount itself.

Ripka would have spent more time admiring the place, if it weren't her prison.

"She cannot keep us cooped up here," Ripka said, as she paced the narrow lane between the door and the room's small, singular window.

"But she is." Honey sat on the edge of the bed, her sturdy legs not quite long enough to touch the floor, so she swung her feet in small, rhythmic arcs. Ripka gave her a solid side-eye, genuinely not able to tell if the woman were being sarcastic or not.

A polite scratch at the door interrupted Ripka's train of thought. She scowled at the thick plank of wood, knowing it was locked, and forced herself to sound somewhat amiable. It wasn't the guards' fault she was locked up here.

"Come in."

A key clanked in the lock, and the door slid open to reveal a rather contrite-looking Tibal and Enard, a black-clad guard their constant shadow.

"You have half a mark," the guard said, then ushered the men within and shut the door behind them.

Enard moved forward immediately, barely checking himself from gathering Ripka up in his arms. Tibal lingered behind him, a surly shadow, arms crossed as he scowled around the room as if he could find fault in the furniture for all the misfortune that had yet befallen him. Despite his body language, it was Tibal who spoke first.

"As, despite my best wishes, you have successfully drawn me into your mess of a scheme, you had better tell me the details."

His posture, she realized, was not wary acceptance of his fate. Though Tibal had his arms locked down around him, he had a slight forward lean, a subtle gleam in his eye. He might pretend annoyance, but Tibal was intrigued by whatever Ripka had dragged him into. Despite the weariness of a long night, Ripka felt a little lighter. This was the first time she'd seen a spark of the old Tibal re-emerge since Detan had left them behind at the Remnant.

"The part regarding the Valatheans you know well." He grunted, a disgusted agreement. "The rest I have uncovered mostly recently."

She launched into her early suspicions that Thratia would use similar methods to those she had used in Aransa to such great effect, and her first investigations into the cafes, and what she found there. The forum seemed to spark some interest in Tibal, his brows raising high in appreciation, but she didn't bother lingering long on that feature of local politics.

Keeping her voice carefully controlled, she explained the events of the night. Their run-in with Dranik at the Ashfall Lounge, and his subsequent confession to her that his movement for freedom was not as pure as he had thought.

With every word laid down, Ripka only had eyes for Tibal's response. She felt Enard stiffen near her, but his reaction was a known quantity. It was Tibal who had proven unreliable in recent months, and Tibal's help they needed now. Ripka was clever, Enard calm in a crisis, and Honey a willing accomplice, but Tibal had bent his recent years to the very type of subterfuge they must attempt to flush out and befuddle Thratia's vile network.

By the time she was done telling the tale, Tibal was still as a boulder, every hard line of muscle stiff beneath his dusty, grease-stained clothes. While Hond Steading's future had not previously roused him to any emotion at all, being confronted with the very human reality of it – of people disappearing, and Thratia's network at hand – had clearly unsettled him. Tibal wouldn't fight for a city, any city. But he would fight for a city's people, and that was the distinction he'd drawn sharp as an obsidian blade.

"I see," Tibal said, and managed to lay into those two simple words the full scope of his intention. He saw, and he would help, and he would not stop until he'd fixed what he saw was broken.

"We must get away from our jailers to do any good at all," Enard said.

She flashed him a small smile and squeezed his arm. "Escaping jails is something we have recent experience in. But you're right, and the sooner the better. If I miss my meeting with Dranik tomorrow I fear he'll go to ground, and that will be a hard trust to rebuild, if we can even find him."

"That sister of his," Enard said, "is she in it, too?"

"Hard to tell. She's an exuberant woman, and often disgusted with her brother's melancholy nature. She brushes off his obsession with things political, but..."

"She knows," Honey said, soft as always. "Women like that know everything that goes on in their house."

"What time are you due to meet him?" Tibal asked.

"Nightfall, at a place very near the lounge I spoke of."

Tibal puffed his cheeks up and blew air out in a great gust. "Not a lot of time to get us out of here. Six guards on two stories of building, and we haven't been here nearly long enough to know their habits."

"And these two need rest." Enard glanced pointedly at Honey, whose head was lolling to one side, though her eyes were open. Ripka had to admit that the very thought of making any escape now, when her muscles were still screaming from her earlier flight from the watchers, made her feet feel like anchors.

"Daybreak, then," Ripka said. "No doubt our guardians will rouse us early for a meal. We'll take account of things then, and wing a plan if we must."

Tibal asked, "Are you prepared to follow my lead, if it comes to that?"

A week ago, she wouldn't have trusted him to lead her anywhere but a bottle. But he had a spark back, one she hadn't seen since he and Detan had joined their heads together to figure out the best way to get Nouli out of the Remnant.

"You're the expert," she said.

He grinned like a rockcat who'd caught a viper for his supper, and tipped his singed, floppy grey hat to her. In all his surly rebuke of Detan's abandonment, he hadn't stopped wearing the hat they'd fought over as long as she'd known them both.

A heavy pounding on the door startled them all – well, all except Tibal. While she and Enard and Honey flinched from the sound, Tibal just smirked, eyeing the door with quiet contempt. He was in his element, and the very sight of his confidence buoyed Ripka's worn-down spirits.

"Time's up." The guard who'd let the men in opened the door and stood glowering at them all, a false bluster that may have fooled a child, but told the four in the room only one thing: the guard was tired, and anxious, and resented her post. Ripka turned her head to hide an instinctive smile.

Hond Steading had no idea the force it harbored. She hoped, deeply, that if its people knew then they might be grateful.

CHAPTER 25

Detan found food in his room, a cold plate of hard cheese and crackers left sometime in the morning. The sustenance wasn't much, but he'd eaten worse fare, and the solidness in his stomach was enough to spit some vigor back into his veins.

Best not to think about veins.

A niggling itch had anchored itself in the crook of his elbow. Nothing based in reality, he knew it was little more than his mind reminding him of what it was missing. Still, hard to ignore a figment of your imagination when it was working up real, physical distress. He caught a glimpse of himself in the mirror and froze.

Cursed skies, he was a mess. Passable for any working man of Aransa, sure, but that was hardly the point. His hair, still wet from the wash-water, slumped across his forehead, and though his clothes were fine he'd put no care into wearing them. They hung untucked and loose, rumpled and just as ragged as his face. He looked the part of a drunkard and a wastrel, not a lord of high station. Certainly no fiance to Thratia Ganal.

And his image mattered now, make no mistake. He'd

hardly enter into any con game playing a nobleman in a state like this. Why was the simple fact he was playing at being himself any different? Tibs would have slapped him upside the head, to see him now. This was not how the game was played. Loose and by ear, surely, but not sloppy. Never that.

With renewed vigor he straightened his clothes and made close acquaintance with a comb. Now he was ready. People were keen to let a man in a crisp suit go wherever he wanted.

Down on the dock, where so very much of his recent life had turned for the worse, he paused for a quick reconnaissance. Aella's ship, the *Crested Fool*, drifted lazily from its rope ties. The ship was a solid transport vessel, but Thratia's dock had been built for a grander ship, for the *Larkspur* he had once stolen from her and handed into Pelkaia's care. The *Crested Fool* looked like a child's toy in comparison. It just so happened that this particular toy belonged to one demented child.

No guards made their presence known on the dock. In fact, the place was practically deserted. Detan huffed and tugged his freshly ironed lapels. All that work to prepare himself, and he didn't even have a keen-eyed servant to charm his way past. Such a waste of his brilliance.

As he jogged up the gangplank, it occurred to him that someone had gone to a great deal of trouble to make it look as if this ship was of no consequence.

"Ahoy!" he called, pausing while his voice echoed throughout the apparently empty ship. No response. Not even a board creaked under his boot to welcome him. He eyed the ship from keel to bowsprit, recalling what little he'd had access to during the long transit from the Remnant to Aransa.

Aella had kept him cooped up in his cabin at the aft

end of the ship, allowing him time to roam the deck but otherwise corralling him to his room and her laboratory. Both rooms were in the ship's aft. And though Aella'd never struck him as a particularly reasonable girl, it did make sense that she'd cloister those things which she did not want him stumbling across toward the fore.

He shoved his hands in his pocket and affected a merry saunter so that anyone who happened across him would think him out for a stroll, not a snoop. The *Crested Fool* stretched long and flat, looking more like the worn leather of an old shoe than an airship. Its buoyancy sacks were practical things, a careful network of sewn and waxed leather held snug under a knotted net of flax rope. All of the cabins were clustered in the center of the ship, a smaller mirror of the vessel's overall shape. Some stroke of genius had inspired the maker to be certain the buoyancy sacks kept the cabins in their shade for most of the day, shielding weary travelers from the harsh desert sun.

A cute little ship, purpose built for hauling people, but not a ship he'd ever want to steal. Pity, that. He was itching for a good heist.

Casting a glance around to make sure he was still alone, Detan strolled along the cabin building, testing doors until he found one unlocked. The hall was dark, the lanterns shuttered tight, but not yet coated in dust. Detan frowned at the nearest lantern, grabbing it from its loop. They hadn't been in Aransa long, but dust was quick to settle in this city, and someone had gone to a whole lot of trouble to make it look like this ship was being neglected. Certainly the servants weren't popping on board to give it the occasional dusting. Someone used this lantern – recently, and regularly. But whoever that was, they hadn't been kind enough to leave behind a flint.

He glared at the cold wick and gave the lantern a shake, just to hear the oil slosh in its base. He didn't dare go back to his room, or leave the ship to trouble a servant for a flint. No one knew he was here, and every chance he took had to offer a really fucking great payoff to be worth it.

But with the door shut behind him, as it must be to hide his presence, the hall was pitch black. He glared at the hall, glared at the lamp. Neither obliged him with a solution.

He wasn't carrying a flint, but the selium Aella had given him to practice with was still tucked into his pocket, returned there on a whim after he'd washed and changed. Aella'd worked him until his senses were numb, but still... He had been practicing, and improving, hadn't he? And what good was all this work, all this pain and sacrifice, if he could not use the things he'd learned to further his own goals?

He was not stressed. Not angry. No one was about to watch him struggle at his work. The shadows certainly wouldn't judge him. Before he'd consciously made his decision, he breathed out, long and slow, forcing some of the tension out of his muscles.

The selium bladder was no bigger than the palm of his hand. The kind of thing rich families used to send strips of painted paper into the sky at celebrations. He extended his senses even as he whisked off the cap, holding the selium in the bladder against its will to rise. He sectioned off the tiniest fragment he could imagine and still control, a sliver no larger than his pinky nail, and floated it free before clamping the cap back on.

Easy, now. With deliberate movements he slipped the bladder back into his pocket and let awareness of it fade from his mind. For just a breath his senses threatened to extend to the mass of selium hidden in the ship's buoyancy sacks above, but his long practice with Aella allowed him to shunt the greater mass away and focus on the smaller sliver.

It came so simply to him he almost shouted with triumph, but the surge of pride threatened to overwhelm his control. Easy, he reminded himself. Smooth and focused.

Measuring his breathing, he steadied himself. He'd trained for this so many times, been taunted by Aella every time he failed. Now, on his own, when he truly needed his power, it would not fail him. He would not allow it. Fingers calm as stone, he flicked open a pane of glass on the lantern and crouched to set it on the floor just in front of him. He stayed in that crouch, sweat seeping through the back of his shirt, but ignored the dual exertion of mind and body.

His senses screamed for finer control still. Never before had he been so keenly aware that his senses were deadened to the reality around him, never before had he felt the ache of that loss. Callia's injection, and later Aella's, had opened up a world to him that he had never even imagined might be real. Coss's world. A world suffused with selium on every level, so small as to be invisible to the naked eye.

Skies, but he missed that extension of his power. Curse Aella and her games – for that's what they were. The girl played cool-hearted, she even had keen-eyed Misol fooled, but Detan noted the subtle pleasure she took in fencing with him, and winning. No body numb of heart would bother with such an endeavor. No matter what Aella thought about herself, or tried to present herself as, that girl could feel, deep down. Maybe not as strongly as the rest of the world, but without motivation driven by emotion she would have been an automaton long ago, a husk bowing to whatever Callia ordered of her.

Instead, the girl had poisoned Callia into helplessness, stolen her and her subjects away to serve under Thratia, and usurped her position as researcher of deviant sensitives. What that had to say about Aella's emotional core… well. Detan knew he'd be well to never trifle with that young lady. Their verbal fencing aside, to truly raise Aella's ire would be a death sentence – no, not that. She'd find something worse for him than death. He'd never claim she wasn't creative.

He shuddered and snapped back to himself. Focus, it seemed, would forever be his greatest obstacle. That, and controlling the flow of his rage.

He reached for his anger. It leapt to him, ready as always, a stoked bed of coals deep in his chest hungry for outlet. Even in his most serene of moments he'd known it was there, hiding beneath his flesh, lurking in the shadowed corners of his mind. He liked to think he was not a hateful man. Liked to think that his desire to do good with his skillset was proof enough that his anger was not his master.

But he could never get away from it. No matter how powerfully Aella made him focus, or meditate, his mind was never truly empty. He could not change the manner in which his deviant power affected selium, no matter how much she hoped otherwise. He could move it, shape it, and urge it to tear itself to shreds.

He wondered if that meant that he secretly wanted to tear himself to shreds, too.

But that line of thought was not helpful now. One task. He'd set himself one simple job – find Clink and Forge and engender their help. Aella's lessons yoked his every thought, but he could not allow them to master his every movement.

He was stalling. Avoiding applying his carefully measured anger into the little sliver of sel that he had, without conscious thought, floated over to rest on the wick in the lantern. It shimmered there, its pearlescent structure evident even in such a small amount, taunting him. A flame that shone but cast no light.

Aella had taught him the benefit of physical movement, a mirror of his intention, and so he visualized himself snapping his fingers to ignite the small globule and then, giving himself no more time to worry nor secondguess his ability, made the movement in truth.

Snap. Anger. Shut it down.

The speck of selium tore itself apart, and with a muted *whoosh* lit the wicked-up lantern into life.

He jumped to his feet and pumped the air with a fist, very nearly knocking the lantern over in the process. He bit his lips to stifle a cry of triumph. Such a simple thing, that tiny flame, but that thing existed at the very edge of his control. It'd been harder for him to light that wick than it'd be to blow the bulk of selium floating the ship. Or, at the very edge of his sphere of awareness, the massive firemount that loomed near Aransa, and all the secret pockets of selium bubbling within.

That froze him in his celebration. At the moment he'd reached for the sliver, his awareness had expanded, wider than it ever had. Standing here, toward the peak of the mountain that housed Aransa, he could feel all the small and large pockets of selium hidden beneath the solid stone of the firemount a half-day's walk away. In all the time he'd spent in this city in the past, never before had he been able to reach so far with such accuracy.

The thought chilled him to the core, snuffing the sparks of his victory.

Never mind that. Focus on finding the girls.

The lantern cast sharp shadows as he scooped it up and sauntered down the hall, testing every door handle he passed. Locked, all of them. But he wasn't here to snoop behind locked doors. He was here to find two trapped women. Each handle he made sure to jiggle, until at the fifth down the line an irritated voice called, "It's locked, you moron. You locked it your damn self."

Detan grinned, recognizing the exasperated tone. "That you, Clink?"

Shuffling behind the door, then a soft thump as someone clunked their forehead against the wood trying to get a good look through the crack between door and jamb. "Well I'll be fucked, it's the Honding. Come to threaten to blow us up again?"

The lantern in his hand felt a little heavier. "I had no say in that. And, hey, I picked the right pouch, didn't I?"

"Our hero," Clink drawled. "The creepy little witch with you?"

Detan caught himself grinning at the blank face of the door like the madman he probably was. He could see why these two had gotten along well with Ripka. "It's just me."

"And a lockpick, I hope."

"Uh, about that…"

A soft groan, then Forge said, "I told you he was a coward."

"Hey, I'm not saying it won't happen, I'm saying it's not the right time." He scowled at the door, wishing he could see their faces, wishing he could show them his face, and all the well-practiced expressions of assurance he could dance across it to help convince them.

"Talk to us when you got a plan, soft man," Clink said. Forge didn't bother hiding her laughter.

"That's what I'm here for." He threw an enigmatic smile at the door, then rolled his eyes at his own showboating. Tibs would have pissed himself laughing at that little move.

"Cute. More talk, less dancing."

He bit his tongue to stifle a quip and cut to the meat of the matter. "I want to set you free."

"Funny you should forget the lockpick, then."

He grimaced and thumped his forehead against the door, letting them hear it. "I told you, I can't manage that just yet. It's too dangerous. You're in the heart of Thratia Ganal's compound, in Aransa. Did you know that?"

A pause, then Forge spoke, "No, we didn't. We haven't seen the sun since Aella dragged us aboard this ship, and frankly we're starting to think we're going to die before we get to see it again. I understand she's keeping us on hand to keep you in line, but she forgets us sometimes. No food last night, and this morning she didn't even mention it when she brought our rations. We had more freedom on the Remnant."

"Fiery pits, I had no idea she'd forgotten about you."

"Really," Clink drawled. "And we were fresh on your mind, were we?"

That hit the mark so soundly he nearly dropped his lantern. Figured Ripka would ally herself with women clever enough to see right through to the core of him. "I can apologize all night, but that won't help you. What I can do, is promise you this. We're moving to Hond Steading soon – I don't know when. A week, probably. In the meantime I can work on Aella, make sure as the skies are blue that you both get moved there with us. Hond Steading's *my* city, I... I can help you better there. Send you to ground in a safe place, to escape the chains that bind you here."

A soft snort, then a murmuring of voices as the women conferred. Forge said, "And what do you want in return?"

"I never said–"

"Didn't have to, Honding. Cut the goatshit. You need something from us, something in Hond Steading. What is it?"

He flushed, embarrassed they'd seen through him so easily. "You in particular, Forge. I will have need of your special talents."

"And if I help you, that will see both Clink and I free?"

"You have my word."

"Fat lot of good that does us, but I suppose we don't exactly have a better offer at the moment."

"Freedom in Hond Steading, a stipend to see you well established, and, if my guesses are correct, a possible reunion with your other friend that escaped with Ripka – Honey, I believe you told me her name was."

Silence, then, "We like her well enough when she's chained. Not sure the girl's worth the risk when she's loosed. But we'll take your offer, Honding. Pity we can't shake on it."

"I'll make sure your meals are remembered. Take care."

"Don't get killed before you can spring us," Forge said.

He grinned, and rapped twice on the door in affirmation before taking off back down the hall. It seemed a pity to snuff the lantern after he'd gone to so much trouble to light it, but he couldn't very well take it with him. He blew the flame to death and hung the lantern, then stepped back onto deck. The sun was high, just beginning to trail over the other side of Thratia's compound where it would eventually go to rest for the night somewhere

behind the firemount that was Aransa's twin. He blinked
in the brightness, settling his vision, then strolled toward
the gangplank, circling around to the other side of the
cabins.

As soon as he turned the corner, he froze.

Thratia stood on the dock, a small entourage of
very armed men and women at her side, deck hands
scurrying about the opposite side of the u-dock in an
effort to make those ties ready. She spotted him there,
cocked her head in mild curiosity, but seemed otherwise
uninterested in his presence. The *Crested Fool* was Aella's
ship, after all, and its contents were the girl's business.
Detan wondered if Aella had ever bothered mentioning
Clink and Forge to Thratia. By the bored expression on
the woman's face, he doubted it. There was no irritation
in her posture, no tension that he might have stumbled
across something he wasn't meant to find. Thratia was
not at all interested in Detan's presence on the *Crested*.
She was, in fact, staring straight over his shoulder.

With a sinking feeling in his gut Detan turned, slowly.
A ship larger than any he'd ever seen blotted what was
left of the fading light, a massive bulk of wood and sail
headed by a sharp, cutting prow. The mere proximity of
all that selium made Detan's skin itch. It loomed toward
the dock, slow and steady, aiming right for the space
alongside the *Crested Fool*.

Detan scurried off the smaller ship before the larger
could close the distance. He'd never been keen on
trusting his safety to the piloting skills of others. Thratia
acknowledged his presence with a distracted nod, her
gaze stuck on that hulking mass. He sidled up to her,
daring to take the place at her right side, and asked,
"What in the pits is that thing?"

She shot him a fierce grin. "That is my new flagship,

and our transport to Hond Steading."

It drifted closer, the voices of the dock hands rising in panic as they scrambled to make ready for the leviathan's arrival. Detan's throat grew dry, his stomach heavy, as he began to make out the fine detail on the ship's deck. Massive harpoons dotted the rails, and structures the likes of which he'd never seen before adorned the silk-smooth deck. Whoever the ship's captain was, they were a deft hand, for they sailed the ship with firm and steady grace. Detan swallowed to regain his voice.

"When do we leave?"

"Two days," Thratia said, and there was more passion in her eyes as she looked upon that ship than he had seen all through the night spent in her bed.

CHAPTER 26

The streets of Aransa baked in the heat, but there was no temperature save the killing field of the Black Wash that could ever make Detan feel clean again. He moved with purpose, letting the fancy clothes Thratia'd dressed him in cut a swathe through the city's crowds, and tried, very hard, to ignore the sting of his raw skin beneath those shiny, shiny clothes.

Two nights now. Two nights in Thratia Ganal's bed, and there was no scrub-brush in the world that could strip the scent of her from his memory. Nothing in the world that could undo the betrayal of his body, responding to her need though it turned his stomach.

He couldn't think on it. Not too long, anyway. Every time the memory threatened to surface it slid away into some black pit in his mind, leaving him unsettled and restless but, at the very least, capable of functioning.

Even his memories of his time in the Bone Tower were clearer.

His destination loomed into view, shaking him back into himself. The thing about mercers, even the wealthiest of the bunch, was that they all had the same boring sense of style. Grandon's offices were located in a squat, squared-off building topped with a roof of dark-stained wood. Expensive stuff, that wood, but he figured Grandon could probably afford it. Pits, he'd probably be able to afford another one after the order Detan was prepared to place.

Grandon's lobby sported a prim little receptionist hard at work under a massive mural of the Grandon family crest. She whipped her head up from the file she'd been prodding at as Detan entered, and plastered on a smile quick enough that he almost believed it was real.

"Welcome to the Grandon Trading House. Do you have an appointment?"

He sauntered forward, making a show of pulling his crimson-lined collar straight, and leaned one arm on the woman's desk.

"Not an appointment, exactly. Renold and I are old friends, I'm sure he can squeeze a little time in for me."

She lifted a brow like she'd found something suspicious on the bottom of her shoe. "Then you know that Mercer Grandon is very busy. Is there a general question I can assist you with?"

Right. In his long experience, it was easier to worm one's way past a guard than a sharp-eyed receptionist. He hadn't meant to play this completely straight, it just wasn't in his nature to stick to a single path, but there was only one thing that could get him past those narrowed eyes without her ringing for the watch to escort him out.

"I'm prepared to place a large purchase, and need to consult with Renold directly regarding delivery times."

In one deft movement she plucked a ledger from under her desk and flicked it open to the appropriate page. "In that case, sir, I would be happy to set you an appointment for a future date with Mercer Grandon, or perhaps one of his junior salesmen. Are you free on the third of this week?"

He rubbed his temples as if fighting back a tension headache. "I leave tomorrow, and skies willing won't be back to this city in my lifetime. My old pal Renold would be very, very upset to hear he'd lost this opportunity, miss. And I will inform him – letters don't need appointments, after all."

She pursed her lips and snapped the ledger shut. "I see. I will inquire about his availability directly, then. Who should I say is calling?"

"Detan Honding."

She paled, and he felt like a bigger rockbrain than usual. Figured she'd have heard of him – most of the city had, by now. Thratia'd made sure of that. He could have skipped that whole song and dance and just cut straight to who he was, and what he wanted, and no doubt she would have seen him straight to Grandon's door. Now she had to keep up appearances by asking the man, and Detan feared Renold's surly streak just might see him kicked out the door. Served him right, forgetting his name was just as deft a tool as any other he had up his sleeves.

"A moment, Master Honding."

She disappeared down a hallway, heels click-clacking on the hardwood floor, and it didn't take her long at all to come click-clacking back, a little furrow between her brows that Detan couldn't quite read.

"He will see you now."

Grandon's office was a study in sand and glass. The wall behind him was pockmarked with hexagonal windows, a high shelf encircling the whole room crowded with vials of all the various sands of the Scorched. Detan had never taken the man for being particularly interested in the geology of the region, but then, he hadn't really thought much about what Grandon may or may not like. Save, of course, that he liked his food and his women and couldn't give two shits for anyone serving him.

"You," Grandon said, splaying both his hands on the chunk of wood that was his desk, "better have a very good reason for coming here."

"Why thank you, I will take a seat. Your hospitality is always so refreshing, Grandon old pal." Detan sauntered forward and flopped into the chair across from Grandon's desk, leaning back to kick an ankle up on his knee. He tapped his fingers on the arm of the chair, flicking his gaze around the room. "I'd ask you who your decorator is, but I suspect I'm looking at the man himself, am I right?"

"You have until the count of ten."

"Now, now, aren't you going to offer me a drink?"

"One. Two."

Detan threw his palms up to forestall the count. "All right, all right. Always in such a rush, you mercers are. Time is money, and all that." Damn his tongue. He was stalling, and he hadn't even meant to. He was just loath to speak the words he needed to get his point across. "You may have heard of my impending nuptials?"

Grandon's face went slack. "Everyone has heard."

"Marvelous," he lied, and clapped with pretend joy to cover the sour note in his voice. "Then I'm sure you can help me. I wish to purchase a large quantity of your liqueur for the happy day. A gift to my bride and our guests, to remind her of old times."

The mercer's fingers curled slowly to fists atop the desk. "You may remember that the local supply of honey was severely depleted after... the accident at the Hub."

"Certainly a little explosion wasn't enough to

undermine your entire enterprise, Grandon. This place of yours," Detan gestured to the finery all around them, "isn't suffering from the lack."

"True. My business survived your little fit. But the liqueur has become a dear thing, rare and precious. A top shelf varietal hardly seen outside this city. Steel, you'll find, is the bulk of my business now. Pre-sharpened, of course."

Ah. So Thratia no longer saw a point in hiding her weapons beneath crates of other goods. Figured. "But you do still sell the stuff?"

"For a price."

A price to make even the richest selium trader blush, he had no doubt. This wasn't just about the scarcity of honey in Aransa. Grandon was punishing him. Funny thing was, the abuse gave him a fleeting sense of relief. "I'm prepared to pay."

"Nothing counterfeit, I assume?"

He smiled and flicked lint from the cuff of his pant leg. "Do you think me a pauper, Grandon? I have the routing cipher to the Honding coffers. Any counting house in this city will confirm them."

Grandon raised both brows, greed overriding his anger. "You're prepared to pay so much for a gift?"

"For my darling wife? Nothing but the best."

"Well then." He leaned forward, dragged a ledger open and dipped a pen into his inkwell. "Let's talk logistics."

CHAPTER 27

The guards, it seemed, just weren't going to cooperate. When daybreak streamed through the tiny, most assuredly locked, window in their room, the guards knocked heavily on their door before barging in. Bleary-eyed and irritated, Ripka dragged herself to a seat in her bed, blinking back sleep. Honey sat awake in the bed next to her, gaze surprisingly sharp despite the early hour and late night. Probably a habit she'd picked up at the Remnant. Ripka hadn't been locked in that place long enough to develop the same talent.

"Don't you sleep?" she muttered at the guards who'd barged in, but they scarcely even glanced her way. Maids of the hotel brought in trays of porridge, fried eggs, and garden herbs, along with two tiny spoons, and scurried back out into the hall. Ripka watched all of this, dumbstruck. She'd been hoping for a communal breakfast with the boys, not a few trays delivered before she'd even had a chance to braid her hair.

The guard was beginning to close the door, the maids safely back in the hall.

"I have to use the privy," she blurted, which was true

enough, but she wanted to stop the rush of events, to
have a moment to get her head on straight and possibly
come up with a way to exploit their breakfast. The guard,
a woman with a permanent scowl on her lips, sighed
heavily and jerked her head toward the hall.

"One at a time, no dallying."

Ripka hurried to her feet, and nearly lost control of
her legs as the sore muscles screamed in protest the
moment she put weight on them. Honey shot out a hand
to steady her, and she took a moment to gather herself
while the guard huffed in annoyance. Ripka shot her
a sour look. Such impatience would never have been
tolerated in her watchers.

They were shuffled, one at a time, to a small water
closet stuffed at the back of the floor's hall. Before Ripka
could formulate anything like a plan, she found herself
standing back in her room, the door locked firmly behind
her, her nightshift too thin against the morning cold and
her hair all a tangle.

"Well," she said, scowling at the food that'd been left
for them. "That was disappointing."

Honey shrugged, stuffing her mouth so full with
greasy eggs that her cheeks bulged. At least someone had
the foresight to provide some soothing tea for the poor
woman's throat.

"Eat," Honey muttered around a mouthful, arresting
Ripka in a circle she hadn't even realized she was pacing.

"Ugh." Ripka flopped to the floor, cross-legged
before her tray, and grabbed one of the crusty slices of
bread. She knew she'd need her strength, but she was
so irritated with the situation it was difficult to muster
up an appetite. Yet, as soon as the bread touched her
tongue, her stomach grumbled with anticipation. Honey
giggled.

"All right, all right, you win," Ripka said around a smile and a hunk of bread. Sweet skies, but she hadn't realized how long it'd been since she'd eaten anything. The previous night seemed ages ago.

"What are we going to do?" she muttered around a mouthful. Honey shrugged and pushed a piece of cheese from her plate to Ripka's. It hadn't been a real question, anyway. She was thinking out loud, keeping her voice low so the guards wouldn't overhear.

"Two guards in the hall at all times, it seems. One for each room. I got a look at the building as we walked up last night, and I think the guys' room is the mirror of ours. So they've got a small window, too, but even if the guards wouldn't hear us breaking the glass we'd all be shredded to bits by the time we squeezed through that little hole, and then there's the climb down to deal with, and the walls looked pretty smooth."

"Privy," Honey prompted.

"No good. They're keeping us stuck on this floor, though skies know how that trick of plumbing is being handled. And the window there is open, no glass to let the air in, but just about as wide as my forearm. Even if we could squeeze through, I doubt Enard and Tibal would make it, and there's no way the guards would allow us to enter the privy one by one, each one vanishing just before the next. No. The privy's out."

"Fight?" Honey's gaze had locked on the spoon in her hand. Ripka had seen the shiv Honey could carve from a wooden spoon. She'd hate to see what damage the woman could cause with a metal one.

Ripka winced. "I'd rather not harm the guards. They're just doing their jobs, and not badly. And there's no telling the positions of the other guards. We only know for sure that there are two in the hall – that might be all we have to worry about, or the other four could be patrolling the building, or waiting for us downstairs. Too risky."

"Sick?"

"Now there's a thought. Enard has some apothik training, just the usual first aid variety, but so do I, and they'd know that well enough as they're all aware I was a watch-captain. I bet Tibal could fake an illness, but what we'd really need is an injury – something bloody enough to freak them out and send them into a panic. Make them *run* for an apothik without realizing they've split their numbers. Then we'd be two-to-four, or maybe three-to-four, and have surprise on our side. I'd prefer if they didn't notice we were gone for a while, but that's not looking likely now... Hmm. Yeah, that could work, but how to fake the injury? You got any sauce on that plate that looks red enough?"

"No," Honey said, and stabbed herself in the thigh with the curved end of her spoon.

"Fuck!"

The tray of food flipped and scattered across the floor as Ripka lunged to her feet. Hot blood pumped down the woman's thigh, bare below her nightshift, and pooled on the rug. Bubbles of blood popped, making a little gurgling sound, around the half-embedded shovel of the spoon, but the flow wasn't strong enough to indicate an arterial strike.

"What the everloving fuck." Ripka grabbed a napkin from the spilled tray and shoved it against Honey's wound, trying to staunch the flow. It didn't help much. They needed to get that spoon out of her, and the wound cleaned and packed with wool and salve before they could stitch it and bind it, and then –

Honey closed her hand over Ripka's. "Better call the guards."

There wasn't the slightest tremor of pain in her voice, no beads of sweat-shock marred her brow. The crazy woman was just as calm as she'd been a moment before, throwing out ideas to spark Ripka's imagination. Honey popped a greasy piece of bread in her mouth and chewed, slowly.

"You're insane, you know that?"

Honey shrugged, though her smile was embarrassed.

No time to admonish the woman. She'd gone ahead and carved an opportunity for them all out of her own flesh, and it was up to Ripka to make the most of it. She scrambled to her feet and looked around. Honey kept on nibbling at her breakfast, calm as could be, the pool of blood spreading steadily around her, but not at a life-threatening rate.

They'd both been wearing plain linen nightshifts, and the bright blood looked rather dramatic against the beige cloth. Ripka tore long strips from one of the blankets and stashed them on the other side of the bed, where the guards would be slow to notice them. With the bloodied napkin clutched in one fist, she took a breath, worked up a false hysteria, and flung herself at the door, pounding with both fists.

"Help! Help! She's bleeding out!"

Curses in the hall, the tromp of boots and the rattle of the key in the lock. The door jerked open and Ripka stumbled back from the guard pushing toward her, but not too quickly. She wanted the guard, the same woman who'd overseen their breakfast delivery, to get a good long look at Ripka's blood-smattered clothes, and the dripping rag she held.

"What in the skies?"

"It's Honey!" Ripka yelled straight into the woman's face, working up a good tremble to add to the disturbance.

The guard pushed Ripka aside and her eyes widened at the sight of Honey who had, thankfully, stopped calmly eating her breakfast.

"Ow," Honey said.

"Pitshit." The guard ducked back out into the hall and called at the top of her lungs, "Apothik!"

"Get Tibal!" Ripka snapped. "He was in the Fleet, he has first aid training!"

The guard didn't even blink. She thrust a finger at the guard manning the door to the boys' room. "Get those men over here. We've got an injury."

"What in the pits happened?" The other guard jangled his keys as he struggled to get the door open.

"Fucked if I know."

"I fell," Honey said. Ripka thanked the skies that her voice was too soft, and the guards too frazzled, for them to have heard her half-hearted explanation.

To keep from being noticed, Ripka hung back as the guards ushered Tibal and Enard, still in their bedclothes, blinking into the women's room. They did not stay confused for long. Tibal caught sight of Honey seeping blood, her hand half-heartedly clasped against the wound, and sucked air through his teeth so fast he whistled.

Enard, however, went pale as a sheet the second he spied Ripka huddling between the two beds, her nightshift a mess of blood. He regained his composure in a breath, crossed to her side and took her by the shoulders, holding her at arm's length to get a look at the damage.

"Are you hurt?"

"None of this is mine."

He cringed at the implication, sparing a glance back over his shoulder to Honey. She'd taken up humming softly under her breath while Tibal tried to figure out the best way to extract the spoon from her leg.

"What in the pits happened here?"

Ripka slid her gaze slowly, pointedly, to the pile of sliced rags on the floor alongside the bed. Enard nodded.

"This looks bad," Tibal said, infusing his voice with gravelly seriousness. "Don't one of you guards have any serious medical experience?"

The woman said, "Eshon does–"

"But it's just the two of us today!" the male guard snapped. "Bitter pits, I told them we should stay four on rotation at all times, but no, and now look what's happened!"

Enard and Ripka locked gazes, understanding passing between them in an instant. Just two guards today. Two very flustered guards. They shared a grin.

Then lunged.

Ripka was over the bed in a heartbeat, shouldering the door to slam it closed. The guards shouted – the words didn't matter. The man, who'd been nearest the door, grabbed Ripka's shoulder, jerking her back so hard she lost her footing. No time to be neat about things. She stumbled into him and took the opportunity to jam her elbow, hard as she could, straight into the man's ribs. He woofed air and doubled over.

She gave him no quarter. Clutching his wrist, she wrenched his arm around behind his back and turned with the movement so that she stood behind him, yanking up on that twisted arm as hard as she could. He lurched, his back slamming into her chest, and in that moment she felt him draw breath to cry out. There were no other guards about, but there were certainly enough civilians in the hotel to run and call for help from the local watch.

They needed time. Time they wouldn't get if he got that shout out.

She struck him on the back of the head with the heel of her palm, felt his jaw snap closed and heard his teeth jar and clatter against each other. He gurgled a yelp, and before he could orient himself and try to pull away she stepped backward, overbalanced him, and spun, throwing him face-first onto the bed.

Blood smeared the sheets where his face connected. He bucked, trying to fling her off, but her legs were longer than his and she had them planted firmly while he was bent over, booted toes just barely dragging on the ground. With his face shoved in the blankets, she had control. She glanced up to see Tibal and Enard scuffling with the female guard. Enard pinned her arms back while Tibal tried to get a strip of cloth around her mouth as a gag.

"Keep them silent," Ripka ordered, and though she didn't raise her voice it was whip-strong with the snap of command. Pits below, but that felt good.

Enard and Tibal wrestled the woman to the ground and got her tied off properly, then hurried over to help Ripka with her thrashing charge. With their help, it took no time at all to get the guard hog-tied, gagged, and blindfolded.

"Now?" Enard asked.

Tibal strolled back over to Honey's side and made quick, easy work of removing the spoon and tying off the wound with a few leftover scraps of cut-up sheet. "Got a place to go to ground?"

"Yes," Ripka said, unwilling to elaborate while the guards were within earshot.

"Right. Lass is good to walk, but you'll be hurting a bit, won't you, dear?" He helped Honey to her feet and she shifted her weight over to her injured leg experimentally. Her grimace was all the answer any of them needed.

"I'll carry her," Enard said, "she's light enough."

"Good man." Tibal stroked his chin, eyeing both women. "New Chum and I can stroll out of here without raising any eyebrows, but you two look a mess."

Ripka flicked the bloodied hem of her nightshift. "I doubt either of you could walk out of here. They saw us all walk in, remember? And who knows who's on staff this morning. We'll need to harness the same confusion – use the shock of the blood to our advantage."

"The uniforms?"

"Perfect."

It wasn't easy going, stripping the guards of their uniform jackets, but between the four of them – and a carefully applied knife by Honey to gain compliance – they managed to get all the coats clear without letting either of the guards get too close to escape.

"Sorry about this," Ripka said as she peeled the sleeve off the last of them. The sharp edge to the woman's muffled voice told her all she needed to know to understand her apology was most certainly not accepted.

"You boys," she chucked the coat to Enard, as Tibal was already donning the man's jacket. "Make a good show of things, eh?"

Tibal and Enard shared a grin, and went to work.

They burst down the stairs of the hotel, Tibal dragging Ripka by falsely bound wrists. Her blood-spattered nightshift stuck to the tops of her thighs as she snarled and twisted, making the best show she could of trying to break free of Tibal's hold while he swore under his breath and dragged her along. Her bare feet skidded on the floor, and she was glad the hotel went to the trouble of keeping it swept clean. She was even gladder to know that underneath Tibal's coat was a sack of the woman's clean clothes.

"Make way!" Tibal barked.

Patrons screamed, swore, and generally made a mess of things as they leapt from tables and scurried to the sides of the room, cleaving a wide path down the center of the hotel's common room.

"What is the meaning of this?" A woman with finer clothes than the regular barmaids stalked toward them. She caught sight of Ripka's bloodied clothes, hesitated a step, then pushed herself forward. Respectable, if irritating, woman.

"Got a fight on our hands," Tibal snapped, holding his head to the side and keeping his hat tucked down. "Move off now, injured girl coming."

The woman stepped to the side, peering up the stairs. "Injured? Shall I send a runner for the apothik?"

"A runner!" Tibal spun on her, yanking Ripka's wrists as he did so. "This woman is bleeding, ma'am, she'd be bone dry by the time your runner got there and back. We'll take her ourselves, it's faster. But mark me, don't you dare touch a thing in those rooms upstairs. The two remaining prisoners are restrained, but that's an active crime scene! Touch nothing until after the watch arrives to begin their investigation, and then only after they have told you it's all right to do so. Do you understand?"

"Ye – yes? You're leaving, with prisoners still locked up here?"

"They're contained, I swear it. Touch. Nothing. Now move!"

Their patroness paled and scurried away as Enard stomped down the stairs. He carried Honey in his arms easily. For all that muscle, the woman was surprisingly light. As he strode into the common room gasps sounded all around, every last eye glued to the figure being carried, not to the man carrying her. If they were lucky, no one would realize the two guards who had checked in were a man and a woman, not two men, until they were well away.

Honey mustered up a little groan so pitiful Ripka wondered if the pain was finally starting to get to her. Enard didn't hesitate a breath. He strode right past Tibal, hustling as if the woman's life depended on it, and kicked the door of the hotel open into the brilliance of the day.

The street in front of the hotel was lightly trafficked, and every eye that landed on them was quickly averted. The black cloak of the Honding family's private guard was enough to grant them some degree of anonymity. No one would look too hard at a Honding guard, and they certainly wouldn't stop to question one.

Still, as they progressed through the neighborhood, Honey whispering subtle directions into Enard's ear as he held her, Ripka's skin began to itch with the attention they were drawing. A palace guard may be untouchable, but the presence of two in the city was something to remark upon. And two of them escorting two bloodied women even more so. She imagined rumors spreading outward from their position like wildfire, and shivered.

"This can't hold," she whispered to Tibal.

He nodded, grim-faced. Probably he'd realized that from the second they stepped into the street, maybe even before. This type of game was his speciality, after all.

"We'll find a quiet place to adjust in," he said, then coughed subtly to alert Enard to fall back to his side.

They abandoned the path toward Latia's house, winding though it was, and decided to veer in the opposite direction, lest the rumor of their presence eventually lead their future pursuers to Latia's doorstep. At the first sight of a narrow alley free of windows and nearby pedestrians, they ducked down the shadowed street, and took a moment to catch their breaths.

Ripka and Honey changed as best they could, covering their nightshifts in long, thin robes that they'd found in the hotel chests. They didn't look like proper day clothes, but they covered the blood well enough, and neither one of them had anything to wash with.

"The jackets?" Enard asked.

"Ditch them," Ripka said. "They draw more attention than we'd like."

"The four of us draw more attention than I'd like." Tibal stripped off his jacket and tossed it in a heap against the alley wall. The men, at least, wore thin trousers and shirts, if not any shoes. Luckily going barefoot was not an uncommon sight in Hond Steading – their streets were smooth and free of firemount glass.

"You've a point," Enard said. "Especially with Honey's injury and both of your, ah, appearances. Forgive me." He flushed.

Ripka snort-laughed. "We're a mess, it's true. All right. Honey and I know where we're going, so we should split up with you boys. Honey, Enard's about your height, do you think you can walk if he gives you his shoulder?"

"That's fine," she said, poking at her leg absently.

"Don't overdo it." Honey just looked at her, doe-eyed, so Ripka turned to Enard and said, "See that she doesn't overdo it."

He gave her a flimsy salute and offered his arm to Honey, who hobbled over to accept it. Tibal watched her intently, no doubt understanding that she'd split them this way to keep him by her side. She had no reason to doubt Enard and Honey's loyalty, but Tibal was another story. Despite his recent interest in her plans, he could just as easily disappear into the city right now.

And if he did that, she knew deep down that she'd never see him again.

"See you there," Enard said, oblivious to the tension thickening between her and Tibal. The pair shuffled their slow, painful way out into the street.

"Better give it a moment," Tibal drawled. "Wouldn't want anyone seeing us come out right after."

"Right."

"Or you could tell me where we're going, and it'll look even less suspicious, us waiting to leave one right after the other."

There it was. The challenge she'd felt was coming since he'd given her that hard look while she bundled Honey off with Enard. She straightened the lay of her robe's tie. "Better if we stick together, in case of trouble. Two sets of hands are better than one."

"You expecting trouble?"

She held her arms out in a gesture that illustrated just how ridiculous she currently looked. "You seen me lately? I'd half expect the watchers to pick me up to evaluate my mental health if I were walking around alone."

He snorted. "And if we get separated?"

Well then. She didn't have anything to answer to that, aside from the fact that she feared that he'd fake separation just to get away from her. But subterfuge was Detan's game, and she was tired of being on delicate footing with Tibal.

"Would I ever see you again?"

He blinked at her, real slow, the most surprised expression she'd ever seen on his weathered face. Took him a moment to register she wasn't fencing with him any more: she'd laid the tension between them bare at his feet and bade him have a long look. So he did, in his own mind, tugging on his whiskery mustache with one hand while he thought. It occurred to her then that he hadn't shaved since the Remnant.

"What's for me, there?"

"You know what," she said, unable to hide her frustration. "I'm trying to do right by this city. Trying to keep it from falling into the same pit Aransa did. We have a chance here. We're prepared. To walk away now… I could never live with myself." And I don't think you could either, she didn't say, but the words stretched out between them anyway. Some things didn't need to be said to be clear as a spring rain.

"City's not my responsibility."

"Isn't it, Tibal Honding?"

His head snapped back, those dark eyes narrowing, and for just a moment she thought she'd triggered his well-hidden temper. But no, that wasn't anger ghosting his features. That was pain, pure and simple. She'd hit him. Hard.

"That ain't my name."

"The Dame seems to think it is."

"You think everything the Dame says is gospel?"

"Convince me otherwise."

"Not my job to put your head on straight, and we don't have time for this nonsense."

"I'm making time. Talk, Tibal. What in the fiery pits is your relation to the Dame?"

"Why are you so damned desperate to know?"

"Because you told me a story." She stepped toward him. He stepped back. "Don't you remember? At Thratia's party, you told me all about how you and Detan met. How he stumbled across you, and you found common ground in trying to control your tempers. You earned my respect with that story, before I ever knew you. And I'm wondering now – how much of the time we shared together was based on lies? If your tempers are mirrors, then…" She let her gaze slide to the shadow of a firemount.

"You think I got the power, too?" He yanked his hat off and slapped it against his knee to clear the dust. "Woman, haven't you been paying attention? What Detan's got is rare, I can't shift sel any more than the Dame can. And anyway." He twisted the brim of his hat between his fingers, picking at the singed spot that had been Detan's doing.

"What I told you was true." He held up a hand to stop her asking more questions. "I wouldn't lie to you now, and I didn't then. You want to know what the Dame knows? Fine." He blew air through his whiskers hard enough to make them flutter.

"Rew Honding is my father by blood, though I never met the man. Some uncle of the Dame, old feller, but my ma liked him well enough for a night and sent him along the next day. Didn't know who he was at the time, till the Dame came along collecting any information she could about Honding bastards. Eletraia – that's Detan's mother – had just died and the Dame wasn't one for birthing her own heirs. Anyway, she made a note of my existence and moved along, ma never heard from her again. But I did.

"She came by the settlement I'd ended up in after the Fleet had let me go 'cause the war with the Catari had gone cold. Ma was doing well enough, running her tavern, and I didn't have any taste for that work, so I'd found an engineer to take me on repairing airships.

"One day the Dame shows up, real quiet like. Came

in on a small ship with just a pilot and a single guard, a man named Gatai. You've seen him around the palace as the keymaster, but I always suspected he was more than that."

He tipped his head back, squinting at the sky as if he could see his past painted in the clouds. Ripka held her breath to keep from peppering him with questions. This was the most she'd ever heard him talk all at once.

"Anyway. She wasn't dressed up fancy or anything, but I knew her, and she looked bad. Real tired. Said her heir had been in some trouble, maybe lost his sel-sense, and was rambling the Scorched a lost man. But she'd been keeping tabs on him, and he was flying straight my way. Asked me to keep an eye on him, help him pull himself together. That if she were to lose him then I was the only one of the bloodline left, and it had to be maintained. Was real animated about that. I told her to go suck gravel. But..." He sighed and shook his head. "Detan showed up the day after she left. I ain't never seen a man so much the mirror to me before. Never met a soul who understood... Shit."

He shoved his hat back on hard enough to cover half his forehead. "That's what you wanted to know, anyway."

"I didn't know," she said, quietly, and reached out to touch his arm lightly in comfort. He shook her off.

"Now you do, and I don't want to hear a damned thing about it again, understood? This ain't my city. Never going to be. I mean it, this city ain't my responsibility."

"Is your conscience your responsibility?"

He pursed his lips, spit on the dry ground, and grated out the words, "Wherever it is you're going, Leshe, I'll be there."

Leshe. He never called her that. Captain, sometimes,

and mostly Ripka. But her last name... There was only one person she knew of he consistently called by his family name, and it was, she thought, maybe the greatest honor he could hand her.

"See you there, then," she said, and told him the way to Latia's house – how to mark it, by its shape and its color and its position against the side of a firemount. Then she left him in the alley, stomach churning with uncertainty, to begin the circuitous route to Latia's.

Leaving him there, not knowing for sure whether he'd come or not, was the greatest leap of faith she'd yet taken in this city. She hoped they both landed on their feet.

CHAPTER 28

Detan made a point of hiding in his room as the *Dread Wind* approached Hond Steading. He did not want to watch the city of his birth roll into view. Did not want to stand at the prow alongside Thratia as he bore witness to whatever defense the city he'd sworn to serve with his life had mustered against her coming. Did not, most of all, want to see familiar faces in those forces, and know that they believed him on the other side of the line Thratia had carved into the whole of the Scorched.

Thratia, of course, had other plans.

"Honding." Misol's voice boomed as she thumped the door to his cabin with the butt of her spear. "Get your lazy ass out here."

"I'm airsick." He made a few attempts at a retching sound. Misol just laughed.

"You can't possibly expect me to believe that."

"Food poisoning?"

"Naw."

"Moral quandary heavy enough to progress to physical illness?"

"Not a chance."

Figured. Detan grunted as he pushed himself to his feet, taking a moment that he told himself wasn't stalling to rub the ache from his knees. That ache was getting more and more frequent, lately. Probably his desire to stay far away from Hond Steading locking up his body, while the ship carried him steadily onward. Though he'd hoped to stay hidden, he hadn't relied on the fact. He'd dressed himself in the soot-grey finery that Thratia had provided him with, the ochre-orange trim hinting at a threat he didn't feel himself capable of.

Ever since Aella'd taken his injections away, he'd spent half of every night sweating himself cold, struggling to rein in his sense so he wasn't so keenly aware of the great balloons of selium transporting the *Dread Wind* through the skies. Cursed child had just laughed at him when he told her he was on the verge of blowing them all to bits.

Misol wasn't alone. Aella smiled at him as he opened the door, all sweet politeness, and swept into a slight bow. Misol gave him the once-over he now knew was her way of checking for weapons. Funny she should be worried about him packing a knife. He couldn't wield a knife against anything bigger than a steak, and he had all that lovely selium above his head to use if he really felt like sticking it to them all.

Probably it was a force of habit for her. Just like giving her a once over – checking for loose pockets, poorly fastened jewelry, and anything likely to steal – was a habit of his own.

"You are required," Aella said the words like she'd been practicing them.

"Thratia giving you etiquette lessons, little squirt?"

A scowl crossed her face – fleeting, but definitely there – and he allowed himself a brief smirk. Wasn't often he was able to get the wind up that girl.

"We are entering a tenuous, diplomatic arena. Please try to remember that you were born for just these types of negotiations, despite your more recent… adventures." Her smile returned, flashing with real pleasure so that he knew she was about to say something truly nasty. "We'd hate to have to resort to violence because you flubbed the diplomacy."

"Have I ever told you what a charmer you are?"

She rolled her eyes and turned her back on him. The girl had ditched the white coat at Thratia's request, but Detan knew well enough that a viper could be painted as plain as a garden snake, and its fangs were still loaded with venom.

They escorted him toward the prow of the ship. Every step he took, his legs felt heavier, until he was just a single step away from Thratia and he could have sworn his boots were made of lead.

He knew what he'd see at that prow, and he didn't want it. Didn't want the city of his birth burned into his mind's eye from this angle, didn't want to go to sleep at night seeing it from the sky, knowing he was about to descend upon it to work out the final throes of his battle with Thratia.

For that's what this was, he realized, as he stood a step behind her, letting her long, straight back fill his vision so that he did not have to look upon the city she eclipsed so fully. From the second he set foot in Aransa, he'd loathed her and goaded her. He'd known so little about her then, only the rumor of her exile, her reputation for viciousness. Those two things were all the excuse he'd needed to justify taking her flagship, the *Larkspur*, out from under her nose.

Had it really been just the prize of the ship that'd lured

him, then? He doubted that truth now. He'd seen her, a proud and impervious woman, kicked out of the same empire that'd turned against him – that'd split his flesh for curiosity's sake – and loathed her for the freedoms she claimed for herself.

He'd been jealous of her, and wanted to take something from her. And in doing so he'd kicked a hornet's nest, roused the specter of the whitecoats to chase him again and stumbled into the horror of Thratia's bargains – deviants for weapons, though she claimed her reasons were worth that tribute.

He could not reconcile her. He hated her, even as he admired her, and knew he must defeat her here in Hond Steading even as, deeply, secretly, he knew that her winning here might not be the worst thing to happen to his city. Valathea taking full control – that would be the real pitfire. And Thratia's attention was no doubt drawing the empire back to Hond Steading like moths to a flame.

He imagined pushing her over the prow. Imagined her breaking, fragile as glass, against the bedrock of his homeland. Imagined her entwined with him, too, taking control of his body and his life as the new Dame of Hond Steading by marriage and – and... And some cowardly part of him welcomed that; thought, wouldn't it be easier, to let this woman who was so sure of herself make all the hard choices? Wouldn't it be so much cleaner, to let her take control and do as she claims – kick the Valatheans out of the Scorched? He could sympathize with that sentiment. Wanted it, desperately.

But he knew how she'd go about it. Knew she'd trade innocents for the future betterment of many, knew the way she gambled, knew the way she played her hands. And at the heart of everything she did there was blood, and pain, and hadn't he seen Aransa? Quieter than it'd ever been, people taking to the streets only to go where they absolutely must, and then as quickly as possible.

Thratia's reign was one of control, of fear and blood, and bargains he could never bring himself to make.

He did not know if he could do better than her. But he had to try.

She turned. Though he'd been standing perfectly still, he felt frozen all the same. Cursed woman had a way of looking at him that made him feel as if she'd stripped every thought he'd ever had bare and laid it out under a microscope for the sort of cold examination she was capable of in all things.

That stare was momentary, though. She smiled, and though he knew the expression was faked, that was the danger of Thratia – how natural it seemed, how gentle and kind and impromptu. If he had not been staring at her in the moment when she'd speared him with that first glance, he'd think she was genuinely delighted to see him. Thratia was a woman of bargains, even in her own mind. And now she'd decided to trade on being gentle with him. That chilled him more than her cruelty.

"Stand with me," she said, and extended her hand to him. He could never look upon that hand without imagining Bel's blood on it, but this was just one more move on the board toward his victory, and his city's freedom. He took her hand, and ignored the deep-seated cold of her flesh.

"The *Dread Wind* made good time," he said, for he'd long considered small talk the easiest way to pry away at a person's true thoughts.

"It was made for this day."

And many more to come, no doubt. He held no illusions that Thratia would be done with the Scorched after she took Hond Steading. She could call the hulking thing her flagship, but it was first and foremost a warship built to last.

She drew him forward. He forced himself to look.

Hond Steading, from above. He loved this view. Had loved it all his life. And for just a moment, he shoved aside the reality of his arrival. Ignored Thratia's cold hand, fingers folded like spider's legs around his.

Here was the bedrock of his birth. The great valley of the city, sprawled between the trailing arms of five massive firemounts. Larger and more vibrant than any other city the Scorched had to offer, Hond Steading drew its water from a delta to the north, aqueducts the likes of which hadn't even been seen in Valathea transporting that precious fluid south to support the citizenry. Three firemounts bounded the south of the city, the two larger loomed to the northern edge. Each bristled with metal fittings, all five mines active as the sensitives of Hond Steading drew forth its surplus of selium. Some of the richer districts had taken to building with sel, as was the fashion in Valathea. Great platforms held by thick guy wires added extra levels to the estates of the wealthy, many lush with gardens.

His heart clenched with joy. His city, his home, had thrived in his absence.

And then, inevitably, he looked for the Honding family palace.

It spread up the steep slopes of the city's largest firemount, set further forward than the rest of the city, the district at its feet a patchwork of beauty in architecture. Its grand spires were hemmed in by walls that were more decorative than functional. And, from its many airdocks, a fleet like none he'd ever seen before took to the sky.

Auntie Honding had spared no expense in the defense of her city. A great wall of ships lifted, staggered throughout the sky in such a way as to make their numbers difficult to count. His stomach sunk, seeing the Valathean banner flying from many a mast, and he knew just where his auntie had allocated much of the funds – straight from the empire's coffers.

She wouldn't have had a choice. Even with their selium surplus, they could not bend time to make so many ships before Thratia's arrival. They'd have to borrow them from somewhere. And yet, he'd hoped...

Thratia squeezed his hand. She leaned forward against the railing, her other hand gripping the smooth metal, her gaze avid as she flicked it over the opposing fleet. There was a hunger so deep in her it unsettled him. The very defense his auntie had mounted enticed her, pleased her. Here was a woman so in love with domination that to see her victim squirm and lash back gave her deep-rooted pleasure. He suppressed a shudder.

"Boarding flags!" A crewman called out.

"Let them close," Thratia commanded.

Detan squinted through the mass of ships. A larger vessel pulled away from the rest, cutting the sky with delicate ease. Four figures stood on the prow of that ship, a mirror to Detan and Thratia's own position. Detan leaned forward and released Thratia's hand so that she would not feel his heart thundering through his palms. Dame Honding he knew at a glance, but the others... Ripka? Tibal? He was not sure he could stomach admitting his betrothal to Thratia Ganal with those eyes watching.

The ship sped closer. Detan took a halting step back, making a low keening sound in his throat. Misol and Aella pressed the space behind him instantly, Aella's power flowing over him like a balm – he hadn't even realized he'd reached out his senses.

He could not yet see the face of the woman standing next to his aunt, but the shape of her was forever burned into his memory.

"What is it?" Thratia asked and, skies curse the woman, there was genuine concern in her voice.

"Ranalae," he said.

She hissed and turned back to watch the ship's approach, while Detan stood stock-still, a slow pain spreading in his chest.

"Breathe," Aella whispered.

He did. The pain eased.

"Keep me leashed," he begged, and she nodded with such serious concern he could have hugged the little witch.

The ships eased alongside each other. Each thud of a gangplank snapping into place was a nail through Detan's heart.

CHAPTER 29

Ripka arrived first of the group. Latia had drawn her curtains, but still a warm, homey light escaped around the edges. Ripka wanted nothing more than to drag herself to that door, to pound on it and throw herself on Latia's fussy ministrations. But it was a bright day, and Latia had drawn the curtains. Whatever was going on inside those walls, she wanted no one to see.

Enard and Honey could not have possibly made it to Latia's house before Ripka, hampered as they were by Honey's injury, and Tibal would not risk knocking on a stranger's door. Which meant that something else had happened. Something Latia did not want the average gravel of the city to see.

Ripka leaned her back against the wall of a closed tavern and caught her breath. Silence pervaded the neighborhood so early in the morning, its bohemian residents still in bed or off to see to more mundane chores. The scarce population was a false wind, so far as Ripka was concerned. There were fewer eyes to note her presence, but she stood out like rain on a summer day. Especially standing about in her hotel robe with hints of blood beginning to seep through around her thighs and hips.

Footfalls alerted her to a passerby, and rather than being spotted she ducked down into a service alley that ran alongside the tavern. It stank of stale ale and fouler things, but Ripka's watcher training had long ago bashed any squeamishness out of her nostrils.

She angled herself to see who approached, and nearly cried out with relief when she spied Tibal strolling alongside Enard, Honey supported between them.

"Here," she said, stepping out of the alley.

"Ran across these two on my way in, and weren't many eyes around to see us," Tibal said. She couldn't blame him for assisting, even if a group of three was more conspicuous. Honey's cheeks were pale enough to have turned beige, her lips wrinkled with dehydration. Despite her assurances that she knew what she was doing, the woman was still in need of care. Crazy didn't make you invincible.

Honey looked at Latia's house and said, "Something's wrong."

"I know." Ripka explained for the guys, "She usually leaves the windows wide open during the morning. She's a painter, and loves the natural light. We don't have much choice, though. We've got to have her help. Ready?"

Honey nodded, curls hanging limp around her cheeks, and the four set off at a hobbling, stunted pace. Ripka steeled herself, and knocked.

The door flung open. A red-cheeked Latia glared out at them, mouth half-opened in defiance, then recognition caught up with her, and her jaw dropped all the way open.

"Sweet skies!" She flung the door wide and stepped

aside. "Get in, get in. You see?" She hollered over her shoulder. "Told you there was a good reason she didn't show!"

Dranik stood in the frame of Latia's patio door, jaw agape as he watched the four pile into Latia's small sitting room. Dranik could wait.

"Honey's injured." Ripka put some command into her voice, and Latia jerked as if someone'd yanked on her arm. "Skies! A moment – I have fresh cloth around here somewhere. Dranik, make yourself useful and boil some water. How bad?"

Latia became a whirlwind of activity while Ripka helped Enard ease Honey onto one of Latia's many lounge chairs.

"It's shallow. She's just put too much weight on it, too soon."

Enard and Tibal wisely stepped back from the rush around Honey, putting their backs to the curtained windows while Latia and Ripka peeled Honey's robe away and set about stitching and binding her wound. Dranik came scurrying into the room moments later, a steaming kettle of water hissing in his hand.

"What in the pits happened?" he demanded, as he knelt alongside Honey and offered the hot water to Latia to clean the wraps before binding Honey's thigh.

To this, Ripka had no good answer. She hesitated only a moment, then decided to err on the side of truth. If they were going to work together, they had to trust one another, and Ripka couldn't very well expect him to let her into his inner circle if she lied to him now. She couldn't think of a convincing lie, anyway. The truth would be enough of a stretch.

"We were detained overnight in the Hotel Cinder by the Honding family guards. Honey's injury allowed us an opportunity to escape this morning. I am sorry I missed your meeting, Dranik, but–"

"Pits take my meeting." He bounced to his feet, shooting the men a hard look. "How did you get detained? And who in the pits are these two people?"

"Friends of mine, I trust them both with my life."

"That's all very well and good for you, but–"

Ripka was on her feet before she'd realized it, closed the distance between her and Dranik and pressed her face so close to his he had to step back or be headbutted. Her robe fell open, revealing the smears of blood on her nightshift, and she watched with perverse satisfaction as his throat bobbed.

"I have had one pits-cursed night, in no small part because of my efforts on behalf of this city. They are my friends. They are trustworthy. Their names are Enard and Tibal. You will treat them with the same courtesy you have shown me, or I will walk right the fuck out that door and leave you to unravel your own shitpile. Am I quite understood?"

"Yes," he squeaked.

"Say hello to Tibal and Enard."

"Uh, I… Hello, Tibal and Enard."

"Smile."

He did.

She slumped away from him, took an unsteady step backward, and tried very hard not to laugh at the ridiculousness of the situation.

"Pardon me," Latia said, "that was all very convincing, and you four are very welcome in my home but, with all respect, what the fuck happened?"

"A few days ago I took it upon myself to intercept a message the Dame Honding sent to her Valathean contacts. That interception was discovered sometime yesterday, and we were apprehended last night and detained until the Dame could figure out what to do with us. That clear enough?"

Latia's eyes were wide as saucers. "You stole information from the Dame?"

"I would steal her knickers off her wrinkled ass if it meant I could keep this city safe. Do you understand me now, both of you?"

"I..." Dranik mustered a shred of dignity. "Why? Why do you care so much about this city?"

Ripka looked at the mess she'd made. At Latia and Dranik, pale with fear. At Enard, pushed away from her so thoroughly that she hardly thought his name unless it was in the context of saving the city. And Tibal, whose friendship she'd nearly lost for good due to her own anger, her own rash decisions. Even Honey only tolerated her out of some misguided sense of loyalty to Ripka's violent streak.

Hond Steading's fate had so consumed her, her loss of Aransa so undermined her confidence, that she'd been working this job from the wrong angle. Taking on Detan's mannerisms, his panache for misdirection. That'd almost gotten them all beheaded at the Dame's hand. It was time to play this game on a more comfortable footing. And time, too, to make some pretty hard apologies. But those would have to wait. Now, she needed Dranik on her side. Her *real* side.

"My name is Ripka Leshe, and I was watch-captain when Aransa fell. I have lost one city to Thratia Ganal. I will not lose another. Do you see that I am quite serious, and that I mean to help you all?"

"I never doubted your intent," Dranik stammered, "but when you didn't show up–"

Latia swatted at him. "Stop simpering and find these

people some fresh clothes, and draw some bathwater, for skies' sake. I take it you four don't exactly enjoy wearing all that blood."

Ripka shot Latia a fierce grin. "Red's not my color."

"Skies, but I must paint you."

"Later. Now, we have a city to save, and very little time to do it. Valathea is already moving in, and I'd bet anything Thratia's forces will arrive in full within the week. Dranik – those contacts of yours, can you take me to them?"

He paused halfway to the patio to draw fresh water, frowning hard. "They were annoyed when the new recruits I promised them didn't show, but–"

"But consider how much more pleased they'll be with four new sycophants."

"Ah. Yes. That could work." He scurried out the door, bucket swinging from one hand, and let out a startled yelp.

"What is it *now*?" Latia was on her feet in an instant, but Ripka made it to the patio first. There was no one there, just Dranik, bucket dropped at his feet, head tipped back as he stared at the swathe of blue sky above all their heads.

A sky that wasn't so blue any more. A fat shadow spilled over Latia's garden wall, swelling with every inch it claimed across the tiles. Ripka swallowed once, then followed Dranik's gaze to the sky which was pristine just a few moments ago.

The largest ship she'd ever seen marred the clouds. Though she could only see its belly and a sliver of its deck, it still managed to blot out the sun. Structures dotted the side that she could see, the ship twisted into a three-quarters view that rapidly dwindled as it slithered into position. It took her a moment to place those structures, as she had never seen so many clustered in one place before – harpoon guns, all of them, and the largest of their kind.

It approached the city from the west, its accordion wings throwing shadows so wide they almost ate up the entire city. Valathea, she knew, would come from the north – across the sea and over the delta. The only thing west of Hond Steading was Aransa.

Was Thratia Ganal.

Enard and Tibal came to flank her, and their combined shadow formed a smaller version of the great ship's: Ripka as the body, Enard and Tibal as the splayed wings.

"She comes," Dranik said, voice quiet with tension.

But there was more than Thratia Ganal on that ship, and only the two men who stood beside her knew that with the same certainty she did. A greater threat, or savior, arrived in Hond Steading this morning.

Thratia Ganal was expected, counted upon, prepared for. She was a force of nature, but one that could be predicted and moved against with enough time and effort.

Detan Honding, however, was a wildcard. And though Ripka believed in the deepest recesses of her heart that he'd only bent knee to Aella to save them all from the fate he'd since endured, she could not know what that fate had done to him. Could not know what plans he made now, what schemes were spooling out from his lips all across the city. After spending half a year as a willing captive of Thratia and Aella, she could not even be certain that he still counted those two his enemies. For all she knew, he came to bend Hond Steading to Thratia's will.

But no. He wouldn't. She knew that man, in the way she knew herself. Knew that despite all his gruff games, his quick tongue and his light fingers, he was wrapping himself in deception to hide the core of goodness in him. The core that had been bruised by the Bone Tower so badly it had retreated to the deepest recesses of his being.

"So soon," Latia murmured. "I thought we'd have some time yet to prepare."

"There's no preparing for what's on that ship," Tibal said. Ripka had never agreed with him more in her entire life.

"What do you mean?" Latia asked.

Ripka said, "Detan Honding has come home."

"Skies help us all," Tibal whispered, too soft for anyone but Ripka to hear.

CHAPTER 30

Thratia did not make Dame Honding board her ship to speak terms, and Detan found that strangely kind of her. Whoever held the ground, held the upper hand, and he knew sure as his nerves were on fire that Thratia was aware of that fact.

But she was a crafty rockviper, his bloodthirsty betrothed, and he suspected that she saw some other upperhand to be gained in dealing with the Dame on her turf. For his part, Detan wished deeply that she'd decided to deal with them on the solid deck of the *Dread Wind*. Not that he wanted Thratia to have any advantage – he simply wanted to know all the good hiding places, should his dear auntie lash out at him in the way he expected.

He was also convinced that Thratia'd allowed Aella to bring along Callia just to put Ranalae on edge. Disgusting little move that it was, he hoped it played true. If anyone in the whole of the world needed her nerves shaken, it was the mistress of the Bone Tower.

What a sordid little party they made, tromping across the gangplank to his auntie's flagship. The boards thundered under his boots, the wind pushed at him as if urging him to turn back. He wanted to tell the wind to mind its own pitsdamned business.

Thratia dragged along a selection of her honor guard, and Detan was just now getting the sense that she'd planned their wardrobe to complement his and hers both. They wore the slate grey coats he'd seen hidden under crates of booze in Aransa, but they'd been trimmed with piping of ochre-orange, like his own coat, and bloodstone red like her tunic. Such a small thing, but it was these deft moves of which Thratia was truly a master. Without so much as saying a word, their entourage presented as a cohesive unit, Detan's importance on par with Thratia's own. His auntie wouldn't take long to figure out what hand Thratia was about to deal her.

Ranalae stood at his auntie's right. For a breathless moment, she was all he could see, though she spared him little more than a cool glance. Auntie Honding, however, appeared to be trying to render him into mush with the sheer force of her glare.

"Well met under blue skies, Warden Ganal, nephew." Auntie Honding had gotten her smile back on, and made a perfect show of bowing over her upheld palms.

"Well met, Dame Honding," Thratia replied, and Detan bowed in sync with her to hide his smile at her casual dismissal of Ranalae's presence. At least they were of one mind when it came to that nasty piece of work.

She could not be ignored for long, however, as she had sighted the withered form of Callia at the end of Aella's leash. Her face twisted with disgust, smoothed away in haste, and she smiled with all her teeth at Aella.

"What have you done?"

The question took Detan by surprise. He'd expected shock, revulsion, anything except immediate acceptance.

He had not considered that she would assume Aella had been the source of Callia's ailment. Poor foresight, on his part. Just because he'd taken the little tyke for a normal child on first sighting didn't mean those around her had missed the signs. Aella had the blood of a killer in her veins – and she didn't even enjoy the act like any other self-respecting psychopath would.

"I have taken care of my ill mother," Aella said with impressive poise. She stroked Callia's hair, and that woman tilted her head to accept the affection. Whatever was left rattling around inside Callia's skull, it didn't appear to recognize Ranalae. Maybe it just saw another coat, and that was the extent of things.

"A strange illness."

"Callia's condition is unfortunate, but we are not here to discuss your past employee's health," Thratia interjected, cutting the rising tension between Aella and Ranalae short. "We are here to discuss the future of Hond Steading."

The Dame's brows lifted. "Are we? The future of this city is my prerogative, Warden, and I do not recall inviting you to offer advice."

Thratia's smile was slow as a rockcat who'd just slapped a paw down on its favorite prey. Detan steeled himself, knowing what was coming.

"And mine, sooner than you'd think. Your heir and I are to be married. We have come to celebrate the nuptials with you, and the handover of the city into his care, of course."

His auntie's gaze snapped to him, pure shock registering for just a moment before she managed to compose herself. Detan forced himself to stand still and tall, his face impassive, as Dame Honding took in the situation in full. Her gaze did not fail to linger on the harpoons lining the deck of the *Dread Wind*, and for that he was proud of her.

"An interesting travel arrangement for a wedding procession," she said dryly. "Tell me, nephew, is this... arrangement to your liking as well?"

If the pits opened up and swallowed them all right at that moment, he could die a happy man, but they'd never been likely to do what he'd wanted, and today was no exception. He plastered on the breezy smile of a spoiled aristocrat, content to have a headstrong spouse take the reins, and shrugged.

"I cannot think of a stronger match." Which was true enough, in a literal sense. He'd bet damn near anything that Thratia could arm wrestle half the women in the Scorched into submission.

"I see. I would like a moment alone with my nephew, if that is all right with you, Warden?"

She flicked a dismissive hand. "He is his own man. Take your time. Ranalae and I have much to discuss."

Detan was a little insulted to realize Thratia didn't think he had the balls to say what he felt in private, but then, she probably believed he had acquiesced in truth to her plan. The very sight of a whitecoat had once been enough to make Detan leap, blindly, from Thratia's dock. She had no reason to doubt that the threat of them taking the imperial throne, and ultimately Hond Steading, would be enough to win him to her as a reluctant ally.

Fool of a woman.

Detan followed his aunt to her private cabin, doing his best to ignore the sideways stare Ranalae had locked on him. Let her stare all she liked; he was beyond her reach, now. Thratia's protection aside, if she so much as grabbed for him he'd drop this ship from the sky, and he'd bet anything that she knew it, too.

His auntie's cabin was sparse, but well-lit, which was rather unfortunate, as the sharp light emphasized every line of the scowl that marred her usually genteel features.

"What in the pits are you doing, young man? I haven't seen a sliver of you since you left Valathea, and now you show up on my doorstep with an invading army – the commander of which you, apparently, intend to wed? Is this how I raised you?"

"*Left* Valathea? I fled that nightmare, Auntie, and if you haven't seen a trace of me since that day then I assure you it was for your own safety – and that of everyone in Hond Steading."

She drew back, her hip knocking the edge of a shelf, and in that slightest of movements, that wrinkled fear around her too-sharp eyes, Detan knew.

Dame Honding: the only family he had left, the woman who had raised him after his parents' deaths, the singular protectress of all Hond Steading, knew what he was. Knew what had really happened on the side of a firemount all those years ago, when he'd blown a selium pipeline to smithereens and all the miners with it. She knew, and she'd sent him willingly to the Bone Tower. There was no other reason for her to be afraid of him now. He'd never been one to strike out – but a man of his power with his ire up around so much selium could be a deadly thing indeed.

"You knew. You fucking knew, and you told me nothing." He wanted to raise his voice, to clench his fists and shout the sky down around her, but he simply didn't have it in him. Oh, the anger was there, he could feel it bubbling just beneath the surface of his skin, but it seemed a distant thing to him now, the sting of her betrayal hollowed by time and distance. And Aella's training, he'd have to give her credit for that.

"I guessed, I did not know."

"And you?"

She stared down her nose at him. "I have no sel-sense, as Eletraia was always quick to remind me."

That name, so long buried, opened a sinkhole in his heart. "Do not blame any of this on my mother. If you even suspected, you should have tested me earlier – told me what I was capable of. You sure as the pits are black shouldn't have sent me out on the fucking line to endanger everyone!"

"Your mother – and I will say my sister's name as I please, boy – was supposed to pass the knowledge to you, and if not her then your father after her. I had no way of knowing she'd failed in her task."

"She was dead before I was twelve! And my father damned near jumped into the grave after her – she – she tried, I think, but there was so little time."

"And what was I supposed to do with you, after I'd discovered her failure to teach you restraint? She'd never deigned to tell me her techniques, even though the fire she held consumed her from within, so when Ranalae offered to take you in and teach you discipline, how was I to decline? I am sorry I sent you away, but it was far too dangerous to keep you here, you must see that. And spreading the rumor that you'd lost your sel-sense kept you safe, kept your people open to loving you should the Bone Tower ever teach you well enough to return. But when I heard you'd run away from them–"

He thrust a trembling hand between them. "Stop. Just. Stop. Teach me discipline? Run away? Have you no fucking clue what Ranalae is, what actually happens in the Bone Tower? It's not named for its pretty white walls, Auntie. It's named for the experiments-turned-corpses buried at its feet."

"The empress would never–"

"The empress is dead!" Shit. He hadn't meant to say that, hadn't meant to clue his auntie in to Thratia's little tale of a political coup. He needed his auntie blind to Thratia's motives, needed her to keep Ranalae around so that the imperial fleet's presence would perform as a stopgap to keep Thratia from swooping right in. Without Ranalae's numbers here, bolstering the city's defenses, Thratia may not even need him to take control.

And then he'd be given over into Aella's complete care. Thratia's loyalties were to her own power, and the second she didn't need him as an heir she'd relegate him to specimen.

"Don't be a fool," she snapped. "I received a letter from her just this morning."

Delivered by Ranalae's couriers, no doubt, but he wasn't about to press the point.

"You washed your hands of me. You cut me loose, bundled me away to the whitecoats and never gave it a second thought. Did you ever write to them to ask how my so-called training was going? Did you ever inquire after their methods of teaching? No, you fucking didn't, because as strong as you are, as clever as you are, I think you knew.

"Not wholly, not the complete picture, but a smart woman like you should have a pretty good idea of what an empire would do with a man who could be turned into a walking weapon. But you saw a solution to your little problem, a way to clean up the mess you felt my mother left behind, so you shoved me away behind those walls, across a sea, and thought no more of me.

"Were you afraid, when you'd heard I'd escaped? You must have had an idea as to why." He stepped forward.

She stepped back. He let the words course through him, let the old hurts bleed out through his lips, and marveled, silently, that he didn't feel the slightest urge to tear the sky to pieces while he rode his anger.

"You must have wondered if I might come home, looking for vengeance. Is that why you only ever wrote to me of banal things? Is that why all your letters were about who married who, and what crops were doing well that year? To keep an eye on my mental stability without ever asking outright? Not once. Not fucking once, did you ask what had happened to me there. Did you ask if I was safe? If I was hurting? You let the rumors swirl about a disgraced lord who'd lost his sel-sense and turned to conning for food and fun, and stuck your head deep in the sand.

"If you're angry at all that I've come here with Thratia on my arm, you have only yourself to blame. You cut me loose, left me to suffer, and didn't so much as send a bouquet of flowers, but you couldn't be bothered to renounce me as heir, either, and now it's biting you straight in the ass, isn't it?"

"I didn't abandon you," she whispered, and he felt ill to see a sheen of tears building in the corners of her eyes. "Tibal was supposed to–"

"What the fuck do you know about Tibal?"

She pressed her lips shut hard, as if to snap back the words. "He never told you?"

A knock on the door made them both jump. "Everything all right in there?" Aella's voice, smooth, but tinged with warning. His senses had reached out without his conscious agreement at Tibs's name, he hadn't even noticed. Some wounds were just too fresh to risk picking at. Whatever his auntie thought she knew about Tibs would have to wait.

"Fine," he grated, reeling himself back under control. Aella must have jumped out of her skin when she'd felt him reach out like a shockwave. His sphere of influence was beginning to unsettle even himself. It seemed every time he reached, he reached farther than before. Not necessarily a good thing, when one was surrounded by five active selium mines. He'd better get off this ship, before his auntie got them all blown to bits.

"Did Pelkaia make it here?" he asked. She blinked, the change in subject sudden enough to take her off guard.

"Yes – and your friends, Tibal, Ripka, and those others. I don't like that Honey woman."

"I don't really care what you like." The words were out before he could stop them, his temper still high though he'd reeled in his power. As a young man, he would have rather cut his own tongue out than speak this way to her. His auntie had been the domineering force of his life ever since the day his mother had died – for his father's spirit had fled on that day, as well – guiding, but always firm. Now, he'd discovered there were greater terrors in the world. And he'd faced them, and won.

And would again.

"You really are just like Elatraia. Careful it doesn't burn you up from the inside, too."

He ignored the jab, and fell back on formality. "We will bring the *Dread Wind* to the palace to begin preparations for the marriage ceremony. See that my friends come to see me."

"They have fled into the city, or so my guards tell me. I have no way of contacting them."

"Fled?"

A flicker of uncertainty crossed her face. "I had placed them under house arrest at the Hotel Cinder until this whole silly invasion of your betrothed was over. They took poorly to the treatment."

He snort-laughed. "I can only imagine. Why in a clear sky would you ever find it necessary to lock them up?"

"They intervened one too many times in my methods of preparing the city."

"Do you know how you can be certain you've walked down the wrong path?"

"I suspect you'll tell me."

"Ripka Leshe disagrees with you."

"This is my city."

"For now," he said, and sighed, reaching up to drag a hand through the hair he'd worked so hard to arrange into nobleman perfection. "Be safe, Auntie."

She reached to him, fingers curling to clasp his shoulder, but he had already turned, and felt little more than the brush of her fingertips against his sleeve. The air had grown cooler while he'd been in that cabin, the sunlight muted by a lazy drifting of clouds. He shoved his hands into his pockets and strolled over to Thratia's side, sliding his affable smile back into place like slotting a key.

"Auntie Honding has offered us use of her private dock for the *Dread Wind* while you and I prepare for the happily-ever-after."

Thratia's brows lifted, but Dame Honding had followed him out just close enough to have overheard, and she nodded mute agreement.

"This is preposterous," Ranalae insisted, her color already up as she continued on whatever argument she and Thratia had been having before the Hondings reappeared. "Dame Honding does not wish to relinquish control of her family's holdings to you, Thratia. We all know this wedding is a farce. To the pits with your heir, Dame, this is an invasion – though a subtle one. Our fleet is well equipped. If Thratia wishes to claim your city, then let her try to take it from us."

Dame Honding looked at Ranalae like she'd discovered a stray dog digging up her garden. "Hond Steading stays in the Honding family blood, and Detan is my only heir. Who he chooses to wed is his own business."

"You wrote to our empress asking for protection from this woman, and now you spread your arms and welcome her to your family bosom?"

"Are you blind, or just stupid?" Detan said, keeping his voice level lest Aella get jumpy over him arguing with a whitecoat – with *the* whitecoat.

"Excuse me, boy?"

"Boy?" Detan snorted and pulled himself to his full height. All this bickering was beginning to wear on him. "I am heir to this city, Ranalae, while you are little more than its guest."

"This city is defended." She spread her arms to indicate the ships she'd brought with her, mingled in amongst Hond Steading's regular fleet. It made him ill to see them there, the weapons of a monster arrayed like spike pits around the city he loved.

"By me." Detan held up a hand, a casual gesture, and poised his fingers as if ready to snap them. "Would you care to do battle, Ranalae of the Bone Tower? You know what I am, let's not forget that, and you know who's been training me. Tell me, do you think your ships could answer your call before I dropped them all from the sky? You are correct – this negotiation is a polite farce. But it is a farce because we could wipe you from the sky without a thought, you dribbling sycophant."

"You would destroy all those lives, just to prove a point?"

"Ranalae, I would burn the very ship I stand on now

if I could be assured no trace of you or your forces would be left on this world."

He turned, taking Thratia's elbow firmly in hand as if he did so all the time, and called over his shoulder. "Make the dock ready, we will arrive before nightfall."

When they were back on the heavy deck of the *Dread Wind*, Thratia extricated her arm from his grip and raised a brow at him. "Impressive performance, Honding. I almost believed you'd burn us all myself."

He closed the space between them, set both palms against the cabin wall to either side of her face, and leaned down, over her. "That was no performance, lover. If I have a chance to burn that woman and all that would continue her work from the world, make no mistake: I will take it, no matter the cost."

CHAPTER 31

Hond Steading buzzed with rumors under the shadows of the invading fleet. They pressed Ripka on all sides, fragments of whispers and declarations of doomsday following her down every street. Her only consolation was that Tibal, Enard, and Dranik looked just as wary as she did. Though she missed having Honey at her side, she was glad they'd left the injured woman with Latia to rest. The streets hummed with tension, and Ripka held no doubts that Honey would have itched to add to their song. She hoped Latia kept Honey well sedated while they were gone.

A beggar woman stepped into Ripka's path. Rags impregnated with dust draped her body, and she clutched a paper-wrapped bouquet of hastily plucked pricklebrush flowers, their petals drooping and only half the thorns stripped from their stems.

"Flowers for the royal wedding?" she asked, shoving one hand forward with a cupped palm for grains.

Foul breath gusted against Ripka's cheek, but she'd spent more than enough time working with the beggars of Aransa to be put off by such a simple thing. "What wedding?" she asked, digging in her pockets to make the woman linger.

"The only rumor that's true!" the woman crowed. She glanced left and right, then leaned forward and brought a hand up to shield the side of her lips as she whispered. "The Lord Honding has returned and is to wed Thratia Ganal."

Ripka froze. "That can't be right."

"Got it off the palace guards themselves." She wiggled her hand, and Ripka deposited a copper grain into it mechanically. The woman moved to give her a flower, but she waved her off.

"For the information," she said, and the woman gave her what might have been a sarcastic bow before trundling away to find her next mark.

For a moment, all four of them just stood there, contemplating the woman's information, and Ripka was glad for the silence of her companions. Her gaze dragged across the dusty streets of the city and found the massive shape of Thratia's new flagship, the *Dread Wind*, drifting with slow precision toward the towers of the Honding family palace. Her fleet remained on the edge of the city, poised for action, but not invading. Not yet. Why should they, when their mistress was prepared to marry the city's heir and take the throne through legal means?

Clever bitch. She'd spent years positioning herself in Aransa to be elected to the Warden's seat, nice and smooth, when the position finally opened up. Ripka had assumed she'd use Detan as a weapon, if she could force him to do her bidding. She had not considered that she might force him to her bed.

Nausea gripped her at the thought, and she shook it away. Detan was in a dire position, but he was not without teeth of his own. And yet…

He was her friend. Her friend was up there, on that ship, just out of reach. Being paraded around like a trophy. Subjected to... perhaps, well. Her stomach clenched. She could not form the word in her mind. Just thinking around its edges made her want to rally all of Hond Steading's watchers and storm that ship, rip Detan from Thratia's vile hands.

"We have to get word to him, somehow, that we can help..."

"Not exactly on friendly terms with the palace," Tibal said.

"We're not, no. But Pelkaia is."

"Last she saw him, she looked willing to rip his face off, and I don't think this news will smooth matters over much."

"Are you saying we shouldn't try?"

Tibal's head dropped as he kicked at the ground and tugged his hat down to hide his eyes. "No, Captain. Just sayin' we don't know where his mind is."

"You really think he's skipping through fields of flowers hand-in-hand with Thratia?"

"No." The word was harsh, bitter. "But I'm not sure us interfering would help him any, and we got our own troubles to manage."

"You're certain he doesn't want her?" Dranik asked, a deep furrow between his brows. Ripka coughed over a laugh. Of course he wouldn't know any better. None of the citizenry of Hond Steading had heard anything but wild rumor about their heir for the last few years, and none of it added up to make Detan look like a particularly stable individual. Marrying a bloodthirsty tyrant just might seem like a grand ole time to him, as far as they knew.

"There are few people in this world Detan hates more

than Thratia, and I'm reasonably certain that the only reason she doesn't return the sentiment is because she can't be bothered mustering up the energy to care one way or another. He's a tool for her to gain the throne legally, nothing more."

"Why would he agree to such a match, then?"

Tibal snorted and stared pointedly at the heavy ships spread across the sky like ink stains. "Because he doesn't want bloodshed in this city any more than we do. Damn fool is probably arrogant enough to think he'll retain some control of his throne after he's hitched himself off to her."

"I pray he's not stupid enough to bed her, then," Dranik said.

Enard, Ripka, and Tibal exchanged a look. It was Ripka who managed to ask, "Why is that?"

"If she cares so little for him, then once he gets an heir on her he'll be useless to her."

"Shit," Tibal said.

Ripka closed her eyes and rubbed the bridge of her nose with thumb and forefinger. "We have to get a message through to him, somehow. If she casts him off…"

"Aella will catch him," Enard said.

The three shivered. Dranik looked thoroughly put out. "Who is Aella?"

"A nasty little friend of Thratia's," Ripka sighed and opened her eyes. Time to focus. "Come, let's get this meeting with your people over with, Dranik. Maybe they'll have some information we can use."

Dranik led them to an inconspicuous door along a street full of mercer houses. Judging by the sweet scent emanating from within, they were at the trade room of a bright eye berry distributor. Not the most nefarious of locales, but Ripka knew from long experience that a posh setting often hid the darkest of dealings.

Dranik scarcely knocked once before the door swung open. A barrel-chested man with a moustache drooping down past the line of his chin set a wary squint on them all.

"Dranik tole me two ladies were comin'," he said, and jabbed a finger at Tibal. "Unless you're particularly ugly, miss, you and your manfriend there are unexpected company. Not much a fan of uninvited guests."

"We need all the help we can get," Dranik shot back, throwing glances over both his shoulders. No one would have had reason to be suspicious of a plain trading house until he started up that darting glance nonsense. Ripka sighed and stepped forward, extending her hand to the man.

"I understand and respect your caution. My name is Ripka, and I can assure you these men are of the same mind as I."

He took her hand and squeezed it a touch too hard. "Name's Calson, and I appreciate your forwardness, but I'd like to know just what mind you're of. Dranik gave us warning you were coming, and told us why, but I'd rather hear it straight from your lips, miss, if you don't mind my saying so. Lot of tension 'round these parts. You understand."

Not only did she understand, she was absolutely relieved that someone had a suspicious bent in this group. If they really did accept her without so much as a sideways glance she'd be wondering if they really were working for Thratia.

She squeezed his hand with equal measure. "The three of us were all present when Thratia took Aransa."

The words *when Aransa fell* were on the tip of her tongue. She forced herself to bite them back. "And we'd like to help see her succeed here in Hond Steading. There are four of us, another woman as you were told, but she's recovering from an injury. She should be with us at the next meeting."

"Funny thing, leaving Aransa after the takeover if you felt positively toward our warden."

She shrugged. "We're wanderers by nature. Some souls just can't sit still."

"And anyway," Tibal interjected, "Thratia's people got a hand on Aransa. It's Hond Steading that needs help."

"True enough," Calson said. It was a marvel, the way Tibal could speak something he thought was true but have it mean something entirely different to the person he was speaking to. No wonder he and Detan had worked up quite the reputation as con men across the Scorched.

"Time's wasting," Dranik said, "and we have a mission tonight, don't we?"

"So we do. Follow me, then." Calson waved an arm, and they trailed after him down a long hallway.

The meeting hall for Dranik's underworld compatriots looked like it was more accustomed to meetings of accountants than thieves. Pyramids of the bright eye berry seed dotted the floor along the wall, their aroma sharp and tangy in the air. Massive scales served as the room's only decor, taking up half the surface of the long table the conspirators were now gathered around. After she was seated, Ripka found the presence of the scales irritating, as every other time she glanced to face whoever was speaking, the polished bronze threw light into her eyes.

"These here are the extra hands Dranik promised us," Calson said, then rattled off a list of names of the six around the table so quickly that Ripka didn't manage to catch a single one of them.

"Thratia's here, it's time to begin," a scarred woman with two prominent front teeth was saying. Ripka hadn't caught her name, but she figured it probably didn't matter. The woman had a high, whining voice, and smelled faintly of donkeyshit.

"We haven't received word from any of our contacts yet. It's too soon, we must be patient," Calson said in his slow, placating voice.

"Did you not have a mission prepared tonight?" Enard asked, all oblique innocence. The group shifted uneasily as one. Dranik may have vouched for them, and they were obviously in need of the numbers, but still the presence of the newcomers made them uneasy – especially with their mistress close to hand.

"Thing is," Calson drawled as he leaned back in his chair and settled his arms over the curve of his belly, "I haven't decided if you're invited yet."

Dranik's cheeks grew crimson and he laid both of his palms down on the table as if he were holding himself in place. "We need the help, and these three are better suited to the work than we are. Do you remember what happened last time? Kleesie nearly got her head torn off, and I remember you damn near shitting yourself."

"No language like that in this room," Calson said. "Your concerns are noted, Dranik, but you're telling me these three new friends of yours are practiced at violence, right? Well that just makes me even jumpier around them – sorry, folks, but things are just too tense and I can't trust new blood with the more delicate matters. You understand."

"I don't, actually." Ripka leaned forward, folding her hands together on the tabletop as if she were entering into a negotiation. Or an interrogation. "We're mercenaries, and we've expressed our intended loyalty. You know anything about mercenaries, you know they don't buck a job until it's done. We wish to see Thratia get what she deserves, and frankly I don't think your little group here has what it takes to pull that off."

"Mercenaries, is it? Thought you were all just wanderers. Mercenaries get paid, lass, what're you asking in payment?"

Enard flashed a grin she'd only seen him muster once before – when he'd faced down his old Glasseater gangmates on the beach of the Remnant. "We're not in need of grains, if that's what you're asking. Sometimes, people like us, we just like to take a little pleasure in doing a job well. Understand?"

Tension webbed the wrinkles around Calson's eyes, his hands flexed on the tabletop. Everyone in his group was looking at him, save Dranik, who stared at Enard as if he'd never seen him before. Ripka couldn't blame him. The first time she'd seen Enard switch from affable, sweet New Chum to the hard-boned man who'd been a valet for the Glasseaters she'd damned near choked on air, too.

"Telling me you're in it for the love of the work?" Calson said.

"I'm telling you we're in. That's all you need to know."

"He's got a point," a scrawny man with a surprisingly well-tailored suit said. Ripka'd pegged him as the owner of the counting house. "We're not fighters, Calson. And we need some to do right by our assignments."

Tibal isn't a fighter either, Ripka thought, but judging by this group she had no doubt he'd handle himself a whole pits lot better in a sticky situation than any one of them.

Calson sighed and leaned back, letting his arms go slack at his sides. "All right then. Dranik, we'll let your friends play tonight. As a trial only. Anything I don't like happens and you're all out – you too, Dranik."

Dranik nodded. "You won't regret it."

The bucktoothed woman snorted, proving herself more astute than she let on.

"We're agreed, then," Ripka said, "now let's hear what's expected for this job."

Calson ruffled his hair, grimaced, then pulled a leather-wrapped bundle of papers from his interior jacket pocket and dropped it on the table with a puff of dust.

"Orders came in this morning. Got a new mark."

"Another deviant?" the wiry man asked.

"Aye," Calson said.

Ripka stiffened, and listened to the details of the woman they were meant to sell into slavery for Thratia Ganal.

CHAPTER 32

Detan was home. The *Dread Wind* listed in the dock at the Honding family palace, its bulk throwing shadows over the finely manicured courtyard below. All around him servants and crewmembers darted to and fro, moving crates of supplies and essentials off the ship and into palace rooms. Thratia had disembarked some time ago, seeking a room high in the palace's most prestigious tower. Aella had probably scurried after her, seeking living arrangements that didn't sway with every breeze.

But Detan just stood there, rooted to the spot at the fore rail, watching the hustle and bustle of the ship's arrival. Rumors of his impending nuptials drifted on whispered conversations. Wary glances came his way, then darted aside at the slightest hint of his notice. He ignored them.

He was home, and he was not, and what was worst of all, Tibal's flier, his flier, the *Happy Birthday Virra!* drifted, tethered to a narrow spire of the palace. His chest ached to know that Tibal was not in the room beside the craft.

"Do you require assistance, young Master Honding?"

A man in the tight, black livery of his family approached him. Salt-white hair curled over his temples, storm-blue eyes peering out at him from within sunken walnut skin. Detan knew those eyes, though the face holding them was much older now. He knew the restrained amusement in the old man's features, too.

"Gatai?"

The man winked and bowed. "Forever at your service, young master."

Detan damned near giggled with glee. To the pits with decorum, he threw his arms around the old man's shoulders and gathered him in for a tight hug. Gatai grunted, peeling himself away with reserved dignity.

"Gatai! You old codger, I can't believe auntie hasn't kicked you to the streets yet. Weren't you dogging the maids' skirts last time I was here?"

Gatai's brows rose. "The other valets' coattails, more like, but I've settled down with a man nearly my own age now."

"You, romancing someone your age? I can hardly believe it."

Gatai bowed his head. "It's true, young master. We've adopted a little girl together. Trella. But I hear you are prepared to settle down yourself, now?"

The quick twitch at the corner of Gatai's lips was all Detan needed to understand exactly what he thought of the match, and Detan really couldn't blame the man. If someone had told him just a few months ago that he'd be swinging into matrimony with Thratia Ganal, he would have lost his lunch all over their shoes.

"Politics does funny things to a man," Detan said, casting his voice low so that they would not be overheard.

"Ah. I'm sorry to hear it, then."

Detan slung an arm around his old valet's shoulders and steered him down the gangplank. When his boots hit the hard stones of the Honding palace's dock, a faint shudder rocked through him, one Gatai was polite enough to pretend he hadn't noticed.

Gatai's discretion was legendary, his charm a veritable force of nature, and if Detan hadn't had him in his life in those early years after the passing of his mother and father he was certain that he and his auntie would have torn one another to pieces before he'd ever gotten old enough to manifest his deviant ability. If there were anyone he could trust in his old home, it was Gatai. He hoped.

If things had changed so much for the worse that even Gatai would betray him, then he wasn't convinced the victory he sought was worth having.

"You see and hear everything that goes on in these halls, don't you, old man?"

Gatai quirked his head to the side in a shallow attempt to hide a prideful smile. "Keen listening is very much a part of my profession, young master. As you well know, it is my duty to be ready to meet your needs before you've even expressed them."

"And to think we use such a marvelous ability for little more than seeing our clothes are laid out and our schedules managed."

"Some more astute members of the household have experimented in varied uses of my skill sets, young master."

"Ah, yes, I do remember how deftly you can shin up a tree."

He shifted, embarrassed. "A good valet is able to manifest the skills the moment requires."

"A school of thought, I confess, I stole from you."

"And has the young master taken up the valet profession?"

Detan flashed him a sharp smile. "If the occasion suits me."

"I had heard much to that effect."

He didn't much like the idea of dwelling on just what, exactly, Gatai had heard in the years after he'd escaped the Bone Tower and wandered the Scorched in search of something – anything – to make him feel safe and whole again. Something he still hadn't found.

"And we return to those marvelous ears of yours."

With firm pressure he guided Gatai down the paths he remembered were little used in the palace, and after a moment's observation Gatai returned the pressure, easing Detan down hallways he didn't recognize that were blissfully empty. Detan could have kissed the man, if he weren't worried he'd cut his lips on that razor beard of his.

"You have, perhaps, a particular sound you were considering?"

"It has been a long time since I've been home," his voice caught over the final word, the word he'd been trying to keep out of his mind ever since Thratia had forced him to watch the skyscape of Hond Steading roll into view. "And I'm sure there have been many changes, many things I've missed. I have heard, for instance, that friends of mine stopped by in my absence but were treated with poor care by my dear auntie. We know she tries, of course, but running this city of ours can just be so stressful."

His heart thundered so that he felt certain Gatai could hear the frantic thump of it straight through all the layers of clothing Thratia had draped him in. Some things just couldn't be hidden by finery. This was it. If Gatai brushed him off now, he'd know himself to be truly alone in this palace that was meant to be his.

"The Dame, great though her wisdom is, may have overreacted in the case of your friends. Tensions are high in the city, of course."

"Of course," Detan agreed quickly. "And I, as her devoted nephew, would love the chance to explain to my friends that her hostility was not cause for scorn..."

Gatai was not leading him toward his rooms. Though he'd been gone years, he'd scrambled up and down the steps to his suite of private rooms countless times in his life. He knew, no matter where he was in the palace, where his bed lay – like an extension of himself, a phantom limb. His rooms had defined his world as long as he could remember, the time of sharing a bed with his parents lost to the fuzzy memory of early age. They had been his sanctuary. And Gatai was leading him in the other direction.

He tensed, preparing to push Gatai away should he need to free himself. "Has auntie moved my rooms?"

"Not at all. But Cook Rachie has sweated all morning over your favorite handpie, and I won't see her effort gone to waste. The pantry, if you remember, is this way, young master."

"I remember."

Which was, of course, an understatement. If his room had been his sanctuary, the pantry had been his hideout. He didn't care to remember the amount of times Gatai had found him there as a young lad, escaping punishment, or hiding away so that the staff of the palace would not see his tear-puffed eyes. It was not exactly an auspicious place to hold a meeting. But it was the quietest room in the palace, a place where a young boy had once secreted himself away to cry and rail at the frustrations of his mother's illness.

Gatai, that clever old goat. He had something to tell Detan. Something he didn't want half the household eavesdropping on.

Buried beneath the palace, the pantry never quite shook off the cold of the earth. Detan shivered, glad of the fine coat Thratia had given him – then desired nothing more than to rip the garment off and set it alight. He crossed his arms to still his hands while Gatai assured himself the place was empty and the door securely latched.

"This place has grown ears," Gatai said.

"That's a biological impossibility."

"You know very well what I mean, young master."

Detan paced a tight circle around a fig barrel. "I expect no less from my dear auntie and Thratia both. I've assumed myself eavesdropped upon from the moment I…" Bent knee to Aella. He swallowed, waved away the rest of his sentence as if it didn't matter. "I am used to playing a part, Gatai. Don't worry about this rockbrain."

"You do not understand." Gatai wrung his hands together, the most worried gesture Detan'd ever seen from the usually composed chap. "It is more than the usual listening – yes, and more than Thratia's spies as well. Ranalae has threaded her own people throughout the palace, throughout the *city*. Nothing happens here nor out there that she does not know about. Young master, forgive me, but… What are your intentions for Hond Steading?"

Detan swallowed. He'd already been less than enthusiastic with Gatai regarding his entanglement with Commodore Throatslitter, but to reveal all just might see him bound by a noose instead of a wedding band. Gatai's forehead furrowed in worry, re-creasing familiar lines. Lines Detan himself had given the poor man.

"To see it safe."

"Define safe." His old eyes hardened. He'd always made Detan say what he meant, instead of his usual dance around the particulars.

"No Thratia. No Ranalae."

"You?"

"I would prefer my auntie continue as she has, until she no longer can."

"And then?"

He hedged a glance toward the door, imagining the scuffle of feet, the rustle of cloth as an ear pressed against the door. Paranoia, plain and simple. The servants held this part of the house, and unless things had changed drastically since Detan's time, they were all fiercely loyal to their keymaster.

"I don't know. I suppose I'll ask the people, when it comes to that."

Gatai smiled slowly, and a tremble in his hands that Detan hadn't noticed before stilled. He was not asking Detan of his plans out of old friendship, then. He was asking because he had a daughter. Trella. Detan committed the name to memory.

"I always knew there was more than gravel between those ears of yours," Gatai said.

"Yeah, piss."

Gatai snort-chuckled and shook his head. "Language, young master. And be assured, the staff here is with you in whole. None of us wish to see a changeover in power, and we are all quite certain the majority of the city feels the same way. No one wants a coup into the hands of the likes of Ganal, or that Ranalae woman – she disturbs us all."

Detan went cold. "Has she harmed you, or any of the staff?"

He shook his head. "Not to my knowledge. It is not what she's done, so much as…" he waved a hand. "The way she looks at the world. It is difficult to articulate with care. Cook Rachie said she 'gives her the heebies', and that is as succinct as I can make the matter."

"If she shows too great an interest in any of the staff, alert me immediately."

Gatai bowed his head. "You have experience with this woman?"

"Experience I would like to forget." Detan shook off

the shadowed claws of Ranalae and pivoted focus to the slim glimmer of hope in his life. "There are two women on the *Dread Wind*, prisoners of Thratia's assistant, Aella. She has kept them as leverage against me and I – I have promised to see them freed, if I can at all manage it. Their names are Forge and Clink, and they are, to the best of my knowledge, the only prisoners traveling with Thratia's fleet. I need to find out where they're being held."

He bowed. "Consider it done. If they are in the palace, we will find them."

Relief washed through him. "Thank you. I will need them both, if anything I attempt to do here is to work."

"And what is it you will attempt to do?"

Detan cast his gaze around the spacious pantry, taking in the barrels of staples and delicacies both. Foodstuff that would soon be repurposed for his wedding feast. At least the booze would be good, Auntie Honding always stocked the best stuff. He blinked, staring at a barrel of mulled cider, the edges of an idea taking shape in his mind.

"I have a few options." He flashed Gatai a grin, but the stodgy old man seemed unimpressed. "Once you find the women, Gatai, if you could..." he swallowed, fearful of asking. "Do you think it possible you could find my friends? The ones auntie tried to lock in the Cinder?"

Gatai frowned. "Searching outside the palace is more difficult, especially for a group of people who have, no doubt, gone into hiding. I will send feelers out, and let you know what is discovered. Do not pin your hopes on the results, young master."

Detan sighed until he was completely deflated. "I am just so tired of working alone."

Gatai squeezed his shoulder. "Young master, you're not alone any more."

CHAPTER 33

Pelkaia dropped, feather-light, from the rope ladder dangling off the side of the *Larkspur* and stifled a wince as her bones jolted from the impact. Cursed city had to go and pave all its roads and walkways with the stone they'd carved out to make room for homes. She missed the soft dirt roads of Aransa. Bad for heavy carts, but at least they'd been kind to her joints.

Above her the crew of the *Larkspur* slept, and before her the nightlife of Hond Steading thrummed. In the wake of the warden of Aransa's death, that city had gone quiet – the citizens scurrying to their homes as quick as they could, doors locked and windows shuttered. This city, this place that had remained independent from Valathea and had its own long pride, went out to dance in the shadows of their invaders' ships.

Pelkaia prowled amongst them, wearing a stranger's face. She'd gone to a lot of trouble to get the set of her cheekbones just right, the tilt to her eyes and the small pucker of her false lips, hair carefully scraped back so that she didn't have to worry about it brushing her skin. She'd gone for forgettable, indistinct. But the truth was she couldn't shake the firmness of her walk, the confident lift of her shoulders.

It wasn't her own body language seeping through. She'd always been a furtive woman, careful and secretive. Such things had been required to survive as an illusionist so long in a society wherein that inborn talent meant death.

But something of Ripka Leshe had rubbed off on her, and she found she didn't want to shake it, though it made her illusions more difficult to perfect.

In every tavern, revelers toasted the health and good fortune of the happy couple. A practice Pelkaia had no stomach for. She could not even pretend to toast Thratia Ganal, even if it meant ingratiating herself within a likely group. She paced the streets, looped round and round neighborhoods, seeking a building with its lights on but a decidedly more somber crowd.

She found one at last, in a dark little corner of what she guessed to be an artisan neighborhood. Bright lights gleamed in the windows, and figures moved within, but with decidedly less pleasure. They sat hunched over their glasses, not clinking them together nor shouting lewd cheers.

Perfect.

Pelkaia slipped inside, remembering to round her shoulders to look less intimidating, and slouched her way over to an empty barstool. A few glanced her way, but quickly wrote her off as beneath notice.

The bartender gave her a sour look until she slid her a couple of copper grains, then the woman shrugged and poured out what was probably a short glass of cheap ale. Didn't even say a word to her. Pelkaia'd never met a quiet bartender in her life, but she didn't mind. Gave her a chance to listen in on the rumble of conversation in the room.

Which was, decidedly, less positive than the rest of the city. No surprise there – these weren't exactly happy folk – but the glum tenor she'd expected was laid over barely restrained anger. At the table nearest her, a man with shoulders that'd barely fit through the door clutched his mug like he was strangling a throat and didn't bother to keep his voice down.

"I'd kill the bitch myself, given half the chance."

"Good fucking luck," his friend said. "Don't call her Throatslitter for nothing."

"Fuuuck that. She think she can just roll over our city, sack up with the Honding heir, and everything's fucking grand? Everyone who's not a moron knows it's a sham anyway. Ladies don't usually show up for their wedding days with a fleet and a big ass warship, do they?"

"*My* kinda' lady would."

"Yeah. But you're an idiot."

Pelkaia let their bickering fall to the background as she considered her options. This man was obviously no fan of Thratia's – and by the looks of him he was used to violence – but could she use him? He wasn't a deviant, but having some dumb muscle on hand might be useful.

When the man wobbled for the door, Pelkaia trailed him on instinct, sticking to the shadows and subtly altering her face each time she was hidden so that he wouldn't recognize her from the tavern.

If the crew of the *Larkspur* wasn't willing to bring arms against Thratia, then she needed to find support elsewhere. This big bastard seemed as good a place as any to start.

She tracked his wobbling steps to a dusty apartment complex, one of many hunkered along the stone roads of Hond Steading. Such proud and foolish people, to build so high out of stone when they lived so near to firemounts. Not even the builders of Aransa were quite so arrogant as to build over two stories of stone.

While the man fumbled with the latch on his door, Pelkaia slipped around the side of the building and hunkered in shadow, considering. To approach the man now might be too forward – she would startle him, and lose his trust.

A hand closed around her arm.

She jumped, wrenching herself free, and spun around, hands dropping to the blades tucked beneath her jacket.

Coss frowned at her out of the dark. He shoved his hands in his pockets, shoulders hunched. "Pell. What in the skies are you doing?"

She eased her hands away from her weapons, trembling slightly with the flood of adrenaline, and smoothed her coat back in concealment. "Almost stabbing you, apparently. Why are you following me?"

He scowled. "Don't evade the question."

"Seeking recruits, if you must know."

"That man a deviant?"

She waved off the question. "I'm not sure."

His scowl was back in full force, his voice tight with restrained anger. "Just a random thug, then."

"Who wants to see Thratia out of his city. I think that's fair enough."

"Brutes from off the street? Is that what we do now? Is that how you plan to protect the people you claim to have saved, by dragging banal muscle on board? What if he's anti-deviant – did you even consider that? We're not exactly on stable footing here, Pell. The Dame tolerates us, but there's no telling how long that'll last if the public gets wind. Not a lot she could do against a mob."

"Exactly. We're weak, we must strengthen our numbers–"

"For what?"

She clamped her mouth shut, almost bit straight through her tongue, and grated, "You know what."

"Thratia. It's always about thrice-cursed Thratia."

"She murdered my *son*."

He grimaced and stepped back from the force in her words. "I know. I know. But that was a long time ago, and you have other charges now–"

"Charges? Deviants, Coss. We're all a bunch of fucking deviants. And always will be, unless we tear down those who would label us as such."

"We talked about this. They're not your soldiers."

"Which is why I'm out looking for willing hands! Yes, we did talk about this, and I've listened – I'm trying something new, aren't I? But you cannot expect me to do nothing. Gods beneath the dunes, Coss, Thratia is *here*, a half-mark's walk away from where we stand. If I didn't know that palace was brimming with Aella and her lot I'd saunter right in and take the woman's head with my own hands. But I can't, you know that. But neither can I let this opportunity pass. She's *so* close. Something must be done."

"Must? And you would risk the whole crew to get your revenge?"

"I never said–"

He held up a fist. "You didn't have to." He sighed and shifted his weight, tugging his coat close though the night was warm and held only a gentle breeze. "Take the night, Pell. Think it through. We're going to have to talk to the crew, you and I, about all this."

"We? It's my crew, Coss. My ship."

"Yeah," he said, and the sadness in his eyes was a punch to her gut. "And remember we can leave your ship any time we'd like."

"It's safer for us all, there."

"Is it?"

Before she could muster up an answer he turned and stomped back down the alley he'd used to sneak up on her, heavy coat flapping at his dusty heels.

Pelkaia glared at the shadow of the *Dread Wind* looming in the cloud-streaked sky above the palace, spit in the dust, and went in search of a room at an inn for the night.

CHAPTER 34

Her name was Sasalai, and Ripka had come here to steal her and sell her into slavery. Though most of the Honding staff lived in the palace, Sasalai's advanced age and long service had given her a home of her own in the expensive palace district. A humble house, by local standards, but a respectable construction of mudbrick faced in stone. A warm, clean little place in which she had raised her children and, later, her grandchildren.

She lived alone, now. That would make the kidnapping easier.

"I don't like this," Ripka whispered. She lounged alongside Enard on a bench in a nearby park. The slight knoll in the rock garden's center gave them a clear view of Sasalai's path home. Twilight settled on the land like a blanket, bringing with it a soft northern breeze and a brilliance of stars. The night was too lovely, too peaceful, to shelter such horrendous work. Enard squeezed her hand, twining his fingers in hers, and she squeezed back.

"We won't let them sell her off," he whispered in return.

"We can't promise that."

"I am promising that." His voice had a sharp edge to it that had been seeping out more and more since their time together on the Remnant.

"I believe you."

His shoulder eased against hers, tension releasing, and she leaned into him, just a touch. If she closed her eyes, or glanced away from the grandmother making her way home, Ripka could almost imagine them out to experience the night together for kinder reasons. But that was a path she dared not let her mind walk. Whatever grew between them, neither could risk the entanglement now. Not with everything drawing so close, so quickly. The slightest distraction could spell either of their deaths.

But it was nice to pretend, just for a little while.

"Here they come," Enard murmured.

Tibal and Calson strolled down the path toward Sasalai, two well-to-do gentlemen out for a midnight ramble. They slouched, gesturing broadly as they pretended at some good-natured argument, looking for all the world like they were meant to be there, like they were at ease. Tibal did, anyway. To Ripka's trained eye, Calson looked ready to bolt like a sandrat in a hawk's shadow.

"He's too tense."

Enard leaned forward, the muscles of his arm firm against hers. "She'll see through that."

"She's a grandmother. Her eyesight might not be the best."

"She's a grandmother who spent her whole life hiding a deviant ability while working in the Honding family palace."

"Good point." Ripka slipped her fingers free of Enard's so that she could settle them on the weapons at her waist. Not that she'd use any of them – even the cudgel seemed exceptionally cruel on a woman as old as Sasalai – but the threat of them might be enough to cow her.

Might be, but probably wasn't. In Ripka's experience, grandmothers feared nothing except running out of honey taffy.

Sasalai's persistent shuffling step slowed as she approached the gentlemen strollers. Her arm tightened around the cloth sack slung across her chest and shoulders. She thought them raucous youth, Ripka decided. Possible thieves, definite annoyances, but nothing more troubling than that. She leaned on her cane, tightening her grip in silent threat or anxiety – Ripka couldn't tell.

Ripka held her breath as the men approached, biting back a cry of warning. This moment was the very type of thing she'd trained most of her life to stop. She tried to tell herself this was little more than a demonstration, of sorts. The woman would be fine. Enard had promised her that, and Tibal would never cause her harm. But Calson was down there too, a wild card she did not know, and her teeth clenched and ground as the distance closed.

Tibal swayed, affecting drunkenness, and bumped Calson hard in the side. Calson stumbled sideways toward the woman, arms outstretched to right himself. A brown arc flashed through the air, the heavy crack of bone echoing over the sharp edge of a cry. Ripka was on her feet in an instant, Enard at her side, pounding down the knoll toward the scene.

It took her a moment to process. Calson lay on the road, curled up in a knot, both hands clasped around a shin that looked… Wrong. Ripka's stomach clenched as she realized the bone had been neatly bisected under the lash of Sasalai's cane, the skin intact but the limb itself clearly stepped down in one spot.

"Fiery pits." She skidded to a stop on the dusty road and dropped to one knee beside Calson while Enard looped around to help Tibal restrain the struggling granny.

"How bad is it?" Calson hissed through his teeth. His people crept toward them, hesitant steps shuffling on the dirt as they peeled themselves from their hiding places. Tibal and Enard had the woman well in hand, her mouth stuffed with a gag and her hands tied. If her glare had been able to cut, it would have, but for the moment she was restrained.

Ripka peeled one of his hands away and tried not to let her shock show as she examined the break. "The skin's not broken," she said, the most positive comment she could muster, "but you need an apothik."

"Shit shit shit," he groaned, and thumped the back of his head against the road.

"You." Ripka jabbed a finger at the buck-toothed woman. "Do you know where the nearest apothik is?"

"Just down Lighten Way," she said.

"Good, then you lot," she waved a hand at all those approaching. "Get a litter together to carry your boss, will you? Sooner this gets set, the better his chances of survival."

"Survival?" Calson asked, all the color draining from his face.

"Broken bones are dangerous." She mustered all the gravity she could and layered it thick into her voice. Clearly this man hadn't experienced so much as a cut requiring a stitch in all his life.

Enard, that beautiful man, was quick to catch on to her plan. "Hurry up," he said, stripping his jacket off. "Take my coat, it's long enough. If one of you grabs each corner, you should be able to carry him."

"But what about the mark?" Buck-toothed asked, squeezing Enard's jacket between her fingers.

"Kill her," Calson growled.

"Hasty," Ripka chided. She pushed to her feet while the others hesitantly set about laying out Enard's coat and rolling the writhing man onto it. "The job still holds. Dranik knows where to find your contact. Don't worry, we'll get her there."

Wariness lined Calson's face, but shattered under pain as they jostled him onto the coat. "If she fights you–"

"I have her," Tibal said, letting his disgust with Calson's need for revenge show plain as a clear sky.

Calson sneered, but whether it was due to pain or Tibal, Ripka couldn't tell.

"Aren't you glad you brought us on after all?" Enard said, flashing Calson a smile, and that time he definitely did sneer.

"Hurry, he's looking too pale," Ripka threw in, just to get Calson to shut up and get his lackeys moving. With nervous glances all around, the awkward litter-bearers shuffled off with their wounded boss, throwing glances back over their shoulders at Ripka all the way. She had to resist an urge to flash them a rude gesture.

"Well," Enard said once the others were out of earshot. "That worked out well."

The old woman scowled around at them all.

"We should probably get off the main street, anyone could see," Dranik piped up. Sweat dotted his forehead despite the cool night air.

"Which way then, lad?" Tibal drawled, and the color came back into Dranik's cheeks full force as he flushed with embarrassment. "Right. Right. This way."

He angled toward the south end of the park, a narrow little lane Ripka had scouted on her way in and found mostly deserted at this time of night. A good enough move for now. She allowed herself to relax, just slightly, eyeing the woman Tibal led along by her bound wrists. She wanted to peel that gag from her lips, to explain herself and her friends – to tell the woman she was safe, and that her only trouble tonight was a bit of momentary discomfort and fright. But, despite Enard's confidence, Ripka was not so sure. They needed inroads to Thratia's network, and every time you knocked on that woman's door you risked losing the hand you knocked with.

"Who is this contact, anyway?" she asked as they padded along the dark lane.

"We don't know her name," Dranik said, "she's called the Songstress."

"Fuck," Ripka said.

CHAPTER 35

Detan told himself he wasn't hiding. He was regrouping, settling in, recovering, preparing himself for what was to come.

He'd never hide when there was work to be done. No, not Detan Honding.

He pulled a blanket over his head, and stared at the false stars his adjusting eyes made of the light seeping through the fabric. He breathed deep of the musky-warm aroma of the blanket. The harsh soaps of his childhood filtered through to him, reminded him of sneaking through the laundry rooms as a child for a hint of what went on in that mysterious, steamy place. And the memory of being cuffed on the back of the head for getting in the washers' way.

Bundled away in his old bed, the mattress permanently dented in a shape that was much like his own, only smaller, he could pretend for a while that stealing a sweet pie was going to be the greatest adventure of his day.

But then reality had to go and ruin it all.

In the hall outside his door footsteps picked up as

the lunch hour grew near. The whole staff of the palace must be bending their backs to accommodate the sudden influx of Thratia's entourage. The longer he lay here, the sooner someone important would come and find him. Thratia, Aella, Auntie Honding. He tried to imagine which one it would be, or who would send a servant first to collect him, and decided to the pits with waiting around for that.

Detan threw the blankets off himself and swung his feet to the ground. He yanked his boots on and tugged his charcoal jacket straight, running a hand through his hair to set it to rights.

He opened the door, and damn near tripped over Misol.

"Come to invite me to tea?" he asked.

She looked naked without her spear, hands folded defensively across her ribs. At least his auntie had put her foot down about Thratia's people running around the house while openly armed.

"Aella wants you."

"And do you just hop right up and do whatever she asks?"

She cocked her head to the side. "She's my boss."

"She's your jailer."

Misol bared her teeth at him, but said nothing.

"Make no mistake, she's mine, too."

"Thought that was Thratia."

"Had to tell where one begins and the other ends."

"Honding," Misol's voice took on a hard edge. "Are you going to make this difficult for me, or will you shut your trap and come along?"

"I'll come, but I can make no guarantees about the state of my trap."

"Marvelous." She stalked off down the hall. Detan

pattered along like a good little prisoner, chafing at being ordered about in what was meant to be his own house. Never mind that being in control of anything at the moment was an illusion. He still had his ego to think of, after all.

Misol led the way to a wing of the palace generally reserved for the most important guests his family hosted, and Detan grew more annoyed with each step he took. Sure, Thratia deserved to be put up with a bit of polish, but Aella? That little monstress was likely to leave a few bloodstains on his auntie's nicest carpets. She was more suited to a dungeon than a suite.

He recalled the narrow tower Thratia had purpose built in her compound for his arrival, and winced. Maybe it was better that his auntie treated her like a normal guest. At least a regular room was less likely to give him a case of the shivers.

And wow, had his auntie ever put Aella up in splendor. Each step they took Detan noted the change in decor, and dredged up old memories of this wing. If Misol wasn't lost, Aella'd been tucked away in one of the nicest rooms in the place. Probably even nicer than what his auntie had handed over to Ranalae, and that made him grin. If Aella was being over-honored, at least Ranalae was being insulted in the process.

Misol knocked once on a door at the end of the hall and swung it open before waiting for a response. Detan's power fled him, a numb, wooly feeling indicative of Aella's will taking its place. He stepped hesitantly into the room, wondering what fresh nightmare Aella had created to test him now, and choked on a scream.

Aella sat in a high-backed chair at a small round table, glancing over the gilded rim of a teacup to the woman who sat beside her. Ranalae. Their postures were mirrored, elegant and firm, but while Aella glanced to Ranalae, that woman's gaze was locked tight on Detan. At their feet, Callia huddled, the silver chain which Aella used to guide her puddled between her shoulder blades.

Detan turned, heart thundering, but Misol barred his way, her sturdy frame filling the doorway. She caught his eye, held it, and there was something like regret in her expression. Whole fucking lot of good her regret would do for him now.

"Leaving so soon?" Ranalae mused.

Detan breathed slowly, deeply, straightened himself, and turned to face them both. "What do you want from me?"

Ranalae inclined her head to an empty seat at the prim little table. "Sit."

Hers was not a voice he was accustomed to disobeying. He sat.

CHAPTER 36

During Aransa's fall, the streets had gone quiet as grainmice, the people locked away inside their homes until the bulk of the conflict was over. Hond Steading was handling things a bit... differently. People crowded the streets, drinking and reveling, throwing rude gestures at the ships that shadowed their sky and singing even ruder songs to toast their new ruling couple. Ripka found she much rather preferred Hond Steading's method of coping. At least with all the confusion on the streets, their little party was less conspicuous.

"You're certain this woman is the contact?" she asked Dranik.

He threw her an insulted glance. "The other night..." He cleared his throat. "Yes. That is who we brought the last one to."

The last, and the first, as far as Dranik's group was concerned. But how many other deviants had Thratia's network scraped up and delivered into the songstress's hands?

"The woman who sings at the Ashfall Lounge?" she pressed again. Dranik let loose an irritated sigh.

"Yes, the very same."

Enard kept stealing glances at her, sensing her agitation. She debated telling them what she knew, that the woman who sang at the Ashfall Lounge was Laella, the young Valathean girl that had come to Hond Steading on Pelkaia's ship.

She was supposed to be one of Pelkaia's rescues, a noble girl who came into her deviant ability in her late teens and hid them well enough, until rumors began to leak and Pelkaia came knocking. She was adept at her craft, one of Pelkaia's fastest learners, but Pelkaia's prejudices against Valatheans weren't an easy thing to hide. Even in the short time Ripka had been aboard the *Larkspur*, the tension between those two had been palpable.

"Care to share your troubles?" Tibal asked. She flinched. While she'd felt Enard's curiosity, she'd been oblivious to Tibal's sly observations.

"Just questions," she said by way of explanation.

"Maybe you should let us help you chew them over."

That was fair enough. Tibal had proved she could trust him, and she doubted Dranik would understand half of the implications. "The Songstress is Laella Eradin."

"Whoa," Tibal said. "You sure?"

"Saw her myself."

"When was this?" Enard asked.

"I looped around the back of the Lounge to shake the watchers after Dranik set them chasing us. She was on the back patio, half in costume, smoking."

Tibal whistled low. "Pelkaia's got herself a leak."

"Or Thratia's network has already been compromised."

"Who are these people?" Dranik asked.

"Deviants working to get other deviants to safety."
Ripka flicked her gaze to Sasalai, whose brows were

raised high in curiosity. She'd stopped dragging her feet, and leaned more easily on the cane Tibal kept tucked carefully under the woman's arm. She should be terrified, but she appeared a strange combination of pissed off and intrigued. Ripka thought she'd like the woman, under different circumstances.

"And this Laella person works for Pelkaia?" Dranik frowned so deeply in thought that Ripka imagined his lips might slip clear off his face.

"Honestly? At this point, I have no idea. But we're about to find out."

The Ashfall Lounge was empty for the evening. A little light filtered through the upstairs windows, seeping out around the edges of pulled curtains. Someone was home, someone who was making it pretty clear they didn't want any company.

"Rules say we go around back and knock the pattern," Dranik said.

Enard gestured the way. "After you then, sir."

Dranik quirked a brow at his use of "sir", but crossed the distance anyway, leading them through the burnt-out remains that gave the theater its sense of danger. He knocked three times, a rather boring pattern in Ripka's opinion, and they waited tense as rockcats.

The door swung open, and the Songstress stood there in her full get-up, wig and all, but now that Ripka knew what she was looking for the girl couldn't hide her face.

Laella drew a deep drag from her cigarillo, flicked ash to the floor, and gave the party on her doorstep a long, appraising look. After a moment, she sighed and shook her head.

"I should have known this would happen after you saw me on the patio. Can't let a mystery lie still, can you, Captain?"

"'Fraid not," Ripka said.

"Well, you'd all better come in and have a chat. Is this the deviant?" She tipped her chin to the gagged grandmother.

"No, this is how I treat all my friends."

Tibal snorted behind her, and Laella narrowed her eyes. "You spent too much time with that Honding man. Now get in, before you're seen, will you?"

Ripka didn't much like the idea of entering Laella's lair without knowing the girl's motives, but she could hardly quibble with her logic.

"After you," she said, and Laella rolled her eyes as she spun around, leading them all into the dreary half-light of the theater's back rooms.

CHAPTER 37

An empty third cup waited by Detan's seat at the table, and he was proud his hands did not shake as he poured the pricklebrush tea into it. Misol stationed herself by the door, a threatening phantom, her hands loose at her sides though he could make out no weapon on her body. Not that she needed one. Detan wasn't exactly handy with, well, his hands, and Aella had his sel-sensitivity locked down tight. That lockdown, more so than the presence of Ranalae, made his skin crawl. Whatever was about to happen here, Aella wanted to be certain Detan couldn't fight it. Which was pretty rude of her, considering all the time she'd put into honing his abilities.

"It is *such* a pleasure to see you again, my lord. I hope your time in the Scorched has treated you well?" Ranalae smiled at him over the rim of her cup, all polite formality. Detan wanted to smash her smug face into the table between them, but he forced a cheery smile and put on his hapless-lord persona. He was not about to let her beat him at his own game.

"I find the wide-open skies suit me better than tower walls."

She flashed him a toothy grin. "Such a pity. I had hoped you might come to enjoy my little tower. We were just beginning to know one another, before you took an early leave of my hospitality."

Detan raised his cup to her. "Your hospitality, it must be said, has improved some since those days."

"Oh, dear boy, I think you'll find it hasn't. Aella has been telling me *so* much about the progress you've made."

He shot the girl a sharp glance. "Traitor."

She rolled her small shoulders. "Oh please, you can't be that forgetful. I am, as I've told you, only interested in what I might learn."

"Your little friend here was preparing to vivisect me, last I saw her."

Aella frowned delicately. "Well, we can't have *that*. You're no use to anyone dead."

"Certain conclusions can be drawn from corpses," Ranalae corrected with the same casualness as if she were discussing the weather. "But I find your methods thus far fascinating. This injection of Callia's devising, what does it do for the deviant?"

Detan cleared his throat. "The deviant is right here, you know. You could ask him."

Aella inclined her head. "The injection does not work for me. His experience may be more valuable than my observations."

Aella had tried the injections, and they did not work. It took all his long-practiced control to hide his shock. At least he hadn't been Callia's first test subject. Pits only knew what went on between those two before they'd apprehended him, and Aella clearly held no love for her adopted mother, as the withered form at her feet attested.

Aella's self-assurance, her cool distance and easy taunts. If Callia had done to Aella half of what Ranalae had done to him, then... Then he could not find it within himself to blame her for the way she treated Callia.

"Well?" Ranalae prompted. "If you are here, then explain. What does the injection do for you?"

"Increases my irritation with pushy bitches."

That was probably not the smartest thing he'd ever said. Aella coughed to hide a strangled chuckle, but Ranalae was too busy glaring needles through Detan's eyes to notice.

"Manners, please, my lord."

"Manners?" He stared at the teacup in his hand, at the crisp line of his sleeves' cuffs, so thoughtfully lined in flame-orange. He might be used to playing a part, to putting on a face and dancing to the tune. But usually he set the tune. And this... This twisted mirror of a tea party was just too much.

There was no thought to his impulse. He crushed the teacup in his hands, felt the satisfying give of the polished material shatter beneath his fingers. Hot tea spilled over them, trickled down his palm and forearm, scalding, blending with the blood small lacerations drew forth from his hand.

"Fuck your manners."

Misol moved, but for once in his life Detan was faster. He grabbed the table by its lip and flipped it while he burst to his feet.

"Restrain him," Aella snapped as she stood and brushed streaks of spilt tea from her robes.

"Stop," Detan growled. Misol hesitated, hands up, ready to grapple him into submission. But Detan wasn't moving toward either woman. He made his body language peaceful, inert. Let the anger in his expression do what he needed it to do to let the women who surrounded him know he was having none of their shit.

"Enough of this pageantry. You brought me here for a reason, Aella, brought me here to meet with this – this monster – to what purpose? Let's get this horror show over with, and you two both stop pretending you're anything but the twisted specks of humanity you really are."

"Well," Ranalae tsked. She stepped away from the flipped table and stood with her hands on her hips, surveying the damage to her room's decor with a mild pout of annoyance. She had the look of a woman whose pet had just pissed on the rug. "I thought you had learned control."

"Control and patience aren't always bedfellows."

"Clearly." Aella shook her head and picked her way around the wreckage to pat a whimpering Callia on the head. The gentle stroking of the desiccated woman's hair made Detan's stomach lurch. "We had better begin, then, since the subject is so eager."

Despite his bravado, Detan's mouth went dry. "Does Thratia know about this?"

Ranalae said, "My dear, she does not care."

Selium he could not sense while Aella kept him locked down poured from Ranalae's sleeves, a neat little trick that he suspected was part of the latest Valathean fashion. He stepped back as the cloud billowed toward him, the raw glimmer temporarily blinding him.

"When did he last have his injection?" Ranalae asked. He could only see pieces of her now, a flesh of arm, a curve of a cheek, through the swathe of selium coalescing around him. He wanted to scream, to swat it back, but he knew that they wanted him to fight. Knew that, to test his control, they were going to make him suffer.

Damned evil thing, having your deviant sensitivity tied to your anger. He wished his mother would have lived long enough to tell him how she dealt with their burden.

"Right before we left for Hond Steading. I wanted to test how long the effects would last, and his ability without regular maintenance."

"Hmm, interesting. You have the capability to make more with you?"

"Of course. I have a fresh vial on me, in fact."

"Wonderful."

He could scarcely hear them over the thundering of his heart. The realization came to him, rather belatedly, that he had not had much direct interaction with Ranalae in the Bone Tower. He had no idea what her sel-sensitivity was like – deviant, or imperial standard. If she were deviant, than the sel getting close and personal with him now was real bad news.

He opened his mouth to protest, to ramble, to stall whatever was about to happen, and choked as sel poured down his throat.

"Ah, there we go," Ranalae said. "Knew he couldn't keep from speaking for long. Are you prepared?"

"I am."

"Trigger Callia now, please?"

"Certainly."

Detan clawed the air in front of him, indistinct wisps of selium tickling the fine hairs on his hands, the aching cuts in his palm fading now as his mind burst with panic. They would not kill him here, he told himself. Not intentionally.

But all his calming techniques had been stripped from him – his deep breaths, his distracting banter. His coping methods crumbled around him and he wanted to scream but the breath just wouldn't come and he fell to one knee, eyes bulging, clawing at the ground as if he could dig his way to clear air. Nails bent back, cuts opened wider, a little pool of slick blood spread beneath his hands and he'd be pits-cursed if he wouldn't rather be drowning in that than sel and he tried, tried so damn hard, to open his senses. To grasp the sel being shoved inside him and rip it out and bore it straight through Ranalae's thrice-cursed eyes and oh holy fuck he was going to die here bug-eyed and useless and what was the fucking point after all–

Callia's ability hit him.

Perversion. That was what she was. Long before Aella's poisons had reduced her to a withered husk of a woman, Callia's deviant ability had been the corruption of everything good – an extension of herself, if Aella's theory of deviancy was true – and the poison had only concentrated that vileness.

He roiled with it. Every muscle in his body twitched and shuddered and clenched and cramped as his body fought against what Callia did to the selium inside him. It was not changed, not fundamentally, and he kept on telling himself that but all his body knew was that the selium inside him was now poison – rot and bile and decay – and he had to get it out.

His throat spasmed as he tried to scream though he had no air to do it with. Limbs he only vaguely recognized as his own twitched and writhed on the floor he'd bloodied.

He was dying and he knew it and something inside him broke.

A fire in his veins. Fire that was not his, had never really been his, that simply coexisted with him because it had no choice, burned within him hotter than anything he'd ever felt in his entire life. Some distant part of him wondered if this was the fire that had eaten his mother up – not bonewither, not after all – and was silenced. The fire would not die with him. It wanted release, and Detan was a whole pits-lot stronger than anyone had ever expected.

Aella's will held his sel-sense in check, that part of him that he had mastered, in a sphere of influence. He was aware of her range now as if it were his own, as if he could see a fine gleam of a soapy bubble wrapping them both, keeping him from affecting any selium within its volume.

But Detan's sphere, the fire's sphere, was bigger. A lot bigger.

He fought it as he realized what was happening, what was going to happen. Clamped down on everything that he was, everything that he could be. But his body panicked and reached without his consent and–

Screaming. Curses. The floor juddered under him, the thunderous crack of stone filled the air and not just nearby – it was heavy and hollow and huge. And the whoomph of what came next shook him to his very bones.

The selium withdrew in a rush, the perversion with it, and all his strength fled.

He lay limp and shuddering, overworked muscles pinging and twitching with jelly-soft weakness. For once, just once, his mind was truly blank, as if everything that he was had been siphoned free, drained out in that one terrible moment.

"What have you done?" Aella demanded. Her small hands grabbed his shoulders and shook him until his eyes slid open. Real fear etched her young face. He'd never seen anything like it before.

He tried to say something, anything, but his mouth

was mealy and his lips wouldn't obey. Misol crouched at his side, grabbed a fistful of his too-fancy coat and dragged him to his limp feet. He wanted to fall, everything in his body wanted to fall, but she wouldn't let him. She shoved him along until his hips rammed into a windowsill.

Ranalae stood next to him at that window, her fingers clutching the rail as she leaned forward to see better. If he had any strength left in him, he would have pushed her out.

"I had him shut down!" Aella protested against reality, stomping her small foot.

People were running in the halls. The air tasted of ash. He squinted against the light, too dark for the hour, and saw –

The firemount nearest the palace had awoken. Grey soot spilled from its mouth, illuminated from underneath by the orange-red smear of molten rock. Same color as his cuffs, he thought bitterly. Thratia had gotten that much right.

The echo of its awakening thrummed in him still. A pocket of selium, near to the conical plug, had been his target, and now the people at the base of that firemount were paying for Ranalae's experiments. He wanted to ask how bad it was – if there was anything he could do, anything at all, that might help, but his mouth still wouldn't work and it was getting really hard to keep his eyes open.

"Beautiful," Ranalae murmured.

Detan vowed to make her suffer as he slipped into unconsciousness.

CHAPTER 38

Ripka was less comfortable with the stability of the upstairs floor than she was with the entire situation. Every step they took the boards creaked in protest, and some of the steps up to the second floor swayed alarmingly. By the time they reached Laella's office, she was sweating, and it had nothing at all to do with the mild weather.

"This place is a deathtrap," Ripka said.

Laella threw herself backward into an overstuffed chair, arms splayed out across the cushions, and shrugged. "It was what I could afford, and the natural ambiance is a draw for the well-to-dos around here. They feel like they're getting away with something, even though the place is legally owned. I'm no squatter."

"This is all fascinating," Tibal said, "but could we perhaps discuss the deviant in the room?"

All gazes turned to Sasalai, who was looking a touch peaky. Ripka shooed Laella out of the only seat and eased the older woman into it. She looked grateful, but Ripka still made sure to move her cane out of striking distance before getting too close.

"This deviant in particular, or deviants as a whole?" Laella plucked her wig from her head and tossed it onto a stand on the room's only table.

"Laella," Ripka said, and watched the girl cringe at the use of her real name. "Stop dancing around. Get to the point already. What are you doing here? Are you working with Thratia?"

She flicked her gaze to Dranik and chewed the corner of her lip.

"He's fine. He's with us," Ripka said.

Laella let out one long, drawn-out sigh and slumped against the wall with her hands folded across her stomach. "Listen, it didn't take me long to figure out what was going on at the bright eye berry cafes after we arrived here, all right? I knew Thratia was working through them somehow, or at least using them as a way to collect people sympathetic to her cause, so I went poking around. Turns out, looking like a posh Valathean gets you some cred." She flashed a bright smile. "And it was easy enough to twist a few arms into thinking I was in tight with our dear commodore. Once I'd delivered a few likely 'messages' from the girl on high, I started changing tack. Asking for things – supplies and such for a stockpile, I claimed. Eventually I hit upon the idea to use them to snag the local deviants out from under the empire. Look, I know it's messy, but–"

"You don't work for Thratia Ganal? At all?" Dranik's jaw hung open, his eyes wide as saucers.

Laella sniffed and tossed her hair. "I'd rather lick a shit-smeared shoe."

"Skies above," he murmured. Enard gave him an awkward pat on the shoulder. Ripka wasn't feeling quite so charitable.

"So I spent the last couple of days working to get close

to Pelkaia's network? Pits below, why didn't you lot tell me what you were up to? I could have helped."

"Uh, yeah, about that." She twisted an already braided chunk of hair around one finger. "Pelkaia doesn't know about any of this."

Tibal whistled low.

"It's not like that," Laella insisted. "I'm not selling them or anything. I found a place, a safe place, for them to live, and used my resources to set up a system to get them there. Valathean-founded cities just aren't safe for deviants any more."

"And the *Larkspur* isn't a safe place?" Ripka prodded.

Laella winced. "I… don't know. Pelkaia hasn't been herself, lately. She's ill, but she's trying to hide it, and Coss isn't… well, he's pretending everything's all right, and it's not. She can't stop talking about putting an end to Thratia, which is well enough, but her level of obsession isn't. We didn't sign up to be soldiers." She glanced to Sasalai. "And I don't think anyone should be conscripted just because they're deviant and have nowhere else to go."

"Perhaps we should ask Sasalai what she wants, now that her ability has been discovered," Ripka said.

Tibal took a knee before the elderly woman, his hands braced on the arms of her chair, and tried his best to look contrite.

"Now, ma'am, you know we're not here to harm you. Your deviant sel-sense has been discovered – not just by us – and we want to keep you safe. I know it wasn't right of us, grabbing you like we did, but if you'd like to hear us explain it all we will. I can promise you this: no one in this room means you harm." He half-turned over his shoulder. "Isn't that right?"

A chorus of agreement all around. The woman's eyes

softened, just a touch, but as Tibal reached for her, her back stiffened and she leaned away, angling herself out of his reach. Ripka shook her head.

"You've got her pinned there. Here, shoo." She nudged Tibal away from the woman and stepped around behind her, sliding her thumbs under the knot on the gag to keep it from tugging too much against the woman's face as she wriggled the knot loose. She'd done the maneuver enough times as a watch-captain, it came easily to her now, though she was out of practice.

"You'll feel a slight tug–"

The floorboards shook, jarring her hands. Shouts echoed from the bottom floor of the theater, deep and controlled – a pattern she recognized.

"What is this?" Laella snapped, springing toward the door. Ripka grabbed her elbow and yanked her back.

"Watchers," she hissed, low so that she wouldn't be overheard. "Stay quiet. Don't step heavily, all of you. Laella, is there another way out of here?"

Her eyes were huge. Skies above, the girl was so young. Stupidly brave, for doing what she'd done. Brave and bold and reckless, assured in her own success. She had probably never even considered the possibility of being caught. From the look in her eye, she was considering the consequences in depth, now.

"There's a fire ladder outside the window," she whispered almost too low for Ripka to make out.

Thank the skies for that. "Tibal, can you handle Sasalia's weight? Enard will go down first, and I'll be last out."

Enard frowned at this, but did not protest. The two of them were the only hands in the room with any real fighting experience, and things could get messy on the ground just as easily as they could in this room.

"I have her," Tibal said.

Sasalai yanked her gag the rest of the way free.

Laella gasped, Tibal lunged for the woman, but it was done so quickly the scream was out of her lips before Tibal's legs had even begun to move.

"Up here! Help! Help!" Sasalai's lungs were surprisingly robust for her age. The stamp of footsteps turned their way immediately, pounding up the stairs. Ripka had only a moment to stare at the woman, who risked being hanged if her ability were discovered, before the watchers burst through the door.

"Hands high! All of you!" a sturdy male voice she was grieved to recognize bellowed.

Ripka lifted her hands to the air, fingers splayed, as all the others did, and turned, slowly, to face Watch-captain Lakon. His eyes bulged. She really couldn't blame him.

"Leshe?" he asked, bewildered. The crossbows pointed at her chest from his flanking watchers, however, did not waver.

"Long story." She tried an embarrassed smile, but his expression just hardened into a firm mask.

"I'll have it all from you, then. Restrain them."

The watchers of Hond Steading were quick to act on their captain's orders. They flowed into the room, filling it with blue, and made no comment as they went about binding the wrists of everyone save Sasalai, and divesting them of weapons.

"Are you all right, ma'am?" Lakon picked up Sasalai's cane and offered it to her. She took it in trembling hands.

"They kidnapped me."

Ripka bit back a protest as Lakon threw her a questioning glance. "I see. Can you walk? We'll need you to give a full statement at the station house."

"Boy, I'd sprint to the station to file this complaint.

I've never been so rudely manhandled in my life."

Lakon helped the woman to her feet and handed her off to the care of a watcher, keeping his own crossbow ready at his side as they ushered the group down the creaking steps, one at a time – it seemed Lakon was just as wary of the building's construction as Ripka – and out into the night.

She took in the area on instinct. Low light, little to no foot traffic, plenty of twisting streets and vague garden walls and alleys to obscure her way with. If she zig-zagged, and used the alleys and rock walls, she'd be nearly impossible to hit with that crossbow. But then, there were the others, and she couldn't be certain they'd be so lucky. Couldn't be sure Laella would even think to run if they all made a dash for it. She told herself she'd escaped from worse situations – near death on the Black Wash, the fortress of the Remnant. But each of those times, she'd had help coming for her: Detan.

Detan was in the city now, but she very much doubted he'd be of any help to her this time around.

She grit her teeth and glared at her feet, struggling to work up a plan.

For the second time that night, the ground shook. She blinked at her feet, wondering for just a moment if she were going mad or about to faint. Little plumes of dust swirled around her toes, and gravel jittered against her boots.

Slowly, reluctantly, she lifted her head and looked around. Everyone was scanning the buildings, the sky, looking for the reason why the ground had shrugged and shuddered, then fallen still.

A crack broke the night, louder than anything she'd ever heard – ever felt – in her life. It slammed her ears and vibrated her teeth, made her heart jump with fear.

The watchers spun in uneasy circles, seeking the threat, eyeing the fleet of ships which blotted the sky with wary eyes.

Enard said, "There."

They all turned to his voice, followed the line of his sight.

An orange smear bled across the underside of the clouds, seeping out from the eastern ridge of the largest firemount's puckered mouth. Ripka went cold, straight to the bones, her stomach dropping out from under her.

She'd never seen anything like it before, but she knew what it was instinctively. Had been told scary stories of such a thing as a child.

The ground shakes. The firemounts crack open their mouths. And then, the fire. The soot and the smoke and the boiling, pooling ash.

People screamed, ran from homes, watched horror-eyed through their windows, knowing that if the flow was coming their way they were already dead. The stories were pretty strict about that: once you'd seen it, it was already over.

"How..." Lakon trailed off, leaving his mouth half-open on the aborted sentence.

The largest firemount of Hond Steading had been dormant as long as there had been a city here. This should not be happening. But, of course, the records were imprecise, and firemounts unpredictable.

Pearlescent wisps drifted in the orange glow of the lava, flickering out as they dissipated, consumed by some internal fire. Selium. Burning.

Tibal hissed through his teeth. Ripka went stiff all over.

Not a natural event, then, if the talents a man were born with could be disconnected from nature. Detan had done that. Someone had pushed Detan to do that. Which was, in a way, a good thing. This was not a complete eruption event. He must have blown a pocket near the surface of the firemount's mouth, and that glow... It could be lava. It could be fire from Detan's handiwork. There was no way to tell for sure.

What she was sure of, however, was the drumbeat rumble of stone cascading down the side of the firemount, toward the eastern edge of the palace and its connected residential quarter.

"Those people will need help," she said, struggling to keep from sprinting toward the destruction with every crash that echoed through the night. Screams rose up to meet those breaking noises, and they jarred her all the way through. They could not just stand there.

Lakon frowned. He lowered the crossbow and tugged at his mustache, gaze stuck on the cloud of dust rising from the falling rocks.

"Protocol says we wait for the dust to settle. Could walk into a pyroclastic flow."

"This is not an eruption event," Ripka snapped. "And those people can't wait."

"What in the pits else could it be?"

Tibal threw her a sharp look that she ignored. "I know Thratia, and I know her weapons. That was not an eruption."

Lakon chewed his lip while his watchers shifted uneasily, eyeing the destruction.

"Those people need help..." a young female watcher said.

Lakon closed his eyes and leaned his crossbow against his leg so that he could rub the heels of his palms against his eyelids. He blew air through his nose so hard his mustache puffed outward.

"I know you, Captain, or of you, anyway. I don't know what was happening here tonight, but, no one appears hurt–" Sasalai opened her mouth to protest and he shot her a glare. "And those people definitely *are* hurt." He locked his gaze on Ripka. "You are sure? You stake your life and your reputation on this not being an eruption?"

"I know what caused that. I swear it."

"Very well. Remove their bonds, men. We'll need the hands. I suspect we're going to have a lot of digging to do."

CHAPTER 39

Detan did not know how long he slept, but when he woke the world was dark and still. The faint light trickling in under the curtain barring his window was enough to give him a pounding headache. He groaned and rested his forearm across his eyes. His arm was enclosed in a silken sleeve – someone had gone to the trouble of changing him. He felt a pang of sympathy for whoever had suffered that nasty little chore. He was pretty certain he'd fouled himself in those final moments. So very much of his bodily control had fled.

And he didn't have it all back. Parts of him radiated numbness like a nimbus, the center of a spot perfectly deadened while the area around it grew steadily in feeling. With care, he began flexing every toe to its max extension, letting them relax, and repeating the motion with every muscle all the way up his body until he was pretty sure he still had all his parts intact.

Not that he deserved them.

Memory of that terrible flailing of his power filled his mind, insisted to be recognized lest he bury it completely. In a rueful way he welcomed the change. After he'd blown up the mines by accident here, that first time, he'd buried the guilt and the memory beneath layers of pain.

His new mental exercises would not allow him that luxury of self-deception. He needed to know everything he possibly could about his ability, and though the pain had been immense he had learned a great deal during those terrible moments.

He tried to catalog them with remote interest, to remove himself from the memory of his agony and the outlet that agony had eventually found.

One: the injection did not affect Aella. He was not yet sure how he could use that, but it felt significant to him. Some tiny sliver of weakness he could pry at.

Two: His sphere of influence was much larger than expected. Large enough that it dwarfed Aella's, and she could not keep him fully contained if he decided to reach outside of her range.

Not that he wanted to. Though he'd desperately attempted to rein himself in, he held no illusions about what he'd done. He'd blown a pocket of selium at the opening of a firemouth. People died. How many, he was terrified to learn. But his fear was irrelevant in the face of the pain and terror he'd caused. He needed to move. To help. To fix something.

He peeled the arm from his eyes, swung his feet to the bedroom floor, and nearly fainted from the exertion. Rather annoying, having a body that wouldn't obey him. Not nearly as bad as having a mind that wouldn't.

Someone had the gall to knock on his door, and he was halfway through reaching back to chuck a pillow at the intruder when his auntie stepped into the room. He froze, mid-swing, and hesitantly brought the pillow down to rest in his lap.

"You're up," she said.

"Your powers of observation never cease to impress me."

She propped a tray against her hip, and sidled awkwardly through the door to keep from rocking its contents. Clay plates rattled as she snatched a guttering candlestick from the tray and set about lighting, one at a time, the candelabra near the door. The warm light made his eyes ache, and he considered asking her to douse the flames, but he'd have to face the day eventually.

He only wished the flames did not remind him of what he had done.

"I would say I taught you to speak better to your elders, but I don't believe those lessons ever stuck."

"Your efforts were valiant, but in vain."

A streak of sadness marred her features, gone as quickly as it came, her stern expression replaced in a flash. He wondered if that ability were a family trait, too. Acquiring a mask for all his various roles had always come easily to him.

She settled herself in a chair alongside his bed and set the tray on his nightstand. Warm tea muddled with cactus fruit steamed beside him, a delicate roll of paper-thin egg wrapped around a huge variety of local vegetables and meats next to it. His stomach grumbled, loud enough to echo in the quiet room. Auntie Honding tipped her head to the plate without comment, and he dug in. When half the food was gone and washed down by tea, he ventured to ask the question he dreaded.

"How bad?"

Her eyes closed, fingers knotting the skirt over her knees. "The fire was contained, but rockfall struck the palace district to the east. We're still sorting through the remains."

The food tasted bland and caught in his throat. "I never meant…"

"I know." She reached out and squeezed his knee. He couldn't remember the last time she'd touched him. "But the damage is done."

He brushed her hand away. "Ranalae pushed me to it. Aella would not have dared without her prodding. If you had not invited her into our home–"

His auntie laughed, a soft, bitter sound he'd never heard from her before. "And do you think I have any choice in the matter?"

"You sent for them."

"They were coming anyway. From the moment Thratia seized Aransa it was only a matter of time before the empire wondered just why it'd let our little family rule this jewel for so long. My invitation was an attempt to save face, to retain some semblance of authority over what happens here." She cast him a sly look. "Not entirely different from your marriage."

"Ranalae is a monster."

"And so are Aella and Thratia and, some would say, you, dear boy."

"Then we should all of us be turned out."

She sighed wearily and leaned back in her chair, allowing her eyes to slip shut. She'd never looked so old before. So tired. Fine lines ran the length of her face like spider-webbed glass, just waiting for the final blow before it shatters.

"Maybe," she agreed. "But we are all this city has, for the moment."

"We aren't the only ones working to protect this city."

Her eyes snapped open and she stared hard at the ceiling their ancestors had built. "You mean your friends. That watch-captain, and the others."

"I do. You did them a terrible disservice, trying to lock them out of the fight. I sent them to you – sent you Nouli – and you threw away all those opportunities to scrape your knees before the empire."

"Threw them away? I protected them, you stupid boy. I tried to lock them where even Ranalae's spies could not find them, and then they went to the wind. Do not think, not even for a moment, that they were not being followed from the moment they stepped off the *Larkspur's* decks. Ranalae may have arrived a few weeks ago, but her spies have been here much longer. The ex-watch-captain of Aransa is a target too juicy to miss."

"And you are doing what, exactly? This city is under siege by disparate forces. You cannot tell me the only thing you've done to protect it is to call for the empire and lock some friends of mine away for their own safety. If you want to lose this city, auntie, you're doing a real good job of it."

The fine lines of her face smoothed away as she drew her expression taut with bitten-back anger. "I've done what I can. I created the forum, to allow our people their voices, in the hopes that they would become their own force if it came to that. I've threaded my own people throughout the city – people looking for your friends *now*, might I add, to make certain they are safe –and flew my little birds to catch any whispers. I have not been *idle*, as you imply, but I have been hamstrung. How can one secure a city's future, without its heir?"

He was on his feet in an instant, the dizzy flash of sudden movement fading beneath the storm front of his anger. The Dame moved, a futile attempt to grab his sleeve, but he was already around the bed, reaching for the curtain the servants had drawn against the evening. Drawn to hide what he had done.

The cloth tore as he yanked it back, revealing the hazy light of a late evening choked in dust. Though his room was not angled to the best vantage, the damage was plain enough. Stonefall carved a swathe of destruction through the palace district, the scents of bloody iron and choking dust still hot in the faint breeze swirling ash against his windowsill.

"This," he grated, "this is what this city's heir brings."

"Aella said–"

"Aella says whatever she damn well pleases to get what she wants. Pitsfucking damnit, auntie, I'm trying to keep it together, damn near making myself mad with all her lessons and experiments upon my 'control' but half the fucking time I suspect she's pushing me to test herself, or to see what she can get away with. I've got the Honding fire, but I've got the family temper, too, and those two nasty cousins should never mingle. I would have rather choked on my own blood than do… do… *this*. But look. Fucking look and see how successful I was."

"Language," she snapped.

He dragged his fingers through sweat-damp hair. "This ain't a time that calls for pretty words, auntie. This is something that deserves words so ugly I haven't even dreamed them up yet."

"While you busy yourself with your vocabulary," she said as she pushed to her feet and straightened the robe that trailed her like midnight, "I came to tell you that Gatai is insisting you have your friends returned to you, and I find I agree. Though you will not take me into your confidence–" she held up a hand to forestall an argument, "– it is clear to me that you must have someone. I have done all I can to keep this city safe, and have reached the end of my ability. If you require my assistance, you have it through Gatai. I suspect the less I know of your true motives, the better."

He swallowed around a dry throat. "And just how will you hide them here, if they even agree to return?"

She flashed him a smile. "Your old auntie isn't beaten yet, boy. I have a few tricks up my sleeve. And you'd be amazed how easy it is for one to overlook the details of a face when the body is wearing servant blacks."

He slouched against the wall beside the window, turning away from the destruction he'd wrought. "I want to help..."

She crossed to him, gathered both of his hands in her boneraw fingers. "I know. You can't. Not me, anyway. My time here is... short, nephew. Now, if you'll excuse me, I have a wedding to prepare for." Her voice was grim as she squeezed his hands. "Make your mother proud, boy. You've already made me so."

She was gone in a moment, aged legs carrying her with the same speed and grace they always had. Must be nice to not be susceptible to bonewither, he thought, then chased the thought away. His auntie had done her best for a family lineage she was, by lack of a genetic inheritance, kept apart from. Though her actions were flawed, her motives were pure. She'd done what she could. The rest was up to him.

Skies save them all.

CHAPTER 40

Hond Steading burned. Ash and screams choked the air, and by the time Ripka arrived at the heart of the terror she and all the others had torn strips of cloth from their clothing to tie around their mouths and noses, lest they breathe in all that had once been stone. And flesh. A certain sweet, meaty smell tinged the air that Ripka tried very, very hard not to think about.

The watchers spread out, using their whistles to coordinate in a pattern so familiar it made Ripka's heart ache. She wanted nothing more than to join them, to shrug on a blue coat and heave to with the others, to be a human bastion of order and safety for the confused and injured populace.

But she'd lost that place. Given it up for a cause, and now this vague edge life was all she had left.

Not so little of a life that she couldn't do something with it, though. Sometimes the greatest leverage for change could only be obtained from outside a system.

The eastern edge of the palace district lay broken across the wide road that had once been its major thoroughfare. Stone and wood and bodies lay scattered

like chaff across the road, cries of distress, pain, and
requests for help merging into one great wail. The belch
of the firemount had stopped, but the horror was just
getting started.

Halfway toward the rubble, she realized she'd lost the
shadow of Tibal at her side. She cast around for him, saw
him standing just on the rise where they'd first caught
sight of the destruction, his hands trembling at his sides
and his face as pale as death. Enard hesitated alongside
her, but she waved him on. Wasn't likely having a crowd
around Tibal would do him any good.

She jogged up to him, aware always of the groans
and cries in the neighborhood behind her, and turned to
stand at his side, looking out across the damage, not at
him. She doubted he'd really see her even if she held his
eyes open and shoved her face right under them.

She said nothing, kept her presence steady and solid
and silent, while he worked up whatever it was he
needed to say.

"Detan did this," he said after a while.

"Didn't mean to."

"Who would make him?"

Ripka kept quiet. Wasn't a real question, anyway.
Eventually Tibal rolled his lips round, working up some
saliva, and said, "Ain't seen nothing like this since the
war." Sweat gleamed across his dusty forehead, tracking
runnels through the grit that dusted them all.

"Won't be likely to again, if we can help it."

"That what we're doing here, preventing horrors like
this?"

"It's what I'm trying for."

"Working out well."

She winced, and he blinked, drawing back into
himself. He tugged on his mouth-wrap with those rangy

fingers of his, didn't quite seem to know what to do with his hands so he tugged on his hat, too. A little avalanche of dust and soot rolled off the brim. Ripka decided not to think about what that dust might have been just a few marks ago.

"Don't know if I can do it," he said.

"You don't have to. Could go back, give Honey a hand."

He pursed his lips like he'd tasted something sour. "They need help."

"Indeed."

"Could give it to 'em. Had training in the Fleet."

Training from the same Fleet that'd brought him through so much carnage that he stood here now, one of the bravest men she'd ever known, shaking straight through the ground for the fear this all brought rushing back.

"Could do," she agreed.

"You could, too."

"Plan on it."

"What are you dicking around with me for, then?"

"Saw someone needed my help, and offered it."

He gave her a sly, sideways glance that she could feel crawl against her cheek, but she kept her gaze straight ahead, stuck on the destruction, mapping out the points of the most hurt, guessing where best she could bend a back and lend a hand as soon as Tibal had himself settled.

"Guess we'd better get to it, then."

"Suppose so," she agreed.

He hesitated, his body canting forward while his feet stayed stuck. She couldn't dream of what kind of demons he was fighting, couldn't even conjure up a ghost of them, but she had to give him credit. He put one foot in front of the other, grit his teeth, lengthened

INHERIT THE FLAME

his stride, and picked up speed. By the time they hit
the bottom of the little ridge he was all cool confidence,
barking orders to those clearing the rubble just like he'd
been trained. Wouldn't sleep well tonight, that man, but
Ripka doubted any one of them would ever sleep well
again after this.

Ripka ran toward the pain. What had once been an
apartment building lay shattered on the ground, spilling
out across the road far enough to block all attempts at
bringing carts through. People had thrown their backs
into clearing that rubble, whickering donkeys dragging
carts over to haul away both broken men and stone.

Hard to tell the screams of men from the complaints
of the animals. She let her training take over. Rockfalls
were always a worry for the sel-mining cities of the
Scorched, firemount eruptions a distant but ever-present
threat. And so the watchers trained, and made plans, and
grinned at each other and boasted about how prepared
they were, how easy it would be to set things to rights.
Their plan was iron. Was stone.

But in the desert, all things grow brittle and break,
and all that planning was no different. She moved
rubble, peeled away sheets of stone and twisted wood
and there under the debris was a woman, just as broken
as her home. Her arm twisted up above her head, bone
poking through the skin like a white flag of surrender.
Sallowness suffused her skin, but her heart beat and her
breath came slow and easy, so Ripka stabilized the arm
as best she could and hauled the woman to the street to
line her up with the other injured.

The night went that way. Whether that woman was
the first or the last she didn't know, couldn't remember
through the haze of faces made indistinct by blood, ash,
and tears. At the end – which wasn't the end, couldn't

be, was just a pause because the screams in the rubble had stopped and something has to make you stop, or you end up in the line with the injured – she sat hard on the knoll where Tibal had frozen with fear of the past, and thought about all the future fears that were always coming. Things could always get worse.

Was a time when Ripka thought the worst thing that'd ever happened in her life was her father coming home from the Catari war, mute and with a look in his eye like all he could see were shades of red and charcoal. Then he walked off, into the scrubland, and never came back. She'd carried the guilt of how relieved that'd made her feel her whole life. Right up until this moment, feeling and knowing some shade of what his pain had been, and hoping there was something could be done to heal that pain. Because if there wasn't, she was a dead woman walking.

Tibal found her soon enough, sat down beside her, those long legs of his crossed in sharp angles that made her distinctly uncomfortable. His fingers were raw, nails ripped back and skin bloodied, probably torn to ribbons. Hers were, too, but she hadn't really realized until she'd seen the mirror of it on him. Didn't matter to her, though. Wasn't the worst thing she was feeling.

Enard came up, looking the same as them all, and that little warmth she got in her chest every time she saw him stayed snuffed. Probably for the best, that. Any hint of happiness she felt now might just make her vomit from the contrast.

Dranik found them, and Captain Falston too, and soon they were all sat there, made indistinct from each other by smears of dust and blood, and for a moment they looked with one set of eyes on what they'd done, and what they hadn't been able to do, and each one of them – each and every fucking one – moved their personal bar for horror up just a little higher.

Sometime during the night Falston turned to her and was himself again, distinct from the group, hints of his blue coat showing like smudges under all the dust. "We need to talk."

"Been wondering when you'd say as much," she said.

They stood as one and, the previous events of the night seeming of trifling importance now, headed to Latia's house. Ripka hoped the woman had strong wine waiting.

CHAPTER 41

There were a lot of things Detan could have done in the day after he let the firemount roar. The household staff tiptoed around him, and he didn't see a hair of either Thratia or Aella. Or Ranalae, and his dear old auntie. That one visit, it seemed, was all he was going to get. He was on his own, which he knew, but it was real frustrating waking up with a pounding headache and knowing people were counting on you to get them out of one right tangled mess.

The reason he had that headache, he decided to shove aside. To dwell too long on that particular nightmare might just set off a whole fresh horror. Aella had given him an injection, returning some of his control, but he didn't trust himself to light a candle with his power now. Not while he could still hear the rescue efforts going on outside.

He could have run. Could have weaseled his way up the towers of the palace and gotten himself onto the *Happy Birthday Virra!* and broken for the inland, or the sea. He could almost convince himself that fleeing was the best possible route, that what Pelkaia had said was true: the best thing he could do for this world was to run, to find some barren, sel-less place, destroy his flier, and stay there.

If Callia hadn't dipped that needle into his vein, he might have believed her. Might have tried just that. But he could see it, now. That infinitesimal world beyond the ken of unaltered eyes. Sel wasn't something that one could run from, not on this world, anyway. It was in his blood and his air and his bones, and even if he fled clear to the other side of the world, he suspected he'd find it there, too.

Running just prolonged the inevitable. He paced the length of his room, juggling options, when a solid knock on the door made him damn near jump out of his skin. He cleared his throat to get his dignity back, and said in the most authoritative voice he could muster, "Enter."

A parlour maid he didn't recognize let herself in, and offered up to him a thick package wrapped in coarse linen. "Master Gatai said I should bring this to you, straightaway."

"My thanks." He took the bundle from her, tucked it under his arm to the sound of rustling cloth and paper. She bobbed her head and made a dash for the door, then paused halfway out with her hand still on the knob, a little worried wrinkle dimpling her chin.

His stomach sank as she glanced back over her shoulder at him, eyes a little wide with worry. "My Lord?" she asked.

He forced himself to smile, knowing what was coming. She'd ask about the eruption. She must know his secret, probably the whole city did. Thratia certainly wasn't trying to hide his deviation. Would she be so bold as to claim the destruction he'd wrought in his name?

Despite the stew of fear in his head, his voice was

cool, calm. "Yes?"

"Nice to have you back, you don't mind my saying."

She flashed him a grin and darted out the door in a rustle of skirts. Detan nearly burst into a fit of anxious laughter. Gatai had said the servants were with him. There must be outliers, of course, people bought over to Ranalae or Thratia or who just plain didn't like him. But, skies above, to have any support at all was a balm.

He made quick work of the package and found two servants' black uniforms with a folded note tucked inside. Gatai's precise handwriting greeted him.

> *My Lord Honding,*
> *Your guests await you in the eastern wing, and*
> *have a lovely view of the oncoming monsoon winds.*
> *Recent events require my attention, but I trust you will*
> *handle all things with care.*
> *Your Servant,*
> *Gatai*

A lot could be hidden behind servants' black, or so his auntie had said, and Detan grinned as he thumbed the fine material. While all eyes were off him, it was time to make a few social calls.

CHAPTER 42

Latia welcomed the watch-captain of Hond Steading into her home with little more shock than a slight widening of eyes and what was, perhaps, a rather heavy pour of wine into her own glass. Honey was less pleased with the situation.

"He tried to arrest you," she protested from the divan Latia had propped her up in with heaps of pillows, and teas that, no doubt, made her tongue looser than usual.

"Won't make that mistake again," Falston said with a smile that never quite reached his eyes. He kept on looking at Honey like he knew her, which was, as far as Ripka could reckon, not a good thing. She'd never pressed Honey on what had landed her on the Remnant, but she could damn well guess, and if the captain had any prior knowledge of her exploits his friendliness might well fade in a hurry.

"What happened tonight," she said to draw his attention to her, "may be only the first demonstration."

That got his attention. His head whipped around like the wind, eyes narrowed. "Demonstration? Is that what you call tonight's horrors?"

"Me? No. But you bet your ass Thratia Ganal does."

She wasn't sure, of course, but Detan had been the source of that explosion – and there was just no way she could allow herself to believe he'd done it of his own free will. Someone pushed him to it, and Thratia had both the means and the access. Whatever power struggle was going on in the Honding palace, Thratia had just made the breadth of her arsenal very, very clear to her opponents. Ranalae was probably wetting herself with excitement at that little display.

"And why in the hell would she want to wound and scare the ever-loving shit out of the very people she claims she wants to rule with a benevolent hand?"

Ripka's smile was tight and sad. "Never said it was a demonstration for the people, Captain."

He knocked back a heavy swallow and squinted at her. "Cut to the point, lass."

"This marriage of hers to Detan. It isn't what you think it is. Isn't what the whole city thinks it is."

Tibal cleared his throat roughly and she cut him a look to shut him up. They needed the watchers on their side if they were going to protect the people from whatever struggles were going on in that palace, and if she had to expose Detan's deviation, then so be it. Wouldn't be much longer he could keep that information under wraps, anyway, no matter what he did. Either Thratia'd let the cat out of the cave, or he would do something rather dumb, and rather public.

"That accident, three years back? The one he lost his sel-sense in?"

Falston nodded. "Whole city knows that story, lass. Dame sent him to Valathea to see if he could recover his sense, but he left there and went rambling, causing trouble for the empire. Truth be told, the city is fond of their heir. Not a lot of love here for the empire, you understand. What with us being independent and all. We get the shit end of their trade taxes."

Ripka found her lips had grown heavy. She took a long swallow, closed her eyes, and breathed out real easy. There was no going back from this. But then, they were already in the shit up to their eyeballs.

"Wasn't his sel-sense he lost, just his freedom. He's a deviant, Captain Falston. He didn't mean to, but he caused that explosion, and he was sent to the Bone Tower to figure out just how that trick of his worked."

Falston sucked air through his two front teeth, gapped just like his little girl's, and stared at the silty bottom of his empty glass. Latia scurried to refill it. He took another long draw. "Heard rumors of that nature. Never counted 'em for much."

"And?" she pressed, stomach sinking.

"Heard rumors of the Bone Tower, too, and those I thought likely enough. Nasty shit, there. Is it true?"

"Worse than the rumors know."

"Pitsdamn. What is our Dame doing, letting those vipers in her house?"

Ripka shook her head. She wasn't quite sure she knew herself, but the last thing she wanted was the watchers turning against their Dame now, when everything was on the line.

"Couldn't rightly tell you. I think they got into her head, Detan told me–" She had to clear her throat. "–told me they talked her up with ideas of curing him, of making him safe again. I think she bought it all. Regrets it now, more than like, but he hasn't been home since he went to that tower. I don't know that they ever talked about it." Her gaze tracked to the window, toward the blown head of the firemount. "Bet they're talking about it now."

"What in the fiery pits is he doing back here, then, if

his power's so unstable? I'd want to stay far away from firemounts, in his position."

Tibal snorted, and Ripka cut him a look. Falston might be tired and a touch drunk, but he picked up on it in an instant. "What's that you've got to say then, man?"

"Now's not the time for this," Ripka urged.

"Pits it isn't." Falston set his glass down and gripped his knees with both hands as he leaned forward. "You're telling me a mountain of a tale, Captain. I got a lot of respect for you, you know that, but something this big, I gotta make sure I see all the faces. Tell your part then, man."

Tibal nudged back his ashy hat and frowned at them both. "Detan was a friend of mine, long time now. Just reckoning that he ain't ever been known for his sense."

Falston grimaced. "All that power, and no sense? We got to get him the pits out of this city."

She could see the notion dancing around in his red-webbed, glassy eyes. Quick as he said the words, his mind caught up with the possibility. If they couldn't get him out safely, they'd have to kill him. To protect the city. After tonight's demonstration, Ripka'd be thinking the same thing if their roles were reversed. If Detan had so much as made the firemount of Aransa hiccup while she'd been the city's watch-captain, she'd put an arrow in his eye and mourn the loss as necessary for the greater good.

Even now, she didn't know the man's state of mind. Had only her own intuition and experience with him to rely upon, but she had to believe he hadn't done tonight's damage on purpose. The man she'd known, the man she *knew*, would rather run than risk an innocent. Which meant he was cornered so hard he had nowhere to flee.

"He's a prisoner," she said slowly, rolling every word over in her mind before she spoke. "What happened tonight? That was his doing, but not his will."

"You can't promise that," Falston protested. "He's a Honding. Solid leaders, but known for their tempers."

She couldn't promise him, not really, and it tore her up right to the core. She struggled with something else to say, something to convince the man that keeping Detan safe – and getting him away from his captors – was the best possible course of action. But every one of those paths was a lie, and the words died halfway to her lips.

Silence stretched, and with every passing moment an empty maw inside her grew, gnawing up her hope and her sympathy. Removing Detan – *assassinating* Detan – was the best thing for this city. Thratia wouldn't have her pawn, her weapon, and the city'd be safe from his outbursts. It made terrible, terrible sense.

"I promise it," Tibal said.

He pushed his hat all the way back so the room could see his eyes, the mudcrack fractures of wrinkles radiating from the corners. In the dim candlelight, caked all over with the dust of rubble, he seemed older. Ancient. Something in the sharp edge of his wiry jaw reminded her of Dame Honding when she was putting on her game face.

"Forgive me, sir." Falston swung around to face Tibal. "But who the pits are you to guarantee such a thing?"

Tibal thought a moment, lips pursing as he chewed over an answer. "His friend. And that's all that should thrice-damned matter."

He cut Ripka a glance that made her wince. "Tibal's right. Doesn't matter what Thratia's done to him, Detan's no killer. He's a prisoner, and he needs our help. I've no doubt he's planning to undermine Thratia before this is all done. He'll need the watch's help, too."

Falston leaned back, wicker creaking, and stared hard at Tibal for a while. If he saw the family resemblance, diluted though it was, he didn't say anything. Just chucked back the rest of his drink and nodded.

"Right, then. We have an awful lot to plan, and very little time. When do you lot suppose he'll make his move?"

Tibal snort-laughed. "The wedding, no doubt. Damn fool likes an audience for his self-diagnosed cleverness."

"Hmm." Falston stroked his whiskers and frowned. "Watch is looking kind of thin lately, and the wedding'll draw out a big crowd. Hard to keep our corners covered, especially with a chunk of the inner wall down."

"Wedding's a week out," Ripka offered. "Not a lot of time to train, but we could get some bodies on board all the same."

Dranik jumped to his feet. "A citizen's brigade!"

Falston frowned. "A what now?"

"Citizen's brigade," he over-pronounced each word as he paced, rubbing his raw hands together. "After the quake tonight, it should be no trouble to get people interested in joining up to protect their neighborhoods. Tell them it's a preparedness plan, in case of emergencies natural and political. They'll get it, I'm sure. So many people in this city are just looking for a way to help it themselves. They love their homes, Captain. Let them throw in."

"And how would we go about getting the word out about something like that?"

Dranik beamed from ear-to-ear. "The forum, of course. Tomorrow is a free speech day, you won't even have to sign up in advance, Ripka."

"Me?" She coughed on a drop of wine gone down wrong. "Need I remind you I'm a fugitive of the palace?"

"Bah," he waved a hand, "everyone around here's heard of the watch-captain of Aransa. And I bet Captain Lakon's watchers will be just too busy with the rebuilding effort to go after you. Isn't that right, Captain?"

Falston grinned. "Better her up there than me."

CHAPTER 43

Coss insisted she was being paranoid, but what in the Black did he know? The crew avoided her. Barely spoke to her. Kept their eyes averted every time she passed. She might be a sick woman in both bone and brain, but she wasn't stupid. Never that. Paranoia ran in her blood but it didn't own her. Nothing did. Not even the land that'd birthed her.

She reveled in the silence of the light step she'd spent her whole life cultivating as she paced back and forth across her cabin, back and forth, hands clasped tight behind the small of her back, head pointed down. She wasn't foolish enough to risk catching another glimpse of her naked face in the mirror, not after what she'd seen last time. Her mother's face, staring back at her, young again and eyes bright with the madness that had taken her grandmother to her grave. Sweating and raving and beating her breasts.

Pelkaia stopped pacing, realized she'd forced her hands up and was pulling at her hair, clumps of dirty blonde strung between her fingers. She flicked them to the floor and strode over them. Silent. Silent. She was a hunter, an agent of revenge. In one night she'd brought Aransa to its knees for what its officials had let happen to her son. Why should she shy away now, now, when the ultimate author of her son's death – the real author, the woman who had signed her damn name to the paper – was near at hand?

There was nothing for it. Her crew was against her. Thought her mad. Wouldn't so much as lift a finger to help her. Their laziness made them complacent. No, worse, implicated – yes, she was sure that was the word. In doing nothing they were as much a part of Thratia's schemes as her militia was.

Maybe, if she could prove to Coss that they were working against her, working for that bitch Thratia, then Coss would see. Would come over to her side of things. Beg forgiveness. Help her knock Thratia from the sky and into the dirt.

The obvious choice was Laella. That girl was pure Valathean aristocracy, though she did her best to hide it around Pelkaia. But you couldn't hide who you were from her, oh no. Pelkaia had made a life of studying the mannerisms of others so that she could copy them. Could pick and choose what she needed to construct a new, false persona or imitate an old one. Laella was good, but no one was good enough to hide from Pelkaia. She saw every twitch, every hidden smirk, every lofty mannerism. That girl was full of herself. And hiding something. Didn't she sneak off the ship at all hours?

Where was she now?

Chill night air blasted against her skin as she opened the door, the scent of ash and fire heavy on the air. Pelkaia threw an annoyed scowl at the sky. Her crew, all of them, milled around the deck of the *Larkspur*, peering over the rails, pointing and talking in low, worried voices.

"What's happened?" she demanded, stalking up to the rail to stand alongside Coss. He shifted his coat from his shoulders and settled it over hers. She hadn't even realized she'd strode out into the night in little more than her leggings and shift. But then, half the crew looked like they'd been rustled out of bed, too – mussed hair and coats thrown over nightclothes. Had something awakened her? She couldn't even remember.

"Trouble with the firemount by the palace. Had a small blowout a few marks back, but seems to have settled down now."

"Thratia."

He raised both brows at her. "Really? And what would she have to do with a perfectly natural occurrence?"

"Don't be daft. She has the Honding. I told him to leave this place before he did harm. How bad?"

Coss looked away from her, hunkering his shoulders so that he leaned slightly back from her side. "Hard to say. Relief's been at it all night. Some of us wanted to go lend a hand, but looters come out on nights like this. Didn't want to leave the ship unwatched."

Pelkaia stifled a need to point out that such decisions were hers to make. She'd had her fill of arguing with Coss as of late, and though she balked at his supposition that she had grown untrustworthy and unwell, a tiny piece of her, some calm core separated from the manic desperation that hummed through her, wondered if he were right. If she should just hand over the ship's control to him, and seek help. Or lay down to die. Was it too soon for that?

She'd forgotten how old she was, again. That couldn't be a good sign.

The dock they'd hired berthage at creaked as a single pair of footsteps pattered toward them. Laella. Her hands were white with dust, her hair and robes streaked with more of the same. In the faint lantern light of the docks, a heavy mask of makeup had been smeared across her features, sweat and grit mingling on her skin in sticky clumps. She walked like a woman exhausted, a woman defeated, but not a woman who'd been injured.

Pelkaia's eyes narrowed. That the girl had been out was no surprise, but that she'd been out on a night when Thratia's little demonstration was made, well. Thratia knew damned well the type of people living aboard the *Larkspur*. Though the Dame had given them express permission to stay in the city, there was nothing stopping Thratia from reaching out to a wayward deviant who spent more time off the *Larkspur* than on it.

Wouldn't Thratia just love that, too? Twisting the mind of a woman Pelkaia had saved. Stealing a human being's loyalties from the woman who'd taken her ship. Laella'd be the perfect mark. Leaving all the time, already closely tied to Valathean nobility. Gods beneath the dunes, the two might even know each other through previous social circles. Laella's family had been high-born, rich mercers. The kind of people Thratia loved to use.

Her fingers curled protectively around the *Larkspur*'s rail. There would be no spy of Thratia's aboard her ship.

"Where have you been?" she demanded when the young woman had mounted the gangplank.

Laella's step stuttered as she dragged herself the rest of the way up onto the deck.

Coss moved toward her, hesitated, then stopped. "Are you all right?"

"I'm fine," Laella said.

"What happened?" Jeffin piped up.

"*Where have you been?*"

All heads snapped to her, eyes wide and white in the

pale light. Laella reached up, tried to straighten an ashy braid, and quickly gave up. "Wading through the pits," she said. "It's a nightmare down there."

"What happened?" Coss pressed.

"One side of that firemount – I don't know what it's called. The big one by the palace. Anyway, it went up. Not too hard. Just a puff, I'd guess, but it was enough to kick off a landslide that took out half the residences of the palace district. I was in the theater district when it happened. Saw the whole thing, close as one could without being crushed, anyway."

"You're certain you're all right?" Coss pressed.

She nodded, but when Essi dragged a crate over to her she sat down like it was the plushest chair she'd ever touched ass to.

"Lucky place to be," Pelkaia said dryly. "Why were you there?"

Laella stared hard at her for a long moment. "In the theater district? For the theater."

Essi snickered. Pelkaia cut her a look and the little brat shut right up. "Seems you've been going there a lot, lately."

"Not like there's much to do here," she snapped.

Pelkaia stepped toward her. Coss put a hand on her shoulder but she shrugged it off. He'd kept her from tackling this treacherous girl long enough.

"Bored, are you? Filling your time with other ventures, then? Ones that put you in safe range of one of Thratia's little demonstrations?"

"What in the ass-licking pits are you talking about?" Laella shook her head in denial, and though she was playing tired and exasperated to all those aboard, Pelkaia could see the truth in the details of her expression. The tension along her jaw, the flicker of irritation in her eyes. She felt challenged, cornered. The girl was hiding something, and Pelkaia was pretty damn sure she knew what that was.

"You expect me to believe that all your ventures off this ship have been innocent – what – tourism?"

Laella's eyes widened. "You think I'm working for Ganal, don't you?"

"Do you dèny it?"

She barked a near-hysteric laugh. "Skies fucking above, Captain, you really have gone off your nut."

A few snickers from the crew. Pelkaia shot them all a hard look, and they weren't so quick to quiet this time around. "You traitorous fucking bastards. I dragged you – all of you! – from the edge of death, and you think I've lost my mind? This girl hasn't been traipsing around the city changing up her appearance every time for nothing."

Coss swore. Laella sucked in a sharp, angry breath. "You've been following me?"

"I have a right to know where my people are."

She stood in one fluid movement, whatever energy skulking around the city had taken out of her flooding back in one great rush. "Fuck you, and your twisted menagerie, Pelkaia Teria. You're a paranoid old woman with a hard-on for vengeance. You didn't save us. You *collected* us, and I for one am sick of being a token on your insane gameboard. Do. Not. Look. For. Me."

"Lael–" Essi reached a hand toward the woman, but she had already turned and was halfway down the gangplank. Pelkaia snorted.

"Good riddance."

Coss shook his head, long and slow. One by one, her crew went to their beds and locked their doors, leaving her alone on the deck, staring at the ashy footprints Laella had left behind, shaking as the mania that'd gripped her earlier faded to little more than shivering exhaustion.

CHAPTER 44

The bundle of servants' blacks made an obvious bulge beneath the front of his coat, but Detan figured no one would bother to comment on their lord's new paunch. They had other things to worry about. Not that anyone was about to comment, anyway. The palace residence wings were as empty as a whorehouse come the dawn. Normally he would have resented the lack of an audience, but today he welcomed the solitude. Every gaze he'd caught lately housed a question he just wasn't able to answer. Not yet, anyway.

By the time he reached the east wing of the palace he was jumping at shadows, expecting a trail from Misol or any other one of Thratia or Ranalae's cronies to make themselves known at the most inopportune of moments. This was the area of the building his auntie had handed over to Thratia, and each time he turned a corner he half expected to see her narrow eyes glaring him into a puddle.

Lady luck, or at least someone pretending to be her, was smiling on him. The empty halls caused him to wonder just what exactly Thratia was up to while he was sneaking about. He had a real nasty feeling that that'd spell trouble for him in the future.

The future. Hah. Ripka had rubbed off on him. He'd never worried about planning for the future before. Options, flexibility. These were the circumstances he created for himself.

Not that his previous habits were doing him a whole lotta' good now.

Detan strolled along like he belonged there, and probably he did. He could get away with explaining he'd come to see his darling betrothed, if pressed by any wanderers. Thratia wouldn't buy it, of course, but it's not like she could kill him until after the happy nuptials.

He decided it was best not to think about what she could do to him that was worse than killing.

Gatai had said the girls were being kept in a room with a view of the monsoons, and there was only one he could think of that fit the description. A lot of windows faced the same way 'round this side of the building, but only one room had been built at an unfortunate angle from a nearby tower that forced the winds to howl incessantly against its exterior, making the balcony all but useless. His auntie stuck guests she didn't like in that room.

Whether Thratia knew that or not, he couldn't guess, but the fact was the winds were likely to keep escape via the window a remote possibility, and the howling would keep any shouts for aid real quiet. She was a clever one, his bloodthirsty little wife-to-be.

Casting around one last time for visitors, he leaned against the door as if gathering his thoughts, tucked a hand up under the small of his back, and tapped on the wood. No response. Those winds weren't doing him any good, either. Nothing else for it, then. He gave the door one solid kick with his heel.

"What the fuck you want us to do, invite you in? Not like we can open the door," Clink's familiar voice barked.

Detan grinned. "I'm not entirely sure I can either, my dears."

A pause. "Is that you, Honding?"

"There are two Hondings in the building at present, but I believe I'm the one you're referring to."

She snorted. "And are you going to be any use this time around?"

"That's the idea." He wished Tibs were with him as he turned his back on the hall and slipped the two picks he'd brought with him into the lock.

"For fuck's sake, man, pass *me* those things. Ain't named Clink for nothing, you know?"

He blinked owlishly at the door. "Oh. Right."

Though the door was nearly flush with the floor, he managed to wiggle them under just enough to feel Clink snatch them away. Immediately, rattling issued from the knob.

"Keep it down, yeah?"

"There's two ways to do this: quiet and slow, or quick and loud. So shut up, I'm concentrating."

In Detan's experience, slow was the only way to go about picking a lock, but he didn't count himself dumb enough to argue with a woman who'd taken the name Clink when it came to lockpicking. He bit his lips and crossed his arms to keep from fidgeting as he leaned against the door, hoping the muffle of his back would silence some of the rattling. It didn't.

"Black skies," he muttered, and was promptly hissed at through the door. Irritable women, these friends of Ripka. But then, he'd probably be pretty pissy too if he'd been locked up to use as leverage against a man he didn't even know.

The lock gave with a clatter and he nearly fell ass-first into both women as they pulled it wide. Clink grabbed him by the scruff, dragged him the rest of the way in, and eased the door shut behind him.

"Skies above, I can't believe the captain was a friend of yours. Damn incompetent."

He made a show of straightening his clothes. "This incompetent has just sprung you both, thank you very much."

Clink and Forge exchanged a long look, then glanced pointedly toward the door. "Really? And just how are we getting past, oh, I don't know, a whole household full of unfriendlies?"

He patted his protruding belly. "I have an answer for that. But–"

Forge jabbed him in the chest with a finger. "You want a favor, is that it, Mister Altruism? Thought you were going to set us free out of the goodness of your little heart."

He winced and held his hands out in supplication. "You're in an unfriendly city that's being threatened with war on all sides. Tell me you wouldn't go looking for the captain, as you call her."

Forge narrowed her eyes. "We might at that. None of your business, noble-boy."

"Agreed. But, if you do see her…" He pulled a leather-wrapped packet about the size of his palm from his pocket and passed it over to Clink. She eyed it, weighing it with care.

"Bit heavy for a love-letter."

He snorted. "It's a few things she might need, that's all. But don't worry, I didn't forget gifts for you ladies, either."

He pulled the parcel of servants' blacks from beneath

his coat and laid it out flat on one of the two thin, hard beds that filled the room. The women fingered the material, frowning.

"Servants' uniforms?" Forge asked, holding one up to her body. The fit was reasonable enough, if a little large.

"No better way to go unnoticed in a palace," Clink said with a little grin.

"Except by other servants."

"Ah, but they are very much on your side. You have only to make it to the central pantry, and you will be smuggled off into the city from there."

"And how do we get to this pantry?" Clink asked, eyes narrowed.

"I will escort you, of course."

"The pits you will. Nothing doing, Honding. We appreciate you've gotten us this far but you're a peacock in this nest. Servants may go unnoticed, but everyone notices you."

Blasted woman was right, no matter how he hated the fact. The role he'd chosen to play here wasn't exactly one conducive to sneaking about. And the lord of the palace caught skulking with a couple of maids, even if they weren't recognized, wouldn't do him any good either.

"Fine," he said. "But I'll precede you to the end of this wing as a lookout."

"Deal."

He explained the way to the pantry in broad strokes, steering them clear of the populous areas. The girls made quick work of changing their clothes. Detan was relieved as anything to see Forge slip the packet he'd given them for Ripka securely on the inside of her crisp top. It was no guarantee, but it was something. Enough to ease the tension coiled within him.

"Ready?" he asked.

Nods from both. No time like the present for a little skullduggery, then. He pressed his ear against the door, listening for a few slow breaths to be sure they wouldn't troop straight into some random's path, then cracked the door just a sliver. All clear.

A peacock, they'd called him. He could work with that. Shoving his hands in his pockets he sauntered into the hall, a pleased smile slapped across his features and what he hoped was a jaunty tilt to his chin. Tibs would probably tell him he looked stupid but, this time around, that was the point.

The hall was clear right to the end, then Detan damned near tripped over a man strutting about in one of the grey coats of Thratia's militia. His heart jumped clear to his throat.

He over-exaggerated a stumble, forcing the man back down the hall that intersected the one the others were in, and threw his arms out to puff his coat and obscure any tell-tale signs of black. Servant's garb or not, if they stumbled across someone who knew their faces, it was all over.

"Whoa," the militiaman said as he put an arm on Detan's shoulder to steady him. "You all right, sir? Look like you seen a ghost."

"Didn't hear you coming, good man. This wing of the palace is dreadfully quiet. Why is that? Where is everyone?"

The man's face scrunched under the one-two punch of questions, trying to find a place to latch onto without overstepping his position too much. Detan made a show of straightening his clothes while the man thought, flapping about and generally being an annoyance.

"Lots to be seen to, sir, and it's still early yet." Was the answer he eventually arrived upon. Which possibly told Detan more about the militiaman than he'd intended. Bloodshot eyes. Droopy, sallow cheeks. Detan knew the look of a man sneaking away for a nap when he saw one.

"Indeed." He put on a lofty tone of voice, looking down his nose at him. "And with so much to do, what are you doing back at the apartments, then, forget something?"

"Oh. I. Uh, er..."

Detan put an arm around the man's shoulders, turned him back down the hall from which he'd come, and lowered his voice to whisper conspiratorially. "I understand, man, I do. Thratia's one pits-cursed taskmistress, isn't she? But I can't just let you saunter on. Hurry back to your duty, and I'll have the servants bring you some bright eye berry."

The man swallowed. "You won't report me?"

"Me? Nah. Truthfully, I understand. It's been a long couple of days, hasn't it?"

"Yes, sir. Thank you."

He bobbed his head a few times in an awkward half-bow, half-salute, and trundled off down the hall as quick as his leaden legs would let him. When he was well and truly gone, Detan let out a huge sigh of relief and grinned to himself. Still got it.

"Way's clear, ladies." He grabbed the corner of the wall and swung around to face them.

They'd already gone.

CHAPTER 45

Ripka had stood in front of a lot of crowds in her time as watch-captain. Had given her fair share of speeches, most of them structured in the formal trappings of her station. Each time she'd felt calm, assured. She knew her place, and the people she addressed knew it, too.

Now, her stomach coiled in knots. The forum was a much bigger venue than Dranik had made it out to be, and after the eruption the people of Hond Steading had come out in force to discuss the matters of their city.

On the edge of the palace district, shoved up against the backside of the main market, an amphitheater had been carved into the ground. Bright morning sunlight spilled across the hundreds of eager and wary faces crowded into the stone-cut benches, the steady rustle of cloth and murmur of voices reduced to a low hum by the fine acoustics. As Ripka lined up with all of those who wished to speak along the side of the stage, half the eyes in the place clung to her like thorns. Of all those lined up, she was the outsider. The one speaker the citizens did not recognize as a regular.

No different than quelling a riotous crowd, she

told herself, and had to stifle a wolfish grin lest those watching think she was mad. At least these people were less likely to try and tear her limbs off.

"Next up," the organizer boomed from above the podium. "Ripka Leshe, of Aransa."

Game time. Her fear fled in a flash, anxiety melting from her limbs as her focus narrowed to the podium, and the crowd. There was nothing else in all the world.

Dranik followed her, standing a respectable distance behind her as she placed her palms on the cool stone lectern and leaned earnestly forward. He was not there to speak. Everyone who frequented the forum knew him, and knew that his physical presence was a silent endorsement of what she had to say.

"People of Hond Steading," she began, thanking the sweet skies for Latia's knowledge of tea that her voice was smooth and without hitch. She pitched her tone low, going for carriage, and the clever acoustics of the forum did the rest. "I am the watch-captain of Aransa, or was on the day that city fell, and I have come to tell you of what happened in the streets that day."

Outbursts in the crowd, indistinct but clear in tone: shock, smug recognition. She held up a fist to silence them and, to her surprise, they quieted immediately.

"The day Aransa lost its right to determine its own warden, its own leadership, the streets were flooded with coats of grey." She tipped her head to point toward the shadow of the *Dread Wind* over the Honding palace. Any citizen aware enough of the city's events to attend this forum must have seen Thratia's militia about, their grey uniforms a ghostly contrast to the ruling family's black.

"It was my job, my duty, my honor, to protect that city's right to govern itself under the guidance of Valathean law. I failed that night. I failed in the weeks leading up to that night. And I have come to you, today, to tell you all the ways in which I have failed. So that you – so that we – may not fail again."

She gathered breath to dive into her next point when a man shouted from the front bench, "Who says a city has fallen just because Thratia Ganal governs it?"

Murmurs of assent spread out around him. The organizer scowled and stepped forward, intent on silencing the man, but Ripka held up a hand to stay him. If she did not face criticism head-on, she would win no one's mind or heart today.

"Speak your name, dissenter," she said.

He stood, a thatch of grey hair set aglow atop his head by the angle of the sun. "I am Hammod. All who attend this forum regularly know me."

She ignored the scorn in his voice, the hint that because she was not a regular here, she was not welcome. "Hammod. Have you met someone who has lived under Thratia's rule?"

His cheeks flamed red. "Cowards calling themselves refugees is all we've seen come through Hond Steading. Opportunists seeking succor from the Dame's teat, more like. Anyone with any grit has stayed in Aransa. She was elected, as you know. Fair as a calm sky."

"Elected? And who counted those votes? Commodore Ganal stepped into a power vacuum that her own games had caused–" Ripka carefully danced over the issue of Pelkaia's involvement. "–and assumed control without the consent of the people. No voting ever took place when I walked those streets, and I left on the day she decided to call herself Warden."

"Left? I heard you were run out. A traitor made to walk the Black Wash. Why in the pits should we listen to you?"

Ripka hadn't counted on that story making it to Hond Steading, but of course Thratia would have it spread. She'd been in the city long enough to set her people to whispering – and even before then, Ripka had no doubt that Thratia's counterintelligence were working hard to keep Hond Steading's loyalties divided. Explaining the circumstances of that walk, her so-called execution, would take too long – and muddy the waters. She needed something quick, sharp, if not entirely truthful, to clear her name.

"If I had walked the Black, would I be alive to stand before you today?"

Awkward shifting from those in the front rows who had murmured on Hammod's behalf. No one survived the Black. That was common knowledge. And if she had, then she certainly didn't fit Hammod's mold of a cowardly opportunist trying to take advantage of the Dame's hospitality. Before Hammod could gather himself for another volley, she pressed on.

"This is what Thratia does! She gives herself all appearance of legitimacy, pretends to legally hold the things she's actually taken. Do you think she came here simply for a wedding?"

Ripka jabbed a finger at the sky, and the silhouetted fleet hanging in it. No one could doubt those ships had been outfitted for war, not romance.

"Do not let her poison your minds. Do not let her assume control through your complacence. We have already seen a demonstration of her willingness to cause destruction to achieve her desires – yes, I place the blame of last night's eruption at her feet. Do you not think she has a weapon capable of demonstrating such power aboard that fortress ship of hers?

"That was a message for the Dame and her troops. But

it was a message you, the people of Hond Steading, must hear. The watch is not enough to keep these streets safe, I promise you that. More souls are needed. Able, quick-minded individuals who want to keep their home, their city, safe. There is no telling what Thratia will do next. I cannot guarantee anyone's safety.

"She will try to take this city legally – by marrying its heir. And I tell you this, he wants no part of that plan. But your ruling family is being held prisoner. Their hands are tied. It is up to you to protect yourselves, now. The time for polite discourse has passed."

A few whoops from the audience gave her heart, but the crowd was mostly inclined to quiet chatter. Her heart sank. This was the wrong audience for this. These were people who wanted to talk out their problems. A good and noble thing – but Thratia Ganal would let you talk all day while she maneuvered a crossbow behind your back.

Hammod scowled and stomped off toward the line to speak, cutting her a hard glare. Ripka closed her eyes a moment, head bowed over the podium. She knew the rules. Dranik had explained them to her. If she stood mute for more than a minute, she would be removed, and the next in line would have a chance to speak. They could go back and forth like this all day, bickering over the ethics, the legality, while Thratia's warship had a speargun pointed at all their necks.

She laughed, loud enough to be heard, and lifted her head, letting her tired eyes roam those gathered. When all had quieted, she lifted her hands, her raw and bleeding fingers, and examined them in the harsh morning light.

"Last night I dug the bodies of your fellow citizens from the ruin of their homes. Forgive me if I am short of words." She put her hands back down, gripping the edge of the podium. "If you wish your city to survive the coming weeks, come see me. Otherwise, make use of this forum while you can. Thratia will not let you keep it long."

She strode off the stage to profound silence, and did not bother to stop to sign her name in the speaker's log as was tradition. Her hands shook with anger at her sides, her focus so narrowed that all she could see was the route out of this place – this place of pointless bickering.

Once out on the street, she tipped her head back and glared at the sun, then flicked her eyes away before they could ache. She was going to lose another city to Thratia Ganal. She didn't know what she wanted to do more: strangle someone, or drink herself stupid.

A footstep crunched behind her, hesitant. She spun, expecting Dranik.

A young man she didn't recognize jumped back from her sudden attention, pupils wide. "Captain Leshe?" he asked.

"Miss Leshe suits me fine," she said by reflex.

His grin was fierce. "Not to me. Not to us."

She blinked. Over his shoulder, a few dozen youths filtered out of the forum, shifting anxiously in the dusty street, each and every one trying to get a good, long look at her. She forced herself to pick her head up, to push her shoulders back, but found she'd never left that posture behind after all.

"What can I do for you?" she asked, not daring to hope. They weren't all young, some grey heads mingled in the group, their numbers swelling until Ripka couldn't keep count.

"Where do we sign up?"

CHAPTER 46

After Clink and Forge so rudely abandoned him to seek their freedom, Detan paced the empty residence halls of the palace, wondering just what in the pits everyone was up to, but not quite curious enough to go find out for himself. It'd be just his luck Ranalae was planning some new heinous experiment for him. Or worse, his auntie and Thratia were busy picking out decorations for the wedding.

Thing was, he knew where he was going from the moment he wandered away from the east wing. Knew where his feet were leading him, though he didn't allow himself to approach the thought. There was one place in the palace he'd avoided since coming home. One room he hadn't dared to poke his head into.

Tibal's.

The door swung open easily under his hand. Unlatched, unlocked. Left ajar, as was often Tibs's way when he was head-deep in a project and couldn't be bothered with niceties like closing doors and bathing. A fan of dust cleared away in the wake of the door. Not even the servants had bothered to touch his room. Detan couldn't blame them. Last time he'd tried to polish a wrench Tibs hadn't talked to him for a week.

It'd been the longest they'd gone without talking, before the Remnant.

He stepped inside. His fancy, polished boots felt strange clicking across the gritty floor. Tibs's sheets were a twisted mess on the narrow bed, his tools spread out around the room in a pattern that made perfect sense to Tibs, and no one else. Detan reached for a hammer, thought better of it, and pulled his hand away before his fingers had brushed the surface. Touching Tibs's tools pissed him off, and though he'd probably never be privy to Detan's little saunter through this room, the habit was ingrained. Living as close together as they had on the flier had given them both clear boundaries to be respected. Mostly so they wouldn't kill each other.

He shivered. Tibs had left the door to the airship dock open, probably never bothered to close the thing the whole time he was here. Damned man never felt the cold, not even during the harshest of winter nights in the highlands of the desert. Despite the airflow, the subtle scent of machine grease and leather clung to the fabric in the room. A phantom of Tibs's presence.

A long, dingy linen curtain hung in the doorway to the airship dock. It fluttered in the faint breeze, kicking up swirls of dust. He pushed it aside, and stepped onto the dock.

The *Happy Birthday Virra!* was in the best shape he'd ever seen her. Her woodwork had been polished to a high, glossy sheen, her brass fittings bright as flame. Tibs had tied her sails and pulled in the wings, but he didn't need to see either unfurled to know they'd been replaced with better stock, the broadcloth sails gleaming with wax, the stabilizing wings webbed with fresh, supple leather. This was a ship ready to fly.

Tibs could have taken off at any time. Could have turned his back on everything that'd gone wrong between them. But instead he'd waited, and worked, and cleaned up the old bird until there was nothing left to polish.

"Where are you?" Detan asked the breeze.

The deck swayed under his step, a familiar sensation that almost made him choke up from pure longing. Without thought, he moved to the captain's podium, ignoring the empty nav deck behind him, and put his hands upon the primary wheel, set his legs in the wide stance he took while piloting.

He could leave. The flier was ready to go. There were probably provisions in its hold, and all his old clothes and trinkets. Money, too, and the means of making more counterfeit grains. Without him, Thratia would have no legal claim to the city. She'd have to take it by force. And he had no doubt she would.

He sighed and stepped back from the podium, peeling his hands away from the warm wood reluctantly. A corner of paper caught his eye, wedged beside one of the smaller wheels.

He plucked it free, annoyed that debris had gotten caught there, and nearly choked on his own spit.

Sirra scrawled across the outside in Tibs's sloppy script. He opened it.

> *Knew this would get you. Just couldn't resist the old bird, could you? Pains me to leave her here, but the Dame's getting itchy with me and I can't stick 'round much longer. I think Ripka's got some sort of plan, but she's mighty pissed with me, so I don't know if she'll let me in.*

*Sirra. Detan. Look. You know I ain't good with
words. I don't even know if you don't already know
what I'm trying to tell you. Thing is, Dame's getting
itchy because she knows my parents. Knew my pop,
anyway. You remember your old uncle Rew? I'm his
bastard, sorry to say. Not many knew, only my ma and
the Dame. But when you went to the Bone Tower the
Dame went a-huntin' for Rew's blowbys and found
me. Heir and a spare, you know? But I don't want it.
Never had. Keeping you out of too much trouble kept
my sorry ass from getting branded for next in line, and
I'm sorry for that.*

*Thing is, keeping your sorry ass out of trouble may
have been the deal I made with the Dame to start, but
that changed. We ain't cousins. We're friends, and
that matters more than any blood. If you can't see that,
you're dumber than that rock you got for brains.*

*Guess you know why we got matchin' tempers, now.
Don't do anything too stupid. I'll see you soon.*

The paper trembled in his hand, and it didn't have a
thing to do with the wind.

"Honding, are you in here?" Thratia asked.

Detan near jumped out of his skin. He folded the
paper and shoved it in his pocket, trying desperately to
gather himself. She was across Tibs's room in a moment,
shoved the curtain aside and squinted at him with tired,
dull eyes. They sharpened in a hurry, though, as she
focused in on him standing on the deck of the flier, just
behind the captain's podium.

"Leaving so soon?"

"Just checking her fitness," he said and shrugged,
strolling across the deck. It took everything he had to
jump down to the dock while maintaining nonchalance.

"By the look of you, you're the one preparing a run. Getting cold feet, dearest?"

Not so much as a frown. She gripped his elbow and steered him back into Tibs's room, out of the light and into the gloom. She looked even more haggard in the half-dark.

"While you've been checking on your toy, I've been working with the Dame to secure aid for those damaged by your little outburst. It's taken damn near every apothik I brought with me, and supplies are running low. What in the pits did you do?"

The words fell as a blow to the chest. Thratia hadn't been doing anything nefarious while he'd been running around getting Forge and Clink freed. She'd been hip-deep in the rescue relief, working alongside his auntie to get the city tidied up. She'd been right where he should have been, if he had any sense at all.

"You want to know what I did," he grated, "ask Aella and Ranalae."

"I did. I want it from you."

"They ambushed me. Pushed me as hard as they could thinking they could control me, and it turns out they couldn't. That enough for you? To know your nasty little friends tried to make me choke to death on selium and I damn near tore the city apart because I couldn't help myself?"

That wasn't tiredness in her eyes, he realized now. That was regret, plain as the sky was blue. She'd counted on Aella's ability to control him, counted on her own, probably, and now she was looking at him like he was a defanged snake who'd grown new teeth.

"Can you control yourself in the future?"

"You keep that bitch Ranalae away from me, and we'll see," he snapped. But it was the wrong thing to say, and he knew it the moment it was past his lips. Her eyes narrowed, her jaw tensed. The second she was done with him, the second she had a marriage contract or an heir in her belly or whatever the fuck else she wanted off him – he was dead. Or worse, she'd hand him over to Ranalae to make nice with Valathea while she gathered herself for another push in some other Scorched city.

"I'll instruct her to avoid you."

"You'll instruct the diplomat of an empire in which you hold no standing, to stay away from a man in a house where you also hold no power?"

"No power?" She snorted. "A formality that will soon be resolved. The wedding's in a week, Honding. Try to leave us a city to rule in the meantime."

"Us? Don't pretend to me, of all fucking people, that I'll have any say in matters once you have your contract signed."

She sighed and shook her head, the sharpened pins she wore in her braids clinking. "I'd prefer a partner, at the very least. You know my motives."

"Am I not a prisoner, then?"

Again, that tension in the jaw. "You never were."

Technically. He wanted to scream *technically* into her calm face. But that was how she did things. Pushed people around until she'd gotten them positioned to do the things she wanted of them of their own will. But she'd given his leash a bit of length, and he wasn't about to lose it.

"Then I'm free to leave the palace?"

Her gaze flicked to the *Dread Wind*, positioned to destroy the city if she decided to take it by force. Subtle, but effective in chilling him straight to the core. That was the thing about Thratia. Her best threats were the ones she never said out loud. "You are."

"Excellent. I have an errand to run." He turned from her, strode toward the flier like he had every right in the world to take it.

"Honding," her voice held an edge, a warning.

He threw a cheerful grin at her over his shoulder and blew a kiss. "Fear not, sweetums, I'll be back before dark. Feel free to smash the city to pieces if I'm not."

"Honding!"

But he was already on the deck of the flier, the tie-ropes kicked free. The day was calm, his sel-sense was keener than it'd ever had been. He didn't even need the sails as he unfurled the flier's wings, and took to the sky.

CHAPTER 47

Falston gave the watcher training grounds over to Ripka, and a single watcher for each dozen recruits that came for the citizens' brigade. They were slow to learn, sweating in the sticky desert sun, the monsoon winds blowing in off the northern coast heavy with moisture. But they were passionate, and brave, and in the end that was all Ripka could expect of them.

She sat on one of the benches lining the training ground, watching the last of them get put through their paces in the safe use of a baton, a bandana wrapped around her forehead to keep the sweat out of her eyes. Soreness suffused her, but she couldn't remember the last time she'd been this at peace.

Lakon spotted her sitting there, broke off his conversation with a watcher administrator, and strolled over. "Pleased with the results thus far, Captain?"

"Better than I could have hoped for. They're green, that's for sure, but they've got more passion than most first year watchers I ever saw. At least this lot isn't in it for the pay."

"Got a lot of opportunists like that, in Aransa?"

She shrugged. "No more than usual in any city. Living in the Scorched isn't an easy life. I don't begrudge them signing up if their heart isn't in it, so long as they do the job and do it well."

"Those tend to learn to love the work, in time."

"If they have a strong leader."

"If they do."

He cast her a sly look, and she tipped her head back against the wall, chuckling.

"Enough patting ourselves on the back. What are you doing for dinner tonight, Leshe?"

She blinked. "Me? Back to Latia's, more than like. I owe that woman a fistful of grains for the care she's given me."

"Kalliah, my little girl, wants you to come by to eat with us. Been talking about that 'lady captain' since the day she saw you come by the station house."

"Me? Why?"

"She's six years old, doesn't have to have a reason. And anyway, the wife and I would like to have you."

She glanced sideways to the courtyard, where Enard and Honey were putting a few late-night recruits through some basic combat training while Tibal looked on. Falston must have caught the look, because he snorted and said, "They can spare you a night. You've done a lot for this city. Let us give a little back."

"All right, all right. Let me clean up first, I'll meet you there."

"Don't keep us waiting," he said, and passed her a note with a hasty diagram on it outlining the directions to his home from the station house. She took it and raised both brows at him.

"Sure of yourself, aren't you?"

"Always am." He shot her a wink and headed back

toward his people, barking orders with every step.

Ripka shook her head as she stood and waved farewell to Honey, who cocked her head but otherwise didn't seem to mind. The woman had people to train how to fight. Ripka'd never seen her happier. Well, maybe once, but she was determined to scrub that memory for good.

She washed up in the watcher locker rooms, found some extra clothes kicking around the spares room, and followed Falston's map to a quaint little mudbrick home with creeper vines growing around the doorway. She hesitated on the walkway, listening to the soft talk and occasional laughter of those within.

Ache filled her from head to toe, every muscle protesting the use she'd put it to over the last few days. She didn't belong in a house like that. Never had, really. Even when she'd been a part of her family, just her mother and her father, they'd lived in a little one-bedroom stick-built thing way off on the edge of town. Only plant life her mother ever bothered tending was cacti and ground-roots for food, and even those withered after the war. Left to her own devices, Ripka'd only ever taken rooms or rented apartments; she'd even spent a few months in an inn, once. Curtains and vines and girlish giggles just weren't her thing.

The map crunched in a fist she hadn't intended to ball, but there it was. And it was getting late, anyway. The others knew where she was, sure, but she was tired straight to the bone. Falston would understand.

Before she could get halfway turned around the door banged open, and Falston came rumbling out, dressed in plain brown clothes instead of his watcher blues, a long pipe dangling from his lips.

"There you are! Was just about to send out a search party. Don't tell me you got lost?"

"No, Captain. Just took longer than I'd meant to clean up." She tried to cover the fact she'd been turning around by shifting her weight. The squint he gave her told her that particular effort had been wasted.

He let out a long, smoky sigh, and chucked his head toward the door. "Come on in now, monsoon's getting sticky and the rains'll come tonight. Mata says so, and Mata always knows."

"Mata?"

"My wife! Mata!" He bellowed the last over his shoulder and flowed back into the household. Ripka clenched her jaw and followed. She wasn't sociable by nature, but there were certain flavors of rude she wasn't willing to stoop to.

"No yelling in the house," came a woman's sharp reply. Mata stuck her head around a hall corner, caught sight of Ripka shuffling across the threshold, and broke into a grin like a thunderstorm.

"There she is!"

"Hey, you said no yelling." Kalliah, the little gap-toothed girl she recognized from Falston's office, bounded after her mother, twin braids swinging.

"It's your father's bad habit, dear, we're allowed."

Falston harrumphed, but hid his smile by taking another long puff of his pipe. "Mata dear, this is–"

"I know who this is." She bustled forward, scooped the girl up in one arm, deposited the child on her hip and stuck her hand out for Ripka to clasp. Ripka stared. Mata'd moved faster than any trainee she'd seen that day. "Nice to meet you, dear, now come in and sit down. Food's just getting hot enough."

Ripka gave her hand a wary squeeze, mindful of her callouses, and was surprised to feel matching ones beneath Mata's fingers and palms. Mata winked in recognition, then swept away back to the kitchen.

"Pitfire of a woman," Falston muttered to himself. "Wouldn't have it any other way."

"She…" Has hands like a warrior, Ripka wanted to say, but settled on, "seems nice."

Falston roared with laughter, clapped Ripka on the shoulder, and practically dragged her down the hall to the kitchen table.

The rest of the house was little more than a blur, but the family table spilled over into the kitchen, giving Mata just enough room to maneuver about her business, even when she had Kalliah clamped to her hip. Falston sat Ripka down on a chair with its back to a window and a clear view of the exit. Whether he'd done it intentionally or not, she appreciated it all the same.

"Fal tells me you've been doing great work with these new recruits of yours."

She blinked, taking a cup of sweet-smelling liqueur from Mata's hand. "They're quick learners."

"Great teachers make quick learners," she insisted.

Falston hauled a huge pot of roast gamebird off the oven-top and placed it with a clunk in the center of the table. Ripka's stomach rumbled. Audibly. Mata laughed. "Thank you, dear."

Ripka covered her embarrassment by taking a quick sip of her drink. Honey liqueur. Laced with selium bubbles. She nearly choked.

"Are you all right?" Mata came around the table in a second and patted her firmly on the back. Ripka waved her away, wiping tears from her eyes.

"Fine, fine, just… Where did you get this?"

Falston narrowed his eyes at her. "The open market this morning. Some Mercer from the west makes it."

"Renold Grandon," she said, rolling the cup around

in her hand.

"Grandon, that's the name. You know him?"

"He's Aransan. Long-time ally of Thratia. This been coming into the city for a while?"

"A day or so," Mata said.

Falston and Ripka exchanged a long, heavy look.

"No business at the dinner table," Falston said.

She nodded, understanding. When Ripka had arrived in Hond Steading, Grandon's liqueur had been nowhere to be found, and so she'd focused on the bright eye berry cafes. If Thratia had now begun slipping weapons into the city, it was probably too late to stop them. She'd tried. And she'd missed.

"Can I get you something else?" Mata asked.

"No," she smiled as she took another swallow without choking. "This is wonderful, thank you. The little bit of home surprised me, that's all."

Mata gave her a look that said clear as day she didn't believe her for a second, but wasn't about to argue with a guest in her own kitchen.

Kalliah clambered atop a chair and propped her fists on her hips, head high. "I'm gonna be a lady captain too!"

The adults laughed while the girl looked put upon, and the evening fell into small talk and praise of the food. Ripka grew warmer with every bite and sip. By the time they were finished, Ripka felt heavier than she'd ever felt in her life.

She made her goodbyes and dragged herself to the door, sluggish with sleep and food, Kalliah dogging every step she took with made-up stories of the little girl's exploits as a captain.

Mata ushered the girl off to bed, then rejoined Falston and Ripka on the front step, and pretended rather smoothly not to notice that their topic of conversation had switched from watcher business to the clearness of the night the moment she appeared.

"Pleasure to have had you," Falston said and clapped her hard on the shoulder.

Mata swooped in, gripped her hand and pulled her into a half-hug, leaning close to whisper lightning quick so that her husband wouldn't notice, "Look after him."

She was away in an instant, but the words clung to Ripka like cactus thorns.

"Thank you for your hospitality." She managed a smile, hoped it looked genuine, then made her escape before Falston could pick up on the shift in her mood. She didn't want to explain to him that his wife was worried for his safety. Even less, did she want to explain to Mata that what they were doing now was very, very dangerous?

And she'd begun it. She'd reached out to Lakon for help and stood in that forum, swaying the people of Hond Steading to hand over their wellbeing to protect a city that might not be savable. In a week's time, they could all be dust. And that'd sit on Ripka's shoulders, if she hadn't gone and joined them.

A steady monsoon of rain began to fall, warm and thick. She was soaked through before she reached Latia's house, and all she wanted was a dry change of clothes and a warm bed. When she opened the door, however, what she found was a full house waiting up for her in the living room. Every head swiveled towards her as she stepped inside.

"What's happened?" she said, reaching instinctively for her weapons belt.

"Nice to see you too, Cap'in," an all too-familiar voice drawled.

Ripka pushed rain-drenched hair from her eyes and squinted through the low light. Forge and Clink sat alongside Honey on the couch, their grins a mirror of one another's.

"Holy shit," Ripka said. "What...?"

"Got a package for you. From that Honding idiot."

Clink pulled a bundle from her severe, black uniform – a Honding servant's uniform – and handed it out. Ripka crossed the room shakily, not quite believing what she saw, and undid the string. A handful of heavy, fine parchment with the letterhead of house Honding fell out. Along with a thick, brass signet ring. Detan's. Had to be.

Forge whistled low. "Guess he's got ears after all."

"We're going to a wedding," Tibal drawled, and Ripka didn't know whether she wanted to laugh or cry.

CHAPTER 48

The flier's wheel beneath his hands, the cool air pushing back his hair. These things combined to ease in him a tension he hadn't realized he was carrying. Despite returning to his familial home, this was where he belonged. The sky was his real home, the selium in the buoyancy sacks above his head an extension of himself. Nowhere else had ever made him feel so whole.

The only trouble was, he had an unfortunate habit of setting the whole thing on fire now and then. Had been his habit, he reminded himself. His control was growing by bounds every day. Even without active training, he knew he had begun to outpace Aella's expectations. He could see it in the hunger in her eyes. Girl might be cold as a fish most of the day, but any progress on her research lit her up like a firemount.

Best not to think of firemounts, just now.

He steered away from the palace, put his back to the vista of the city that was both his duty and his burden.

He hadn't known what he was going to do when he took the flier. Had only been acting on an intense desire to get away from Thratia, from the palace, from the hulk of responsibilities and terrors that rested on his shoulders, penning him in. But now that he had the wind in his hair and the wheel beneath his hands, he was able to think clearly in a way that'd eluded him ever since he'd found himself bending knee to Aella on the Remnant.

If Thratia thought she'd bag him as a husband, roll up his city in some neat little farce of a contract, and kick him to the whitecoats to deal with, she was fucking delusional.

He yanked on the wheel, listened to the wind scream as he brought the flier hard around and pointed it straight toward the northern coast. He wasn't running. Not this time. Not ever again. But he couldn't do what he set out to do alone. There was only one person left in Hond Steading who could help him pull this off without major bloodshed.

It was just too bad for him that she hated him with a burning passion.

Detan brought the flier, smooth as oil, alongside the sleek figure of the *Larkspur*. The ship'd been docked on the north edge of the city, far away from the population center, but that hadn't hidden it from his view when he'd flown in on the *Dread Wind*. A ship like the *Larkspur* was hard to miss – it drew the eye, the heart. Thratia had good taste in ships, that was for sure. Too bad she had terrible ideas about everything else.

"Ho, *Larkspur*!" he called, and waited. And waited. No one seemed to be aboard, or no one who wanted to talk to him, anyway. He guided the flier to the opposite side of the dock, dropped a handful of grains in the porter's lockbox and tied off.

The *Larkspur*'s gangplank tongued the dock, and as he strode up it he wondered who in the pits had been dumb enough to leave it down with a non-responsive crew on board. Ships like the *Larkspur* drew a lot of eyes, and sticky fingers, too.

He mounted the deck, ready to ream some lackey of Pelkaia's for poor ship management, and stopped cold. Pelkaia herself sat in the center of the deck on a lounge chair tucked up under the shadow of the mainmast. Her head was tipped back, eyes stuck on the empty sky, a plethora of bottles scattered across the deck around her. Pools of shadow gathered in her sunken cheeks and, for just a heartbeat, he thought she was dead. Her head lifted. She squinted at him a moment, slow to recognition, and snort-laughed.

"Of course it's you."

"Skies, Pelkaia. What's going on here?"

He crossed to her side and toed an empty bottle. Not booze, as he'd first thought, though there was a fair amount of that kicking around nearby. The distinct tang of medicine – sedatives, painkillers – hung on the air, clinging to Pelkaia like a cloud despite the soft breeze.

"They left," she said.

"Who left?" He hunkered down into a crouch beside her and reached to check her pulse via her wrist. She didn't so much as flinch when he touched her. The beat of her heart was sluggish, but steady.

"Everyone."

Shit. Coss, the crew... Coss. No wonder she was drinking herself stupid with anything she could find. He hadn't been with those two long, but even he could see they'd cared about each other, and Pelkaia'd seemed considerably less nutty with Coss around to keep her stable.

"You gonna let their leaving kill you?" he asked.

She squinted at him. "You are such an idiot."

"So I've been told. Come on now. Sit up. I'm not your biggest fan, Pelly my dear, but I'll be damned if I let you waste away on the deck of this ship. You know how hard it is to clean a rotten body stain off hardwood?"

"Tip me over the side, then."

"Pits." He wrangled an arm under her shoulders and hefted her more or less upright, got her legs slung over the side of the chair so she'd be forced to bend them. Every move she made her joints crackled, and it was real hard to ignore just how firm her bone-braces had gotten since last he'd seen her. If Coss leaving wouldn't kill her, the bonewither soon would.

After she was more or less stable, he went rummaging through the ship for some water, and came across cactus pulp juice. Good enough. She probably needed the extra nutrients.

By the time he returned she was looking a little more clear-eyed, but not much. Still managed to sit up straighter when she saw him, though, so that was something. Pride could get a body through a lot of things.

"Drink this, you damn fool of a woman."

He helped her sip down half the bottle before she started spluttering.

"Why do you care?" she asked.

"Saved your ass once or twice before. Seems I'm making a habit of it."

"Honding." The sharpness was back in her voice, the subtle edge of exasperation. He grinned at her, and her frown just got deeper. That was as good a sign as any.

"Need your help."

She snorted and reached for the juice. He handed it off to her, watched her throat bob as she forced a bigger swallow than she was ready for. "What is it this time?"

"You still want a shot at Thratia?"

There it was. She was back in a heartbeat, everything about her sharp and alert. If Detan knew one thing for sure about dear, crazy Pelly, it was that revenge would keep her walking and talking long after she'd been buried in a deep grave.

"Explain."

"I'll need you to work with an old friend of mine, name's Gatai. He'll handle most of the logistics, but he'll need your particular talent. Once you've finished, you'll have to return to Aransa, then wait for Thratia to come crawling back with her tail between her legs."

"You think I can make it to Aransa in this shape?" She flung an arm out, taking in the whole of the empty *Larkspur*. Her arm trembled from the effort, and he wondered if she'd meant that to be part of her little display. Probably not.

"Gatai will get you a flier you can handle. You'll be out of the city, en route to Aransa, long before the party even begins. You're in poor shape, Pelly dear, but we both know you can rally yourself for one last push if it means a shot at Thratia."

Her eyes narrowed with suspicion, but she nodded. "I'm listening."

He gathered himself, and explained his plan, such as it was. She listened with rapt attention, eyes growing brighter as each word fell into place. When he was finished, he didn't need to ask her what her answer would be, but she provided one anyway.

"I'll do it, but not alone."

"Gatai will provide you with–"

She kicked one of the empty bottles hard enough that it shattered in a puff of glass shards. "Your wedding is in two days. That is no time at all to prepare what you ask, even with your friend's help. I need a favor."

"Anything."

Her brows rose. "I doubt that. But all I need is for you to deliver a letter to Nouli. Can you?"

"Absolutely." If he couldn't do it himself, he could always hand it off to Gatai.

She took a moment to scrounge up some paper from a pocket and scrawled something brief, folded it, and passed it over. He put it in his own pocket and stood, offering her his hand. She eyed him a moment, then took it and allowed him to heft her to her feet.

"Chances are I won't be seeing you again, I think," he said. Skies, he wasn't very good at this good-bye goatshit. Pelkaia was a walking nightmare for him more often than not, a crazy murderous nightmare, but he still had a soft spot for the nutter. At the very least, he understood her reasons.

She squeezed his arm, a soldier's grip, and offered him what might be the first real smile he'd ever seen on her naked, true face. "Good luck."

"And you."

He left her to prepare, and waited until he was halfway back to the palace before taking a peek at the note she'd written Nouli.

The favor I must ask of you is, as it turns out, for all our benefit. I will come to discuss matters with you soon. As a token of my faith, here are the coordinates to a Catari meeting place. I will leave you once our task is complete, but if you travel to this location, leave a message in my name – Pelkaia Ariat Teria. The shamans will come for you, and share their knowledge. May you find your cure, as I could not.

Skies keep you.

CHAPTER 49

A week after Ripka's plea to the forum, the Honding palace rang out a peal of bells to mark the day of Detan's wedding. Birds roosting on the roof of the stationhouse took to the air, sending the citizens' brigade members – Ripka included – ducking for cover lest they be shat upon.

"Oh happy day," Tibal said, to the nervous chuckles of many of those gathered. At least something had broken the tension.

"For those attending the festivities." Forge removed a carefully wrapped parcel containing four wedding invitations she'd counterfeited with the supplies Detan had sent them. One each for Ripka, Tibal, Enard, and Honey. Watch-captain Lakon had received his own, legitimate, invitation the day before.

Ripka undid the bundle and handed them out to her well-dressed companions, feeling stiff and awkward in her own fine, carnelian dress. At least Thratia's taste in fashion made wearing a high slight and leggings beneath acceptable. Mobility would be key tonight.

Latia'd procured somber black suits for the men,

subtle pleating allowing them a greater range of motion, and a dye-dipped dress of oranges and reds that made Honey look like she was the smoldering wick of a candle, her hair the golden flame.

All in all, Ripka'd much rather be wearing her street clothes and staying close to the brigade. But Detan had sent those invitation blanks for a reason, and she wasn't about to let Enard and Tibal walk in there without her.

"Dranik," she said. The young man snapped to attention. He'd really bent himself to the task in the last week, and had earned himself a position at the top of the pack. "Keep our people distributed evenly, no clumping until trouble spots can be identified. Use your whistles to communicate, as we taught you. No weapons unless you receive the signal from the palace. Keep yourselves hidden, and safe."

"Yes, Captain." His salute was a mess, but well-meaning, so she let it slide with a smile.

"Now," she said, "let's go crash this party."

Carriages clogged the streets of Hond Steading, all the well-to-do of the city coming out to be seen, but not get their feet dusty. They skirted the crowded streets, and Ripka wondered if her invitation was the only one growing a bit damp in a sweaty palm. It was one thing to break into a large celebration like this. It was quite another to do so when many of the attendees were very likely to recognize you. They'd done their best to obscure their features with carefully applied makeup and different hairstyles, but there was only so much they could do to hide their faces – without Pelkaia's tricks, anyway. Too bad Detan hadn't thought to demand his wedding be a masquerade.

The palace's great doors had been thrown wide, a contingent of black-clad guards lining the flower-strewn steps to check for invitations and weapons. Ripka squinted against the sun, and her heart beat a little faster. They weren't all Honding guards. Many wore the grey coats of Thratia's personal militia, the same damned uniform she'd seen flood the streets the night she took Aransa.

Enard squeezed her hand, just for a moment, and she breathed a little easier. They were prepared. They could do this.

They mounted the steps as a group, Ripka at the head, Tibal trailing in the rear as he was most likely to be recognized – even without the hat. Honey stuck close by Ripka, her over-the-top outfit and beauty doing a whole lot of good to keep the guards from looking too closely at anyone else. It worked. Their invitations were checked, the corners clipped, and they were in.

Ripka gasped. The grand hall of the palace, where all the people of the city were welcome to visit at any time for refuge, had been transformed into a glimmering garden of light and flowers. How the Dame had mustered all this up on such short notice, Ripka had no idea. But the walls were festooned in garlands of flowers, the ceiling a waterfall of lanterns made of glass in all possible colors. The Dame might not be pleased about the match her nephew had made, but she wasn't going to let that keep her from sending him to his nuptials in Honding style.

The hall was packed, but not quite as packed as she would have liked it. Servants moved among them, deftly presenting trays of drink and small bites to the guests as they waited for the couple's arrival. The contract, she knew, by tradition would be signed before the ceremony even began. The moment Detan stepped into this hall, he would already be legally bound to Thratia. The binding of hands before those gathered was only a formality, a way to publicly display their intentions. Marriage contracts were meant to be a private, intimate affair. Just one more thing perverted by Thratia's aspirations.

A servant swooped down upon her and she took a glass of something red and citrusy, even though her stomach ached at the thought of what Thratia was putting Detan through. A guest refusing refreshment would be remarked upon.

They spread out a little, though Honey stuck close to Ripka's side. The crowd was thickening as the day grew late, morning marching steadily toward midday, when the couple would make their appearance. No one recognized her, and so no one tried to make small talk. She was an unimportant fish in a very, very big social pond. She kept herself busy checking exits, bottlenecks. At the end of the hall the guests clumped up, getting as close to the ceremonial altar as possible. She'd want to stick to the edge, toward the back, to best be able to maneuver through the crowd, but still be close enough to the center aisle that Detan could spot her when he entered. If she and Honey pressed just a little further to the right…

A hand fell on her shoulder.

Dame Honding stood behind her, resplendent in teal and navy blue silk piped with her family's black. Ripka swallowed, forced a small smile, opened her mouth to say something, anything, but found no words. She braced herself for the guards to be called.

The Dame winked, nodded once, and disappeared back into the crowd.

Ripka's knees were jellied.

A lilting harp took up a slow waltz, and the couple entered.

CHAPTER 50

The weird thing was, Thratia didn't even try to slip anything untoward into the marriage contract. The wording was as straightforward as you could get – the usual bindings of house and fortune, the special paragraphs detailing the split rule of Hond Steading, and how the last word ultimately fell to the blooded heir – Detan himself.

He thought it strange, until he realized the actual wording was pointless. The whole thing was a farce, anyway. She'd label him dangerous or mentally unstable – or both – first chance she got and ship him off for Aella to play with. Or worse, Ranalae. He really didn't like the way Thratia was looking at him after his slip with the firemount. Like he was a wildfire that needed to be snuffed, and fast.

The marching music, as he thought of it, struck up, and he was proud of himself for not trembling as he took Thratia's arm in his. Thratia wore flame red, her hair piled with vicious pins, and she'd gone ahead and stuck him in the same charcoal-and-ember style she'd filled his wardrobe with, if cut a little tighter and a little fancier for the occasion. Maybe she didn't much like the truth about his power, but she was willing to flaunt it, for now. He thought he looked ridiculous, but then he figured even at a normal wedding the groom wouldn't have much say in his attire.

Servants pulled the doors. They stepped into the hall. Detan's breath caught as he took in what his auntie had done for this day, for him. She didn't know his plans. Didn't know that he still held out hope that he'd figure out a way to wriggle free of Thratia's stranglehold. All she knew was her nephew was getting married, and to the pits with the reasons or the bride. She'd decorated the hall like she meant it and, in her own strange way, he knew she was telling him she loved him. Maybe even that she was sorry.

The long aisle to the altar was as red as Thratia's dress, making her seem omnipresent, somehow. As if she could reach out and control the whole of the room with only a thought. Detan put a little saunter into his walk, because why the pits not, it was his wedding, after all, and escorted his evil little bride down the aisle with the fakest grin he'd ever mustered in his life.

The crowd was silent, polite, whispering behind their hands if they talked at all. All eyes were on him, on Thratia, and there was a tension in the room – a thickness that crawled over his skin.

He found the source in the little grey dots breaking up the guests, members of Thratia's militia in their uniform best, but their uniforms all the same. No doubt the only people allowed weapons in the entire building tonight. Aside from Detan himself, anyway. He could never truly be denied his power. Not now that he knew the injections did not work on Aella.

Halfway down the aisle, he almost tripped.

Ripka. Ripka and that blonde-haired woman he'd last seen her with at the Remnant were in the crowd.

She stood a little ways back from the aisle, angled so that he could see her, but otherwise making herself inconspicuous. She'd done a bit of fancy work with her makeup and hair, but he'd know her anywhere. Could see in the set of her shoulders, the slight wrinkle around her eyes, that she was up to something. Planning, preparing. For what, he hadn't a clue. But if Ripka was here, his other friends might be, too. He glanced away to avoid Thratia following his eye, and scanned the crowd quickly. No sign of Tibs or New Chum that he could see, but that didn't mean they were absent.

If Thratia noticed the sudden lightness in his step, she gave no indication.

They reached the end of the aisle, where his auntie waited with a misty look in her eye that he tried very, very hard to ignore. The altar was a simple thing, a hip-height pillar of stone with a copper basin in its center. Knowing his auntie, it was probably the same one Detan's parents had been married with. He hoped not. They'd been through enough trouble in their lives without him sullying their memory by dribbling Thratia's blood into their altar. The knife that matched the set was already in his auntie's hand.

"Thratia Ganal. Detan Honding. You have been bound by paper. Do you consent to be bound by blood?"

"We do," they said in unison.

A quick slice on the palms, a clasping of hands above the copper bowl, and it was done. Over in a flash and the faintest of stings. The audience burst into cheers and applause.

Detan stood opposite Thratia at the altar, his bleeding hand clasped in hers, dripping a mingling of their blood into the bowl, and was stunned at how simple a thing it all was.

He had married Thratia Ganal.

CHAPTER 51

The marriage thus sealed, apothiks swooped down upon the couple to bandage their hands, and Ripka was astonished to see Detan not so much as blink as an apothik in a sharp white apron rushed at him.

"He has calmed," she murmured.

Servants brought out tables and chairs for those who wanted them, and the altar was cleared away to make room for a long banquet table at which Thratia and Detan were sat, dead center, Dame Honding to Detan's left and Aella to Thratia's right.

Most of the guests stayed on their feet, mingling and chatting and generally trying to get as close to the couple's table as possible. Ripka eyed those gathered with fresh insight. Their city had just been stolen out from under them, but for the higher-ups of Hond Steading, life went on. And that meant making alliances with this new couple that ruled them, slotting themselves into places of importance in whatever system would emerge in the wake of Thratia's takeover.

And everyone knew this was Thratia's city now, not Detan's. The amount of people trying to get close to her while ignoring their blooded lord's existence bordered on pathetic. Hond Steading fancied itself the most future-looking city on the Scorched, but its people were still born of the homesteading tradition. These were hard people, and they would do what needed to be done to survive. Ripka only hoped that translated into fighting for their future, if the opportunity would arrive.

"Bunch of vultures," Enard whispered as he sidled up to her.

"They're scared," she said, shrugging.

"Cowards, then."

"Can't argue that."

A young man in a very sharp blue suit stepped in front of Honey. "Good evening, my dear. I fear we have not yet met. You are...?" He extended a hand to her, eyes wide with question. Honey pursed her lips and stared at his hand like she'd never seen one before. His eyebrows drooped. "Ah, do you not speak Valathean?"

Honey turned to Ripka. "I don't like him."

Enard chuckled into his drink. Ripka grimaced and inserted herself between the two, nudging Honey gently behind her. Curse Latia for doing too fine a job making Honey distractingly beautiful.

"She doesn't take well to strangers," Ripka explained, hoping her apologetic smile might soothe whatever wounds the man's ego had taken.

"I see. And how would one get to know her?"

Enard stepped forward then, his voice low, but polite. "Not happening, friend."

The man huffed and stomped away. Ripka let out a breath and gave Honey a side-eye. "Well done," she drawled.

Honey brightened. "Thank you."

Enard took one look at Ripka's exasperated expression

and almost choked on his next drink. His amusement lifted her spirits, and she caught herself grinning into her own glass. That crinkle around the corner of his eye, the little way he smiled – just tight enough not to be noticed unless one were really looking. Skies. Everything about Enard calmed her.

"Enjoying the festivities?"

Ripka turned to find Nouli Bern behind her. Someone from the palace had fetched him appropriate clothes for the evening, and, all cleaned up in his fresh suit with straightened glasses, he almost looked like a well man.

"Nouli–" she bit back an apology. After the Dame had thrown her out of the palace, she hadn't even thought of the man she'd risked so much to steal from the empire. She'd left him here to stew, to prepare for a war she hoped they wouldn't have to fight, without so much as a word. And yet, he looked more relaxed than she'd ever seen him. Her brow furrowed.

"Whatever you're going to say, my dear, it's quite all right." He drew a hand through his hair, messing up the careful style a servant had no doubt worked hard to achieve. There was a glint in his eye, a sly amusement that she wasn't quite sure she could trust. "I was hoping to see you here, in fact, so that I could thank you."

"Thank me?" Enard slipped up alongside her, hands easy at his sides, his glass dangling from his fingertips should he have to move in a hurry. If Nouli noticed the implicit threat in his posture, he said nothing about it. He smiled and tipped his head to Enard like he were an old friend.

"For the introduction to Pelkaia Teria. Fascinating woman. We had much to discuss. Information that proved very fruitful for my particular needs." He held his glass out to her, and she brought hers up hesitantly to clink them together. His grin was a wolfish thing, taking over his whole face. "I'm leaving Hond Steading tonight, I'm afraid, to continue my research elsewhere."

"You're well?" she asked, breathless with surprise.

"On my way to it." He leaned forward, squeezed her shoulder in his hand, and spoke softly so that only she and Enard could hear. "My parting gift to you, my dear: mind the sweet stuff."

He flicked his head toward Detan, who had his head together with Gatai, the keymaster of the palace, whispering. Ripka frowned, not understanding, but before she could muster up a question he winked at her and slipped away into the crowd.

"What in the pits did he mean by that?" Enard asked.

Honey said, "Watch."

Ripka had seen it, too. Gatai nodded, solemnly, and passed on whatever Detan had told him to another servant. And another. The information spread between them, each pausing to tap another on the elbow and whisper something – lightning quick. Ripka cast around for a nearby servant, hoping to eavesdrop, but the information had already finished spreading

New bottles appeared on their trays, deep green and hauntingly familiar. They circled the guests, handing out drinks when asked, but pressed the militiamen to join in the celebrations with a sip or two. Ripka hadn't met a guard yet who'd turn down a free drink at a party.

Detan clapped, a whip-crack above the polite murmuring of the crowd. All heads turned to the bridal table. He stood, bowed elaborately to Thratia, then motioned for Gatai to step forward. The man had his own tray now, one of the green bottles and a glass the only items on it.

"A gift to you, my lovely bride." Detan's voice was

firm but gentle. Even Ripka couldn't detect a hint of sarcasm in it. "To remind you of all the time we've spent together."

Gatai poured. He placed the glass before Thratia. Even Thratia, a known teetotaler, couldn't turn down a gift from her husband on their wedding day. She forced a smile and took a small sip.

"Fond memories of Aransa," she said, loud enough to carry. The crowd applauded as Detan sat back down, the long line of well-wishers clustering forward once more.

"Is he getting them drunk?" she asked.

"Seems like." Enard waved down a servant who had just finished topping up a guard. They each took a glass, and a small sip. Ripka wrinkled her nose.

"Grandon's honey liqueur."

"Indeed," Enard agreed. "But something else, too, something bitter…"

"Golden needle," Honey offered.

Ripka swirled her glass, took a long sniff and another, careful, sip. "Fiery pits. She's right."

"He's not just getting them drunk. He's knocking them all out," Enard said with admiration. And Thratia, who never drank alcohol, wouldn't have the slightest clue the brew was off. The hint of sedative was just faint enough that Ripka doubted even the heaviest of drinkers would notice. Golden needle was a strong flavor… Nouli and Pelkaia must have worked out a means to cover it. She grinned fiercely.

"That won't take long to work. We should be ready."

Enard nodded and sat his still-full cup carefully down on a passing dish-tray. Ripka and Honey followed suit. "I have a feeling there's little we can do until the action starts. With luck, the Lord Honding will inform us further."

"Have you seen Captain Lakon? I should warn him."

"Sir, please, wait your turn," a guard was saying firmly at the front of the room. Ripka pressed to her toes to see over the heads of those around her. Tibal stood in front of the couple's banquet table, swaying with drink, a cup still clutched in one hand. Not the honey liqueur, thank the skies, but it seemed Tibs hadn't needed the extra kick to get drunk in a hurry. He pinned a hard stare on the guard and slurred. "I'm family."

"Shit." Ripka dropped back down from her toes.

"What?" Enard pressed.

"When did you last see Tibal?"

"He was right behind me during the ceremony."

"Drinking himself stupid."

"Oh. Shit."

"Right."

"It's all right," Detan's voice echoed through the hall. He hadn't seen the man was Tibal yet, couldn't have. Ripka swore and elbowed her way through the crowd, but she was too far back. There was no way she could peel him away in time. "Let the man give his blessing."

The crowd broke in front of Ripka. Tibal sauntered forward, set his cup down on the table in front of a slack-jawed Detan, and smirked.

"Congratulations on the nuptials, cousin."

CHAPTER 52

Detan couldn't shut his mouth. He knew it was open, knew he should probably do something about that. This was his wedding, after all. Walking around catching flies in his wide-open trap was probably not the done thing. But he couldn't help himself.

Tibs. Drunker than he'd ever seen him. And cleaner, too, in a pretty neat-looking suit that Detan wished he could swap him for. And he had just declared himself Detan's cousin. In front of Thratia. Worse, in front of Ranalae and Aella who, even though they were seated down Thratia's side of the table, Detan could tell clear as day were practically salivating at the thought.

"Tibal," Thratia said, with a surprising amount of grace. She held her hand out to him and, to Detan's great horror, Tibs took the clawed thing and bowed politely over it. "Always a pleasure to see you."

"Welcome to the fucking family," Tibs drawled.

Detan cleared his throat. Hard. Tibs didn't seem to notice, the damned fool. Where was Ripka, anyway? Someone desperately needed to reel Tibs back in, and it couldn't be Detan.

"I am delighted to hear you're a part of our little family. The Hondings are so sadly small in number." Thratia continued with the whole polite-elegant act. Detan gripped the handle of his fork and considered sticking it in her eye. He could probably get away with it. At least until her guards punched him full of arrows.

Detan stared hard at Tibs and willed him to keep his trap shut. Tibs was just as inclined to listen to Detan's attempt at psychic orders as he was his verbal ones.

"Bastards aren't hard to come by in any family, Commodore."

He snapped her a salute that was, under the circumstances, pretty crisp. Detan supposed Fleet soldiers had a lot of practice saluting their superiors even while toasted.

"A bastard, you say?" Ranalae leaned toward him across the table, dissecting him with her eyes. "What side? Who are your parents?"

"Tibs," Detan said quickly, "is merely *like* family. More like a brother to me, than a cousin."

Tibs rounded on him, and from the surly look in his eye Detan knew he was about to open his mouth and ruin the whole damned thing by insisting they were blood-related.

The first militiaman dropped. Wasn't as dramatic an affair as Detan would have hoped. In the interests of not tipping their hand, dear Pelly had laced the last shipment of honey liqueur lightly. But it was laced, golden needle pumping through the veins of every grey-coated guard in the building, thanks to Gatai's deft efforts.

The first guard, standing just a few paces away from the table, wobbled a bit, his knees going loose as string. His head tipped back and down he went, all that fancy armor making a mighty racket as he connected with the floor.

There was a pause. Then a scream. And the guards began to drop, one by one, some unfortunate guests following suit. Chaos erupted.

Detan let out a woofed sigh of relief and slipped his hands behind his head, leaned back in his chair, and kicked his boots up on the table. "About damned time."

Thratia sprung to her feet, fists planted on the tabletop, glaring down those gathered as if she could scowl her guards into getting back on their feet. "What have you done?" she hissed.

"Me, personally? Not much, really. Just sat around and waited. You really should have disciplined your guards better."

Black-coated servants moved through the crowd, pretending to see to the fallen militiamen, but surreptitiously binding their hands and ankles so that they would be no threat when they eventually roused themselves. Detan figured there were probably a few knocked heads in the crowd, maybe a few broken bones, and that was a shame. But still a whole pits-load better than an all-out war.

Thratia was on him faster than he could blink. She had him by the front of his jacket in one iron fist and yanked him to his feet, sending his chair flying. The tight buttons of his coat and shirt scrunched, constricting his throat as she dragged him face-to-face with her, his legs too tangled to gain any purchase. He knew she was strong. Hadn't counted on her being powerful enough to toss him around like a doll when enraged.

He sputtered, tried to suck a breath down but she gave him a shake. "You damn fool of a man. This could have been peaceful. Now your city will have to bleed. But you, first. I've seen what you're capable of. I was an idiot to ever let you come within a stone's throw of a firemount."

He tried to squawk out a protest, but there was no air left in him. He got his feet under himself, found purchase, prepared to kick away from her grip and reached out, grasping for her other arm. The arm holding the knife pointed at his gut.

"Hey, Thratia!"

Thratia half-turned. Ripka decked her so hard a tooth flew.

CHAPTER 53

The most satisfying feeling in the whole of Ripka's life thus far was watching Thratia's gore-smeared tooth pop right on out of her smug mouth. The pain in her fist was well, well worth it. Thratia twisted, hit the ground with a meaty slap. Ripka was on her in an instant, grabbed her by the arm and flopped her over onto her stomach while Detan scurried backward to get clear of the scuffle. Not that he'd ever been any use in a fight.

Thratia kicked back, hard as a donkey, and all the wind left Ripka as her stomach exploded in pain. Detan got ahold of himself, then, darted forward and whacked Thratia across the back with a chair. Not the cleanest move, but considering the legs broke clean off the chair, he'd hit her with enough force to do some damage. Thratia cursed up a bloody storm and shoved her hands under herself to get upright again, but Ripka was already there, forcing her down, digging her elbow hard into that tender spot Detan had made.

The guards at the door had checked her for weapons, but they hadn't been bothered about the silk ties around Ripka's thighs and upper arms. It didn't take long to have

Thratia hog-tied and gagged, for good measure. Spitting mad, but subdued all the same.

"Got the bitch," she said, when she'd tested the ties and they held.

Before she could get to her feet Detan swooped her up in both arms, let loose a mighty whoop, and spun her about, laughing. Her ribs sang with pain.

"My boy," Dame Honding said, "the poor woman is injured."

He pouted a little as he sat her down. "Sorry, sorry. Are you all right?"

"Nothing a little rest and wine won't heal." She inclined her head to the Dame, who returned the gesture a little deeper than was strictly necessary.

"Captain!" Enard ran up to the table, sweaty-faced and panting. "Fighting on the steps. Seems those guards didn't take their medicine."

"New Chum!" Detan had never looked so deliriously happy.

Enard grinned and inclined his head. "Good to see you again, sir."

"No time for reunions," Ripka said. "Who's on the steps?"

"Honey and some watchers."

"My guards?" the Dame asked.

"In the mix too, ma'am."

"Good."

Figured Honey went straight for the bloodbath. Damned good thing she was on their side. Ripka vaulted over the table, pausing long enough to pick up a meat-knife, then spun around slowly to survey the situation. The wedding guests had mostly fled when the fighting broke out, and now all that was left in the ceremonial hall was a pile of grey-clad militia being overseen by the servants of the palace. No Ranalae. No Aella. No Callia.

Tibal let out a little groan and crouched down by the banquet table, drawing up his knees as he shoved his head into his hands. Ripka and Detan converged on him, her fingers going straight to his pulse while Detan knelt alongside him and rocked back on his heels to watch.

His pulse was slow, but steady, his forehead warm and clammy with sweat.

"You got into the booze early, didn't you?" she asked.

"Coulda' warned me," Tibs growled at Detan.

"And missed your stunning display of welcome to my new ex-wife?"

"Ass," Tibs muttered.

Detan put a hand on Tibs's shoulder to steady him. "Missed you too, Old Chum."

"Did you drink any of the honey liqueur?" Ripka demanded.

Tibs squinted at her through bleary eyes. "I'm still standing, aren't I?"

"Technically–" Detan began, but she cut him off.

"Right. You handled?"

Detan glanced to the servants, caught sight of Gatai coming his way, and nodded. "I've got this. We'll start moving the militia to their ships."

"Ships?"

His expression darkened and he glanced over at Thratia, still thrashing against her bonds. "I want none of this stain to remain in Hond Steading."

"Understood, Lord Honding." She saluted him with a wink and dashed after Enard, discarding her meat-knife for a few of the blades from the pile the servants were busy collecting from the sedated guards.

The doors to the stairs stood open, and she could hear the fighting even from the far end of the hall. The sun had sunk to the other side of the palace by the time she made it to the stairs. Knots of men and women contested in shadow, hard-fought but, from what Ripka could see, the matter was almost settled. There were a great many more grey coats scattering the ground than black or blue.

She caught sight of Honey down toward the bottom of the steps. Cursed woman hadn't even stuck around long enough to pick up a proper weapon. She was ducking and weaving, dancing under longer cutlasses to score hit after hit with a meat-knife. Singing at the top of her battered voice all the while. Alone as she was, she had her contestants well in hand, so Ripka jumped into the nearest fray.

Some grey coats had pushed two watchers against the flat wall of the palace's opened doors and were hammering them with sloppy blow after sloppy blow, but time and numbers were on the militia's side. They were four against two, and the watchers they had penned were growing tired.

Ripka darted in, opened up the side of one and leapt away before the other could get turned about. One of the watchers closed that opportunity, took a hit on the hip but shrugged it off to ram her cutlass guard-deep into the chest of her opponent. Ripka winced at the pale look on the watcher's face that had nothing at all to do with exertion.

Watchers didn't see a lot of death, not by their own hands. They were trained to subdue, if at all possible. But it was damn near impossible to subdue a determined killer with a sword without doing mortal damage. She'd seen the results of knock-out blows to the head. If it were her, she'd rather be run through than knocked silly.

The second watcher moved in and between them they made short work of the last grey coat. Ripka gave a little thanks to Thratia for making her people so easy to pick out. It'd come as a surprise in Aransa, where the sudden flood of supporters had frightened everyone into their homes. Here and now, the coats only served to make her angry. And to give her a target to hit.

She spun around, looking for a new mark. Honey'd done her work and was on to another knot of fighting, Enard at her side. Where the fuck was Tibal, anyway? Not that he was handy in a fight, but still. If he'd run off to drink some more after that little display of his she'd pull his tongue out far enough to slap him with it.

Midway down the steps a couple of the Dame's guards fought back to back with Falston, a bunch of his watchers busy taking the last hits on their own battles. Ripka jogged down the steps, intent on joining Falston in his defense.

The watch-captain slipped.

His heel caught the back of a step, bloodied from the battle, and as Ripka pumped her legs as hard as she could, urged herself to move faster toward him, his legs went out from under him, boots kissing the air. He let one short cry break free and then he was down, the hard stone steps knocking the air out of him, maybe even breaking his back.

"Falston!" she yelled, trying to get the watchers' attention. Trying to get anyone, anyone at all, who was closer than she was to step in. To help. But the Dame's people were hard pressed, now that they'd lost their third. But the grey coats weren't.

Easy as you please, a militiaman turned, stabbed down, took Falston right through the heart. Ripka screamed defiance, flung herself at the man, connected hard and went tumbling with him down the steps. Somewhere in the tangle she got her legs around the man's waist from behind and dropped her weapons, grabbed the man's head and smashed it, hard as she could, into the edge of a stair. His body spasmed beneath her, jerking in a way that didn't mean resistance – only death. She did it again. Again.

Enard grabbed her arm and wrested her to her feet. "What –?"

"Falston." Every speck of her body ached, elbows and knees scraped and bleeding. Something clicked alarmingly in her foot when she stood. She shook Enard off, pushed through the pain to jog up the steps. The militia was dead, or subdued. Silence cloyed thick in the blood-heavy air. Somewhere, Honey sang a lullaby.

His watchers had already gathered around him, a semi-circular wall of blue. She shouldered through, vision blurry at the edges with fear and disbelief. Falston lay as he'd fallen, cheeks puffing with bloat as his blood flowed down the incline of the steps into his face. She dropped to her knees, scooped his head into her arms.

The life had already fled him.

CHAPTER 54

Dark had fallen on Hond Steading by the time they managed to pack all of Thratia's ships full of her people. She had not brought many, so assured was she of her victory, but it had been enough to take up more than half the night. Some, he was sure, had skinned themselves of their uniforms and escaped into the city. Aella, Callia, and Ranalae, of all people, had disappeared in the fray. He would have to deal with them sometime soon, that reckoning had always been coming for him, but not tonight. Tonight he was ridding himself of the monster he'd brought here with him.

Detan no longer knew the time, and he didn't care. He was worn through, tired down to a core of himself he hadn't even known existed. Every time he glanced at Ripka, a little worm of guilt burrowed even deeper inside him.

He'd never met the late watch-captain of Hond Steading, but he had meant something to her. And that meant he had been a good man.

A man accustomed to blood, surely. A man who'd signed up for a violent life, who knew someday he might die in the service of the city. But a man who hadn't had to die tonight, of all nights, on the steps of the palace he served, in a hard-fought battle that was, ultimately, Detan's doing. Detan could have just married Thratia. Could have given himself over to her scheming. Could have thrown himself from the roof of the palace, too, and tonight's bloodshed might not have happened.

But he had chosen to fight back. And the consequences, though smaller than all-out war, had been dire. And he was not yet done.

"Bring her in," Detan ordered. It was a strange thing, to hear easy authority in his own voice when he wasn't intentionally faking it.

He'd had a team of the Dame's pilots take the *Dread Wind* away from the palace after it had been loaded with Thratia's people, save one, the woman herself. Now, his auntie's flagship pulled up alongside the *Dread Wind*, and found a handful of her soldiers had already freed themselves and were pointing harpoons at his ship. Detan sighed.

Thratia stood alongside him at the rail, wrists bound behind her back with chains and her ankles sporting matching jewelry. The gag had been removed, but she'd been silent. Until now.

"I could order them to knock you out of the sky."

"You're on this ship too, Thratia."

"And are you so certain I wouldn't find that acceptable?"

He chuckled and shook his head, leaning forward to rest both hands on the rail. "You forget, O wife of mine, that I've come to know you better in these last few months. You won't take that route, because it's final. I'm setting you free. You can go home to Aransa, regroup if you'd like, but you can't do that if you die here, tonight. And you're never done, are you?"

"And knowing this, you would let me go?"

"You will not come here again."

She shook her head. "I am not trying to encourage you to kill me, Honding, but you cannot be that daft. You know I will come for you. And this time, there will be no play at peace. I will have this city. I will have this whole cursed continent. I tried to play nice with you. Tried to show you why I do what I do – but if you will not bend, then I will be forced to break you."

"Ah, Thratia." He raised his hands to the sky, wide apart, as if to hug all of the ships of her fleet hanging there in the night. "I could snuff every last ship of yours from the sky, right now, and not break a sweat. Did you know that? What your pet whitecoat was training me to do? Control *and* strength. That is what I have, now, thanks to you. This city is protected. Never forget that."

He nodded to Gatai, who signaled his guards to take Thratia, one arm in each hand, and steer her toward the connected gangplank. He watched her go, something like melancholy coming over him. Such passion. Such strength. She could have been marvelous, if she hadn't decided to be a monster instead.

With Thratia removed and the gangplank retracted, Detan held out his hands as he had when he spoke to her. All around him hushed. He'd made no secret of his deviation after the wedding. Hadn't even bothered to lower his voice as he spoke to Thratia about dashing all her ships from the sky. There was no point to that, not any more. If Hond Steading were going to get its lord back, they were going to get him in the full light of what he was. Maybe they'd accept that. Maybe they wouldn't. He wasn't even sure he was prepared to stick around to find out.

He knew what they must be thinking, watching him now. That they suspected him of preparing to do the very thing he'd threatened Thratia with. Why else would he make them move all the ships in her fleet over the empty, eastern flats outside the city?

He didn't mind the speculation. Truth was, he wanted Thratia to worry a little. His sel-sense expanded. Slowly, deliberately. Not the desperate grab he had made when he sent up the firemount. No, this time he really had learned control. It helped that someone wasn't currently trying to choke him to death, of course.

Thratia's fleet was massive, but his sphere of influence covered it easily. He held all those buoyancy sacks in his mind, explored them with care, felt his way around their valves and internal workings. Then pushed. Hard.

Gasps from the deck all around him. The fleet shot away, arcing out into the night, shouts of surprise from their decks dwindling with distance just as quickly as the ships dwindled from sight.

On each and every ship, he'd vented just enough selium to accelerate them a day's flight away in a matter of a few marks. And depleted their reserves enough that they'd have no choice but to return to Aransa.

Detan slumped against the rail, sweating, panting. Explosions he could do without breaking a sweat. Fine work, careful work, was another matter entirely. Those selium sacks weren't the only thing he'd depleted. He'd never been so worn through in his life. But he was done, now. It was over. And the thing he wanted most in the world at that moment was a long, hot, bath. They'd still be around when he was restored, and the very thought made him grin.

Auntie stepped up to his side and laid a blanket over his shoulders. Her small, bony hand patted the small of his back.

"You've done well today. Come on, let's take you home."

CHAPTER 55

Ripka stayed close by Detan as the ship shuddered against its dock, returning them all to the palace. He'd made a show of being fine. Of being hale. His normal, cheerful, wisecracking self. But when she caught him at off moments, when he thought she wasn't looking, his face creased with pain, with sadness. Whatever had been done to him while at the mercy of Thratia – whatever he'd been forced to do – would be a long time in healing. If such wounds could ever heal.

Right now, it was easier to worry about Detan's state of mind than her own. Everytime she closed her eyes – every time she so much as blinked – she saw the faces of Falston's wife, his daughter. Heard the echo of her whispered plea to keep him safe overlaid with the rattle of his final breath.

"Something's wrong," Honey whispered.

Ripka tensed, and leaned against the railing to get a better look. The palace seemed fine, if dark and a little quiet... Which didn't make much sense, now that she considered the fact. The palace should be alive with light, the servants busy cleaning up the mess, and the Dame's guard rooting out any of Thratia's leftovers.

"Detan," she said quietly.

He paused, one foot on the gangplank. She chucked her head toward the palace and he looked, really looked, and hissed quietly to himself. "What in the pits is it *now*?"

He turned, taking on an air of command she'd never seen him employ before, and pointed to the Dame's guards. "You two, forward positions, weapons out. We may have hostiles. Auntie, my dear, I suggest you stay aboard the ship with an honor guard, just in case."

"And you?"

He looked grim. "I kicked this hornet's nest. I'll see it through."

Ripka and Honey fell into step behind Detan, the two guards taking point. Ripka itched to be in their place, but Detan had given his orders, and she wasn't about to start undermining him now that he was showing some initiative as a leader. She was half-worried that if she drew attention to herself, he'd order her back. And then she *would* have to defy him. Some orders, she knew from long experience, were just plain stupid.

Weapons readied, the guards opened the door and edged inside. "Clear," one called.

Detan held out a hand to indicate those on board the ship should hold position and followed the guards inside. Ripka drew a cutlass she'd collected from some corpse or another and saw Honey do likewise as they followed him into the faintly lit chamber.

The entrance foyer for the dock was dark, but the space beyond – to the hall where the wedding had been held – was bright as day, bleeding light across the floor. A beacon. A lighthouse warning of dangerous rocks.

The first guard across the threshold went down, blood fountaining from his neck, legs kicking as the life poured out of him. The second moved to forward position, brought his shield arm up and swore as something heavy thundered against it.

"Fucking imperials," the guard barked, retreating.

Detan grabbed the man's shoulder and hauled him back, out of the line of fire that had taken down his comrade. An arrow skittered across the floor in his now-empty place. Honey drifted forward, pulled by the promise of violence, and Ripka snapped a hand out to grab her arm and stop her. She pouted, but hung back anyway.

"What's the situation?" Detan asked.

The guard stared at the kicking corpse of his friend. Detan swore and dragged the man further away from the door, physically turning his head to look him in the eye. "Report, soldier."

The soldier snapped to his senses at the command in Detan's voice. "They've got the hall secured. The exterior doors appear to be barred, though I couldn't get a good look at them. Armed sentries on every internal door."

"Uniforms?"

"Light blue." Ranalae's imperials. Wonderful.

"Numbers?" Ripka demanded.

"I don't know – fifty?"

"Shit," Detan said. Ripka had to agree. He thought a moment, pacing as he tapped his forehead. "How'd she get them in? Thratia's been watching those ships to the north like a bloodhawk, not a one's made a move. They even turned some back a few days ago."

"Oh," Ripka said, feeling rather stupid.

He spun on her. "What? What is it?"

"I thought… Pits. I thought I was working on infiltrating Thratia's network. It all looked the same – talk of political change. Weapons smuggling. Deviant smuggling. Never quite caught up with her, turned out I was knocking on a false door, but there *was* something going on in the city. I should have remembered where she learned her tricks."

"Ranalae's got people. In the streets. Same as the night Aransa fell?"

Ripka nodded, slowly. "I'd bet my life on it."

"You might have to." He tugged at his hair, scowling, then turned on the guard. "How many of you in the palace?"

There was a time, Ripka recalled, when Detan would have been horrified at being so near the man dying on the ground beside him – out of reach, beyond hope of medical aid. Now, he scarcely glanced the man's way. And when he did, there was only a faint flicker of pain in his expression, quickly overrun by angry determination.

"No telling what's left after the imperials swept the place, if they even did, but there were two hundred of us before tonight's, uh, celebration, sir. Lord." The soldier cleared his throat.

"Right. Go back to the ship, warn my aunt – ah, the Dame – of what's going on and leave her with a guard, at least five, then take the rest and go round up your fellows. Gather together in this room in no less than a mark, do you hear me? It's imperative we use our numbers to regain control while we have the chance."

Detan caught Ripka staring and blinked at her. "What?"

"You... have a plan."

He grinned. "Rippy, ole girl, I've changed. Hopefully for the better. Now go."

"Wait." Ripka stepped in front of the guard. "We're not alone here. There's a whole citizens' brigade outside those walls, just waiting for a chance to aid their city.

They're no soldiers, but they've had a week of watcher training. They just need a signal to converge on the palace."

"Rippy! You're brilliant!" He reached to scoop her up again and she ducked away, swatting at him.

"Don't you dare. Soldier, there's no time to do the signal properly. Can you use a bow?"

"Yes, ma'am."

"Good. Fire lit pitch arrows at the northern garden trees. That was our backup plan for tonight."

His eyes widened. "Those trees are very tall, ma'am."

"Yes, and bordered by stone walls and not near any domiciles. That's the idea. Now *go*."

He saluted them both and took off at a dead sprint.

Ripka eyed Detan. "And just what do we do in this plan of yours?"

"We make a dramatic entrance. And stall like our lives depend on it, because they definitely do."

CHAPTER 56

The servants, skies bless them, still hadn't touched Tibs's old room, which meant Detan found a whole pits-load of sel to work with. He hunkered with Honey and Ripka in the foyer where the first guard had fallen, looking pretty ridiculous as they each carried a massive balloon of selium on a rope. Honey was looking at hers like she wanted to stab it. Based on what he remembered of Forge and Clink's stories, she probably did.

"You sure about this?" Ripka asked.

"I saw Pelkaia do something like this once. Worked a treat. Trust me."

"Was it on fire when she did it?"

"Well, no, but have a little faith, Rip ole girl. The Valatheans will shit themselves."

"Charming."

He mimed a noble bow for her. "Miss me?"

She grinned, just a little. "Yeah. Kinda. Don't forget, Enard and Tibal are both in there."

"Pah, New Chum is a marvel with a blade and Tibs is far too crafty to get himself caught in that nonsense. They're probably skulking about these halls worrying that we're in there."

"I hope you're right."

He did, too, but he wasn't about to tell her that. The thought of either of those two stuck in that room with the Valatheans made his blood boil, because he had no doubt they'd be used as pawns against him. The very idea that anyone he cared about would be harmed as a proxy to harming him made him want to tear the whole damned city down. A sentiment he needed to keep on a very, very tight leash.

They'd left those two with Gatai, looking after Tibs's little overindulgence, and if Detan was very lucky then they weren't even aware of the trouble brewing in the wedding hall. He tried not to think too hard on how luck had been playing out for him, lately.

"Think the brigade is in position?" he asked.

Ripka leaned back to glance out a window, where a smear of yellow light graced the clouds from the tree fire. "Any time now."

"Honey, my dear, you don't have to join us. If you'd prefer to wait on the ship–"

Both women stared at him like he'd just started burping up snakes. "Uh. Right. Never mind. Onward."

As one, they slashed the balloons of selium and let the gas coalesce into a shimmering cloud above their heads. Wasn't as much as he'd like to work with, but the only other source was in the flier, and that would have taken far too long to siphon out safely.

He extended his senses, gathered all that gas into a cohesive cloud, and found the center of himself. Calm, Ready. Onward, indeed.

He pushed outward, mentally, shoved that cloud of selium through the door in front of them for all he was worth. Cries of alarm echoed in the room, shouts and stomping of feet. He swirled the gas up, tracking it in his mind, envisioning all those lanterns his auntie had dangled from the ceiling to celebrate his wedding, and pushed. The lights went out with a snuff.

The brigade, skies bless them, didn't need another cue. Shouts echoed as the bedraggled crew stormed the palace, and it wasn't long before the heavy crack of the massive wooden doors breaking down filled the air.

He gave it a couple of beats, just to let the brigade get inside, then muttered, "Let there be light." He reached out, grabbed the selium trapped in the ceiling, sectioned off a small sliver of it, and fed his rage into it. The hall returned to light in a violent burst, and it was a testament to his new finesse that he didn't blow the damned ceiling off by feeding his anger into the remaining selium. Those lanterns still being fed oil caught, burning merrily, while some burst and dripped flaming oil to the floor. Oops.

Ripka and Honey were through the door the second the lights came back on, sabers out, stances ready. Neither of them found shields, but neither seemed to mind. Especially Honey. That girl had taken up singing at the top of her lungs, some ancient mourning rite that gave him shivers straight to the bone, as she waded into the fray.

Detan hung back, aware of his vulnerability when the blades came out, and focused on manipulating what selium he had left. Didn't last long.

"Honding!" Ranalae's voice, firm and irritated. "You have until the count of three to show yourself, or I slit your cousin's throat. One. Tw–"

That was that, then. Time to play a different game. He strolled into the hall like it was his own idea, hands in his pockets, eyebrow cocked like he couldn't quite imagine what they wanted from him. Ranalae and Aella stood toward the front of the room, Callia huddled at their feet, and a rather bored-looking imperial lingered just a step behind them. An unsteady Tibs was held up between two surly looking imperial bruisers in mussed coats. Detan grinned. At least Tibs had gotten a few shots in.

"Hold," he ordered and, to his surprise, the brigade listened. No one quite put their weapons down, but they backed away unsteadily, pointy ends still pointed in all the right places, eyes wary as they examined their imperial contestants. The brigade had Ranalae outnumbered, easily. But she had Tibs. Pits-fucking-damnit.

"Now Ranalae, this is mighty rude of you. You're a guest in my home."

"Spare me the polite-lord act, Honding. Order your men to put down arms."

He rolled his shoulders, trying to ignore the fact he'd just seen New Chum slinking up behind Tibs and his guards, a knife in each hand. Damn man could move like a rockcat on the hunt when he wanted to.

"Naw, don't think I'll be doing that. I think you'll be handing Tibs over, nice and gentle, or I'll rip this place to itty bitty bits."

"You won't," she said, rolling her eyes.

Detan caught Aella's eye, stared hard at her. "Fucking try me."

"He might," Aella conceded. "He has become increasingly more unstable since his time in Hond Steading. I suggest a removal from the local stimulus to enhance further study."

"Suggestion declined," Detan grated.

New Chum moved. Faster than Detan could follow he swooped in, opened the hamstring of one man and plunged his blade into the kidney of the other. Both went down, hard, spasming on the stone, and Tibs stumbled forward, startled by the sudden freedom, lost his footing and skidded across the floor. Ripka was there in a flash, grabbed Tibs by the shoulders and hauled him up and away.

New Chum pivoted, blades flashing, ducked in low and tight for Ranalae's stomach and then – Misol. Detan'd forgotten about fucking Misol, who worked for Aella, not Thratia. The damned doppel dropped her false face as a random imperial alongside Aella, half-turned, and with a casual thrust sank her blade straight through New Chum's loyal little heart.

"No!" Ripka screamed. She lunged forward but Tibs had her now, and that was for the best, because Detan was real sure Ripka wasn't prepared to take on Misol. Not now. Not blind with rage as she was.

Detan was having his own anger problems.

"You fucking monster!" He reached for the sel above his head, shaped it, formed it into a spear twin to Misol's favorite little toy and aimed it straight at her face. In a blink, it was done. The explosive force knocked what was left of Misol's body back against the wall in a greasy, red stain.

Aella's sphere of dampening fell around him, cutting him off. Ranalae brushed gore from her shoe.

"Well, that was disappointing," she said.

His vision fogged. He couldn't look at New Chum. Couldn't look at Ripka. Couldn't stand to see either the tears hot on her face nor the blood pumping, endless, from New Chum's shuddering chest.

Pits below, but he wanted to close that distance. Wanted to tell Tibs to let Ripka loose. They should shove some cloth in that wound, get some salve – something, anything. But that was a killing wound, and he'd only be buying time, and with Ranalae and her nasty coterie hovering nearby Detan couldn't even get close. Couldn't even hold New Chum's palsying hand as he passed to the endless.

"Enard," Ripka said, and her voice was so very cracked and broken that the mere sound of it nearly cut through Detan's resolve.

Pink foam frothed at the corners of New Chum's lips, stealing his voice, stealing whatever he might want to say before the end. But he could still move, if only a little, and he reached, stretched his arm out toward Ripka, fingers curled as if he'd take her hand.

And then he went very, very still.

CHAPTER 57

Ripka lunged, Tibs hauling back on her for all he was worth, Honey singing something dark and dreary and shouts echoed from the brigade all around but Detan wasn't watching. Wasn't even listening, not really. He heard it all, saw it, but he was fighting his own, internal battles, and right now he only had eyes for Aella.

She'd clamped down on him, cut off his sphere of influence. But she knew how well that'd worked last time, and... Detan's vision went white. He pushed against Aella's shield with all he was worth, and then –

At first he didn't understand what he was sensing, what he was feeling. Not consciously – this was not a thing that one could come to realize through force, through effort. As Ranalae laughed, lectured, paced and gloated, Detan sensed, for the first time in his life – for the first time in many, many lives – the world spool out around him.

Aella had him shut down, true. But the injections didn't work on her. The girl couldn't touch, couldn't sense the world he was experiencing now. He'd gone beyond her. So far out of her reach he couldn't even begin to explain it to himself.

Selium. Everywhere. He knew that, of course, in the intellectual way that one knows that sandstone makes brown sand and firestone black sand. Had even caught glimpses of that truth at the height of his control and power. But this. This was nothing like he ever could have imagined. Nothing he had words to describe, to contextualize. Wasn't fair this was happening to him, probably. Greater minds than Detan's gravel-sized noggin could probably glean something of use from this moment. But he tried. He was always trying.

And so back to the selium: to it being everywhere.

He could sense the great, vast network of it. Glimmering fragments – molecules, Aella had called them in one of her many lectures. Yes. That was the right term. Molecules of selium drifted in the air he breathed, the air everyone breathed. He could sense them, tiny as they were – impossible as they were – seep through his lungs, seep into his bloodstream. Seep into *everyone's* bloodstreams.

With his eyes opened it was like he was seeing another world, the true world, laid in false and shifting color over the world he could touch and taste and scent. This world, this true world, wasn't for his eyes. It was an extension of his sel-sense – he must derive a better name for it. Seles? No. Ripka would have a better idea. She always did. But he could *see* it, such as it was, for human brains were adaptable, clever things, and this new rush of information had to be processed somehow.

So it was everywhere. In every pore and breath and cell. He could see it, as he watched Ranalae. She breathed it in, and it escaped her lungs to the flow of her blood and bonded there. Stray molecules of selium which found no blood to bond with leached into her muscles, ate away at her bones instead.

Bonewither. Huh. So that was how that worked.

But the real kicker, the thing that made him breathe slow and easy because he knew – knew now more than he ever had in his life – that the world was about to change for the better, was this: he could see how sel-sense worked. The very thing the Bone Tower had been digging around in bodies for decades trying to puzzle out. He could just look at Ranalae, look at any other sensitive, and *see* it. He would have laughed, if his throat weren't so raw.

As the selium coursed through a body it hit a barrier near the brainstem, something he could make no real sense of – Tibs would have called it a valve, maybe, or a filter. Either way, when he looked at Ranalae he saw the sel course pass that barrier, enter the brain, respond to whatever crazy chemistry was taking place there and then the command reverberated throughout the rest of the selium in her sphere of influence. And her strength was huge. Ranalae's sphere pulsed as she worked at the edge of her ability, slinging selium like it was acid at her enemies. When he looked at Ripka, all that sel that seeped into her body reached that barrier and just... stopped. Coursed back through her blood and escaped through her exhalations.

But he could change that.

And so much more.

His sphere of influence flowed beyond the strength of simple vision. At a certain point the sight of the world ceased, blended into the horizon or a wall or any other everyday obstruction. But he was beyond the lenses in his eyes, now. His senses spiraled outward, a gyrating torrent of awareness that swept from the heart of the palace and out, out, encompassing people and beings beyond his ability to count. Folded in the whole of the neighborhood, the city. Consciousnesses danced like nodes of light amongst the firings of his own mind, prickles of brilliant, beautiful, life. Thousands and thousands, sensitive and not, aged and curled in the womb.

His own reach took his breath away. Even as he spotted the little blots of life he never lost sight of selium itself, omnipresent, trapped in breezes and bellied within the hot, churning core of the planet. Its presence in the air was so thin no unenhanced eye could see it, and only the finest of sensitives could detect it. But to Detan those molecules were as clear as dappled sunlight through leaves, clustering and thinning and occasionally joining together in numbers large enough to break through the eddies in the air and float toward the sky.

But those lights. Those consciousnesses. He selected those with the firm filters, the tightened valves. It took him only a thought, a moment. He breathed in, breathed out, then held the fates of all those banal lives in the wide sphere of his control.

"Ranalae."

Her head snapped up, jerked toward him, eyes narrowed. He couldn't blame her. His voice sounded foreign to his own ears. Calm. Distant.

But he was not calm. Anger boiled in his veins, held at a low simmer, and though his sense had extended to show him something heart-achingly beautiful, a tiny sliver of a voice deep in his darkest mind whispered to him to let loose. To leave this place, this whole city – and maybe the whole continent, if he were lucky – a smoldering crater.

But that was an old voice, smoothed over by time and control. Just looking at Ripka, at her pale and sweat-slicked face, he knew he could never listen to it. Never go back to the temptations that had called to him, siren-like, before. He was not his anger's puppet. He was its master.

He would lash out again, if the need arose. Would burn the whole fucking world if it meant keeping just this city and the people in it safe. He had not *lost* that ability, he had simply grown into another.

And wouldn't Aella be just delighted to study him now.

"This city," Ranalae was saying, and Detan realized she'd been talking while he watched Ripka. "Is under the martial control of Valathea. Order your people to stand down at once."

"You cannot have this place." The place where my mother's bones are buried.

She sneered. "I already have it."

Ah, right, they were surrounded. Funny how easy it was to forget things like that when you were busy having a sense-awakening. "And what is it that you have, exactly?"

"Detan–" Ripka's voice, soft and choked with grief. Tibs hushed her, slipped an arm around her shoulders and pulled her back a step. Sweet, stubborn Tibs. He always knew when Detan was about to do something, and he wondered if his old friend could feel him now. Feel the hold Detan exuded over the whole of this city. If he didn't, he would soon.

His question took Ranalae aback. She scowled down her long nose at him. "A rebellious little city, is what I have. A dog gone feral that needs to be brought to heel. Remember your ancestors, Detan. Remember they founded this city while seeking fertile ground in the name of the empire."

"Did you ever wonder where my ancestors came from?"

"Why in the fiery pits would I? This is inane. You have one minute to disarm your ragamuffins or I will order you all felled. Do not test my patience."

The brigade shifted to ready stances, raising weapons, preparing to pounce. Detan made a soft, negating sound, and they eased back, but only slightly.

"History matters, Ranalae, and this city is the confluence of many historical paths. The founders of my family – the real founders, those whose names we've lost to the erosion of time – were not Valathean. They were Catari. They must have been. And do you know why they came to the Valathean isles? Do you know why the patient, accepting, kind Catari would ever kick a family out?"

Worldbreaker.

"It does not matter. You will be the last of your troublesome line."

He smiled. Folded his hands before his chest and tipped his head back, staring at the blank expanse of the ceiling though his thoughts, his sense, was decidedly elsewhere.

"Because we could do this."

"Detan, no!" Tibs cried. But this time – this time Ripka hushed him.

He didn't fully understand what he was doing. He lacked the vocabulary to describe it. Maybe, after this was all done, he could seek out one of those Catari enclaves Pelkaia was always going on about and ask them to explain it to him.

But he didn't need to know the proper words. There were valves – filters – set to varying degrees of openness in every banal mind he held. The mechanism was endlessly complex, but it had a lever. A button, a wheel, a switch. Whatever it was, whatever he'd later decide to call it – Detan had never met a button he didn't want to push.

He started with Ranalae. Reversing her sensitivity, shutting the valve tight. He moved on to Aella, then Callia. For the rest... He opened them. Blew them wide. Didn't stop until he'd exhausted the whole of the sphere of his influence, and every one of those banal consciousnesses had switched over to sel-sensitive status.

He opened eyes he didn't remember closing. Ranalae managed to look white as gypsum, despite the dark cast of her skin. Callia let out a howl to make a coyote shiver, collapsed to her knees and curled in upon herself, shuddering.

Aella had no eyes for her adopted mother. She stared at Detan, eyes wider than he'd ever seen them, every muscle of her body straining as she tried, tried so very hard, to take back what was hers. What she was just beginning to understand he'd taken from her.

The brigade, the imperials, the Honding guards – they all shifted their weight uncomfortably, and Ripka was staring at her hands like she'd never seen them before. She shook all over, Tibs's support the only thing keeping her on her feet.

"What have you done?" Ranalae rasped.

"See for yourself." He reached out, snagged disparate particles of selium from the air and congealed them into a fist-sized mass. A task that'd once left Coss sweating to drown the desert now came to him merely as an afterthought. He had no time to ponder what he had become, only what he must do next. "Catch."

He threw the selium ball at her. Ranalae flinched backward, holding her hands up instinctively, but nothing happened for her. The sel sailed through her upheld fingers, broke into a thousand tiny fragments and faded as it dissolved into the air.

"I've taken from you your greatest pleasure," he said. "And given it to every single banal body in all of Hond Steading. Most of them will be normal. Many of them will be what you call deviant. But you can't enslave a whole city. You can't send all of them to the mines, and you sure as shit can't collect all the deviants up for your little science experiments now.

"This is not your city, Ranalae. This is not Valathea's city. It is not even the Hondings' city, though I will do what I can to guide it forward into peace. Hond Steading is a city entirely of sel-sensitives. This is something new. Something of hope. And you. Are. Not. Welcome."

Fury gathered in her eyes, in every tight line of her body, in the bulging of her veins and the tendons snaking around her neck.

"I could still cut you down, you fool," she snapped.

He sighed, low and slow, and drew himself up to his full height. "Even if it were your greatest desire, you wouldn't. Not if you think for just a sands-cursed moment." He tapped the side of his head. "Don't you get it? I know how it works. You kill me, that knowledge goes to my grave. I am the only person alive who can give it back to you."

Aella had a knife in her hand in an instant. Detan stepped back, wary, but she turned to Ranalae and placed the silver edge of the blade against the whitecoat's throat. "If you order him killed," she hissed, "you die with him."

Ranalae paled, and fell silent.

The door to the antechamber slung open, cracking in its frame, and Dame Honding swept into the room with a retinue of a hundred guards on her heels. The sight of them very nearly made Detan weep with relief. Bluster aside, he really wasn't sure just how long he could keep convincing Ranalae he had the upper hand.

"You're a little late to the party, Auntie." He beamed at her, and she scowled back as, with a snap of her fingers, her people swept in to detain Ranalae and her entourage.

"You wouldn't happen to have anything to do with the widespread panic on my streets, would you, boy?"

Even with his awareness a glowing, vibrant thing stretching out to blanket all of Hond Steading, even at the peak of his power and control, that razor-sharp scowl still made him flinch and kick at the ground with one dusty boot.

"I, uh, made some… improvements."

Hands on her hips, eyes narrowed enough to cut glass, she dismissed all of Ranalae and her people in one gesture and squared her full attention on Detan. "Explain."

He grinned, reached for sel, and said, "Catch."

To her obvious surprise, she did.

CHAPTER 58

Ripka awoke to find Honey at her side. The woman slept, curled on the rug by Ripka's bed like a puppy, breathing peacefully in the shaft of morning light that fell upon her. Ripka rubbed at her eyes, scraping away sleep crust and tear stains alike, and pushed hair from her face. Had she wept in her sleep? If so, she had no doubt Honey had heard and come to lend her presence, if not her words.

Any other time she would have found Honey lying there creepy. Now, she just smiled. If someone loves you, you revel in as much time with them as you possibly can. She'd learned that the hard way.

"Honey," she said, swinging her legs off the bed. The woman didn't stir. She crouched beside her and brushed her hair, gently, away from her face. In sleep, the woman looked dreamy as a ceramic doll, her features unlined and innocent.

It had taken a great deal of time to scrub the blood out of her hair the night before.

"Come on, girl, rise and shine." She gave Honey a shake, and she blinked awake with a startled, piggish snort.

436 INHERIT THE FLAME

"Are we under attack?"

Ripka sighed and sat back on her heels, dangling her hands between her knees. "No. Not any more."

Honey rolled to her feet and stretched, working the kinks out of her body from having spent the night on the floor. She hummed a little, warming her voice, and while once that would have sent shivers down her spine, Ripka just laughed. Honey pouted at her.

"What?" Honey murmured.

"Your singing..." She trailed off, seeing a dark crease form between Honey's brows. Pits, but that woman was sensitive about her voice. She settled back into a cross-legged position, wincing as her sore ribs shifted beneath the wrap the apothiks had bundled her up in. She was simply tired of not knowing her friends well enough, of keeping them distant for fear of... Of so many things. Maybe Honey really didn't want to tell her. Maybe she just didn't know how.

"What happened?" she asked eventually. Honey's perfectly smooth face scrunched up as she worked through the question.

"I used to sing," she said, quietly, and fiddled with the hem of her nightshift. Ripka reached out, took her hands and turned them over, palm up. The pale flesh there was crisscrossed with countless scars, the marks left behind from many, many knife fights. She'd ignored them when she'd first seen them on Enard's hands, so very long ago now, and been blindsided by his past. Nothing good lay behind those scars on Honey's hands. She wanted to know anyway.

"What happened?" she repeated.

Honey curled her fingers to hide half the scars, head cast down so that her hair fell over her expression. It took her a while, but she found the words eventually.

"I loved to sing. My parents…" Twitch of the lips, as if the word were foreign to her. "I sang for their money."

She fell quiet again, but Ripka had learned the texture of her silences, and this one meant she was building up the words she wanted to say.

"People wanted to give me money for other things, too."

Ripka swallowed and squeezed Honey's hands. Whatever had happened to her as a young woman, Ripka could only guess – and guess well, as during her time in the watch she'd seen some truly horrendous parents – and, in a strange way, she was proud of Honey for learning to sing with her knives. She hoped she could learn to sing without them someday.

A knock sounded on the door, and both women flinched, reaching for weapons they didn't carry in their nightshifts.

"Who is it?"

"Dame Honding."

Ripka gave Honey a sly glance and whispered, "I guess we are still under attack."

Honey smiled. At least she was beginning to catch on to Ripka's sense of humor.

"Come in."

The Dame looked surprisingly hale for having suffered a full night of having her palace ripped apart. She glided into the room, servants carrying trays of hot cakes and steaming bright eye berry tea on their hips behind her, ordered the placement of the meals, and then ushered the servants right back out again.

"Good morning to you both. My apothiks tell me you both suffered injuries, but will recover?"

Ripka pressed a hand over her broken ribs and nodded. "Lots of bed rest in our future, but we should pull together quickly. Thank you for the food, and the use of your apothiks."

"It is, I'm certain, the absolute least I can do."

The Dame grabbed one of the room's chairs and turned it around to face them as she sat, her ankles crossed and her skirt lying just so across her lap. Even in distress, she carried herself with dignity, with passion and grace. It was as reflexive to her as reaching for a cutlass was to Ripka.

"My dear, I know things have moved very quickly here as of late, and I have come to offer you an apology. I tried to hide you away from the trouble, to keep you safe, and that was a mistake. I should have listened to you from the very beginning. My nephew tells that Thratia claims the empress is dead, and that he believes her. I find I believe this, too. The empress I knew would never be so crass as to send her people to invade us, skies forbid. My, ah, people, are putting questions to Ranalae to find out the truth of the matter."

Ripka winced. "I'd rather not know the details of that, Dame. Forgive me, but I've had my fill of Valathean politics."

"Understood. But I hope you will be amenable to politics of a different nature."

Ripka frowned. "Of what kind?"

"Local, my dear. Captain Lakon's death leaves a very large hole in our community. I, for one, would be honored if you took up the position."

Her throat went dry. She'd never dreamed of being a watch-captain again. Never even dreamed she'd be a watcher, or allowed to serve anywhere near them. To have worked with Falston so closely in his final days, to have been welcomed there and honored... That was a treasure. A memory she wanted to keep pure.

And she could never look his men in the eye without hearing his wife's voice: *keep him safe*.

"I'm sorry, Dame. You honor me. But I'm sure there are viable candidates in your local watch. I will help you interview and select, if you'd like."

"I'm sorry to hear you won't take the job, but I will accept your offer to help in the selection process. Things will be busy, around here, for a time. What will you do afterward?"

Now there was a question she hadn't dared to think of. Losing Enard… Her throat knotted. She glanced to Honey, to the open admiration there, and sighed. There was one task she'd promised herself, and Enard too. One thing she had left to do.

"I'd like to return to the Remnant Isle prison. The warden there is corrupt as a sewer line, and I promised myself I'd clear him out and set things right just as soon as I could."

"You are a strange woman, Ripka Leshe, but I see your reasoning. If I can help in any way – funds, transport, men-at-arms, you have only to ask."

"Thank you, Dame."

She stood in one fluid movement and stepped to the door.

"Dame?"

She paused, fingers on the handle.

"Yes, Miss Leshe?"

"Go easy on Detan, won't you?"

She smiled, small and slow and genuine. "I'll do my best."

CHAPTER 59

Thratia's fleet had been spotted that morning, cresting the sandy dunes which hemmed in Aransa. Just a mark out, as the airship flies, the people were saying, and the streets of Aransa were abuzz with the return of their tyrant lord. The fleet bobbed low in the sky, struggling against heavy winds due to a lack of selium to vent. Pelkaia could tell. She had a clear view from the window of Thratia's bedroom.

More than a mark, probably, the way they were fighting that wind. But she could wait. She'd waited years. Her body wouldn't fail her in the next few moments.

She peeled off the servant's face she wore to sneak her way into Thratia's compound, watching her natural face come into view in Thratia's vanity mirror. Sallowness made her skin yellow-pale, deep lines traced every edge of her features. She was old. So very old. And it was beginning to show. She tucked the selium into a small bladder, and hid it away in her pocket on instinct. Everything was ready. She had only to wait.

The knife at her back was almost as old as she was, a

Catari blade of simple make. There was no real ceremony in what she'd come here to do. No real passion, either. It was something she'd been driving toward since they day they'd told her her son, her sweet Kel, had gone to the skies.

She took no pleasure in what was to come, aside from a job well done.

One mark. Two. Thratia must be in the city now, tying up her affairs before returning to her home. It was late. She'd sleep soon. Even monsters needed their rest. Pelkaia most of all, these days.

Pelkaia tucked herself into a shadow between the wardrobe edge and wall, and waited.

Eventually, the door swung open. She'd lost track of time, of course, but days and marks and months and years were meaning less and less to her. It was dark, and Thratia was here, and she was yawning and stripping her boots off and going through the whole night-routine Detan had told Pelkaia she did, every night, step by step.

Such a methodical woman. You had to be methodical to be a murderer. Pelkaia knew that, too.

Thratia sat at her vanity, twisted off the top of her scar cream, and slathered the balm against her cheek – against the mark Detan had left her, so long ago that the memory was growing hazy. But most memories were hazy, now. Pelkaia knew only two things: what she must do, and what would come after.

Thratia stretched out in her bed, wriggling her muscles, settling into the covers. She left a light burning, as she always did, fearful of being surprised in the dark.

Surprise, Pelkaia thought.

Marks drifted by again while the cream did its work. Soaked into her hardened skin and brought with it the Catari poisons Pelkaia had laced it with. Sometime, eventually, Thratia jerked up in bed, gasping, clawing at her throat, eyes wide as she scrabbled about her nightstand for a glass of water. Wasn't there. Wasn't a drop in the room. Pelkaia'd made sure of it.

"No good," Pelkaia said, and stepped from the shadows.

Thratia, to her credit, was on her feet in a moment, blade in hand even though her eyes bugged out and her mouth gaped open, struggling for air that just wouldn't come.

"You crushed my son."

Thratia lunged at her, but the motion was weak, and Pelkaia had no trouble batting it away with her own blade.

"Not you, personally, of course. But you signed off on the papers. Put him there in that landslide for the cover up. Do you know me, Thratia Ganal? Do you know who's killing you now?"

Thratia backed against the wall, barely able to keep the tip of her blade up. Pity Pelkaia hadn't trusted her health enough to take Thratia in a fair fight. She'd like to draw this out, hear what Thratia had to say for herself. But ultimately, none of that mattered. Never had.

Pelkaia slit Thratia's throat. Left her bleeding her last in her own bed. Put the servant's face back on, and waltzed out like she'd never been there.

There'd be chaos in the morning, sure. A city without its dictator would be lost for awhile. But Detan knew what was coming, had sent urgent messages ahead of her to sympathetic contacts in Aransa so that they'd be prepared. Some man named Banch Thent.

Didn't matter to Pelkaia. All that mattered now was the second thing she had to do, *wanted* to do.

Pelkaia walked the Black.

CHAPTER 60

Detan found it rather rude that his auntie sent him a summons while he hung out in Ripka's room, chatting, instead of coming to visit him like she had the ladies.

Tibs a steady presence beside him, they limped their way down the halls, nursing aches and pains and generally taking their sweet time of it. If his auntie wanted to speak with him, she could wait. He was sick to the bone of jumping to other people's needs.

They found her sitting on her big chair – she'd pinch his ear if she ever heard him call it a throne – arms folded across her lap while she listened to Gatai deliver some dire news or other. Detan pictured himself in that same chair, and his stomach dropped.

The moment she sighted them, she waved Gatai away with one hand, leaned forward.

"I hope you both are well?"

Detan exaggerated his limp, just for the pits of it, and Tibs joined in. The Dame rolled her eyes and slumped back in her chair. "Will you two ever stop?"

"Stop what, exactly, ma'am?" Tibs asked.

"You *are* well?"

"We made it down here without fainting, so I suppose that's well enough," Detan said.

"And what will you do now, nephew?" Dame Honding asked, eyes like flints that'd just been put to the spark. Detan looked to Tibs, saw the question in his single, cocked eyebrow, the hint of a smile in the corner of his boot-leather lips.

"Ole Rippy's got a lot of work to do, getting the Remnant into shape, don't you think, Tibs?"

"It ain't an easy thing, keeping a prison in shape, that's for sure."

Auntie Honding cut a hand through the air. "Miss Leshe is perfectly capable of the task she has chosen. What of you, nephew?"

Detan just kept on looking at Tibs, not daring to glance into the smolder of his aunt's expression. "Know what prisons need lots of? Locks, you know. Gotta' keep 'em all in nice and snug – that's the idea."

"True 'nough, can't be much of a prison without locks."

"Will you both stop your inane babbling–"

"Need metal for locks, though. Good iron ore."

Tibs quirked a grin, catching on. "Yes indeed, sirra."

"And I just happen to know that rotten ole' Mercer Grandon is sending a fresh load of the stuff down the eastern caravan route, to a weapons forge on the coast there. Trunk-loads of it."

"Dangerous route, that. Bandits rove those skies."

"Bandits?" Detan faked a shiver. "What's the sky coming to?"

"Heard tell most mercers running routes down that skyroad hire mercenaries to see 'em through."

"But wouldn't you know it, Mercer Grandon is in a pinch. Put a lotta' money behind some venture that fell through – something to do with honey."

"You don't say," Tibs drawled.

Dame Honding threw her arms into the air and let loose an exasperated huff. "Are you even listening to me, boy?"

He gave up the limp and stepped closer to the throne, leaving Tibs just an arm's length behind him. Caught between two Honding futures, he thought, and neither one of them he really wanted.

"I have never stopped listening to you, Auntie. But this…" he dragged his gaze over her throne, tipped his chin to stare pointedly at the family crest carved into the wall above her head. "This is not what I do. This is not how I *help*. Not yet, anyway. The world needs a little time to get used to me in it. And…" He swallowed, thinking of a particular sunset on a particular beach. "I have some promises yet to keep."

Detan straightened, feeling the ache in every joint, and turned toward the door. With his aunt's shadow thrown over his shoulder he hesitated, just a breath. Then Tibs was beside him, offering an arm to take some of Detan's weight. He picked up like they'd never stopped chatting.

"It wouldn't do to leave the mercer in such a lurch, would it?" Detan asked.

"Wouldn't be right."

"Wouldn't be gentlemanly."

"Mmhmm. And we can't leave Ripka without proper supplies. It'd be beastly of us."

"Downright traitorous."

Shuffling, limping, they made their way down the long strip of red rug that spilt like blood from the foot of the Honding family throne. His aunt's shadow did not waver over his shoulder, but it did not cause his knees to quake as it once would have. Outside, the night gleamed on, a bruise-black sky shot through with hundreds of thousands of stars.

His flier waited. The open sky waited.

He was leaving Hond Steading, but he was going home.

ACKNOWLEDGMENTS

The third book in a trilogy is a daunting, exhilarating task to undertake, and I wouldn't have been able to do it without a team of wonderful people having my back.

First, thank you to my amazing fiancé, Joey Hewitt, who makes sure I do things like eat and sleep on occasion.

A huge thank you to all of my writer buddies, whose support and encouragement are invaluable to me: E A Foley, Trish Henry, Earl T Roske, Andrea Stewart, K A Rochnik, Courtney Schafer, Gama Martinez, and Vylar Kaftan.

Thank you to my kickass agent, Sam Morgan, and all of the team over at JABberwocky. And thank you to Paul Simpson, Marc Gascoigne, Michael R Underwood, Penny Reeve, Phil Jourdan, Nick Tyler, and the rest of the Angry Robots for all their insight and support throughout this series.

Thank you too, to all the wonderful bookstores who have hosted me. And to all of the wonderful writers and readers I've encountered along the road: you're too many to list, but you are invaluable. Thank you.

And of course, thank you to all of you readers who have come with me on this journey through the Scorched Continent. I hope you'll travel along with me to many strange worlds yet to come

STEAL
THE SKY

A SCORCHED
CONTINENT NOVEL

MEGAN E. O'KEEFE

*Further
breathtaking
adventures from
the* SCORCHED
CONTINENT,
*from the
peerless pen of*
MEGAN E
O'KEEFE